BRAIN WASH

A DARCY McCLAIN THRILLER

PAT KRAPF

THUNDER GLASS PRESS

ISBN 978-1-941300-00-8 (Kindle Edition)
ISBN 978-1-941300-01-5 (Paperback Edition)

Editing by Caroline Kaiser
Book design by Fiona Raven

Printed and bound in USA
First Printing July 2014

Published by Thunder Glass Press LLC
P.O. Box 93234
Southlake, TX, USA 76092

Visit **patkrapf.com**

To my husband and my giant schnauzers,
for your support and unconditional love.

To the Dallas/Ft.Worth Writers' Workshop,
without you the journey would have been twice as long.

Disclaimer

The author does not promote ownership of the giant schnauzer breed. Every prospective owner of any pet should thoroughly research that particular breed's characteristics before purchasing or adopting the animal. Caring for an animal is a lifelong commitment. Speak to reputable giant schnauzer breeders and educate yourself about this breed before choosing the giant schnauzer.

SUPPORT RESCUE

1

Johnny Duran often contemplated death. How? When? Now he knew where and by whom.

Fear propelled him across the grassy easement; he was frantic to reach the arroyos before his executioners. More than once he thanked God for the brilliant moon. It gave him an edge—not a huge advantage, but a chance to evade them, for the brighter the night, the worse their optivision goggles performed. But if they removed them, they couldn't track him at all.

Behind him, rapid footsteps thundered over the earth, and brittle piñons snapped underfoot. Johnny jerked his head sideways and glanced back, but nothing stirred in the moonlit clearing. He ran on, mouth agape, gulping the frosty air. His tongue darted over the crusted corners of his blistered lips. The metallic taste made his stomach roil. Blood throbbed in his ears, the rhythm punctuated by his erratic heartbeat. He skirted a stand of junipers. A branch slapped his face, but he kept stride, flying along at a pulse-pounding speed. Sweat trickled from beneath his wool cap and stung his eyes, already raw from the icy night.

He spotted his first arroyo and raced toward it. Too late he saw a glint off its edge. Frost sheeted the soft dirt, transforming bone-dry loam into slick clay. He slipped on the muddy rim and catapulted headfirst down the steep slope, his jaw striking a rock as he landed in the arid bed. Stunned, he lay motionless on the frozen ground. The rigid case zipped into his breast pocket gouged his chest, the flash drive a constant reminder of why they were stalking him.

Johnny had never done anything important in his life, nothing he considered brave, until he hacked into LANL's classified databases and downloaded proof of the atrocities in the basement laboratories. Now he regretted his actions.

Orange flashed across the ridgeline: a detector ray.

He squatted and scooted backward into sage snarled with trash. Metal tore a gash in his new parka. White goose down spilled onto his lap and floated upward, cradled on a gentle breeze. He inhaled and held his breath.

Squeak, crunch, squeak, crunch: the familiar sound of feet trudging through packed snow echoed in his ears. His hunters stopped close to where he crouched, then moved on.

Adrenaline turbocharged Johnny's weary body. He broke from the shadows and fled in the opposite direction. The cold burned his lungs and numbed his bare face. He stifled a cough, afraid the sound might pinpoint his location.

Down one side of the incline, across the snaking funnel of the arroyo's core, and up the opposite bank he scurried, as he traversed one ravine after another. Churned-up dirt coated him from head to toe. He breathed into a gloved hand, the dust-laden air suffocating. Every step jarred his knees, but his feet barely felt the rocks, soles desensitized by the bitter night.

He clutched his head. The loud thumps in his temples dulled his concentration. The fork must be close. Around the next turn or . . . The thought became lost in a debilitating fog brought on by exhaustion, for he'd traveled miles at a pace guaranteed to tax even a marathoner. He paused, listening and straining to hear. The silence, normally inviting, troubled him. He squinted into the darkness. A black *Y* sliced the desert floor—at last, the fork in the arroyo and his way to safety.

He stumbled toward the ravine, confused as to which route to take. With no time to debate, he skidded down the bank and headed south, nature's light his guide. One need haunted him: water—if only a sip to ease his parched throat. He surveyed the basin. A frozen puddle about a yard ahead drew his attention, but he blew past it. Stop, then they might catch him.

He jogged to the right, following the curve of the ravine. In the distance, coyotes howled. Their plaintive cries mirrored the burden heavy on his heart. Who would care for Rio if he died? The coyotes' high-pitched yelps escalated to a frenzy, signaling a fresh kill. The hair on his neck bristled. He raised his head and sniffed the air: piñon smoke. People. His spirits lifted but quickly died as a dark figure appeared on the ridge.

The thumb drive. He had to hide it. Keep the data safe. He unzipped his parka, removed the USB, and scanned the area for a suitable hiding place. Not here. Not yet. He rounded a sharp bend. Ice cracked. He slid across the slick surface and crashed into a tree. The memory stick soared into the air. He started after it, but a man blocked his path. Otto. If the boss had sent him, then Duke wasn't far behind. Johnny scrambled up the arroyo wall, nails clawing the soft dirt. When he was halfway to the top, strong hands grabbed his ankles and dragged him back into the ditch.

"Running away, are ya?" Duke raised his fist.

Johnny winced, preparing for the blow. The punch knocked the wind out of him. Doubled over and gasping for air, he somehow mustered the strength to kick Duke in the shins, but the attack had little effect on the big man. He yanked Johnny to his feet and pinned his arms behind his back while Otto snatched the wool cap, a gift from Rio, from Johnny's head and ground it into the dirt. Anger welled in his heart, then sorrow. He'd never see her again. Tears wet his cheeks. His plea for help bubbled to the surface, vibrated, and escaped in a mournful wail that blasted the desert calm. He refluxed bile, and the caustic juice trickled from his trembling lips.

"Gross son of a bitch." Otto cleared his throat and spat. "Hold him and I'll do the honors."

Duke snickered. "Be my guest."

Otto pulled something rigid from his jacket. Moonlight reflected off the glass barrel. Spellbound, Johnny stared at the probe, but not for long. He dug his boots into the ground and sent dirt and stones scattering as he fought back, twisting and flailing.

"Knock it the fuck off." Duke kneed Johnny in the small of the back.

Johnny gritted his teeth and squeezed his eyes shut. The pain eased, and his lids shot open. Otto hovered over him, the shaft of the probe pointed at Johnny's temple. Terrified, he used his only weapon, smashing his head into Otto's. Red blurred Johnny's vision, and bells rang in his ears.

"Shit, I dropped the damn thing," said Otto. "Go find it or there'll be hell to pay."

Duke cursed. "Forget it and just get the job done."

"You got another?"

"Sure, but this time you hold the asshole still and let me do the job."

Johnny summoned every ounce of power he possessed, desperate to break free, but in the end his struggles failed. Paralyzed by fear and fatigue, he lost the will to fight. Rio danced through his dazed mind. Her image made it easier to endure the searing hot probe that bored a hole into his head. Fire scorched his skull, knifed along his spine, and scalded his body. Every neuron in his brain screeched in agony. Drained, Johnny surrendered to life's greatest luxury: death.

2

Sunlight melted the gray slush banked against the sidewalks, turning the sooty drifts into a muddy stream that wound its way to the nearest drainage culvert. In the underground lot, the steady drip of water dulled the roar of takeoffs and landings at Albuquerque's Sunport.

Darcy McClain parked her Toyota 4Runner in an end spot, cracked open the windows for Bullet, and locked up. The subtle click of the door locks triggered a whine session from the giant schnauzer. She wanted to spring him from the crate but didn't dare. The last time he roamed the vehicle while she ran an errand, he snacked on the grab handles, lunched on the steering wheel, and chewed through the seat belts. She returned to find the hundred-pound canine curled in a ball, snoring up a storm. The following day, she bought the ideal restraining device and prepared for a battle, but to her delight discovered

Bullet was crate trained. Poor dog. He'd been through so much these last few months: his master's killing, new owners, and a strange home to settle into.

Darcy ducked into the busy terminal and broke into a fast walk. If the flight was on time, the plane had already landed. She dodged hordes of travelers, maneuvered around luggage, and steered clear of shopping bags crammed with Christmas gifts. After making a visual sweep of the passengers in baggage claim, she hopped on the escalator and rode to the upper level where she'd agreed to meet her sister Charlene. Since Vicky, Charlene's college roommate, had sprung for first-class tickets, the two should be first to deplane.

Darcy couldn't wait to see her sister. Finally, they'd have some time together, even if it meant dragging Vicky along on their vacation. Just the thought of her sister's friend made her pulse skyrocket into the danger zone, but she shrugged off the aggravation and dwelled on more pleasant things, like her plans for the holidays, and after she picked up Charlene and Vicky, a firsthand look at the acreage she'd recently inherited.

What better time than Christmas, when everything seemed magical and right with the world, to mend the rift between her and her sister? It felt like a lifetime since the two had been happy, really happy, and how Darcy longed to feel that way again—or at least to rekindle some of the joy they'd once enjoyed as a family. Not easy with their parents dead, but she had to try.

Upstairs, she scanned the sea of faces streaming from the gateway tunnel like angry ants scurrying from a disturbed hill. The crowd engulfed her and scattered, but no Charlene, not even among the stragglers, and no Vicky.

Darcy hailed the ground agent about to vacate her post at the boarding gate next door. According to the woman, she had the right flight, so she dialed her sister's cell phone and left a message. When Charlene didn't return the call, she keyed in Vicky's number; voice mail picked up.

The half hour ticked into an hour.

Concerned, she phoned her house in San Francisco, tried Charlene's cell again, and called Vicky once more. When no one answered at all three, she texted them. Twenty minutes later and still no one had replied. Worried, Darcy left the terminal.

Halfway across the parking lot, her phone vibrated. She clawed it free from her pocket and flipped open the cover, anxious to hear Charlene's voice. It was her sister all right, but she hadn't called. Darcy stared at the text message. This couldn't be happening. Not again. Not only had her sister stood her up, but she'd also deserted her for Vicky.

Seething, Darcy marched to her 4Runner, fury mounting as she fought the urge to confront her sister. Six months of planning ruined, all because of "better powder in Colorado." From the start, she'd been adamant about this being a family vacation, and Charlene agreed, but not a week later, without asking, her sister invited Vicky to accompany them on their ski trip. Although livid, Darcy had held her temper; if she'd blown up, she only would have alienated her sister even more, something she was good at. So she swallowed her anger and canceled the casita she'd booked in Taos in favor of a larger rental home, one big enough for three women and a large dog. Now she and Bullet would be stuck with the enormous house.

She threw open the driver's door. From the hatch Bullet whined, so she freed him from his crate and belted him in before she jumped behind the wheel and rammed the key into the ignition. If she'd known Charlene and Vicky would be no-shows, she'd have flown and boarded Bullet rather than make the long haul from San Francisco to Taos with him in tow. But Charlene wouldn't hear of kenneling him. "We can't go on vacation and leave him behind. He's part of the family now." Just like her sister. She begs for a dog, the novelty wears off, and who gets stuck with the animal? Ease up, McClain. Remember who brought Bullet home in the first place; quit blaming Charlene.

In a huff, Darcy gunned the engine and drove off, cutting the corner sharp. Damn it. She had her heart set on this vacation. "Vicky this and Vicky that. You'd swear they were lifelong friends, not college roomies for less than two years," she said to Bullet, who sighed as though he empathized.

She sped up the ramp to the I-25. "To think it was my big idea she bunk with someone because she might be lonely in her freshman year. So who does she pick but the ultimate party animal! Tattooed and pierced to boot." At times like these, Darcy wished her parents were alive. Life would've been a lot easier if they hadn't died in a plane crash, leaving her sole guardian of a nine-year-old at age twenty-nine.

The haunting pain of their deaths spilled into the hurt and anger she felt at throwing away a promising career at the FBI to play mother, a desire she never had. Until forced to resign from the bureau, Darcy thought she'd dreamed up the perfect solution: she shipped Charlene off to boarding school. But five years later, her sister had been expelled, a disgrace to the law Darcy had sworn to uphold, so she had no choice but to quit work to raise Charlene.

Life still wasn't easy. Just as she'd done today, Charlene knew exactly what buttons to push and loved pushing them. Even if Darcy tried to have a calm, rational discussion with her sister, it proved pointless. Their talks always escalated into ugly arguments that left both emotionally drained. In the end, their words were hardly worth uttering. The only redeeming factor? Charlene was doing well in school and staying out of trouble—so far.

On the drive north to Santa Fe, Darcy tried to enjoy the scenery, but her sister's budding friendship troubled her. She'd worked hard to steer Charlene onto the right track and even harder to keep her there. What concerned Darcy now was that Vicky's wild lifestyle would derail those efforts.

Her thoughts skipped from Charlene to Randolph Colton, her father's best friend. Hard to believe their surrogate dad had been murdered less than three months ago by a killer bent on revenge. Since his death, loneliness had hung over Darcy like a black cloud, fueling her decision to resolve the differences between her and Charlene.

Miles down the interstate, she exited at Cerrillos and inched through the downtown Santa Fe snarl, but soon the gridlock unwound and she cruised past the opera house, the open-air theater barely visible among the piñon-studded hills.

In the hour ahead, one pueblo sprawled into the next as she motored up the highway, her concentration tuned to the throngs of vehicles flowing from the Indian casinos and adding to the already congested thoroughfare. To her, gambling seemed out of place in this dynamic landscape.

A black spot floated into the corner of her eye. The speck dove below the mesas, then rose high as if carried on a zephyr. A hot air balloon? But a throaty rumble dispelled that notion. A Black Hawk zoomed toward her, roared low overhead, and became a blip on the horizon.

Darcy crested the rise. Ahead, a white truck with flashing yellow lights and "Wide Load" etched across the back chugged up the incline. She braked, darted into the fast lane, and passed the pickup. In front of him, a Ford SUV crawled up the grade. She punched the accelerator. The speedometer hit eighty as she breezed by both vehicles, which quickly vanished in her rearview mirror.

She looked forward just in time to see an identical Ford SUV tailgating an extra-wide trailer. Escorting the convoy was another white pickup with flashing amber lights. As she flew by, Darcy hunted for a company name or logo but saw nothing until she glimpsed NASA's vector decal in the hatch window of the second Ford. The fleet took the 502 turnoff to Los Alamos, and she rolled into Española.

Stalled in rush-hour traffic, Darcy braked behind a low rider spewing caustic fumes and snuck a peek at the map Ann Gilroy, Randolph's surveyor, had included with her letter of introduction.

"Good, right on track."

Bullet barked. The word "track" had a completely different connotation to him.

She left Española and wound her way through the farming villages that hugged the Rio Grande. Below the highway, the bright afternoon sun painted indigo shadows on bare cottonwoods and ignited the river's glassy surface. She gained in altitude, capped the peak, and dropped into a horseshoe canyon that opened onto a vast mesa dusted in white, the pristine snow fractured by a massive escarpment, its chasm barren and black. To the east, dense evergreens carpeted the desert floor and undulated up the slopes to the alluvial fans of the Sangre de Cristo range. In the midst of this splendor jutted Taos Mountain, its crown shrouded in fog.

"Awesome."

Bullet barked.

"Hey, keep watch. We're looking for marker forty. Bad habit, talking to your dog, but you're good company. Better than most humans." He nibbled her earlobe. "Thanks, I needed that. As it turned out, glad you're along for the ride."

With the heater on high, she coasted down Highway 68 to mile marker forty and eased the 4Runner onto a pothole-ridden road with wide shoulders and deep gullies on either side; the trenches were designed to divert water off the easement. She swerved to avoid a huge hole. A sharp jolt shook the SUV.

Bullet growled.

"Hold on. Looks like rough going."

Darcy hadn't gone far when she spotted the turnoff high-lighted on Gil's hand-drawn map. "Darn, this stretch looks worse than the last." She slowed to a crawl, afraid of damaging the undercarriage, or worse, getting stuck in one of the cav-ernous ruts that crisscrossed the road. The vehicle shuddered and groaned as it bumped over the rocky terrain. Behind her, a huge dust funnel obliterated the sky.

The road curved, and a small sign nailed to a stake popped into view: Bandit's Bluff. Good, she was headed in the right direction. "Legend goes," Gil had jotted on the map, "that Billy the Kid and his gang had a hideout near Bandit's Bluff. Some think it was the adobe on your land." Intrigued, Darcy tried to speed up the trip, but the lousy road conditions made it impossible.

In the last jarring miles, the vehicle zigzagged through dense brush. Tree branches clawed the windows and raked the hood. Finally, the onslaught ended, and her 4Runner emerged into a clearing. She switched off the engine, unbuckled Bullet, and climbed out. He landed on the ground beside her. The strong scent of pine and sage hung in the crisp air. She inhaled long and deep. Bullet jerked his muzzle toward the trailhead.

An ancient Suburban, the paint sandblasted off one side and mottled with rust, lumbered up the road and parked next to Darcy's 4Runner. A tall, slim woman stepped out. She gathered up her hair, brown streaked with blonde, and tied the unruly mane into a ponytail. "Darcy McClain?" she called out.

"That's me."

"Ann Gilroy, but call me Gil." A smile lit Gil's weathered face; her dark skin was wrinkled by the strong New Mexico sun but warmed by sparkling blue eyes. "How cool—you own a giant schnauzer!"

Darcy laughed, pleased Gil recognized the breed. "Not many people know what he is."

"I owned one. Shadow—black like yours. He died last year. Broke my heart. But I have a pup reserved from a litter in California. I should have him next month. Miss my old boy." The minute Gil kneeled, Bullet buried his muzzle in her chest. "Hey, big boy."

"A hundred pounds of solid muscle and boundless energy."

"How old is he?"

"Five. I inherited him."

Gil smiled. "Randolph's dog?"

"No, Randolph's killer's dog."

"Oh yeah, Albuquerque's most notorious serial killer. Loved to carve up his victims with a laser. You solved the case, right?"

Darcy nodded, reluctant to go into detail. The investigation brought back bad memories. Even though Paco, Bullet's former owner, had murdered Randolph, a part of her wanted desperately to help him overcome his demons. But fate had other plans for the troubled young man bent on revenge.

"Know anything else about your giant? What kennel's he from?" Gil said.

"Target Kennels in Kerrville, Texas. Defunct now. His registered name is Trajectory, aka Bullet."

"Handsome boy." Gil looked about. "Where's your sister? When we spoke, you said she was coming too."

"She made other plans."

"Sounds like I struck a nerve."

Darcy shrugged.

Gil took the hint and changed the subject by spreading a topographical map across the hood of her Suburban. With a red pen, she outlined one of the parcels. "This is your tract."

Darcy studied the plat map. "Quite a hike in."

"Feel up to it?" Gil slung a daypack over her shoulder.

"You bet. Can't wait to see the place."

"A word of advice: take only what you need for the hike. Leave the rest. I've parked here before and never had a problem, so your stuff should be okay."

Darcy didn't like the idea of leaving her laptop and iPad behind, but her backpack was already heavy with water for her and Bullet, so she concealed each item from view, locked up, and looped her arms through the straps of her Kelty.

Bullet charged ahead. Darcy whistled, and he circled back. "It's not a footrace."

"He listens well," said Gil as she waded into the waist-high sage.

Darcy followed. "I'm considering tracking or search and rescue."

"Good idea," said Gil.

For a while, they trekked on in single file, Gil focused on the route, Darcy immersed in her environs. The only sound was dried vegetation crackling underfoot as they tramped across the dormant grasslands to their first arroyo.

Gil took a compass from her pocket. "Good, right on course."

Darcy peered over the edge of the ravine. Looked like a good thirty-foot drop, maybe more. "Going down?"

"We are." Gil dug her boot heels into the loose earth as she descended.

Seconds later, Darcy slid to the bottom with Bullet tagging along.

"Now, up and out," said Gil. The ascent wasn't as easy as the descent.

For over an hour, under a warm winter sun, Darcy and her companions hiked across land patched with snow and ice. They negotiated another arroyo, shallow compared to the first but wetter. About a half mile down the gulch, Gil shouted, "Up again."

On the ridgeline, Gil stopped to scrape caked mud off her hiking boots. Darcy did the same. "Are we close?"

"Almost there."

A short distance in, a brown adobe appeared among the trees. Gil held back while Darcy approached. The outside mud had crumbled in places, exposing hundreds of hand-molded bricks to the harsh elements.

"Imagine the work that went into this place. Still can't believe it. Sixty acres. Sounds like a lot of land, but you don't realize just how big until you walk it," Darcy said.

Gil chuckled. "I know. I walk that and more every day. Let's go in."

Darcy followed Gil and Bullet through the front door into the dark house. In the living room, an old couch, dusty and threadbare, faced an alcove that made up the kitchen. In the other room, an army cot sat in one corner, the canvas a drab, olive-green and perforated with holes. Darcy pulled aside a tattered curtain, the only source of privacy in the tiny bathroom, and turned on the faucet. Air sputtered from the pitted fixture. She raised the toilet seat. "No water."

Gil poked her head through the opening. "Probably shut off to prevent the pipes from freezing."

"Green slime." Darcy lowered the lid.

"Antifreeze."

"Place needs some work."

"Randolph planned to tear the house down and build new. Seen enough? I really want to show you the view." Bullet bounded after Gil as the two headed for the patio door.

Reluctantly, Darcy caught up. No, she hadn't seen enough. She wanted time to digest everything—the land, the house, the vistas—but Gil was on a mission. By the time Darcy reached the back porch, the two stood on a knoll that overlooked the valley.

"What do you think? Rio Grande Gorge to the northwest,

Taos Mountain to the east, and the Sangre de Cristos due south."
Gil summed up the magnificent views in such a generic way.

The beauty of the land, Randolph's generosity, his murder:
perhaps all three brought tears to Darcy's eyes. She missed
him so much.

"First time I surveyed Wilson's tract," said Gil, "I understood why the old man refused to sell. He had to die to part
with the land."

"Wilson's kids sold to Randolph, right?"

"Yes."

"How'd Wilson die?"

"Heart attack. Hiker found him on the cot in the house.
Hope that doesn't spook you."

Took a lot to spook Darcy. "Any idea what Randolph paid
for the land?"

Gil nodded. "Eight hundred and fifty thousand."

Darcy whistled.

"All yours now. Something tells me you'll respect the land
as much as old Wil did."

"You're right. I wish Charlene . . ." The mere mention of her
sister's name rekindled mixed emotions. Hurt, guilt, frustration—all tumbled forth.

"Talking might help," said Gil, staring straight ahead.

Emotionally compromised, Darcy did something she'd
never done. She spilled her guts to a complete stranger. What
concerned her more than blabbing details to an outsider was
hearing herself admit what an awful parent she'd been to
Charlene—and not much better as an older sister.

"Under the circumstances you describe, I don't think
I would've done any better. As for being angry about this
vacation, can't blame you."

Darcy dug a bottle of water from her pack, cracked the seal,
and polished off half. "I've always bailed her out. Pulled strings

here, begged someone there. Took her years to clean up her act. Then she links up with Vicky."

Gil put her hand on Darcy's shoulder.

Embarrassed by her sudden outpouring, Darcy said, "Sorry. It's difficult to hide my anger when she's done the same thing over and over again."

"Don't let her ruin the day."

On the return trip, Darcy tried hard to keep Charlene from her thoughts. She drank in the landscape, talked to Bullet, and watched Gil weave through the brush. Plans for her property drifted into her mind, but in the crevices Charlene dominated her thoughts. Bullet disappeared from her side. She looked up, surprised to see their parked vehicles. Winded, she leaned against Gil's Suburban to catch her breath. "You're in great shape. I swore I had better stamina."

"It's the altitude. You'll get used to it."

"There's something I don't understand."

"What's that?" Gil filled a small bowl with water for Bullet.

"At his age, why would Wilson subject himself to such a torturous trip when he could cut a road to his house?"

"Because of the cost."

"For an easement?"

Gil wiped water from her lips with a swipe of her wrist. "To pay the attorneys."

An uneasy feeling washed over Darcy. "What attorneys?"

"You're serious, aren't you? And all this time I assumed you knew."

Before Darcy had a chance to ask, Gil said matter-of-factly, "The acreage is landlocked."

A long silence.

Darcy finally broke it. "Great. I own land but have no way to access the parcel legally. Know a good lawyer?"

"Best in town." Gil jotted a name and number on a business

card and handed it to Darcy. "I hate to deliver bad news and then run, but I have a tract to survey on the north side."

As Gil's battered Suburban lumbered down the lane, one word spiked through Darcy's brain: landlocked. Locked out was exactly how she felt. Locked out of her land. Locked out of Charlene's life. She sighed. Another problem to toss on the heap. However, if she had a choice, she'd opt for land problems over Charlene problems any day. And Gil had recommended an attorney even if Darcy's internal cash register had gone berserk. Disappointed, she decided to walk off her self-pity, clear her mind, and think through her dilemma.

Bullet fell in step as Darcy bushwhacked a jagged course through the sagebrush to a stand of piñon. Just beyond the trees loomed the first arroyo. Bullet needed no coaxing. He half trotted, half skidded to the bottom. Darcy hit feetfirst—not as gracefully as he, but without mishap.

Nose to the ground, Bullet immediately set off down the arroyo, confirming to Darcy that he would probably do well in tracking or search and rescue (SAR). As a working breed, he needed to channel his intelligence and high energy, so she'd been kicking around some ideas about how to do this. Some days, he simply wore her out even after an eight- to ten-mile run in the mornings and a long walk most evenings. He certainly challenged her stamina, a trait she prided herself on.

Bullet vanished around the bend in the arroyo. She whistled, then shouted a command, but he didn't reappear. Normally, she wouldn't have chased after him but made him come to her. However, she was in unfamiliar territory, and worry spurred her to act.

"Bullet, come." She rounded the fork in the arroyo at a fast clip, expecting to find him with his leg lifted on a bush, but there was no sign of him. She ran on, stumbling over rocks, dodging small junipers, and avoiding mature piñons. Her anxiety mounted.

The ravine branched. Darcy stopped abruptly. She heard a noise behind her, but before she could turn something large and black appeared in her peripheral vision: Bullet. He stood in the middle of the dry gulch, looking up at her as if to say, "Okay, I came and I've been chasing you. Now what?"

Relieved, she hugged him and started off at a more leisurely pace with him beside her, his nose planted to the dusty ground. He appeared to be after something, so she played along.

He moved ahead of her, took a few steps, and froze, his ears erect and his docked tail straight. He cocked his head, sniffed the air, then glanced back at her.

She crouched beside him. "What is it, boy?" He ignored her, his gaze fixed on some distant object. Her hand slid under her jacket; the holstered 9 millimeter reassured her. Nothing moved on the ledge above, and only silence clung to the noonday air.

He lowered his muzzle to the dry bed and emitted several deep snorts, sucking the essence of the earth into his nostrils. Satisfied with whatever he smelled, he walked on at a steady lope. She kept up, curious as to what he was tracking.

The arroyo arched sharply, and Bullet slipped around the bend. Darcy followed, almost colliding headlong with the huge pile of debris that blocked the gulch. The trash heap looked like someone's private dump. On top of the pile perched Bullet. The minute she reached him, he descended back into the arroyo and forged ahead. He maintained this vigorous gait for several yards until once again he broke stride, as though waiting for her to catch up. The minute she drew near, he bolted.

Losing patience, she yelled, "Bullet. Wait."

He obeyed the command but acted restless and eager to continue on, so she gave in again to his instincts and pursued him as he dashed through the arroyo at a perilous speed, forcing her to leap all obstacles in her path. Finally, the hurdle race ended when he slowed to sniff a rock.

"What's so important about a rock?"

Before she had a chance to leash him, he broke into a dead run. A yard up the arroyo, she found him with his head buried in a clump of sagebrush snarled with filthy carpeting. When he withdrew, white feathers coated his muzzle.

She stifled a laugh. "Bet some coyote had a good meal. I don't know what brought this on, but let's rest." She snapped on his lead and tied him to a stout juniper.

He looped and relooped the small clearing, tangling his leash as he walked in circles. He nuzzled a mound of snow sheltered by an overhang.

"Water?" She filled a collapsible bowl, but he wouldn't drink. "You're acting mighty strange. Ten minutes, then we're out of here." Darcy lowered her backpack to the ground and leaned against the Kelty, her eyes shut and the sun warm on her face.

Bullet nudged her shoulder. She didn't respond, so he bucked her. She sat up. Gold shimmered through his beard. "What do you have?" She held out her hand. "Drop it."

A case fell into her palm. The flash drive looked brand new. Inscribed across the back was "Property of LANL."

3

Even though Bullet had already compromised the integrity of the flash drive by slobbering all over it, Darcy avoided further contamination by snapping on the latex gloves she always carried, a holdover from her bureau days. And as an avid hiker, she also packed Ziploc bags to haul out trash, and a first aid kit for minor emergencies.

"Algonized Zipgig," she said aloud, recognizing the signature gold case. She owned one herself, but hers stored 256 gigabytes, not 2 terabytes. Hefty storage capacity. "Wonder what's on this baby?" Curiosity ate at her. Government property, probably encrypted.

She studied the device. A tiny decal in the lower right-hand corner caught her eye. She pulled a small magnifying glass from her first aid kit and held it to the minuscule letters fanned across the bottom of the seal. "SFI/AIL. SFI/AIL," she said as though repetition would bring recognition. It didn't.

Strange finding a UBS drive in such a remote location, especially one in such good condition and this current. Hadn't been a month since Algonized Industries had launched their new line of terabyte flash drives.

Darcy shifted positions. Sunlight hit the device. A white thread shimmered in the bright rays. With tweezers, she snagged the fiber stuck to the case and placed it in an empty pillbox. Maybe nothing, but experience had taught her not to discount anything.

Somewhere behind her, Bullet rustled in the brush. She turned to see him half-buried in sage, straining to reach something beyond the range of his lead.

"What now?" She shoved her hand into the bush and pulled out a wool hat. Bullet went wild with excitement. "Wow, another find of the century. A dirty cap." She was about to toss it to him as a reward but noticed stains on the inside rim. She touched a gloved finger to the darkest splotch, surprised when a red streak rubbed off. Bullet bucked her arm.

"Sorry, boy, but the hat's mine." Darcy appeased him with his favorite treat, a carrot, while she grabbed a Ziploc bag from the wad in her backpack. The first chance she had, she'd transfer the cap to a paper sack.

On a hunch, she hiked up and down the arroyo, scouring the basin and the slopes for anything suspicious. Perhaps to take her mind off her personal problems, she wanted to believe something sinister had happened in the ravine. Work could be a wonderful diversion from reality, but at whose expense?

Finding nothing of interest, she retraced her steps to where Bullet had found the wool cap and tied several pieces of neon orange surveyor's tape to the adjacent trees. She'd packed the roll at Gil's suggestion, in case she wanted to mark the trail to her property, making it easier to find the house later. "More effective than breadcrumbs," Gil had said. But there was no need for either, for Darcy owned a compass and had a keen sense of direction.

Before leaving, she snapped off some shots. With the site identified and photographed, there was no reason to stay, so she and Bullet set out for her 4Runner.

On the return trip, he again zeroed in on the bush tangled with strips of filthy carpet. Trusting his instincts, she snared a sample of the feathers. "One more." She plucked another. A stinging sensation shot up her hand, and blood beaded on the nasty scratch etched across her knuckles. Only then did she see the metal strip entwined in the shag rug. She fished out the small first aid kit from her Kelty. The cut cleaned and bandaged, she moved on.

Bullet paused as he neared the rock that jutted from the culvert floor. Darcy crouched down for a closer look—nothing but a plain old rock from what she could tell, and too heavy to haul out. "Come on, boy," she said, tugging on his collar. He tore his attention from the boulder.

The arroyo narrowed and Bullet led, keeping stride with her. Both were enjoying the peaceful, sunny day, and all of Darcy's worries were briefly forgotten.

A figure appeared on the ridgeline and quickly disappeared, so fast Darcy wondered if she'd imagined it, but Bullet confirmed the sighting with a deep-throated growl. His hackles bristled, and low rumbles percolated from within him. For a moment she thought it might've been a coyote or a stray dog, but the soft swish of fabric brushing dry sage dispelled that theory. The person, for she detected only one, moved swiftly. She felt trapped in the arroyo while someone stalked from above, so she whispered, "Let's go," in Bullet's ear and scrambled up the bank, reaching the rim as someone in blue blended into the piñons. Darcy gave chase, but the dense sage made it impossible to catch up, so she navigated a different route to Wilson's adobe, the direction in which the person headed.

Cautious, she approached from the southwest and circled the mud structure, surprised to find the front door propped open with a brick. Bullet cocked his head and growled. Darcy ordered him to stay. He obeyed but kept his eyes fixed on the entrance.

She slipped in, tiptoed across the living room, and peeked into the bedroom. The person in blue leaned over Wilson's tattered cot. Darcy stood perfectly still, her eyes glued to the trespasser as he folded the bed in two, rested it against the wall, and squatted. Light glinted off the knife clutched in his gloved hand. She watched for a long time as the hooded prowler chipped away at the dirt floor.

"Looking for anything in particular?" Her voice resonated in the confined space. Even to her it sounded as if she spoke through a bullhorn.

The intruder jumped up. Taller than Darcy by a few inches but slighter in build, he spun to face her, his features shrouded by his hood and large sunglasses. Darcy unzipped her parka, the holstered 9 millimeter visible. "Drop the knife."

A flashlight thudded to the dirt floor. Next came the knife.

"Outside." Darcy motioned with her head, "where I can see you better." She gave him a wide berth as he left the bedroom, crossed the living room, and strolled out the front door.

Bullet's sharp barks filtered into the house. Darcy's stride quickened; she was eager to reach Bullet because she wasn't sure how he'd react to the stranger. She ducked through the narrow doorway and into the strong sunshine, temporarily blinded by the intense rays. As soon as she emerged, Bullet placed himself between Darcy and the intruder. The man flipped back his parka hood. Long, black hair cascaded down his shoulders and framed his face. He yanked off his mirrored wraparound glasses.

Darcy stepped forward. "You're a woman."

The stranger laughed. "Yeah."

Something about her was vaguely familiar, but exactly what escaped Darcy until the stranger said, "My name's Regina O'Neil." She extended her hand.

Stunned, it took a moment for the name to sink in. Even then, Darcy had a hard time choosing the right words, yet she had no doubt. The striking resemblance to Randolph was unquestionable: same fair skin, black hair, and green eyes. "Rio? What a strange coincidence."

Rio frowned. "You know me?"

"No. I've only seen pictures." She meant photos dumped in the trash by Randolph's wife soon after the reading of his will, when the entire family first learned of his illegitimate daughter. Since then, bits of information had filtered through the family grapevine, all of them true, penned in Randolph's hand and taken from his personal diary—confirmation that he fathered Rio and his sworn commitment to always provide for her, but never any mention of her biological mother.

"You're . . . you're Darcy. Darcy McClain. Randolph told me about you. Only months before, before . . ." Her arms outstretched, Rio closed the gap between them. She hugged Darcy.

Randolph's murder had devastated Darcy. Now she felt a piece of her heart had been restored. "Let's see. If my math is correct, you're nineteen."

Rio laughed, an appealing, throaty sort of chuckle. "Right on." The smile faded. "It's so sad about Randolph. We barely had a chance to meet, never mind get to know each other. Now he's . . . he's gone forever."

"I know."

"From what he told me, you two were very close."

Darcy could only smile, the pain of his loss still raw.

"I'm so sorry. For you. For me. Glad you killed his murderer."

Darcy jumped at the chance to set the record straight. "His death was an accident."

"The important thing is, he won't hurt anyone again. So you inherited this land from Randolph. Did you know my adopted parents own the sixty acres diagonal to yours?"

"No, I didn't." When the timing was right, she planned to ask Rio if the O'Neils would consider an easement agreement, but for now, she was more interested in an answer to another question. "I'm curious, what were you looking for in the house?"

Rio's smile faded. "Johnny Duran."

"Who?"

"My fiancé. He's disappeared. Let's go in and I'll explain. I'm cold." After Darcy and Bullet entered, Rio shut the door, then headed straight for the bedroom, at home in Wilson's adobe.

"You certainly know your way around the place." The statement sounded accusatory. "I mean . . ."

"I do, and I'll explain in a minute," Rio called back. She returned to the living room with deck chairs and army blankets. "Don't sit on the couch. It's filthy."

Bullet jumped onto the threadbare cushions, more interested in a snooze than the soiled condition of the sofa. Rio set up the chairs and sat, her long legs stretched before her and boots crossed at the ankles, the soles crusted with dried mud. Darcy felt a true affinity for the teenager, probably because the bond between them was Randolph.

"You were saying," said Darcy.

A pensive look replaced Rio's cheerful demeanor. "Gosh, where do I start?"

4

For a long time, Rio stared in silence at the dirty windows in the dank living room while Darcy savored the moment, happy to be in Rio's company, for her presence alone eased some of the pain of Randolph's loss.

Without looking at Darcy, Rio said, "The sixty-acre parcel north of yours is owned by Enzo Duran, Johnny's uncle."

It wasn't the start Darcy expected, but she listened intently.

"This is Johnny, my fiancé." Rio took a snapshot from her pocket.

A thin, nerdy-looking man with stringy brown hair looked back from the photograph. He wore a blue suit and a gray tie. His smile appeared forced.

Rio held out her hand. "What do you think of my engagement ring?"

Darcy admired the diamond. Questions surrounding

Johnny's disappearance crowded into her brain. When had Rio last seen him? Had they argued about something? But instinct told her the girl would explain in her own time.

Rio put the picture away and went back to her story about Johnny's uncle. "Enzo built a house on his property but lives full-time in California. He hired Johnny to watch the place, so Johnny spends the weekends at his uncle's, which makes seeing each other convenient."

"Where does Johnny live during the week?"

"Los Alamos. He works at the lab."

The reply stopped Darcy. She barely heard Rio's next statement, her mind galloping to conclusions; the flash drive (property of LANL), Johnny's employer, and now Johnny's disappearance. Come on, McClain. Reality check.

"Johnny's a computer analyst, or so he says." Rio smiled. "If I ask questions, he clams up." She combed her hair into place with her fingers. The black strands snagged in her long nails. "He works on government stuff. Hush-hush."

Darcy glanced at her backpack, the flash drive safe in a side pocket. "Why look for him in Wilson's house?"

Sadness clouded Rio's face. "I haven't seen him since last Friday."

The detective in Darcy surfaced. "Is that unusual?"

"Yes. Sunday was my birthday." Her tears brimmed. "We planned to meet here. I waited over an hour, but he never showed up, so I went to his uncle's house. No sign of him there. I called a friend to check his duplex in Los Alamos. Wasn't there either. I even scoured the arroyos around here, thinking he might've gotten hurt."

The comment puzzled Darcy. "Why check the arroyos?"

"About a dozen crisscross this area. In some spots they're almost forty feet deep; the rest are around twenty or thirty. Johnny loves to cruise them, as he puts it. He calls them nature's highways. He searches for salvageable trash." Tears rolled down her cheeks.

Darcy rummaged in her Kelty for tissues and handed the package to Rio. "Have you reported him missing?"

She nodded. "Maddox—he's the new deputy sheriff for Taos County—took the report, but didn't act the least bit concerned."

"What about Johnny's family? Have you notified them?"

"His mother died last year of cancer, and his father deserted them when Johnny was three. No siblings."

"What about his uncle?"

"I haven't seen Enzo in ages." An angry edge crept into her voice. "He's always in Mexico on business. He's no help."

Darcy looked around the cold, dismal interior. "Why meet here?"

"I live at home, and I'm forbidden to see Johnny. This is the only safe place we can meet without half the town knowing."

"Forbidden? By whom?"

Rio wiped her eyes. "My father. I fear him the most. He hates Johnny."

Darcy couldn't imagine fearing a father. She'd loved her own dearly. "Why does he hate Johnny?"

"He's Mexican." The words exploded from her mouth. "It may mean nothing to you, but it's a big deal in my blue-blooded family. Damn racists, all of them."

The outburst left Darcy speechless.

A weak smile lit Rio's face. "Johnny nicknamed me Rio after the Duran Duran song."

The sadness in her voice tugged at Darcy. "I remember the tune."

Rio chewed her bottom lip. "Ever been in love? Deeply in love?"

Great. Of all the subjects she could have chosen, Rio had to choose love. "Can't say I have. I've never taken the time."

"That's a shame. Love can be wonderful."

She'd take Rio's word for it.

"I thought about hiring a private detective to find Johnny, but I don't know any. Besides, I can't afford one."

"You know one now." *What? Are you crazy?* blared in Darcy's brain. What about her vacation? On second thought, what vacation? The trip had already been ruined.

Rio's eyes widened. She jumped up. "So you'll help me? Oh, say you will. Please." Her hand closed on Darcy's arm.

She wanted to help, but nothing Rio had said so far convinced Darcy that Johnny was actually missing. He could've disappeared for any number of reasons.

"You don't believe me, do you?" Suddenly, the room turned very cold, almost as chilly as the outdoors. "Fine." Rio's lips sealed to a thin line, and her jaw jutted forward. "I'll just have to convince you." She flounced back into her chair, drew her knees to her chest, and tucked the blanket under her chin. "He made me promise not to breathe a word to anyone, but vanishing like this leaves me no choice." She shifted positions, signaling to Darcy she was in for a long story, but she really did want to help. "It all started about a month ago, Johnny mumbling in his sleep about dozens dead, sucked dry. Then he'd wake up drenched in sweat or shivering."

Darcy gazed at the grimy windows, which had no window coverings. If she slept in Wilson's shack, she'd shiver too.

Rio must have read Darcy's thoughts. "This was during the day. Not at night. We never spend the night in the winter. Not even a good sleeping bag would keep you warm."

A chill ran through Darcy; the thin blanket was inadequate to ward off the cold. She could have used a good sleeping bag right about now. "Go on."

"Johnny left work early Friday and met me here. Said he had something important to do Saturday, but he'd be at Wilson's around nine Sunday morning. I asked a lot of questions, but he refused to answer. He said he'd make me proud, but I *am* proud of him. He doesn't have to prove anything to me." Anger creased her brow. "I blame his mom for his inferiority complex. She was always calling him a wimp."

Darcy cut in. "Why were you digging in the dirt under Wilson's old cot?"

"I'll show you."

In the bedroom, Rio scooped up the flashlight and the knife lying nearby and raked back the dirt until she exposed a small metal box. "I think this belonged to Wilson. At one time, it locked." She pointed to the rusted latch. "Years ago, we'd leave messages in it for each other. I'd almost forgotten about the box until Johnny brought it up." She replaced the box and covered the top with loose earth. "He's been working weekends, using company resources—his words—to invent computer games. That's what I think he meant when he said he had something important to do Saturday night. I thought he'd lined up a buyer for his games."

"Were you checking the box for messages?"

"No, a flash drive."

A chill pulsed through Darcy.

"He worried that his boss might be on to him, so he planned to download his games from his work computer and store them on his Zipgig."

Computer games! Great.

"A Zipgig is a memory stick," said Rio.

"I know. I own one. Holds about three hundred gigabytes."

"Johnny told me his stores two terabytes."

Two TB, two TB, her brain repeated as if she'd never heard the words before. What if Rio was right and something sinister had happened to Johnny? "Let's assume Johnny is missing."

Rio clasped her hands together. "Thank God, you finally believe me."

"When you reported him missing, did you give Maddox a full description?"

Rio paused. "Like what he wore, that kind of thing?"

"Yes."

"No. Like I said, Maddox didn't seem the least bit concerned about Johnny. He cut me off in mid-sentence."

Odd. "When you saw Johnny on Friday, what was he wearing?"

"Jeans, turtleneck, black sweater, parka, and hiking boots."

"Gloves? Hat?" Darcy asked, doing her best not to raise suspicion.

"Leather gloves and a wool stocking cap."

Darcy's heart fluttered. In as calm a voice as she could muster, she asked, "What color was the cap?"

"Gosh, is it important?"

Darcy avoided eye contact. "I'm sure Johnny's fine and there's a simple explanation for his disappearance, but it's smart to give the police a full description. The color?"

"Blue. Light blue, to be exact."

Sadly, Rio had just convinced Darcy he was missing.

"He's not coming back, is he?" Tears glimmered in her eyes.

"Of course, he is. He'd be a fool not to." But the compliment was lost on Rio.

"He has to come back. He has a right to know." She covered her face with her hands.

"To know what?"

The weeping subsided, and only whispered words hung in the air. "I'm pregnant."

5

After Rio's announcement the only sound in Wilson's frigid house drifted from the worn couch where Bullet snored. At least someone knew peace. She glanced from him to Rio, who had her head on her knees, her eyes shut, and black hair framing one side of her tear-stained face. Darcy wanted to lighten the emotional burden she must be feeling, but how? Thankfully, Charlene hadn't treated her to news of a pregnancy. Stoned on more occasions than Darcy cared to remember, Charlene had somehow managed to avoid conception. For that matter, Darcy had no idea if her sister was still a virgin. The two seldom had serious talks. Most times, they simply danced around a subject. Strange how little she knew about her sister's innermost thoughts and secrets. She shared more with her friends than she ever did with Charlene. It was so easy to blame their problems on the age gap, but Darcy admitted the twenty-year difference had little bearing on the rift in their relationship.

Recalling the past unsettled her. Restless, she wandered to the windows. The sun's rays had waned, and a cold draft snaked its way through a cracked pane. Soon, the temperature would drop even further. Time to rouse Rio.

But before she could, Rio said, "How do you feel about abortion?"

Darcy spun around. The question stabbed her heart. "You aren't serious?" she said without thinking.

Anger fired Rio's face. "Funny, I didn't figure you for a pro-lifer."

"Why are we discussing abortion when we should be talking about finding the father?"

"Have *you* ever been pregnant?" Defiance flared in Rio's eyes.

"We aren't talking about me."

"Sorry I asked. I thought you'd understand." Rio threw off the blanket.

Darcy started toward her. "I didn't mean to sound judgmental."

"To you, abortion might seem like the easy way out . . ."

It is. The answer rolled to the tip of Darcy's tongue. Quickly, she shut her mouth. However, it went against her nature to say nothing. "Okay, so you're in a tough spot, and it looks like there's no way out. But you're wrong. See the pregnancy through, then if you don't think you can care for the baby, give the child up for adoption. I promise I'll help in any way I can."

"You've never been in a really tight spot before, have you?" The tears surfaced. "Don't you think abortion is a tough call?"

"Yes, probably one of life's toughest, but if you make a rash decision you'll regret it the rest of your life."

"Either way, abortion or adoption, the decision will haunt me forever." Rio broke into a sob.

"Adoption will haunt you less," Darcy was about to say, but she didn't want the discussion to become a fight. "Why are we talking about giving the child away? Let's find the baby's father. Let's find Johnny."

"My dad—"

"Forget him," Darcy said in a calm voice. "This is your life. You have a baby to think about, not your parents. Come on. We're both freezing, and I'd like a look at Enzo's place before nightfall."

"Enzo's place? Oh, okay." The distraction seemed to help. "Thanks, Darcy."

"If you don't feel comfortable going home, stay with me. There's plenty of room."

Rio stood. "I can't even afford to live on my own, never mind raise a child."

"We'll deal with that problem when we come to it." Darcy folded the blankets. "Do you work?"

"Part-time, for a title company in town. I'm a gopher. And a high school dropout." Her short laugh ended in a sniffle.

Darcy hugged Rio. "Everything will be fine." She shouldered her backpack, collected Bullet, and closed up.

On the hike back to her 4Runner, she mulled over Rio's dilemma—now Darcy's predicament since she'd volunteered to help. As always, she tackled challenges from two angles: practical and emotional. Working through pragmatic issues was simply a matter of logistics, but when it came to emotions, she fell short. Charlene could attest to that.

Why didn't young people think about what they were doing before they . . . ? Had she at nineteen? No. True, she'd made her share of mistakes, but becoming a single parent? Darcy knew how hard she'd struggled to raise Charlene. Being a parent was, in her estimation, the hardest job in life, and fortunately for her, she didn't have financial worries on top of all her responsibilities, thanks to income from McClain Import Export, the company her parents started.

Bullet barked as if to say, "Are you coming?"

Darcy picked up the pace.

"About Enzo's house," said Rio as Darcy approached. "Mind going alone? I'm tired and I want to go home."

"Not at all. So you're not coming back to the guesthouse with me?"

"No. Thank you. Just drop me at the fork in the road." She climbed into the passenger's seat of Darcy's 4Runner.

When the cutoff came into view, Darcy pulled to the shoulder of the road. "If you need anything, call me." She handed her business card to Rio. "My local number's on the back. Cell's on the front. Do you have a key to Enzo's house? I'd like to go in if I can."

"Sure. Glad you said something. I'm not thinking clearly." Rio handed over a key ring. "The gold one is Enzo's. Silver is Johnny's, in case you want to check his place too. You'll need addresses."

Darcy peeled back the cover on her iPad. "Shoot." She typed in Johnny's address. "What's Enzo's?"

"It's easier to just give you directions. Turn right at the fork and follow the easement to where it dead ends. The drive to the right is Enzo's. The other's a hiking trail. Thanks again." Rio shut the door and started up the dirt road, her shoulders hunched forward and head bowed.

Compassion tugged at Darcy's heart. She wanted to wish away Rio's burden, but all she could do was offer support. She waited a few minutes to be sure Rio hadn't changed her mind, then drove down the lane to Enzo's house.

She parked in the shadows at the far end of the driveway and climbed out of her 4Runner. After a brief pause to check her surroundings, she walked slowly up the narrow path to the portal of the territorial-style home, and glanced about again, the air dead calm. Fading daylight washed the porch, tingeing the sun-bleached patio cushions a soft gold. She peered through one of the strip windows that flanked the entry. No sign of life. Still, she knocked. No one answered, so she slid the key into the lock. Damn, she forgot to ask Rio if the house had a security system—or worse, a silent alarm. This mistake had happened once before, and explaining to the officers who'd caught her admiring a Ming vase in the house of a murdered art collector was difficult at best. Rookie days. She'd wised up since then. Or had she?

Darcy nudged the door open with her knee. Silence. She set her backpack on the entry floor, pocketed a few Ziploc bags, and snapped on latex gloves. Her gaze traveled over the walls, hunting for a switch. She located one near the entrance and flicked the light on. White blazed from a chandelier of deer antlers and tubular bulbs arranged in a circle. The contraption hung above a U-shaped beige sectional that had seen better days. Navajo rugs blanketed the tiled floor, and framed posters of the New Mexico landscape adorned the walls. Nothing appeared disturbed, and not even a single footprint marked the dingy off-white carpeting.

She began her search in the kitchen. No dishwasher, and no dishes on the drainboard or in the sink. She ran a wet paper towel under the lip of the cabinets. Not even a speck of dirt. Her place should be this spotless. The refrigerator disappointed as well. Empty shelves, recently cleaned. In the adjacent laundry room, the washer and dryer stood empty, and no clothes were anywhere.

She poked her head into the spare bedrooms. Again, not a single footprint graced the light tan carpet. Beds stripped in both rooms. Closets empty.

Much of the same greeted her in the master bedroom. Everything gleamed. She entered the bathroom and stepped into the shower. The sharp odor of Clorox made her eyes water. Kneeling, she pried the drain cap loose with her pocket knife and inspected the trap. In the narrow space a silver mass sparkled. She scooped up the wad of steel wool with the knifepoint and inspected it more closely after she noticed brown hairs embedded in the coil. She bagged it.

On her way out of the master, she stopped in the doorway. Something about the bedroom bothered her, so she strolled back in for another look. The bed sat at an odd angle. She crouched down and looked underneath. Near the foot of each bedpost was a deep indentation, the impression discolored a yellow brown. Someone had moved the bed but hadn't returned it to its original position.

"Looking for anything in particular?" A male voice resounded through the house.

Darcy jumped up so fast, her vision blurred.

The man repeated his sentence as he advanced.

6

"Deputy Sheriff Ron Maddox," said the uniformed officer who blocked the doorway. The introduction sounded like a threat.

"Darcy McClain." She extended her hand.

His eyes locked on the exposed shoulder rig.

"I have a permit."

Stone-faced, Maddox caressed his holster, his cold eyes riveted to Darcy's Browning. "You a friend of the homeowner? If not, I'd like an explanation."

She wanted to ask him the same question, but why antagonize the man? Instead, she smiled but failed to thaw him. "I'm a friend of a friend."

He stayed close to the door as though he regarded her as a flight risk. "And the friend is?"

She wondered if discussing the matter with Maddox would

anger Rio, but how else could she carry out an investigation if she couldn't ask questions? "Regina O'Neil."

He snorted. "Oh, her."

The dismissive remark irked Darcy. "According to Rio, she reported Johnny Duran missing several days ago."

"Two." Maddox held up two fingers to emphasize his point.

"What action's been taken on the report?"

"You'd have to check with Missing Persons. If you're done here . . ." He moved aside, allowing her to go first.

She brushed by and looked over her shoulder; Maddox stood inches behind her. "So you can't tell me anything about Johnny's disappearance?"

"I told you, contact Missing Persons. Happy to give you their phone number." He never broke eye contact.

"You aren't convinced he's missing, are you?"

He removed his hat and toyed with the brim, dark eyes fixed on her. Pale sunlight shone off his black hair, the strands slicked back from his tanned face. "What's your interest, Ms. McClain?"

"And I told you. Rio's a friend, and she asked me to help her find Johnny."

He leaned forward, his blank gaze unwavering. "You move fast."

The remark puzzled her. "Beg your pardon?"

He raised an eyebrow. "One day in Taos and already you're good friends with Regina O'Neil. Don't look stunned, Ms. McClain. Taos is a small town. Word travels. You inherited the old Wilson homestead."

"Since you know so much about me, I guess you also know—"

"You're a licensed PI." For the first time, Maddox smiled, the grin forced. "But in California, not New Mexico."

He'd done his homework. "Is that a warning?"

He flashed another stiff smile. "Good advice worth heeding." He put on his hat and motioned to the front door.

She headed for the foyer, surprised Bullet hadn't alerted her to Maddox's presence. No one ever tricked his radar. Unless Maddox had approached the house from the back and on foot, which would ensure he wouldn't be seen or heard by Bullet; this approach made sense if he wanted to avoid detection. For she strongly suspected he had been following her. He knew too much about her and her association with Rio in the short time she'd been in Taos.

Maddox reached for the door handle, hesitated, then turned. "You can take those off now." He nodded to her hands.

She still wore the latex gloves. Darcy stripped them off, stuffed them in her pocket, and scooped up her backpack.

"You always haul that thing around? Looks heavy."

"I like to travel prepared." She anticipated his next question, but again, he surprised her. He didn't ask to search her or the Kelty. Strange. In his position, she would have.

Outside the temperature had fallen.

The minute Maddox appeared on the porch, Bullet exploded in a fit of barking. "Big dog. What kind?"

Why was he interested? "A giant schnauzer."

"Never seen one before."

"Neither had I, until I inherited him," said Darcy, still hoping to strike up a conversation with the Iceman and tap him for more information.

"You seem to have a knack for inheriting things."

"Seems so." Darcy zipped up her parka, locked the front door, and joined him on the gravel drive. She looked about for a patrol car, but saw none. "Must've been a long walk."

Her dry sense of humor had no effect on him. "Night comes early in winter. Goodbye, Ms. McClain. I assume you know your way into town."

Darcy walked leisurely toward her 4Runner, her eyes scanning the area for a squad car. *Night comes early in winter.* What in the heck did that mean? An observation or an omen? Sure sounded cryptic.

She climbed behind the wheel and let the engine warm up, hoping Maddox would leave so she could search the grounds around Enzo's house before nightfall. But the deputy had no intention of going anywhere. He lit a cigarette.

Bullet poked his head through the window and rested his muzzle on the half-open glass. Minutes into his vigil, he growled. Darcy craned her neck to see down the drive. High beams pierced the trees, and a police cruiser rounded the bend. The officer at the wheel killed his lights as he rolled to a stop feet from Maddox, who immediately leaned into the squad car

"Radioing the station, perhaps?" Her question triggered a deep-throated growl from Bullet.

Darcy thought it best to leave, so she started down the lane but was unwilling to give up completely. She spotted a turnoff on her way to the main highway and nosed her 4Runner into a blind to wait for Maddox to drive by. An orange light pulsed from the dashboard. Damn—she needed gas! She shut off the engine.

Ten minutes ticked by, then twenty. The temperature dropped. She wiggled her numb feet and rubbed her hands to increase circulation.

Thirty minutes passed. A bright moon illuminated large flakes as they blew past the windshield. In seconds, snow mantled her hood. Freezing, Darcy shifted into gear and backed out of the brush.

The suv rumbled off one dirt road onto another as she threaded her way off the mountain. In the distance, coyotes howled. Bullet pressed his nose to the glass. A cloud formed on the frosty pane. She slowed as she neared the cutoff, her visibility seriously diminished by the oncoming storm. Bullet jerked his head from the window and stared straight ahead, his muzzle forward and ears cocked. Alerted, Darcy hit her high beams.

A figure dashed into the road.

She slammed on her brakes. The seatbelt cut into her chest. Bullet hit the side door with a thud and let out a yelp. The suv skidded to the right. Darcy cranked the wheel to the left, struggling to keep the vehicle from careening into the ditch that bordered the easement. She downshifted, glided to the center of the road, and gently applied the brakes. The suv slowed to a crawl and stopped. Angry, she flung open the door. Her hands clenched into fists and her heart thumping, she shouted into the blackness. "Are you out of your frickin' mind? I could have killed you."

Someone broke from the shadows. "I had to stop you. I . . . I . . ."

"Rio?"

7

Rio slid into the passenger's seat. "They threw me out. I thought they might change their minds once they knew about the baby, but Mom said she'd never be a grandmother to a half-breed. Their hearts are dead. Dad told me to never come back." She sniffed.

"Things'll get better. You'll see."

"They already have. Thanks." Rio smiled.

"I'm headed to Los Alamos to take a look at Johnny's duplex, but I'll drop you at the guesthouse first."

"No, I'm going with you."

"You sure?"

"Positive."

Darcy gassed up in town, bought hamburgers for the three of them, and sped south on Highway 68. The Toyota descended the steep curve into the horseshoe and flew past Pilar, the river village as black as night. A mile down the road, nature's spotlight broke from the clouds and shone its brilliance on the Rio Grande. The placid surface sparkled in the moonlight, the nocturnal scene a delight.

"How far to Johnny's place?" Darcy asked.

"From here, sixty miles or so." Rio munched a French fry. "Mind if I doze? I'm beat."

"Go ahead." The dashboard clock read nine fifteen. It crossed Darcy's mind to wait until daylight to visit Johnny's duplex, but something in Maddox's demeanor troubled her. Years ago she'd stopped trying to decipher these sparks of intuition. "Don't question it," her mother had advised. "Intuition is your second sight. Trust the feeling more than your own eyes."

As Darcy tooled through the farming towns along the Rio Grande, snores erupted from her travel companions. She envied them. Sleep sounded good right about now. She breezed through Española, traffic thinned by the late hour, and soon spotted the Los Alamos turnoff.

Rio sat bolt upright. "Oh no!"

Darcy jumped. "What? I took the wrong turn?"

"No, I forgot about Ollie."

"Who?"

"Johnny's cat. Last time I fed him was Sunday morning. Poor thing. He must be starving."

Darcy shook her head. "Scare me like that again, and you'll have me on your conscience as well."

"Sorry. When you were at Enzo's house, did Ollie have food and water?"

"I'm sure he's fine. Cats are pretty self-sufficient." Her mind flashed to Johnny's kitchen. No pet dishes on the counter or the floor. None in the utility room. No signs of an animal, period. She changed the subject to keep Rio from worrying but made a mental note to get a description of the cat, then check the local shelters and vet office's. "Now that everyone's wide awake, I have some questions."

"Ask away."

Darcy passed a vehicle and moved back into the slow lane. "Is Johnny a neat freak?"

Rio laughed. "Hardly. Why?"

She carefully phrased her next comment. "Just wondered. Enzo's place looked rather clean for a bachelor's."

"Really?" She sank against the seat. "On Sunday, when I fed Ollie, there were dirty dishes in the sink, clothes on the floor, and an unmade bed. The usual mess. I wanted to tidy up but didn't feel well. How clean was the place?"

"Not that clean," Darcy fibbed.

Rio looked out the window. "We're coming into Los Alamos."

Darcy drove slowly through the mountain community, taking in her shadowy surroundings. Johnny's duplex sat on a secluded cul-de-sac, the street well lit by antique lamp posts and the dormant greenbelts mowed short. She parked in the driveway and switched off the engine. "Nice place."

"Johnny couldn't afford the rent if it weren't for Andrew Silverbird, his best friend and next-door neighbor. Andy bought the duplex from his parents. He works at the lab, in the same department as Johnny."

"How far is LANL from here?"

"Ten minutes or so."

Darcy reached over the seat into the hatch for her backpack. "Wonder if Andrew's home."

"No. He's in Florida, visiting his girlfriend Elena."

Good. "Do me a favor. Stay with Bullet. If he hears the slightest noise, he'll wake the entire neighborhood."

Rio hesitated. "Okay."

The ploy worked. Not knowing what she might find, Darcy preferred to search alone.

Darcy walked briskly up the snow-dusted path toward Johnny's porch but didn't go to the front door. Instead, she cut across the open lot to Andrew's back patio and cupped her hands to a window. Dim light filtered from within. The decor, a mix of mauves, blues, and beige, indicated a woman's touch. She knocked. Although she believed Rio, she wanted to be sure Andrew hadn't returned. The last thing she needed was a call to the police about a suspected burglar. When no one answered, she retraced her steps to Johnny's duplex and strolled the yard, flashlight in hand, until the moon made an appearance.

The home backed onto a canyon overgrown with vegetation, the bronze foliage specked white with frost. A stream ran the length of the property. She crossed to the water's edge and paused on the bank to listen. A brisk wind laced with piñon smoke rustled the cattail-cloaked slopes, and water trickled over the rock dam into the pool below. Only her footprints violated the pristine snow.

She sidled down the incline to the creek bed and wandered the marshy banks, her eyes trained on the slow-moving water. She saw boulders, decaying reeds, and the typical amount of trash but nothing worth noting, so she headed back to Johnny's place and inserted Rio's key into the lock. The door refused to budge. She tried a second time. Maybe she had the wrong key. But how? Each was distinct. When neither worked in the deadbolt, she went to the front door. She had no better luck there. After she snagged her backpack off the porch, Darcy headed for her 4Runner.

Rio opened the window. "Done already?"

"Haven't been in. Can't get the key to work. You're sure this is the right one?"

"Positive. Want me to try?"

"Hang on a minute." Darcy popped open the glove box,

collected a soft leather pouch, and stuffed it in her pocket. To Bullet she said, "Stay. Quiet."

"Wow," said Rio, "He obeys well."

Darcy had just blown her credibility. She covered the blunder with "I'm never sure. He's a rescue."

"Oh." Rio marched across the frozen ground to the front door. Like Darcy, she inserted one key, then the other, but neither worked. She tried again, this time jiggling the knob vigorously.

"Don't think forcing the lock will work." Darcy removed the leather pouch from her parka. "This might be easier."

Rio leaned forward. "What are those?"

"Lock-picking tools." Darcy chose one.

"Cool. I thought you'd kick the door in."

"Why waste the energy when these babies will do the trick? Besides, breaking and entering is a crime." She gave the pouch to Rio to hold and she set to work.

"What's the difference?"

"One leaves evidence, the other doesn't."

Rio laughed. "I like your style, McClain."

"Thanks. This lock's a bear. Is there an alarm?"

"No." Rio shifted her weight from one leg to the other. "I'm freezing."

"So am I and my fingers are numb, which is probably part of the problem. Good, we're in." Darcy pushed open the door and entered first.

"The light switch is over there." Rio started toward the panel. "Should I turn it on?"

"Go ahead."

Darcy blinked; the sudden flare of light blinded her. The layout reminded her of her first apartment: small, sparsely furnished, few pictures on the wall, and a cinder block and wood plank bookcase, this one stacked with video games and a PlayStation, not books. "Stay here."

"Sure," said Rio.

Darcy glanced about the room, then continued her sweep of the first floor by stepping into the kitchen. As with Enzo's house, the duplex had been sanitized. She yanked open cupboard doors and looked in the refrigerator; both areas had been cleaned, and she saw no dishes in the dishwasher.

"Going upstairs," Darcy said.

Rio grunted a reply, her eyes on her smartphone.

Darcy mounted the stairs to the bedroom loft, not surprised to see only a bed and a nightstand. She entered the bathroom. A musty smell lingered in the stale air. She pulled open the shower door. The drain trap sparkled, so she could forget about finding any evidence there.

Back in the bedroom, she peered under the bed. The strong scent of musk wafted from the carpet, the frieze recently cleaned and all clues scrubbed into oblivion. Someone had even been careful about replacing the furniture; not a single telltale depression lingered in the dingy beige fibers.

Downstairs, Darcy paused before Johnny's collection of video game posters. One in particular captured her attention: *Last Man Standing*, a favorite of hers. After the player conquered the world, the sole survivor's prize was to create a new world, one in which the winner called all the shots. Recalling the premise sent a tingle of euphoria through her, but the feeling was soon dashed by a sense of urgency that just grew stronger when she expected it to fade. "We have to go." Darcy grabbed Rio's arm on her way out the front door.

"What's wrong?"

"Don't know. Instinct. Have to get back to Enzo's as fast as I can. Come on."

"Why? What's going on?"

"Told you. Don't know."

Halfway across the front lawn, she pressed her car remote. The locks shot up. She yanked open the driver's door and dove behind the wheel. The engine was idling when Rio got in. "Sorry I sounded short back there. It's a feeling. I can't explain it."

"Then let's go. Got a radar detector in this rig?"

Darcy stifled a laugh. She hadn't seen this side of her new friend. "No, so you're it. Keep your eyes on the mirrors."

"Yes, ma'am. The traffic's light, so it should be easy to spot a cop. Just go slow through Española. There we'll have to watch for them."

Seemed like an eternity before Darcy closed in on the outskirts of Española and an injustice to crawl through the empty town at thirty miles per hour. She made up for the delay by speeding through the farms that hemmed the river. With only one northbound lane and a series of sharp curves, she had no trouble monitoring police activity. From Pilar, she accelerated and zipped up the steep incline toward Taos. The 4Runner capped the first ridge, dropped into the horseshoe, and glided up the road to the last plateau.

"Cop," said Rio. "A local guy, coming from Taos."

Darcy eased off the pedal. The cruiser flew by. "Where's the turnoff? It's pitch-black out there."

"Coming up. As you near the road, cut your speed. There's a deputy camped on the shoulder. It's his favorite hangout."

Rio was right. Darcy crawled past the squad car and inched up the dusty washboard road, giving the officer no reason to stop her. She missed the turn to Enzo's and doubled back. "Glad you're along. I'm in no mood to get lost." She leaned into the steering wheel and searched the night through a bug-specked windshield.

"What's up?" Rio asked.

"Somewhere here there's a blind, a shallow easement."

"Another twenty feet or so up the road. There." Rio pointed out the hiding place.

Darcy parked in the same blind she had earlier and shut off the engine. "Stay with Bullet."

"Not this time, and I don't want an argument." Rio put on her hat and gloves.

"Then keep your voice down."

Darcy led the way up Enzo's easement, retreating to the protection of the shadows as the moon appeared and disappeared with the shifting cloud cover. She stopped to listen. "Thought I heard something."

Rio moved closer. "There's a shortcut near the garage." She ducked into the sagebrush, and Darcy hurried after her.

The meandering trail ended in a field where a vegetable garden once grew. Beyond, floodlights set the desert night ablaze. "Stay while I check this out. No argument."

Darcy slipped into the sage and moved as close as she dared to the lit clearing. A short dark man in a baseball cap, brown hair streaming down his back, paced the gravel drive. She fished out her binoculars and scanned the length of his body, from the NRA emblem on his hat to his regulation combat boots.

Clad in khaki, he strutted back and forth and barked orders to the uniformed officers moving in and out of Enzo Duran's house. She squinted, astonished to see the local cops cart one stick of furniture after another from the home to a white semi parked at the end of the circular drive. She counted approximately a dozen men, but she had a hard time keeping track with them all dressed alike and constantly on the move.

She panned the binoculars over the trailer—no markings and no plates—then back to the front door. Bewildered, she watched two men emerge with a roll of carpet slung over their shoulders. They dodged another two hauling linoleum. The four chucked the flooring into the truck and headed back inside the home.

A twig snapped.

Darcy tensed. She unsnapped her holster and grasped warm steel.

"What's going on?" asked Rio, appearing at Darcy's side.

"Don't sneak up on me. Ever. You could get shot."

Rio nodded.

Maddox sauntered onto the porch and joined the man in khaki.

Rio scooted closer, her breath warm on Darcy's numb ear. "What's happening?"

"See the man in khaki?"

"I'm talking about the men over there."

She lowered her binoculars and looked where Rio pointed. One by one, the officers streamed toward the truck. Each carried or wheeled a fixture or an appliance.

"Toilet, sink. Weird," Rio whispered. "I've never seen a cop pack an Uzi. Any idea what's up?"

"No. Wonder what Enzo will say when he finds his house has been looted."

"You're kidding, right?"

"Why would I be?"

"The man in khaki . . . that is Enzo Duran."

8

Rio's remark took a moment to register. "You're sure that's Enzo?"

"Positive. They're leaving," said Rio.

A truck engine roared to life, and the loud pop of gravel, crushed beneath the weight of a sixteen-wheeler, blasted the night. The grinding gradually died as the rig disappeared down the road, the stench of diesel fouling the air.

Enzo eased into the passenger's seat of a squad car, Maddox already at the wheel, and the car faded into the nebulous shadows of night.

Darcy jumped up. "Come on." She ran for the trees that edged the stone walk and stole up the path to the front door. By the time Rio arrived, Darcy had tried unlocking the deadbolt twice. "Someone changed the locks." She made for the back porch.

Rio caught up. "Locked too?"

"Yes. Dammit. Here, hold this." She thrust the leather pouch at Rio.

"I think it's so cool you can pick a lock."

"Thanks, but it's nothing to brag about." Darcy cursed as she felt a pinch.

"You okay?"

"Hurt my finger. There, the door's open."

"Boy, you're quick." Rio took the tool from Darcy's outstretched hand and replaced it in the pouch.

"Keep watch, okay? Don't turn on any lights."

"Oh, all right."

Darcy rummaged in her pockets for her penlight. Her second tour of Enzo's house went fast because there wasn't much left to search: bare walls surrounding her, cement slab underfoot, and overhead a ceiling with no light fixtures, fans, or vent covers. Even the interior doors were gone, ripped from their hinges, the brass dangling from splintered pine.

She returned to the entry. "Let's leave through the side door."

"Look at the floor," said Rio. "They chipped up the tile."

"I noticed." Darcy locked up and lingered on the portal. The sanitized homes disturbed her. Why the cover-up?

Rio leaned against the wall. "Do you think any of this has to do with Johnny's disappearance?"

"Not sure, but I plan to find out."

"Are you going to confront Enzo?"

Darcy chose her words carefully, trying not to add to Rio's worries. "If I get the chance. If not, I'll get answers somehow."

"Thanks again for helping me."

"We'll find him. Come on. Let's go." Darcy strolled across the side patio and down the steps, eager to reach the rental and settle in. She felt tired from the cross-country drive, the round trip to Los Alamos, plus the stakeout at Enzo's; her body screamed for food, a shower, and sleep in precisely that order. But she'd never rest without first sneaking a peek at the data saved on Johnny's thumb drive, which meant she needed time alone.

She slid behind the wheel of her 4Runner, fired up the engine, and drove away from Enzo's house. Her stomach growled.

"I'm hungry too," said Rio, belted into the passenger's seat.

A week prior, Darcy had the foresight to ask the realtor who leased the home to stock the pantry with a few items in case she arrived late and the grocery stores had closed. Thank goodness she'd planned ahead.

Planning brought to mind her predicament regarding her land. From the moment she learned Rio's parents owned the parcel adjacent to hers, Darcy had wanted to ask Rio if they'd consider an easement agreement. Now she had her chance. "Did you know my property's landlocked?"

"Yes, of course."

The comment came as no surprise. Everyone seemed to know but Darcy. "Which means I'll probably be here a while unless . . ."

"Forget it. Randolph tried but couldn't convince Dad to even listen to his offers. My adoptive parents are assholes."

"What a pain."

Rio sighed. "I agree, but you can put some of the blame on Wilson. When Grandpa sold the land to Wilson, it had an easement to the north between Enzo's tract and the Blackman's."

"Enzo as in Johnny's uncle?" asked Darcy as she motored toward town.

"Yes."

Cozy community.

"But stubborn old Wil demanded one from the south. The landowners said no and stuck to their decision."

Undeterred, Darcy said, "There's a spark of hope. Maybe your grandfather recorded the north easement?"

Rio frowned. "Not to my knowledge."

Still, Darcy persisted. "Tomorrow, point me toward the county offices and I'll check the map books."

"Don't get your hopes up. Taos isn't California. Here, some people still do business on a handshake."

"Maybe I can renegotiate the north easement with Enzo and Blackman."

"Good luck. The Blackman sons own the land now, and they're real . . ."

"Assholes."

Rio chuckled. "You said it."

And who knew what Enzo was up to or where she might find him? "Great."

"You'll need time, money, and loads of patience."

The latter, a virtue Darcy didn't possess. "You said you worked for a title company in town."

Rio hesitated. "Yes."

"Which means you probably have some good contacts and know your way around the recording office."

Rio smiled. "True. Why?"

If Darcy planned to find Johnny, she didn't have the time to bird-dog this land issue; nor did she have the inclination to do so. She wanted to resolve the problem and quickly, so she could do what she loved best—detective work. Darcy needed help, and Rio, in her estimation, needed a better-paying job, one that might take the pressure off her, thereby squelching any thought of an abortion.

"Earth to Darcy."

Darcy laughed. "Sorry. Been thinking through a few details and have a proposition for you. I can't devote my full attention to finding Johnny if I'm sidetracked with this easement issue, so I could use help dealing with the county and the attorney I plan to hire to resolve the problem."

"Who's that?"

"Matt Mackenzie."

"Excellent choice. Best real estate attorney in Taos."

"Good. So are you game?"

"You bet."

"What's the title company paying you?"

Rio looked sheepish. "Minimum wage. I'm only a gopher."

Darcy thought as much. "I'll pay double."

"Really? Oh, thanks, Darcy. How can I repay you?"

"Do a good job."

Rio rubbed her hands together. "When do I start?"

Darcy tapped her iPad, which was sitting precariously on the console. "Take notes. First, call Matt and set up an appointment. The time and date's irrelevant, but the sooner the better. Next, call Dan Gruet, my former partner at the FBI. He's retired now but owns a detective agency in San Francisco. We help each other from time to time."

"Will he help find Johnny?"

The hope in her voice struck a chord in Darcy. "Sure, if he can. His number's in my contact list."

"So you really do plan to look for Johnny?"

"I gave my word."

Minutes outside of Ranchos de Taos, Darcy exited the highway and wound her way inland toward the foothills. "When you have a chance, go to maps."

"To find the rental?" asked Rio without looking up from typing.

"Yes."

"No need. I used to ride my horse all through this area until people gobbled up the land, fenced themselves in, posted no trespassing signs, and bought shotguns. See the light pole up ahead? The Peters live there. Turn to the right."

Another impassible easement, or so it appeared. Darcy eased her 4Runner onto the uneven road.

The Toyota rattled over the rocky lane. A boulder nicked the passenger tire. Darcy steered to the shoulder, the grade flatter and smoother.

"Any minute, we'll come to a bridge. There. Cross and hang an immediate left." Rio wiped condensation off the windshield with a paper towel and replaced the partial roll to the door storage compartment.

Darcy adjusted the vent lever and upped the fan to clear the rest of the glass. "Five secluded acres, the agent said. No kidding. Where's the house?"

"Straight ahead. You can barely see the outline."

As expected, the house looked enormous—far too big for her needs, but she was already committed. She parked the 4Runner outside the compound and climbed out. The passenger door burst open, and Rio, her hand clapped over her mouth, ran into the darkness. Darcy grabbed bottled water and the paper towels. She found Rio sitting on a rock near the bridge, her head down and breathing labored.

"Have you seen a doctor?"

Rio took the towel Darcy doused with water and dabbed at the perspiration beading on her forehead. "Not yet. I feel better now. Honest." She stood but sat down again. "I need a few minutes."

"You don't look good." Darcy held out her hand. "Let's go in where you can lie down."

"Some assistant I am."

"Ease up. You'll be fine in the morning."

"It is morning."

Darcy expected Rio to retire soon after they went in, but she waved away the idea and headed straight to the kitchen to fix tea. "Want a cup?"

"Yes, thanks. I'll warm some soup, if you're interested."

"A little bit." Rio sat at the counter while Darcy heated clam chowder and popped bread into the toaster. She fed Bullet and slid onto a stool beside Rio. The meal over, she waited impatiently for Rio to retreat to her room, but she didn't, so Darcy poured hot water into her cup. The tea tasted bland, drained of its flavor after three cups. She paced the kitchen and acted busy by loading the dishwasher and cleaning the counter. Each time she passed the Kelty, her gaze fell on the side pocket, the USB safely zipped inside. Come on, Rio, go to bed.

Rio yawned. "I'm wide awake now. Why don't we take the grand tour? Looks like an interesting house."

"Okay," Darcy replied, forcing herself to sound cheerful. "According to the realtor, there's the main house here with an apartment over the attached two-car garage, and a small guesthouse at the back of the enclosed courtyard."

"Which bedroom should I take?"

"Your pick."

"The main house. Okay?"

"Works for me. I'll take the garage apartment."

"Big place you rented."

Too big. "I know," said Darcy.

They toured the main house first; the interior was decorated in a disarray of wicker baskets, framed posters, and clay pots. The collection hung from wall hooks or ceiling anchors. Pottery adorned the end tables, Indian blankets covered the pine furniture, and Mexican artifacts graced every nook and corner. The bedrooms were sparsely furnished but neat and clean.

A glass-enclosed breezeway off the kitchen led to the guesthouse out back. One side of the passageway overlooked a stone courtyard. The other faced north with a commanding view of Taos Mountain.

The guesthouse's decor mimicked that of the main house: cluttered. The rooms smelled of fresh paint, scented candles, and potpourri. Darcy sneezed. She crossed the small living room and opened the glass sliding door; the outside air cold and dry. A flagstone courtyard connected the two buildings, and a compound wall approximately six feet high cloistered both structures.

"Well, I've seen enough," said Rio abruptly. "Bedtime."

"Sounds like a plan." Darcy followed Rio back through the breezeway to the main house.

In the kitchen, Rio grabbed her backpack off the floor, said goodnight, and made her way down the hall to the bedrooms. The minute she turned the corner, Darcy snagged her Kelty and took the steps to the garage apartment two at a time, Bullet at her heels.

Upstairs she found two rooms, one furnished as a bedroom and the other as a study with a sofa bed on one wall and a desk and chair near the glass sliding door. Across from them, she discovered a kitchenette and a bathroom. Bullet immediately claimed the sofa bed and fell fast asleep.

Darcy removed her laptop and iPad from her Kelty and placed them on the desk. After she gloved up, she unzipped the side pouch of her backpack and scooped up the flash drive. Her hands shook with excitement, making it difficult to plug the module into the USB port on her computer. On the third try, she seated the drive and slid into the chair.

She double-clicked the mouse. Nothing happened, so she double-clicked again. "Come on." Four folders popped onto the screen. She scrolled to the JPEG file first and clicked on it. Gibberish. Next, she tried the Excel spreadsheet. Same result. The database, the Word file, and everything stored on the device translated to pure gibberish. Ciphertext! Great. From experience, Darcy knew that success at cracking code hinged upon the complexity of the encryption. However, her greatest enemy wasn't skill but time.

9

Too wired to sleep, Darcy slipped on her parka, wrapped a scarf around her neck, and pulled on a wool hat. Awakened by her movements, Bullet raised his head but made no attempt to follow, so alone she stepped onto the outdoor staircase that served the garage apartment and descended to the enclosed courtyard.

Even in winter, the dormant landscape impressed. Tall red and black reeds intertwined with yellow and brown grasses, the combination a striking visual against the white adobe walls and backlit by the subtle indoor lights. She gravitated toward a heavy, weathered wooden gate at one end of the compound and yanked on the handle until it opened. The rusty hinges cried for a good oiling.

Moonlight guided her down the long drive to the dirt ease-ment. She stood there between gravel and earth to enjoy the tranquil night, her mind working on a plan to decipher the data on the flash drive. Dan would be her best bet. Stuck in Taos, she didn't have the means or the time to crack code.

A vapor light, high on an electrical pole near the main house, flickered on. Darcy made her way toward it, eyes surveying the dark shadows along the deserted lane. Noting nothing of interest, she turned at the mouth of the drive to go back.

Movement came from her left. She spun.

A figure in a parka much greener than the rest of the vegetation broke from the piñons and loitered feet from her parked Toyota. Instinctively, Darcy stepped backward into the tree line to watch. The man looked about, peered into the windows of her vehicle, then disappeared into the cover of the night.

Darcy tailed him, darting from one stand of junipers to the next until he came into view. An uneasy feeling swept over her. What if he was after Rio?

Hidden among the trees, Darcy retraced her route to the house. As she reached the vapor light, she paused to check her back. Green flashed to her right—an emerald streak in a sea of olive, the brightness in sharp contrast to the subdued surroundings. He too had retraced his steps and was now stalking her. Not sure if he'd seen her, she ducked under the boughs of a juniper and groped her jacket for the night vision binoculars she kept zipped into her breast pocket.

Took her a few seconds to catch him in the viewfinder, but she found him. He lurked near some sagebrush—crouched down, his shoulders hunched forward and binoculars cupped to his eyes. She panned the terrain around him, searching for whatever he sought but saw nothing out of the ordinary—except him. He evidently had no understanding of the desert or camouflage; his parka was the wrong shade of green.

The minutes passed. Her arms grew tired. As the cold, damp night settled into her tired bones, she leaned her elbows on her knees, praying he'd leave. As if he read her thoughts, the man sprang to his feet and ran off.

Darcy scurried from beneath the tree and chased him to a bend in the easement. She jogged wide, saw the pickup, and increased speed, but too late. Under the glow of the Peters's light pole, Green threw himself behind the wheel and sped off in a cloud of dust.

Concerned about Rio and Bullet alone in the house, Darcy headed back to the compound. The wind shifted direction and snow started to fall, the weatherman's prediction of a cold front right on target. She hurried up the outdoor staircase and entered the garage apartment just as the clock in the hall chimed the half hour.

In the downstairs kitchen, she located the garage door remote exactly where the realtor said she'd put it, then moved her 4Runner into a bay before she grabbed a wineglass and a bottle of sauvignon blanc from the fridge.

Back in her office, she nursed her wine and gazed at the town below, the valley awash in white. Why hadn't Dan called? She slid into the desk chair. Her elbow brushed the mouse. The screen came to life, illuminating her cell phone nearby. "Where are you, Gruet?" She reached for her iPhone, ready to call again, when it vibrated. Finally. "Hey, where've you been?"

"Long damn day. Hope I didn't wake you. Your message said to call no matter what time. Must be important."

"I think so, but what's going on with you?"

Disturbed by her voice, Bullet hopped off the sofa bed.

Dan sighed. "This court case is a bitch, but not worth going into. What's up?"

"Rick, your new hire . . . he did a stint at the NSA, right?"

"Just like you. We nicknamed him Cryptowhiz." Dan yawned. "Sorry."

Good, because she needed someone who had worked at the

National Security Agency (NSA) to break this baby. "I need a top-notch code maker."

"What for?"

"To break code."

Bullet darted under her outstretched legs. Startled, Darcy gasped.

"You all right?"

"Fine. Bullet just scared the crap out of me."

"Hold on. Let me grab my laptop."

She heard him boot up.

"Okay. Go ahead."

Darcy filled him in, ending with, "Every damn file on the drive's encrypted."

"I imagine they'd be if he wanted to protect his data. How come you need Rick? You're not exactly a novice at this."

"Don't have the time or the equipment to crack this baby."

"Sounds like Johnny knew what he was doing?"

"His cryptographic system is asymmetric encryption."

Dan grunted. "Two keys—one to encrypt the data and another to decrypt."

"Which means the recipient, in this case me, needs to use the same application to decode the data Johnny used to encode it. Now how the hell am I going to do that stuck here in Taos?"

"Good point."

"That's why I need Rick."

"Sounds like something beyond his expertise," said Dan.

"Not if he links up with Bill Wilder at the NSA. If I recall, Bill was one of the privileged few who attended the unveiling of CryptoForce, the agency's multibillion-dollar code-breaking machine."

Dan acknowledged this with an uh-huh.

"I'm sure Bill will let Rick use the computer to perform a brute-force attack—for a price, of course."

"No can do. Wilder retired last year."

Her shoulders drooped. Another setback. "Damn. Why don't I send the drive anyway? Maybe you can network with some of our old contacts."

"I can't."

"Why not?" She heard the edge in her tone. "Sorry. I'm frustrated."

"Because NSA's CryptoForce has been upstaged by the next generation, a quantum-speed supercomputer called G-cell."

"I don't care what they call the darn thing as long as it can crack code." Easy, McClain. He's not the enemy.

"I'm not telling you this to piss you off, but G-cell is LANL's baby now."

Darcy groaned. "Wonderful."

"The computer is off-limits to civilians, i.e., us. Not even an act of Congress or God will get you near G."

"Crap." Her mind jumped to her contingency plan. "Do you still have connections on the Hill?"

"Haven't spoken to anyone at LANL in years, but I'll see what I can do."

Bullet growled.

Darcy swiveled in her chair.

Bullet paced in front of the glass sliding door.

"Thanks. Are you still working with Testco?" she asked.

"Sure am. Why?"

Bullet slid gracefully to the tiled floor but remained alert.

"In the meantime, while you're checking your contacts on the Hill, why don't I mail the thumb drive to Testco, have their lab check for blood and fingerprints—assuming anything's left after Bullet mouthed the memory stick," Darcy said.

"Good idea."

"Along with the drive, I'll send the hat and other evidence

I mentioned. Or what I think is evidence. And a few shots of the area."

Bullet cocked his head, then jerked his muzzle to the left. What had his attention? The wind?

"Testco's forensics guy," said Darcy, "the one who does field . . ."

Bullet rose silently to his feet.

Dan yawned. "Clark."

"What?"

"I said Clark. Ed Clark. The forensics guy."

Toenails clicked on the tile as Bullet padded into the kitchenette.

Darcy tried to concentrate. "Can you contact him? And ask if he'll process the site as a crime scene?"

"Sure."

She walked to the doorway. "Now I have to dream up an excuse for him being here."

"Because of Rio?"

"Exactly."

"Missing person's expert. He's there to help find Johnny."

Bullet reappeared. Restless, he looped the bank of windows and trotted out of the room again. Maybe he had business to do.

Dan's voice snapped Darcy to attention. "You still there?"

"I'm here. Good cover—a missing person's expert—but at some point I'll have to level with her. Wish I handled that sort of thing better."

"You mean a heart-to-heart."

"Yeah."

Bullet dashed past her desk, sliding across the wood floor until he reached the windows. His paws on the sill, he peered out.

"You aren't alone," said Dan.

Darcy tensed. "What?"

"You're falling asleep on me. I agreed with you. Heart-to-hearts are tough."

Bullet growled, the sound low in his throat.

"I better go." Her hand closed on the semiautomatic lying nearby. "I think Rio's awake."

"Sleep tight." Dan hung up.

She scooped her Browning off the desk and stood beside Bullet. He stared straight ahead. She touched his flank, but the gesture went unheeded. Deep within him a vibration rumbled and grew.

"Sh," said Darcy.

The hostile growl died. She scanned her office; the rectangular room featured windows along an entire wall. The panes butted up against the sliding door, and her desk was positioned in the center of the room, facing all the glass.

His head cocked, Bullet slunk toward the windows as though stalking prey.

A silhouette appeared on the balcony.

Darcy's heart lurched. "Quiet," she whispered, her mouth close to Bullet's ear.

The person crossed the patio to the row of windows and vanished. Bullet propelled himself into the hall and barreled by the kitchenette, his paws pedaling across the tile as he fought to gain traction. Darcy overtook him, but not for long. He cut sharply in front of her, and she almost fell over him trying to reach the backdoor.

A shadow darkened the outdoor landing. Bullet froze. The person cupped his hands to the glass inset, then jiggled the knob. Bullet charged the door with such force that he rattled the panes in the adjacent windows. Loud, angry barks shattered the night.

"What's going on?" someone shouted.

Darcy turned, surprised by Rio's sudden appearance. Before she could reply, Rio hit the light switch, and the porch spotlight blazed to life, capturing the man in a pool of white. He bolted.

Rio shoved Darcy aside, threw the deadbolt, and clambered down the outdoor staircase. Bullet dodged past Darcy. She chased after them, the pursuit short. The two stood in the driveway watching red taillights recede into the dark.

"I don't understand," said Rio. "Why'd he run?"

"Who? Johnny?"

"No, Andrew Silverbird."

Just as puzzled as Rio, Darcy said, "What was that all about?"

"Don't know." Rio started up the steps to the garage apartment. Bullet tagged along, and Darcy followed.

The minute she entered the hallway, she remembered the USB drive lying on her desk, and her pace quickened. She practically ran into her office. Rio sat on the couch, the flash drive in her hand. Tears welled up in her eyes. "You lied," she said.

"No, I withheld the truth. I saw no reason to worry you."

"You lied . . . because you know."

Darcy frowned. "Know what?"

"The truth." The Zipgig clattered to the floor. "Johnny's dead."

10

An uncomfortable silence hung in the chilly room. Darcy wanted to refute Rio's statement, but she had no proof if Johnny was alive or dead.

Words tumbled from Rio's trembling lips. "You should've warned me. Prepared me. Not given me false hope." She hugged herself and wept.

This was the type of outburst Darcy dreaded. She hated emotional confrontations. She hovered in the doorway, torn between the need to console and the desire to flee. "I'm sorry if I misled you, but who's to say Johnny isn't alive?" She approached slowly, unsure of how to handle the situation. She didn't know Rio well enough to read her. "We have no proof to the contrary, so I refuse to give up hope."

"Oh, Johnny, what'll I do now?" Rio's body shook with sobs.

Darcy reached out, drew Rio close, and held her while she

cried. "Everything will be all right." She must've done the right thing because the weeping subsided.

After a long while, Rio gently pulled free and bent down, her hand within inches of the flash drive.

"No," said Darcy.

Rio jumped.

"Sorry. Too many fingerprints will damage the evidence." If any evidence existed. Darcy crossed the room, yanked latex gloves from her backpack, and picked up the storage device.

"I didn't think about fingerprints. Where'd you find the drive?"

She weighed her decision. Eventually, Rio had to face reality, and the only thing Darcy could do was be there for her. "I found it in the arroyo, not far from Wilson's house."

Rio's sad expression brightened. "When?"

She had to think. So much had happened. "Yesterday."

Rio's brows furrowed, not from puzzlement but anger. "Before you caught me snooping around Wilson's place?"

Darcy nodded.

"You knew then? What a fool I am."

"I understand how you feel, but—"

"Never mind. Being mad solves nothing." She sat at the desk, a far-off look on her tear-streaked face. "Maybe he accidentally dropped the drive and didn't realize it." She stood and paced. "No. Even I don't buy that." She faced Darcy. "Tell me the truth. Did you find anything else? Like blood?"

Darcy considered, then reconsidered. "I'm not a forensic scientist. Someone with experience should check the site." She avoided the words "crime scene."

"Do you know someone?" Hope crept into her voice.

"I do. Plan to call him in the morning."

Rio glanced sideways at the wall clock. "It is morning."

"At a more decent hour than 3:00 a.m." Darcy scooted a

chair to the desk, pleased Rio seemed to have forgotten the question she'd skirted, the one about blood. Why upset her with speculation? The wool cap with the dark stain could belong to anyone. As for blood, she couldn't prove her hunch. Yet.

Bullet raised his head. He groaned, then went back to snoring.

"What a life he has," said Rio. "Not a care in the world. Ever wish you were a dog?"

"More than once over the past few days."

Rio's laugh eased the tension between them. "Have you looked at the files and seen the games Johnny designed?"

"They're encrypted to protect them from being stolen."

"Really? How smart."

After Rio's comment, Darcy didn't hold out much hope for an answer to the question she was about to ask, but she asked it anyway. "About the games being encrypted . . . did Johnny give you a public key, by chance? A public key is—"

"The answer is no, and I know what a public key is because Johnny and I used them whenever we sent each other messages via the Internet."

Her hopes raised, she asked, "Do you remember the keys?"

"Sure, because our public and private keys were related. The public key to encrypt the messages and a corresponding private key to decrypt them." Rio reached for the pad and pen sitting on the desk. "This key locked the plaintext, and this one unlocked it." She jotted two alphanumeric codes on a page.

Darcy's immediate thought? Too simple.

Rio paced the room. "Do you think maybe someone tried to steal the drive? Maybe they jumped Johnny in the arroyo on his way to Wilson's place? They struggled, he dropped it, and they left him there to . . ."

"No, I walked the entire bed and found nothing, but to put your mind at ease, I'll take Bullet and scout it again, go farther in each direction, and scour the ridges."

Rio beamed. "Thanks." She made for the door.

"A question before you go. Do the letters SFI mean anything to you?" Darcy held a magnifying glass to the thumb drive. "There, next to the inscription, 'Property of LANL.'"

Rio leaned closer to the Zipgig and squinted. "The only SFI I know is in conjunction with an *A*."

"I don't follow." Darcy picked up a Post-it note.

"Santa Fe Institute of Art." Rio leaned against the doorjamb and removed her cell phone from her pajama pocket. "I need to track Andrew down, talk to him, and find out what's going on."

Darcy agreed. Until Testco analyzed the material collected from the arroyo, she had only one lead worth pursuing, and something told her Enzo Duran wouldn't help. Andrew Silverbird, on the other hand . . .

"No answer at his duplex. Let me try his cell." Rio rolled her eyes to the ceiling. "Great. Voice mail. His parents' number is unlisted, and I don't recall it, but his aunt's is listed."

"What's her name?"

"Lari Morales."

Darcy surfed the Net for Lari's telephone number then programmed it into her cell. "I've got her number."

"Good. Really strange, the way Andrew acted. Are you going to bed?"

"Soon." Or at least she hoped so.

After Rio's footsteps died down the hall, Darcy tried to decrypt Johnny's data using Rio's keys, but with no luck. At first she suspected he may have double or triple encrypted the data, but he had no reason to because he had used a good encryption algorithm from the start. Disappointed, she changed for bed, then poured herself another glass of wine, the sauvignon blanc warm from sitting on her desk. She padded into the kitchenette for an ice cube and set the bottle in the fridge.

An hour later she felt a tad buzzed, but the self-induced

fog still hadn't chased away insomnia, so she sprawled out on the bed in the other room and stared at the ceiling, her mind wandering. The minutes ticked by on the wall clock. She grew antsy as time wore on. Her brain rewound and replayed the events of the day. Had she missed anything, some clue that might help her find Johnny? No, she'd been thorough.

Her cell phone said 5:00 a.m. Maybe the aunt was an early riser. She dialed.

A sleepy voice answered. "Hello."

"Mrs. Morales?"

"Who is this?"

Darcy chose her words carefully, mindful that word traveled fast and free in this small community. "A friend of Regina O'Neil's, Johnny Duran's girlfriend. Johnny and Andrew—"

"I know who Johnny is. Why are you calling at this hour?"

Bad idea, McClain. "As I said, I'm a friend of Regina's. She asked me to help her find Johnny."

"Why? What happened to him?"

"He's missing."

"Since when?"

"Friday evening. It's the last time Regina saw him."

"Since Friday?" She sounded genuinely concerned. "Why call me?"

"Regina's trying to reach Andrew's parents. She misplaced their telephone number and thought—"

"Why would Andy's family know where Johnny is? What did you say your name was?"

"Darcy. I—"

"Do you have a number where I can reach you?"

Darcy repeated it twice. "If you feel more comfortable having Mr. Silverbird contact—"

The connection went dead.

Darcy hung up, then redialed, but got a busy signal.

"Probably off the hook." She dropped her iPhone on the bed and rolled over.

Her cell phone rang. She grabbed it off the pillow.

"Darcy," the male caller demanded before she said a word.

She hesitated. "Speaking."

"How dare you upset my sister with lies?"

Stay cool. "What lies?"

"I know who you are. You journalists will stop at nothing for a story. Shame on you, badgering my sister for information. You know Johnny isn't missing any more than you are."

"Johnny's disappeared. Regina filed a police report."

"With whom?"

"Deputy Sheriff Ron Maddox," said Darcy.

He calmed down. "How long has he been missing?"

"Since last Friday."

"Hmm, that explains a few things."

The comment piqued her interest. "Such as?"

"When I couldn't reach him by phone, I drove to the lab. HR said he quit. I waited all day at his duplex, but he never came home."

"Why are you looking for Johnny?"

He snorted. "Are you serious?"

"I am."

"I wanted to question him to see what he knows about Andrew's disappearance."

His remark stopped her. "Andrew isn't missing. I saw him tonight, at our rental in Talpa. He took off without a word. Rio chased after him, but he drove away."

She heard dead air.

For a moment, she thought her caller had hung up.

"That's a sick, sick joke, lady."

11

Darcy veered off Cruz Alta onto a lane bordered by huge cottonwoods. At the back of the lot sprawled a chocolate-colored adobe with dark blue trim. She drove past a Chevy truck, the finish on one side sandblasted a mottled red and dingy gray, and parked near the garage. In the still, crisp morning, the only sound came from the steady drip of melting snow as the drops trickled from the *canales*, and the only smell from air burdened by the pungent smoke of too many piñon fires.

Despite an unlisted telephone number, locating Andrew Silverbird Sr. had taken only minutes on the Internet, and she had a good GPS. She found no pleasure in invading people's private lives and hated appearing unannounced on a stranger's doorstep, but if doing so meant she helped someone, then it warranted the intrusion.

Darcy strolled up the walkway to the portal. The second

she set foot on the patio, the front door opened. "Can I help you?" asked the brunette who stood in the doorway. The aroma of rosemary and garlic wafted from the warm interior. The woman's quizzical gaze roamed over Darcy.

"I'm looking for Andrew Silverbird—the son."

"Your name?"

"Darcy McClain. I'm a friend of Regina O'Neil, Johnny's fiancé." She hoped the latter statement helped her case. Must have, because a slight smile curled the woman's lips. Not the reaction Darcy anticipated, but it beat having the door slammed in her face.

"So you're the one who upset Mrs. Morales."

"Elena, who is it?" a male voice called from within.

Elena stepped outside and pulled the door closed after her. "What do you want?"

Surprised to see Elena in Taos when she'd thought she was in Florida, Darcy paused to collect her thoughts. "Regina's boyfriend, Johnny Duran, is missing. I'm helping her find him."

A deep frown knitted Elena's black brows. "He's missing?"

"According to Regina, since last Friday."

Elena motioned toward the house. "Can't talk here. The Catholic church in Ranchos."

"Elena!" the man yelled. Heavy footfalls pounded on a wooden floor.

The woman backed inside and shut the door, but no sooner had it closed than someone flung it open. A silver-haired man waved his fist at Darcy as she made her way down the front walk. "Don't ever come back," he shouted, "or I'll call the police. Do you hear me?"

She walked quickly to her suv and climbed in. She knew she couldn't reason with him, so she drove off to the main highway.

In Ranchos, she parked near the historic San Francisco de Asis Church and locked up. It was a cold day, but the sun

shone brightly. Hot oil, garlic, and roasted chilies permeated
the chilly air. A handful of overdressed tourists, cameras slung
over their shoulders, milled about the parking lot, impatient
for the shops and galleries to open. Locals lumbered out of the
Ranchos Grill. They leaned against their pickups to socialize;
they looked like contractors with time to spare before heading
to the job site.

Darcy wandered toward the front doors of the church.
Cooing pigeons scattered in her wake. She ducked into the
vestibule, dipped her hand in holy water, and blessed herself.
In the middle of the church, she genuflected, slid into a pew,
and knelt. Strong sunlight warmed the interior.

Ten minutes passed, then fifteen. Darcy wondered if Elena's
words were nothing more than a clever ruse to get rid of her.
With every second, she lost hope and grew angrier at herself for
being duped. Still, she clung to a single impression: the concern
in Elena's eyes when Darcy said Johnny had been missing since
Friday. Her apprehension appeared genuine.

New light stabbed the interior. In seconds, Elena marched
up the aisle. She scooted into the pew in front of Darcy, sat,
and took rosary beads from her pocket.

"Thanks for coming," said Darcy in a low voice.

Elena fingered her beads. "Sorry to drag you across town, but
my future father-in-law knows everyone, and I want our meeting
kept secret. If the family knew, it would only upset them. You
see, this time the Silverbirds think Andrew really *is* missing."

Perched on the edge of the pew, Darcy listened eagerly to
everything Elena had to say. "I don't understand."

Elena shrugged. "Until you showed up, I thought I'd simply
pissed him off—which I did—and he went somewhere to cool
down. Same pattern as always. We fight, he takes a vacation
from work, then disappears. Right about the time we begin to
worry, he turns up."

Questions crowded into Darcy's mind, one in particular. Was it possible he and Johnny had taken off together? Before she could ask, Elena continued with her story.

"We didn't give his disappearance much thought until Lari's call early this morning. I answered the phone. The old battle-ax ranted about a woman named Darcy, some friend of Rio's who claimed Johnny was missing. Then you appeared at the door, which lent credence to your concern. Now I'm worried."

With practiced ease, Elena rolled a bead between her fingers. She moved from a Hail Mary to an Our Father and shifted her head slightly to the right. "I live in Florida now. Andy came down for a visit. He was there two days before we started to fight. We argued all Monday morning, then I drove him to the airport in the afternoon. He cut his visit short by four days. Tuesday, I called the lab; he works at Los Alamos. HR said he extended his vacation until the following Tuesday."

"How well do you know Rio?"

"Not very. We met about three years ago and have spoken on a couple of occasions. I moved to Florida shortly after she and Johnny went public with their relationship. Rio's parents are real works of art."

"So I've heard. What did you and Andrew argue about?"

Elena made brief eye contact. "We've been engaged for five years, but he can't make the big leap. Our on-and-off romance was on when he planned his visit. He missed his first flight to Orlando, which isn't like him." She shook her head. "He's been acting so strange. Anyway, he arrived in Florida but left his mind in New Mexico. I had to repeat everything I said. Andy has his faults, but listening isn't one of them. This last visit was the worst. He had something on his mind, but it wasn't me."

Light invaded their sanctuary.

Darcy moved to the back of the pew. Elena knelt, her head bowed. Her rosary clattered against wood.

Nearby whispering voices died.

Darcy looked over her shoulder. "They're gone."

"Darn tourists." After a pause, Elena continued. "I grew up in Taos—the most boring years of my life. A big defense company in Florida hired me straight out of college. I packed up fast. To this day, Andy's been begging me to move back. The firm I work for offered him a management job, but he turned them down. It's a macho thing. I make more money than him. But who cares? It all gets dumped into the same account—or should. We have different views on that subject."

Elena put her rosary in her pocket. "Sorry. My family and friends are bored with my romance woes. They won't listen. You gave me a chance to unload, and I thank you."

After unloading her problems with Charlene on Gil, Darcy knew the feeling. "What made you come back to Taos this time?" She slid off the hardwood pew onto the padded kneeler.

"To reason with him. To give him one last shot at making our relationship work. If he says no to my ultimatum, I'm moving on."

"I'm afraid my conversation with Mrs. Morales went poorly. I called too early."

"Lari can be difficult. As for Andrew Sr., forgive him. He's a gentle, kind man who adores his son. His wife died recently. All he has is Andy, and he's worried."

Darcy leaned forward and watched for a reaction. "I saw Andrew last night."

"What?" Elena turned sideways. "Where?"

"At the house I rented in Talpa."

She looked skeptical. "You're sure?"

"Rio identified him."

"Thank God." She faced Darcy, concern etched on her features. "What did he say?"

"Nothing. He peeked through the window, and my dog

saw him and charged the backdoor with a vengeance. Scared him off."

"I've never known Andy to fear dogs, especially if a door separates them." She lowered her head. "His behavior . . . I just don't understand him lately." She stood. "Gotta go."

"One more question. Did Andrew Sr. file a missing person's report?"

"He will today."

"Here." Darcy dug a business card from her pocket. "My number in Talpa is on the back."

Elena hooked her purse strap over her shoulder. "If you see Andrew again, tell him . . . tell him I love him."

"I will."

The church door closed with a thud, locking Darcy in gray light as the sun hit high noon. She knelt. The wood, plaster, and flooring emitted the faint, musty odor of age scented with incense, the smell as old as the church. She said a few prayers, asking God to forgive her for all the Sunday Masses she'd missed while on stakeouts and those she'd probably miss in the future.

Outside, she strolled toward the shops. A watercolor drew her attention. She paused at the gallery window to admire the piece and noticed the parking lot behind her reflected in the glass. Elena's car was gone. Darcy moved to the next pane, drawn to a vibrant pastel of blue on a black background.

"You have great taste. Are you a fan of the artist?"

Darcy spun. "Maddox."

He removed his hat but not the dark, wraparound Revos that hid those cold eyes. "Enjoying your visit?"

She responded with a stiff nod. "Any progress locating Johnny Duran?"

"No, no leads yet. A shame about your land."

The remark irked her, but she didn't take the bait. "Nothing good comes without a fight."

He lowered his sunglasses and peered over their rims. "Nicely put. Easements can be difficult to secure, not to mention darn expensive."

He'd pushed her buttons, but she played it cool. "So I've heard."

"But why worry if you plan to hire Mackenzie? Best real estate attorney in town. Too many lawyers won't litigate anymore. Litigious state, New Mexico." On went the hat and up went the glasses. Good, she'd be free of him soon.

"With your property landlocked, guess you'll be staying for some time." He leaned closer. "Be careful up there on your land." He grinned, and she longed to slap that smirk off his face. "Hate to see someone as pretty as you . . . get hurt."

12

A burgundy sun fired the turquoise sky, and a rainbow arched over the Rio Grande as Darcy drove across town for her appointment with Matt MacKenzie. She passed Walmart. People streamed from the big-box store, their arms laden with shopping bags, their happy kids in tow. Green wreaths with red ribbons decked the telephone poles, and piñon smoke spiced the frosty air.

With two weeks to Christmas, the same question still nagged her. Would Charlene return to Taos to spend Christmas with Darcy, or would she renege on her promise as she'd done so many times in the past? She recalled Charlene's comment when she suggested the Taos vacation. "You'll be too busy with property stuff, and I want to have fun, not troop around the wilderness freezing my butt off." What Darcy had asked for was two days to settle any land matters, then they could ski, sightsee, and shop, but as usual Charlene had her mind made up. Now that Darcy knew her property was landlocked, maybe Vicky's invitation to ski in Colorado was a blessing in disguise.

Dan replaced Charlene in Darcy's thoughts. She'd called him early this morning, but he didn't answer his cell, so she contacted his office. "He's giving a deposition in a murder case, but I'll pass the message along the moment he calls in," said his assistant Emily.

Darcy pulled off the highway into a cluster of old homes renovated into offices and parked in front of Matt's firm, a beige stucco building with blue trim. Sunlight filtered through the bare branches of a cottonwood. Snow cloaked the porch and icicles hung from the eaves.

For the third time, she checked the side pocket of her backpack for the flash drive. Overnight, the only mishap the Kelty had suffered was from drool when Bullet made it his pillow. Before locking her Toyota, she removed the drive and placed it in her briefcase.

Matt's receptionist Sara showed Darcy into his office and offered her coffee. She prepared for a wait, but in minutes a man appeared in the doorway. He tugged off his gloves and crossed the room, his right hand extended. "Darcy McClain? Matt Mackenzie."

She rocked forward, ready to stand.

"No, sit. No formalities around here, but don't get comfortable. We're moving to the conference room down the hall. If I stay up front, friends drop in to talk or strangers with no appointments show up. After them, I get neighbors seeking quick advice. Never a moment's peace." Matt laughed.

He set his Stetson on the desk, draped his gloves over the crown, and hung his coat on the back of a chair. He smelled of pipe smoke, spicy aftershave, and new leather. His body language said high energy. Darcy liked that.

He collected a pile of folders from his desk and escorted her down the narrow corridor into a room at the end of the hall, a bland space with white walls, bleached wood flooring, and a pine table with ten chairs.

"Sara said Regina O'Neil made the appointment. Is she a friend?" He pulled out a chair for Darcy.

"Yes."

"Are you visiting or living here?" He took a seat opposite her and sorted through the stack of manila folders.

"Visiting."

"Give me a minute to review these." Matt flipped open a file. "They came by courier late yesterday." He put on reading glasses and skimmed the material, tracing the highlighted sections with his index finger. He had slim hands, no rings, and small wrists. Her gaze traveled to his broad shoulders and roamed his face. A frown creased his brow. His hair, the brown strands fine and uncontrollable, fanned his high forehead and poked out at will in some places. Considered individually, his facial features detracted from his appearance, but together, the prominent nose, thin lips, and square jaw made for a handsome man.

He pushed the file aside, and the name on the tab caught her attention. "Were you representing Randolph Colton?"

He looked up. "I thought you knew. Isn't that the reason for your appointment?"

She folded her hands. Not more bad news. "Knew what?"

"Randolph retained me in April to secure an easement for the tract. He wanted the land free of encumbrances because he planned to leave you the property. When Regina contacted Sara for an appointment, I assumed you wanted to complete the process."

Darcy let the news sink in. "Pardon me if this sounds rude, but if Randolph hired you eight months ago, why hasn't the easement issue been resolved?"

Matt shuffled some papers. "Here they are—notes from my last conversation with Randolph. After numerous attempts to persuade the adjacent landowners for a grant of easement, everyone refused—vehemently, I might add—despite what Randolph offered, so we decided to litigate."

A lawsuit. Great. "What about a land swap or a shared easement?"

"No takers."

She leaned on the table. "You can't landlock a person. It's the law, right?"

"Correct. Which means our only avenue of recourse is to seek relief in the courts."

She shook her head, aggravated by the news. "Nothing like ticking off your neighbors before you move in. How long will a lawsuit take?"

"Another eight months, maybe a year."

She could hardly believe her ears. "Why so long?"

"I know, the whole situation is frustrating, but this is what happens when people operate on handshakes and verbal agreements rather than recordation of deeds and easements. Problems are bound to arise."

"You make it sound like an everyday occurrence."

He made a face. "It is."

"What are your fees?" She held her breath.

"Two hundred an hour. I also have three paralegals, who can handle a lot of tasks."

"Mr. Mackenzie—"

"Matt."

"Before we go any further, I need to know exactly what I'm up against."

A quizzical expression crossed his face. "In terms of cost?"

"Issues. Every time the subject comes up, another problem surfaces." She unlocked her iPad, ready to type.

"Very well. They aren't in order of importance."

They! She clenched her teeth. Dollar signs swarmed before her eyes, then vanished into Matt's wallet.

He opened a folder. "Let's see . . . the sixty-acre minimum question has been resolved. Seems one of the adjacent land-owners wanted to subdivide his property into half-acre lots. The Planning and Zoning Commission put an abrupt end to the idea." He put a tick mark in the margin and turned the page. "Good, no archeological sites on your tract. If you ever find bones on your land, keep it to yourself. If they're human, the local Indian tribes will tie you up in court until they can prove the bones aren't from some sacred burial ground. By then, you'll be too old to walk. Or dead."

"I'll keep that in mind." She wondered where flash drives from LANL fit in. "Anything else?"

"Darn—I thought so," he said, his head buried in a document.

Her anxiety level shot up.

"You're land is in the de la Veña grant."

She put her cup down hard on the tabletop. Matt jumped, obviously startled by the sharp crack. Stay calm, she told herself. "Sorry. Which means what?"

He pulled a thick brown binder toward him and leafed through the pages. "This is an official document issued by the United States government to the heirs of the de la Veña family. Without going into detail, your land was once part of a twenty-thousand-acre Spanish land grant."

She couldn't even fathom owning sixty acres, never mind twenty thousand.

"The tract was granted to Antonio Vicente Tolosa de la Veña while he was an officer in the Royal Army of the Kingdom of Spain. Endowed on June 15, 1715. The suit bridges decades, involves more people than a person can commit to memory or even track on paper, spans counties, and lays claim to what's currently Navajo land."

Matt thumbed through his papers. "The metes and bounds cite such markers as—"

"I hate to sound rude, but can we cut to the chase? I've had my share of bad news lately, especially regarding this land." She softened her tone. "I'm sort of low on patience at this point."

He closed the binder. "I understand."

"Not entirely," she wanted to say, but she smiled instead. "Thanks."

"Simply put, the de la Veña heirs want their land back, all twenty thousand acres including your sixty. They've worked their case to the United States Supreme Court."

Mixed emotions engulfed her. On one hand, she empathized with the family, but on the other, the prospect of losing her property upset her. "Could I lose the land?"

"If the American Indians had made the claim," he shrugged, "possibility. As for the de la Veñas, they have two strikes against them. They're but one of many Spanish families who lost their estates during the acquisition of New Mexico, and frankly, I think the government sees the issue as a nonissue. Plus, this is the second time the Supreme Court has heard the de la Veña dispute. Since the argument failed on the first go-around, it's unlikely to succeed this time. There's no new evidence to present; therefore the court will probably rule as before."

She stifled a sigh. "Which is when?"

He opened a calendar. "Late January."

"Okay." What else could she say? "I have a few questions."

"Sure."

"What's involved with cutting—or blading—an easement?"

"Blading an easement means different things to different people. Some of my clients simply clear the area for a road.

Others lay down gravel and crusher fines for a smoother ride and to prevent erosion."

This information she already knew from doing a Google search. "I'm more interested in the cost."

"A lot of factors play into cost. For instance, how many arroyos you have to cross, which means installing culverts. How long the easement will be. Where your utilities are located and whether you'll bring them up your easement. Yours are at the lot line, but if you build too far in on your property then it will cost more to bring them from the edge of your land to wherever you build."

Darcy envisioned a second major drain on her investments, the first being Charlene's education at Stanford. "Gil said Randolph planned to tear down the house."

"That's true. He wanted to build a new home on the property, but his wife refused to leave Santa Fe, so he willed the land to you."

"Are we done for today?" She stood, having heard enough.

He nodded. "I'm really sorry this wasn't resolved before Randolph's . . . his passing."

"I am too."

"His untimely death came as quite a shock."

"Yes." Darcy hoped he wouldn't say more. So far, she'd managed to keep her grief in check.

He walked her to the door. "You don't have to stay in town. We can communicate by e-mail or phone."

"January isn't far off. Besides, I came to ski. Now I'll have plenty of time."

He stopped at Sara's desk. "If you need anything while you're here, call."

"There is something I could use—the name of an office supply store."

"What are you looking for?" asked Sara.

"A printer."

"Call Mike and see what he can do for Ms. McClain," Matt said to Sara.

An hour later, after Darcy purchased a printer at Mike's and ran errands, she turned onto the dirt lane that led to the rental and braked in front of the garage. She pressed the automatic opener. The door whined as it traveled slowly up its railings. She pulled in and closed up just as large snowflakes blew across the drive.

Loaded with grocery bags and the backpack over her shoulder, Darcy shoved open the door that led from the garage into the kitchen and dumped the bags on the counter. Rio began unpacking while she returned to her 4Runner for the printer. She placed the box on the table in the breakfast nook and slid onto a stool at the counter with the Kelty nestled at her feet.

"Good timing. Snowstorm's headed our way," said Rio. "Hot tea?"

"Sounds wonderful."

"How'd your meeting go?"

Darcy groaned. "Tell you later—after a stiff drink."

Rio made a face. "That doesn't sound good." She took the stool across from Darcy. "I've been thinking about Ollie. One night outdoors and, well . . . you know, coyotes."

Darn. With everything going on, she'd forgotten about Johnny's cat. "Why don't you spend the afternoon checking local shelters and contacting vet offices? See if you can find him."

"And if I do?"

"Bullet isn't fond of cats, but this place is big. There's no reason you can't move to the guesthouse out back. The two of you can bunk there."

"You sure?"

"I am. So, start checking."

"Gee, thanks, Darcy. But first your messages. Dan called. He's in court until five and has a meeting until nine his time. And your sister Charlene called."

Darcy inhaled long and deep.

"She and Vicky are on their way to Canada to visit Vicky's aunt. The powder's even better up there."

"Canada!" Darcy blurted.

"Is something wrong?"

She counted to ten. "No, nothing. Now go find Ollie."

Rio disappeared into a small room adjacent to the kitchen, a workstation with a desk, chair, and phone. In seconds, Darcy heard her talking to Stray Hearts Animal Shelter. "No luck," she called to Darcy.

"Keep searching. If you can't find him, then we'll go back to Enzo's and the duplex to see if he's still in the area. I'm going upstairs."

"Thanks," Rio shouted as Darcy raced up the steps.

She stood at the sliding door in her office, contemplating her next move in her hunt for Johnny, but the details failed to gel in her sleep-deprived brain. A good run always jump-started her, but the weather wouldn't cooperate. As she lingered there, a biting wind whorled through the flagstone courtyard. It rattled windowpanes and smothered the mountain ranges in white.

Hoping the storm would clear soon, Darcy napped, making up for the past few fitful nights. She woke hours later to pale blue skies and fast-moving, billowy white clouds. Took great effort to motivate her in cold weather, but her body and brain craved a good run.

At 4:00 p.m., she steered off Highway 68 to the subdivision Rio had suggested as "the best place to run if you want to avoid people and cars, unless you live to suck up carbon monoxide."

An early winter moon hung over the Rio Grande, its brilliance growing as Darcy eased her 4Runner down the steep hill into the El Mira subdivision. She followed the curve of the road through arid terrain thick with sage and dead wildflowers, their auburn stalks swaying in the gentle breeze. The rutted easement crossed over a wide bridge. Massive steel pipes jutted from both sides of the drainage culvert, and in the bed below the white trunks of a dozen aspens gleamed in the fading winter light.

She cruised through the deserted housing tract, the streets bladed and named, utilities to the lot lines, but few homes. No wonder Rio suggested this as a good place to run.

Darcy parked on a slight rise that overlooked the highway and climbed out. Cold air nipped at her. She shoved her hands into fleece-lined gloves and zipped her jacket. What a shame to leave Bullet behind. He loved these runs as much as she did, no matter the weather, but she thought it best for him to stay with Rio in case Green showed.

She warmed up with a fast walk, the distant whoosh of highway traffic barely audible as she reached the end of the lane. What a pleasant change these dirt easements were from the concrete byways of San Francisco. Nothing was above her but blue-gray sky and nothing around her but silence, eerie yet welcome. And unlike the smoke-laden air in town, the air here was flavored only with the faint spice of live piñon.

The high-pitched whistle of a bird of prey alerted her to his presence. She glanced up. A hawk soared overhead, swooped down, and disappeared. In his place, a jet streaked across the heavens, a white contrail in its wake. But her tranquil mood faded as Darcy jogged up Harmony Court, a street littered with construction debris. She jumped piles of loose PVC scattered in the roadway, dodged spools of electrical wire, and ran around concrete pipes. No matter where she went, she couldn't escape man's trash. The upside was that Harmony Court paralleled the snowcapped Sangre de Cristo Mountains, their emerald backs dusted in white. The closer she drew to the mountains, the thicker the vegetation. Sage gave way to dense piñon and juniper, the branches laden with ice. Her steady lope broke into a lung-bursting sprint.

She looped the cul-de-sac, her head slightly bowed, searching for cable or glass. Blue flashed from the corner of her eye. She whipped her head sideways. A man jogged toward her. He wore jeans and a blue parka. He yanked off his cap. Andrew. She came to an abrupt stop, almost tripping over her own feet.

"Hurry," he called as he ducked into the brush.

She jogged after him, her body cutting a jagged path through the tall scrub.

He stopped, bent over, and rested his hands on his thighs to catch his breath. "Ran quite a ways." He panted and coughed.

"There's water in my daypack. Take all you want. How'd you know I'd be here?"

"Keep your voice down." He took two bottles from her pack, unscrewed the caps on both, and drank greedily. "I tailed you from Talpa." He stifled another cough, lowered the bottle, and looked about. "I . . . parked on the ridge. Watched you drive in." The wind picked up, muffling his soft voice. "Found you with these." He patted the binoculars dangling from his neck.

"Where's Johnny?"

"Wish I knew."

"Your family reported you missing."

"Damn." He stomped his foot. "The last damn thing I need—more people hunting me."

"Andrew, what's going on?"

He ignored her question, his eyes on the sky. The hawk had returned.

"Hurry." He grabbed her wrist and pulled her through waist-high sage to a grove of trees where he paused to listen before scurrying under the low-hanging branches of a cedar. Beyond, she found herself in a small clearing sheltered by evergreens.

In the center a fire pit had been dug. She smelled smoke, but no flames lit the wood stacked in the rock-lined cavity.

"Sit." He motioned to the cinder blocks spaced around the site.

She sat. The frigid concrete sent a chill up her spine. She gazed at the kindling piled in the pit.

He rubbed his gloved hands together. "Too risky for a fire. Johnny said you'd contact Rio if anything happened."

Darcy concealed her surprise. "You know who I am?"

"Sure. Megan Real, the investigative reporter from Albuquerque. Johnny planned to give you the flash drive so you'd go public with the proof."

Proof? Not games? Journalist? Darcy didn't bother to correct him on any of this. Not yet. "Back up a bit."

"Don't play dumb. You knew Johnny's plan. He'd download the proof, and if all went well he'd hand off the drive to you. If anything happened to him, Rio was your contact person for the storage device."

"Did Rio know this?"

"Only where to find the device. He planned to leave her instructions. The less she knew, the better."

"Why did you come to the rental?"

"When Johnny disappeared, I went to Wilson's but couldn't find the thumb drive, so I assumed Rio already had it. I wanted the drive."

"But if she planned to turn it over to me, then why bother?"

"After Rio connected with you and no news of the thumb drive surfaced in the press, I became suspicious, so I did some digging. You're a private dick, not Megan Real."

Busted, Darcy opened her mouth to explain, but he cut her off.

"I don't care why you're in Taos or what your agenda is—I just want the drive." He stood, shoulders hunched, eyes bloodshot, and black stubble on his jaw. "I don't have a lot of time. Now where's the drive?"

"At the moment, in my SUV. As soon as First National opens, I'll rent a safe-deposit box."

"No!" The word exploded from his mouth. "It won't be safe there."

"In a bank? Of course it will." No sooner had she spoken than she doubted her own words.

"You have no idea what or who you're up against. They're ruthless." A twitch developed in his temple. "They'll stop at nothing to steal the drive. They killed Johnny." Andrew wrung his hands. "Why do you think I'm hiding? For fun? My life's in jeopardy." A path took shape where he paced.

Was he serious, or was this the ranting of a grief-stricken friend? "Why is your life at stake?"

"Because Johnny confided in me." Again, he checked the sky. "Sort of. Nothing he said made sense, but they don't know that."

"What did he say?"

Andrew shifted his weight from one foot to the next. "Most of the time he just rambled. Something about atrocities at the lab. How he planned to prove it. When the truth was known, no one would ever call him a coward again." The words fell from his quivering lips.

Fear or the cold?

"The week I left for Florida, he really got weird. Always checking his back. I couldn't stop thinking about what he said, so I called him from Orlando to see how things were going. 'The time's come,' he told me. 'I'm downloading tonight. If anything bad happens, Rio will know where to find the flash drive and I'll leave her instructions.'"

Andrew stopped pacing and squatted. The muscles in his face relaxed a bit. "I didn't sleep most of Saturday night and called him early Sunday but never got through. I left Orlando

Monday afternoon—not for the reasons Elena believes, but because I was worried about Johnny."

"Elena?"

"No games. I know you two met at the church in Ranchos."

"Okay, no games." Wonderful. First Maddox, then Andrew. Who else was watching?

As if he read her thoughts, Andrew surveyed the trees. "You packing anything?"

She unzipped her jacket, exposing the shoulder rig.

He smiled. "Good. I remember seeing the gun on your desk." The furrows across his forehead eased. "When I saw Johnny's duplex cleaned out and HR claimed he'd taken a vacation, I panicked and decided I'd better disappear."

She studied him. Something didn't fit. Took more than the situation Andrew had described to drive a person underground. After all, she'd been there herself. "Who are they?"

"Don't know. Not sure."

"Which is it?"

He shrugged. "There's no proof."

"A theory will do. At least it gives me a place to start," she said without thinking.

He looked hopeful. "You'll help?"

"Have been, but you should know. You've been tailing me."

He sat. "Monday night, a little after midnight, I drove to the lab and went straight to Johnny's station. A note taped to his monitor read D1—code for destroy, priority one. I switched on his computer. Immediately, the background went from gray-white to blood red." The muscle in his temple twitched violently, and his hands shook even though they were folded in his lap. "I stared at the message for a long time, hardly believing my eyes."

"What did it say?"

"'Andrew's next.'"

No wonder he ran. "Any idea who sent the threat?"

"No, but he signed it Brainwash."

The wind rustled the pines, and Andrew jumped.

Darcy shivered in the stiff wind. "Brainwash? Does the word mean anything to you?"

"Nothing." He pivoted in a circle, his nervous fingers fiddling with his jacket collar.

"Elena said you called HR on Tuesday to put in for more vacation time."

He stopped in mid-stride. "What? Are you kidding? I was— am—too damn scared to call anyone. After I saw the message, I walked out of the lab and kept going. If I call anyone, it'll be Elena or my father."

"Where've you been staying?"

"That's not important. I want Johnny's flash drive." Not a request but a demand.

"Why? It's safe with me."

He looked incredulous. "Because someone has to read the files—to find out what's on them and what's going on."

She stood and stretched. Her joints ached from the bitter cold. "Your security clearance . . . what level are you?"

Andrew sucked in air and slowly exhaled. His shoulders sagged. "Don't tell me . . . the data's encrypted?"

"Johnny was no fool."

"Then we have to get into the lab and let G-cell read the files. G's a computer unlike any you've ever seen. Capable of—" His eyes widened.

A distant rumble.

Andrew turned toward the sound. He gathered the wood from the fire pit, threw the logs under a tree, and scattered the ashes with his boot.

Darcy tossed the cinder blocks into the sage.

"Under here." He dragged her beneath a juniper. "I'll make contact as soon as I can."

She gripped his shoulder. "You aren't going anywhere."

"If I stay they'll kill me. I won't be any good dead."

She had to let him go. What else could she do? "Be careful."

"They haven't caught me yet. Quick, help me out of my parka." He unzipped his jacket, and she tugged it off. He wadded the coat into a ball and crammed it into the crook of a branch. Underneath, he wore a brown sweater, the color of the New Mexico earth. "This way, I'll be tougher to spot."

Darcy watched him vanish into the dense forest of piñons.

A helicopter roared overhead. The rotor blades whipped trees around and churned up dirt. She shielded her face with her hands. The metal bird soared on as it searched another section of the subdivision. She darted from the blind and played decoy. Andrew escaped to the south, so she ran north.

The bait worked. Behind her, an army Black Hawk stirred up a cloud of dust. The chopper flew low, the hum deafening. The pilot overshot her, circled, and returned, coming dangerously close just as she dove behind the wheel of her 4Runner. The red letters across the silver belly glared at Darcy: NASA.

13

Darcy watched the Black Hawk until the chopper became a blip on the horizon. Freezing, she sat in her 4Runner with the heater on high and stared through the foggy windshield, her mind on her encounter with Andrew, until the chilly interior became too uncomfortable. She pulled off her glove and held her hand to the heater vent. Warm air gushed from the outlet, yet she shivered.

A frosty breeze invaded the vehicle. She raised herself off the seat and looked into the rear compartment. Jagged shards jutted from the windowsill like translucent daggers stacked in a haphazard row. She lunged for her Kelty. The nylon flap hung down, the pocket unzipped on both sides. The Zipgig was gone.

"Damn, damn, damn," she said through clenched teeth.

She threw her 4Runner into gear and sped to the top of the

hill. Binoculars in hand, she climbed onto her front tire and scanned the valley floor. Nothing but green. For over an hour, she toured the streets of El Mira, stopping at intervals to comb the adjacent terrain for Andrew, but it soon became too dark to spot anything.

Cursing her stupidity, she drove into town. The last thing she felt like doing was grocery shopping, but Rio needed some things for dinner, and even Darcy had to eat sometime. Plus, she wanted to mail the evidence found in the arroyo to Testco.

She parked close to the store and emptied the glove box of anything valuable before she locked up. Smith's hummed with activity. Darcy wandered aimlessly up one aisle and down the next, forgetting things and returning to hunt for them. Any small, rectangular object reminded her of the flash drive. She loved to cook when time permitted and usually enjoyed trips to the grocery store, but the stolen Zipgig had ruined the outing.

In the produce department, she chose a red bell pepper and tore a bag off the spool, almost wrenching the holder from its spindle.

"Taking out your aggressions on the baggies?"

She recognized the voice, and her bad mood darkened. Without turning, she asked, "You following me, Maddox?" She dropped the pepper into the bag.

He answered with a question, a habit she detested. "Should I be?"

The lilt in his tone sparked her ire.

He chuckled. "Are you still hauling around that heavy backpack?"

She faced him. "What do you want?"

"A bit hostile, aren't we? I came in for a few things, saw you, and wanted to say hi."

"In case you hadn't noticed, your cart's empty." She moved on.

He caught up. "Won't be for long." He chose a head of iceberg lettuce. "Want one?"

"I prefer romaine."

He pushed his cart across her path and leaned over the bin of lettuce. "Green? Or do you prefer red?"

This sudden display of friendliness put her on guard. "One more time. What do you want?"

He smiled his wooden grin. "You sure are suspicious, McClain."

"Comes with the territory." She maneuvered around him, her eyes on her grocery list.

"See you," he said. "Maybe next time you'll be in a better mood."

Darcy looked up as he whisked the head of lettuce out of his cart, placed it back on the pile, and abandoned the cart near the dairy section. Weirdo.

Done with her food shopping, she wheeled her cart to the nearest battery display to find replacements for the dead volts in her antitheft device. If she'd carried a backup remote like Dan had suggested, she might have heard Andrew break into her 4Runner because the alarm would've sounded.

She scooted into the express lane and paid cash for her purchases. The less information people had about her, the better. Sometimes paranoia was good.

While she loaded bags into her hatch, Darcy kept a watchful eye for Maddox, but the pest never showed. Next stop, UPS.

If it hadn't been for Christmas hours, the store would have been closed. Ninth in line, she studied the people ahead. Most balanced packages in their arms, a reminder of the approaching holiday. She made a mental note of gifts to buy Charlene. Don't dwell on her now. After the morning she'd had, why add to the aggravation? The line moved quickly.

Darcy placed the package for Testco on the counter and said, "Express Critical." She handed the woman the necessary paperwork and paid cash.

Her cell phone chirped. She ripped her iPhone from the clip on her belt, eager to hear Charlene's voice. "Oh, hi Matt. What's up?" Disappointed, Darcy half listened to what her attorney had to say. Something about a status report, and he'd stop by the rental on his way home. She mumbled her thanks. The second she disconnected, her phone rang again, and again her spirits lifted, but not for long.

"Oh, hi Rio," she said, trying to sound upbeat. "What's up?"

"Charlene called."

Darcy braced herself. If her sister had good news, she always delivered it firsthand.

"She and Vicky met up with friends from Stanford."

In Canada? Here we go again.

"They plan to ski all next week. Hold on a minute. I'm having a hard time reading my own writing. She'll fly into Albuquerque Monday, in plenty of time for Christmas."

Darcy tried to curb her excitement; she'd been disappointed too many times in the past.

"And Matt called. Said he'd call your cell. Have you heard from him?"

"Yes. Anything else?"

"Don't forget the groceries."

"Done."

"And no Ollie yet."

"Tomorrow we'll search for him."

On the drive to the rental, Darcy racked her brain for a plan to steal back the missing drive. But where to start? After all, not even Andrew's family knew how to contact him, and if she found him, could he be persuaded to hand over the USB?

Darcy's 4Runner rumbled onto the lane toward the main

house. She remembered Rio's strange look when asked to keep the doors locked. "Bullet will protect me," she'd said nonchalantly. "Besides, who would come all the way out here to rob us?" Darcy didn't mention Green.

She braked outside the garage and pressed the remote. The double door groaned as it slid upward. No sooner had she parked and closed the bay when Rio stumbled from the kitchen door into the garage, eyes red and swollen.

"What's wrong?" Not bad news about Johnny, Darcy hoped.

Rio sniffed. "The news is on all stations."

"What is?"

"Johnny's disappearance."

Great. Exactly what she needed, a team of reporters snooping around Taos. She hugged Rio. "He'll show up. You'll see. Did Johnny ever mention a woman reporter named Megan Real?"

A skeptical expression clouded her face. "No. Why?"

"I thought I saw her at the grocery store," Darcy lied.

Rio dabbed at her nose with a tissue. "Never heard of her."

"Any mention of Andrew on the news?"

Rio's sorrow dissolved to indignation. "Yes. The damn reporters made a big deal out of not being able to find him for an interview. Then the newscaster attacked the Silverbird family for refusing to talk to the press."

Good, no interviews. Darcy didn't need more publicity.

Bullet bounded into the garage and leaned into her. Darcy showered him with affection. "Easy, big guy, or you'll knock me over. Rio, leave the groceries. I'll unload them. Go in. You'll freeze out here." Darcy wasn't in the mood to discuss the broken window or the missing drive. Some things were best kept to herself . . . for now.

"No way." She marched to the back of the 4Runner. "I'm pregnant, not an invalid. And as far as being cold, I'm wearing enough layers to be the Michelin Man." She reached into the open hatch, her hand outstretched, and stopped in mid-reach. "Your window's busted."

Darcy hooked her hands through several plastic bags. "I found the window broken when I returned from my run at El Mira." She hurried into the kitchen to discourage further discussion.

Rio entered. "Really? I've never heard of vandalism up there. Anything stolen?"

"Nothing. Certainly surprised me." She abruptly changed the subject. "On a more important note, have you called for a doctor's appointment?"

"Tomorrow at one. A friend will drive me. Thanks for caring. About your broken window . . ." Rio crossed to the wall phone. "What's your insurance deductible?"

Darcy wrinkled her nose. "Too high to mention, even on auto glass."

"So you don't plan to file a claim."

"Not worth the trouble. I'll have the window fixed tomorrow. Any suggestions as to where?"

"Sure. Hang on a minute." She dialed. "Hey, Sam, Rio here. Fine. A friend of mine has a broken window. Passenger side, rear. Toyota 4Runner. Today at three? Sounds good. Take Highway 68 to . . ."

Darcy mouthed thank you as she left the kitchen for her office, where she placed a call to Dan, hoping he'd found someone by now on the Hill to clear her for access to LANL's restricted operating systems. If she had an in, next time Andrew made contact (assuming he would), she might be able to convince him to accompany her to the lab to read the data. Ifs, maybes, assumptions. She shook her head, growing more irritated the longer Emily kept her on hold.

"Sorry, busy day. You're holding for Dan, right?" Without waiting for an answer, Emily launched into her canned response. "He's out of town. Do you want to leave a message?"

Darcy sighed. "I'll page him or try his cell." The dial tone droned in her ear.

Dan didn't answer his page or his cell.

As the afternoon wore on, the gravity of the missing drive sunk in, and Darcy's carelessness weighed heavily on her mind. She had to come up with a plan to get the storage device back.

Guilt could be a powerful motivator, and it was another reason for helping Rio find Johnny. Darcy had never forgiven herself for not saving Paco, so if she could save Johnny, assuming he was still alive, it might make up for Paco's loss in some small way.

Bullet trotted in. He stared at her with those soulful brown eyes. She gently tweaked his black nose. He responded with a lick to her hand.

"Darcy," Rio called from the hallway before entering the bedroom, "Matt Mackenzie's coming over later with some files."

"Oh, yes. I forgot. Okay. Shower time. Everyone out." Darcy started to shed her clothes.

Bullet barked.

The doorbell chimed.

"Sam." Rio said as she disappeared from the doorway.

Dressed only in thermals, Darcy wiggled her feet into slippers and walked to the windows in the kitchenette to confirm the visitor's identity. A van with "Sam's Auto Glass" stenciled on the side was parked in the driveway. Rio greeted the man, who wore denim overalls, and both stepped out of sight, leaving Bullet in peace to anoint Sam's tires before Rio reappeared to retrieve him. Darcy crossed the hall to the bathroom.

Halfway through her routine, the door opened and Bullet entered. He took up his post outside the shower, and she had to straddle him to grab a towel. She was zipping up her jeans when the doorbell chimed. Bullet tore out of the bedroom like someone had poked him with a cattle prod.

Darcy paused on the landing. The stolen flash drive, her stupidity—both made her stomach churn in sync with her brain. The last thing she wanted to discuss was land issues.

Matt sat on the sofa. Across from him, Bullet hogged the recliner, and Rio perched on the arm of the chair.

Matt stood when Darcy came down the stairs. "Hi. I brought those files I mentioned." He put the stack on the coffee table.

Dismayed, Darcy eyed the pile.

"I spoke with all of your neighbors except one—haven't been able to locate him."

She thumbed through the documents, some paper clipped, the thicker ones clamped. "Which one?"

"Enzo Duran."

Darcy glanced sideways at Rio, who raised her eyebrows in response.

"Sara's been trying to track him down, but no luck." Matt resumed his seat. "As far as the rest of the neighbors go, the bottom line is, we'll have to litigate."

"I figured."

"Sorry, but even the O'Neils said no. They claim you turned their daughter against them."

"I what?"

"Sorry, I'm only the messenger."

"Sounds like my parents," said Rio. "They're never any help when you need them."

"Okay," Darcy said, "so we sue. I want this resolved, and soon."

"I'll get started right away." Matt slid out of his chair. "Have to run. Dinner appointment."

Darcy walked him to the foyer. "Thanks for stopping by and for suggesting Mike's."

"Happy to help."

Bullet growled twice. This evolved into a series of loud barks, each more formidable than the last.

Someone knocked on the front door.

"At this hour?" Rio restrained Bullet while Matt threw the deadbolt.

Darcy slid her hand under her sweater, fingers poised over the revolver stuffed in the back waistband of her jeans, but one look at the two men on her doorstep told her neither posed a threat. Dan, the slightly taller of the two, she knew well. As for his companion, she recognized him from a photograph in the *San Francisco Chronicle*: renowned forensic examiner Ed Clark. He looked more like a basketball player than a CSI guy. Tall, thin, and fit, he had wavy dirty-blond hair and blue eyes.

"Can we help you?" asked Matt.

"I'm a friend of Darcy's." The large man with the rugged good looks smiled. "I don't believe we've met." He extended his hand.

"Matt Mackenzie, Darcy's attorney."

"Attorney?" He laughed with the infectious chuckle women adored. "Is she in trouble again?"

Rio giggled. Dan had been here less than five minutes and already he'd charmed her. So like him.

Darcy hugged Dan. "Emily said you were out of town."

"I am. I'm in Taos." Dan smiled. "Told her not to ruin the surprise. I'm on my way to Ohio again and thought I'd drop off Ed and say hi on my way up."

Darcy ushered them in and made the introductions. "Rio, Matt, meet Ed Clark and Dan Gruet."

14

Up early, the stolen flash drive plaguing her, Darcy shuffled into the kitchenette to fix coffee. A blue blur awakened her senses: Dan broke from the cover of the trees and sprinted up the driveway with ease. Half-asleep from a fitful night, it took a second to jog her memory. Yesterday evening, after Matt left for his appointment, she'd invited Ed and Dan to spend the night since she had plenty of room. Both opted for the guesthouse across the courtyard. She wanted to discuss the case in detail, but Rio, quite captivated with Dan, stayed up late, monopolizing his time. However, Darcy did have the opportunity to mention Green on the off chance he showed while Dan visited.

Dan capped the rise on the northeast corner of the property, dropped from sight, and reappeared as he jogged down the dirt easement. The trees gobbled him up. Why hadn't he asked her to join him?

Minutes later, as expected, he came trooping up the road, walking off his run. He wore blue sweats and aviator glasses. Watching him now, Darcy agreed with Rio. He was ripped and hot, but Darcy had never looked at Dan this way, probably because she valued their friendship and couldn't make the leap from a platonic relationship to a romantic one no matter how hot he or any man looked. She loved her independence too much to be tied down.

Dan stooped at the edge of drive. He squatted there for a few seconds, then sprinted to the pedestrian gate, crossed the courtyard, and entered the guesthouse. She was glad he'd flown out with Ed. He had great insight, and she valued his opinion on this investigation as she had on past cases.

The thought prompted her to throw on sweats and pay him a visit. The side door whined as she pried it open and started down the outside staircase. She held onto the railing with a vise-like grip, being extra cautious as she descended the frost-sheeted steps to the courtyard. The enclosed patio was no safer. Navigating the ice-slick flagstones reminded her of negotiating a minefield—not that she'd ever traversed one.

Inside the guesthouse, she walked quietly along the main hall to Dan's room. Behind her, a door opened. Darn, she'd woken Ed. Dan stepped out, a towel wrapped around his waist. "Hey, hi. Ed and I swapped rooms. I planned to call you as soon as I got dressed."

"Why didn't you stop by? We haven't run together in weeks."

"Saw your light on until the wee hours and thought you might be sleeping in."

"Tried, but no luck. This case is frustrating."

"Want to talk?"

"You know I do." She followed him into his room.

"Give me a minute to throw on some pants." He closed the bathroom door and came out within a few minutes. "I didn't want to ask last night in front of company, but where's Charlene? Another disappearing act?"

"Yep." Darcy sunk onto the edge of the bed.

He put his hand on her shoulder. "Sorry. All those plans you made."

"Uh-huh. If I'd known, I would've boarded Bullet, although he travels well and is good company."

"He's a cool dog. I'd watch him anytime." He slipped on a shirt. "Given he's Charlene's dog, the two of you sure have bonded."

"He's a kick. I'm glad he's ours." She laughed. "Mine. I did the right thing saving him from rescue, even if every day he reminds me of Paco."

"Let it go. You did everything you could to save him. His death was an unfortunate accident. Be proud that you did right by Bullet. By the way, on my run this morning, I found a footprint near the drive."

"I saw you bend down to inspect something."

"Might be nothing, but I'd have Ed lift it, especially after you told me about Green."

"Hey, Dan." Ed materialized in the doorway. "Walt, my LANL connection—the guy who can read the encrypted drive—is on my cell. Want me to put him on the speaker?"

"What?" Darcy leaped off the bed and grabbed Dan's arm. "You never said Ed had a connection at LANL."

"I didn't get a chance to say anything last night," said Dan.

"Yes, put him on the speaker," said Darcy excitedly.

Ed pressed the speaker function on his phone. "Walt, I'm here with Darcy and Dan."

Thrilled with a possible breakthrough in the case, Darcy listened intently.

After the introductions, Walt got straight to the point. "For the record, if I don't feel comfortable with your questions, I won't answer."

"Fair enough." Defensive guy, Darcy noted.

"So you want G-cell to decode a flash drive," said Walt. "I have a few questions first."

Ed rolled his eyes.

"Go ahead," said Darcy.

"How'd you come by the flash drive?"

Darcy brought them up-to-date on the investigation but said nothing about the stolen drive, embarrassed by her stupidity, especially after Dan reminded her several times to change the batteries in her key remote.

Papers rustled at Walt's end. "Now this changes things."

The tone of his voice concerned Darcy. "In what way?"

"In every way. Hold a minute. I need to verify something."

The silence drove her crazy. The same sense of helplessness that had washed over her when she discovered the flash drive missing engulfed her again.

"Had no idea Duran and Silverbird were involved." The sound of paper shuffling at Walt's end died. "This puts a completely different complexion on things."

Darcy fought to keep her temper. "Why?"

"You have no idea what you're dealing with. Snoop around, and someone might get hurt—most likely you. I don't think you want that."

Dan flagged Ed as if to say, "You're up to bat."

A frown creased Ed's brow. He folded his hands and bounced them on the desktop. A puzzled expression crossed Dan's face. The thumping grew louder as Ed drummed harder.

"I hear you," Walt said, "but threats won't work. Not this time, Ed. Circumstances are just too damn dangerous. Please, don't push the issue."

Ed's lips folded to a thin line, and the drumming stopped. "I hate to dredge up the past, but you owe me, Walt. Remember Breckenridge?"

A loud sigh broke from the speaker. "Blackmail. Fine, back me into a corner, but you'll regret your decision. Trust me. This isn't the favor you want."

Ed beamed. "Let me be the judge."

A knock on a door came from Walt's end of the line. "Gotta run. I'll call you from the office."

The word "no" formed on Darcy's lips, but Walt had already hung up. She stood abruptly, her fists clenched. "Now what?"

Ed leaned back. "Darcy, you're sure Walt's critical to moving the investigation forward?"

She slid into a chair. "Yes. I have to get inside LANL, find G-cell, and read the drive."

"Aren't there other ways?" asked Ed.

"There are, but there'd be hell to pay, such as losing my PI license. Or worse, jail."

"Especially if Rio's claims are bogus." Dan held up his hand. "I'm not saying they are, but maybe Johnny isn't really missing. He could have left for any number of reasons. No offense."

Darcy agreed. "You're right."

"What are those other options?" asked Ed.

"Agent Hunter with the Albuquerque Field Office is a friend and has connections at the lab, but contacting him will leave a paper trail. He'll insist I follow strict protocol—work through the proper channels, fill out forms, wait for clearance. Not to mention walking the halls with an ID badge plastered to my chest. Do it the feds way. Hell, I might as well pay for a billboard on the I-40." Her voice had risen several octaves. "Sorry. I'm venting my frustration. No, kicking myself for letting Andrew steal the damn drive."

"Steal? What are you talking about?" Dan and Ed asked in unison.

Damn, she'd tipped her hand. "I'm afraid so. A stupid mistake on my part."

When she finished explaining, Ed said, "An honest mistake."

"Could've happened to anyone." Dan's comment lifted her spirits, a bit.

"Drive or no drive, I still have to get inside the lab," said Darcy.

"Let's forget the drive for now and focus on Walt." Ed tapped the table with his finger. "Sounds like we have no choice. I hate holding dirt over a person's head, but . . ."

"Are you referring to Breckenridge?" Darcy said.

Ed kept them in suspense while he groomed his mustache with his thumb and index finger, his eyes focused on the wall of windows. "It's not fair to explain without Walt here, but let's just say we've got an edge."

Not one to play games, Darcy hated being baited and then dropped without an explanation. "Okay, so we have an edge. Where do we go from here?"

Ed pulled a photograph from his wallet and handed it to Darcy. "First off, here's a photo of me and Walt Spears. If you do access LANL, you should know what he looks like."

"Would certainly help." Beside Ed slouched a short, balding man, his glasses perched on the tip of his nose, an award plaque in his hand.

Ed's phone vibrated, and he snatched it up. "Walt? Good. Thanks." He hung up.

Darcy's heart thrashed against her rib cage. "What's the verdict?"

Ed gave her a thumbs-up. "It's a go. He'll call tonight from home and fill you in on the particulars."

"I can't thank you enough," said Darcy.

"Thank me by showing me where you found the flash drive, which is one of the reasons I'm here, right?" He turned to Dan. "Taking off soon?"

"Within the hour. I'll be glad when this Ohio case is over. Good luck with the investigation, you two."

"Thanks. Have a safe flight." Darcy hugged Dan, then strolled out into the hallway with Ed. "Meet you by the garage in forty-five."

Half an hour later, Darcy dumped her backpack into the hatch of her 4Runner and backed out of the garage. Sam, the auto glass guy, had done a good job and for a decent price. She lingered in the driveway to wait for Ed, the bright sunlight a welcome change after the recent snowstorms and frigid temperatures. In minutes, Ed came down the front walk, his JanSport over his shoulder.

"Good," said Darcy, "you brought your backpack. Forgot to tell you we'd be hiking in."

"I had an inkling. How far in is it to the trailhead?"

"Three miles or more." She spread a topographical map across the hood of her suv. "We're here. The arroyo's there."

He traced the creek bed with his fingernail. "Runs straight through the Wilson property. Private land, I presume. Know the owners? I don't take kindly to being shot at. Happened once, and once is enough."

She folded the map. "I own the parcel."

"Really? Lucky you."

She shut the cargo hatch. "Property's landlocked."

"A temporary problem, I'm sure. You can't deny a person access to their land."

He made the solution sound so easy. Darcy slid behind the wheel, and Ed settled into the passenger's seat.

The Toyota bucked and rocked over the uneven drive to the main road. Darcy switched on the radio but kept the music low.

"Dan said you were partners at the Feeb."

Darcy chuckled. "Happy memories—some of the best years of my life."

Ed laughed. "You make it sound like you're ancient."

Sometimes she felt ancient.

"He also said you resigned early to raise your kid sister. How noble of you, considering you were one of the bureau's shining stars."

Ed had hit a raw nerve, but Darcy remained cool. "Tough call at the time." She tried to sound lighthearted. All her young life, she'd wanted nothing more than to be a CIA agent, but she never made the cut, so she accepted a job with the FBI. Then, at the peak of her career, her parents died.

"Sorry, I think I overstepped my bounds."

"Seemed like a big deal then, but in retrospect . . ." In truth, it was a painful decision that had left a lasting scar, but now she just wanted to put the entire matter behind her and not dwell on the past. She wished Dan hadn't said anything to Ed.

The conversation about the agency continued, but in generic terms—nothing personal. Time passed quickly.

"We're almost there." She rumbled into the dirt cul-de-sac and killed the engine.

Ed helped her strap on her Kelty before he hoisted on his JanSport.

"This way." She pointed out the trail.

About a mile in, the path ended, and she had to trek through dense sagebrush to keep the arroyo in sight. The wind kicked up, chilling her to the bone. "If we want to make progress, why don't we find a place to head down? Anything to avoid fighting the brush and this wind."

"Good idea. There's a spot." He motioned to a section where rain and snow had eroded the bank. "I'll go first."

After Ed landed in the dry gulch, Darcy joined him. She

hit heels-first, ricocheted off the arroyo wall, and into a standing position. "Let's see." She unfolded the topographical map. He held one end, she the other. "If I read the map right, our gulch is linked to a much larger fork that splits again to form a junction."

He studied the map. "Appears to be the case. What does the X mean?"

"The proposed crime scene. Marked the location right after Bullet found the flash drive. Also sketched a diagram of the area and snapped photos."

"Smart move. A half a mile or so before the site, let's climb up so I can photograph the scene from above before we process below."

"I'll give you a heads-up." She took the lead, her feet sinking into the soft, volcanic earth. The powdery dirt coated her boots and pant legs, but at least she didn't have to contend with the wind stirring up the dust. She trooped on for about twenty minutes, rounded a sharp bend, and stopped.

"What's wrong?" Ed asked.

"Nothing. Main fork's about a half mile ahead."

"See any place to climb out?"

"There." She scaled the steep bank, her hiking boots gouging the crumbling hillside, and topped the ridge with ease. "Grab hold." She extended her hand. "Your pack's a lot heavier than mine."

"Thanks, but I'll get there." He paused halfway to catch his breath. "Give me a minute."

"It's the altitude. Take your time."

"You aren't panting."

She laughed. "You didn't see me yesterday."

He lagged behind for a stretch, then closed the gap between them. The sun rose high in the sky, its warm rays stripping away the morning chill as they zigzagged through the thick brush. Occasionally, she caught the scent of pine mixed with cedar, the two often overpowered by the pungent odor of disturbed sage.

Darcy picked up the pace. "We're here." She waved him forward.

"How do you know?"

She handed him her binoculars. "The tree closest to us . . . see the orange on the branches?"

He scanned the gulch. "Sure do."

"Strips of neon orange surveyor's tape."

"Again, smart move. I'll unload, and we'll get started." He tugged a thick binder from his pack. "Do you mind being my evidence recorder?"

"Not at all." Darcy eyed the book.

"I know. Looks like overkill, but I'm a stickler about documenting physical evidence. In almost every case, you only get one"—he held up a finger to emphasize his point—"shot at processing the scene properly."

She placed the binder on her Kelty. "Wish more law enforcement officials practiced your philosophy."

He removed a tarp from his backpack. With her holding one end, they shook the folds free. "Now let's unload my gear, if you don't mind."

"Not at all." She helped him unload. "Want me to set up the cameras?" She hung her parka on a tree limb. "Day's warming up."

"About the cameras, sure. About warming up, good. I hate cold weather."

"Me too." Darcy attached his camera, then hers, to their respective tripods. "Are these locations okay?"

"For now, yes. Let's work from up here so I can get the entire picture from above before we head down." He dragged out a daypack and stuffed it with paraphernalia he needed to process the scene. "Let's see." He ticked off items on a checklist. "I don't think I forgot anything."

"Looks like you brought your entire lab."

He chuckled. "Hardly. I notice you've done this before." He pointed to a smaller backpack lying across the trunk of a fallen tree.

Darcy nodded. "Too many times to count. Learned my lesson. Pack everything in something big, but bring something small if you leave your base camp."

"Spoken like a professional." Positioned behind his tripod, he uncapped the lens and went to work. The Canon's motor drive whined.

For over an hour, she and Ed photographed the alleged crime scene from overhead, then logged their shots, processed sketches, and pinpointed the arroyo on her topographical map.

"Let's walk the ridge for a few yards to be sure we haven't missed anything from above, then make our descent here"— he tapped a spot on the map—"and retrace our steps to your orange markers."

"Okay." She hoisted on her pack, snapped the cam lock belt around her waist, and tied orange tape to the bushes growing in an uneven row atop the arroyo.

"What's that for?"

"To warn us that the crime scene's coming up. Down there, things look a lot different."

"You're too smart for me."

"Yeah, right." Darcy shielded her eyes with her hand and glanced at the sky. "We better move it. I'm not sure how long it'll take to process the site, and dusk comes early in winter." The statement brought Maddox to mind. She grimaced.

A few yards up the rim, Darcy skidded down into the arroyo, the heels of her boots chiseling clefts in the soft walls. Ed followed.

"I'll lead," he said. "We want to proceed slowly to be sure we protect the integrity of the site."

He hadn't gone far when the split she described appeared before them.

"I don't see any markers." He searched the ledge with binoculars.

"Too soon. We're only at the first junction." She studied the map. "We need to take the next fork. About fifty feet in, we should see the orange tape."

"That's where you saw white feathers strewn across the sagebrush?"

"Right, but I'm not sure they play a part. Only noticed them because Bullet found them interesting."

"Did he find the cap in the same vicinity?"

"Nearby."

"Between you and me, even though Testco hasn't confirmed the dark stains as blood, I've seen it too many times on too many materials and in too many stages—from fresh to years old—to be wrong. I think you're on to something. Told my boss Ray the same thing after we sorted through the evidence you mailed us. Ray's a skeptic, but he humored me with a ticket to New Mexico," Ed said.

"Thanks for the vote of confidence."

The arroyo narrowed, then dipped. The high walls blocked the sun. Darcy shivered, cold from walking in the shadows. Fresh snow clung to the sheltered corners. Where it had melted, the dusty earth had turned a rich chocolate, the mud slick and treacherous. She walked on, her eyes cataloging the terrain.

She spotted a flash of orange. "Ed, the tape."

He raised his arm. She fell silent, allowing him to dictate his observations into a handheld recorder. When he finished, he called out, "If the real scene is another fifty feet or so, let's set up here."

"If you're eager to start, I'll unpack."

"Thanks, but I need my designated notetaker close by, and that's you." He spread a tarp on the ground, anchored it in place with metal spikes, and emptied his pack.

Darcy fanned through the pages in the binder, the material sectioned into notes, sketches, photographs, and a video log. "You sure are organized."

He smiled. "Any questions?"

"No, I'm fairly familiar with documenting CS work."

"At the bureau?"

"Yes. Had my share of homicides." She closed the book. "I've had a shot at everything from mixing dental stone to packaging evidence for analysts."

"Great. I had no idea. Sharing duties sure takes the onus off me. At the back of the binder, there's a list of items and/or areas I think we should concentrate on. I drew up the inventory based on your letter to Testco." Hunched over his equipment, he mumbled, "Blood, soil samples, if they're still of any use. Ignore me. I remember better if I think aloud."

"Same here. Add fiber to your list."

"Done." He pointed to a box of collection materials.

"The fiber might be nothing more than bird feathers, but you never know. As for soil samples, I agree—by now they may have changed too dramatically to be of much help. Time, plus Bullet and I stomping through the place, probably corrupted the evidence."

"We'll see."

"Meant to tell you . . . the wool cap was damp when Bullet found it. I stored it in a Ziploc with the mouth open until I could transfer it to paper. Hope I didn't contaminate the evidence."

"I checked all of the evidence the minute Testco received your package. I didn't see any mold, and the blood had air-dried nicely, so I doubt there's any contamination."

Good news. "Glad we had freezing temps that night."

"Always been my experience that bloodstains retain their characteristics fairly well in cold temperatures. Give me a few minutes, then we'll start."

From the entry-exit point, Ed photographed the site before he conducted a walk-through examination. Afterward, Darcy helped him sketch the area on his laptop.

"Cool computer program. Where'd you buy it?" she said.

"I didn't. I designed the program for Testco's use."

"Impressive."

Ed blushed. "No big deal." He donned gloves. "I considered an outward or inward spiral search, but in this case, I think I'll opt for a . . ."

"Grid."

"You do know your stuff."

"Let's see, the area is approximately six by six, so a thorough pattern would be north-south, then perpendicular east-west, each step no more than a foot in length." She put the log on the tarp. "Fragile evidence should be gathered first."

"You're right, so let's take soil samples from the immediate area, access, and escape routes. When you're finished, we'll discuss what you've covered and decide if we should take more and from where. Or whether we should vacuum certain sectors," Ed said.

She snapped on latex gloves and picked up a box of plastic pill bottles. "Sounds like a plan."

Time passed. Darcy stood and stretched, the warmth of the sun's rays a pleasant change after working in the cold shadows. Done with the soil samples, she retrieved a pair of tweezers and snagged the first white feather from the dried branches of the sagebrush. She tucked the sample in an envelope and reached for another. Something blue, hidden deep in the bush, shimmered in the strong light. She shoved her hand into the shrub and tweezed it. "Hey, Ed."

He wandered over. "What's up?"

She squeezed the neck of an envelope, ready to toss the blue swatch in after he'd examined the material.

"Electric blue," he said, leaning closer to the square of fabric. "Where'd you find it?"

"In the bush with the white feathers."

"Hmm. I own a down parka similar in color."

She met his gaze. "Are you thinking what I'm thinking?

"Feathers all right, but not from any bird around here."

"I agree." She dropped the sample into the envelope and sealed it.

"How's the soil collection coming?"

"Almost wrapped up. I'm done with the immediate area. Next, the narrow strip along the east side to the bend beyond, and afterward, the arroyo walls."

Ed beamed. "You do know CS work."

"Ease up on the praise," Darcy was about to say, but she didn't. Maybe he felt bad about bringing up her bureau days. Instead, she said, "Every crime scene is three-dimensional."

"Right you are. I'll grab some containers."

An hour later, she showed him the dry bed where Bullet had found the wool cap snagged in the underbrush. He sized up the section. "Area is less than a third of the size of the first scene—should go fast. I'll walk the grid, if you don't mind?"

She shook her head, busy counting aloud. She finished. "While you search the scene, I'll label plastic cups for blood specimens."

"Is this the rock Bullet stopped to examine?"

"Yes."

Ed scooped dirt into several containers, capped them, and labeled each. Then he shot long-range and close-range photographs of the rock, as well as its relationship to the surrounding area.

"Hey!" Darcy shouted. "I found something interesting. We'll need black-and-white film, a linear scale, and Snow Print Wax. Oh, and bring something to mix it in. You know the drill."

He gathered the items and arrived at her side. "What luck, a shoeprint in the snow."

To increase the contrast, Darcy sprayed Snow Print Wax over the impression and allowed the wax to set up before she snapped off several shots. The last series of frames fell to Ed. He adjusted the zoom lens, filled the frame with the print and the scale, and bracketed his exposures to obtain maximum image detail. "Glad you came across this little jewel."

"Me too." She leaned into the bush to force the branches back. "Under there is a partial, but the print's in bad shape."

Ed examined it. "You're right—only the toe. Take a shot anyway. Might be a match."

"I'm surprised the impression survived the weather we've had lately—lots of rain and snow. Maybe that overhang protected the print. Want me to mix the mud?" She reached for the dental stone.

He gave her the plastic bag of dry mix and a bottle of water. "Two pounds should be plenty."

The sun sank low in the sky.

"The light'll fade soon," he said. "We might be waiting in the dark for the stone to harden."

"Pray for the moon. Burns brighter here than anywhere I've been. Must be the altitude." She poured water into the bag, sealed the top, then kneaded the mixture to combine it. Blended, the mud resembled pancake batter. She drained the composite onto the ground next to the impression and watched the mix trickle into the shoeprint until the indentation overflowed.

"You have good technique—no erosion, no detail destroyed. You're a natural. Ever consider forensic science?"

"I'm too old to learn new tricks. Better stick to sleuthing." She poured the remainder of the mixture into the partial print.

Before the stone hardened, Ed inscribed the date, his initials, and some identifying information into the damp compound. "Now we wait. In this weather, the stone will take thirty minutes or longer to set."

"What do you say to a sandwich?"

"I say I'm starving." He stripped off his gloves. "Pass the wine. I'll pour."

She laughed. "You wish."

Interested in the case, Ed asked a litany of questions. Darcy shared her information willingly, for she realized he might have something insightful to offer. She concluded by saying, "Any theories, suggestions, or whatever . . . I'd like to hear them."

"Let me mull over what you've said. Our print should be ready." He lifted the cast, wrapped it in butcher paper, and marked the package for identification. "I'm beat."

"Check this out." Darcy removed her sunglasses, hooked them over her head, and placed her hand on the ground to support herself as she reached into the sagebrush. "I need gloves."

He handed her a pair. "What'd you find?"

"Not sure." She pulled out a long object. "Are your gloves clean?"

He snapped on a fresh pair. "Are now."

She placed the transparent cylinder in his open palms.

He frowned. "Looks like but... What is it?"

15

Darcy stared at the object cradled in Ed's hands. "Some kind of syringe, but what kind? I've never seen anything like it. Have you?"

He shook his head.

She picked up the hypodermic by the plunger and rotated it. "Crystal-clear plastic from one end to the other. Strange that the stylus isn't metal. And why so long? Looks like something you'd inject a horse with, not a human. The barrel capacity is approximately—"

"Twenty-two cc," Ed said.

"How'd you know?"

"A good guess. Hold still." He placed a ruler alongside the needle. "End to end, six inches long excluding the barrel, and with it, eight inches. Keep that pose." He grabbed a magnifying glass. "The distal tip's serrated an entire 360 degrees. Here, take a look."

Ed held the hypodermic while Darcy inspected it. "I'll bet each of those notches is razor sharp. Reminds me of a miniature concrete corer—the type used to cut drainage holes in curbs," she said.

"You mean a core driller."

"Exactly." She took it back.

He puckered his upper lip, his eyes glued to the needle. "I've seen my share of hypodermics, but none like this. Wonder what the silver strip is for?"

"Haven't a clue, but that's how I found the syringe."

"What do you mean?"

"The strip reflected the fading sunlight. Cast a reddish-orange glow over the sagebrush. Otherwise, I doubt I would've noticed the needle."

"What luck. Any markings on the strip?"

She moved the magnifying glass over the needle. "None visible to the naked eye. Odd finding a syringe way out here, and not even the kind a junkie would shoot up with."

He stared down at the arroyo. "But it's a good place to do drugs. No one's around to pry."

A light breeze rustled the boughs of the piñons that rimmed the arroyo. The soft wind stiffened and carried with it the promise of a frigid night. On the horizon, a fireball sun ignited the landscape, coloring the desert rose, lavender, and blue.

"Be dark soon," said Ed.

"How do you want to package this baby?"

"In a plastic tube. There's several in my backpack. They're padded on all sides."

She found the cylinders, slid the syringe into one, and handed it to Ed for labeling. "While you're doing that, I'll finish cleaning up. Daylight's fading fast. Remember, we still have gear above to load."

He nodded, busy scribbling on the plastic tube. He capped the container, hooked his pack over his shoulders, and joined her as she crammed a stuff bag into her Kelty. He strapped on a carbine headlamp.

"Going high tech on me," Darcy said.

He chuckled. "Belongs to Testco." He scaled the arroyo wall and headed in the direction of their base camp.

When Darcy arrived at the site, Ed had already dismantled the camera gear. She packed up the tripods and made a final sweep of the area. "Looks like we have everything."

On the return trip, she led. The day darkened. With Ed's carbine lantern projecting bright light on the vegetation, it made more sense for him to go first, but as he confessed, "I'm no good with a compass," so he swapped his lantern for a flashlight and walked alongside her until a wide stand of junipers forced them to proceed single file.

For a while, Darcy talked in abbreviated sentences, but the wind picked up and snatched her words away. After the gusts died, the constant swish of Gore-Tex against sagebrush drowned all dialogue, leaving her to tramp on in silence.

Yards ahead, the trail gave way to thick patches of blue grama grass, a sign the cul-de-sac lay near. She glimpsed her 4Runner among the trees, and her pace quickened. "Long day." She shed her Kelty.

Ed stowed their packs in the hatch and eased into the passenger's seat.

Darcy fired up the engine. "Hope Walt called."

"Me too." Ed leaned back in his seat.

"Why didn't you give him my cell number?"

"Walt's requirement, not mine. He wanted a landline only."

"More secure?"

"Perhaps. He didn't say. Besides, the less he knows, the better. Trust me."

If Ed didn't trust Walt, then how could she? Darcy backed out of the clearing.

"I've been giving the case some thought," Ed said.

"Anything in particular?" Darcy listened attentively, eager to hear his comments.

"Enzo's gutted house, Johnny's apartment in Los Alamos . . . I'd like to conduct my own search and treat each one like a crime scene. Who knows what might turn up?"

"Don't think you'll find much. Both places were sanitized."

"You never know."

Having seen the homes, Darcy wasn't as hopeful. "We have to pass the turnoff to Enzo's on the way back. Want to swing by?"

"Sure, if you don't mind."

"Will do." Curious herself, she didn't mind at all.

Just shy of eight miles down the highway, Darcy backed off the accelerator and rolled off the paved main drag onto the pothole-riddled easement to Enzo's gutted house. "The home should be right around this bend—" She braked hard. Her seatbelt gouged her chest.

Ed sat up. "Something wrong?"

"I must've missed the turn."

"What makes you think so?"

"Because the house was right there." She pointed to a space among the trees. "Now it's gone."

"Which might explain why Enzo gutted the structure?"

"I don't follow."

"He planned to move the house to another location or scrape it. Let's take a look." Ed jumped out.

"Better take all the samples you need. Way this case has gone, by our next visit someone may have excavated all the dirt from the area." She switched on her flashlight and started across the drive. "The house stood right here." She squatted.

"Notice the difference in color between the earth around our feet and the soil over there?"

He crouched beside her. "Sure do. The contrast from light to dark is obvious."

"So is the texture. The old driveway ended along this stretch. What you're looking at are crusher fines, top-dressing for a dirt easement. Dig down a bit, and you'll come across a coarser base of stone. Over there, to your right, you'll find gravel."

"You're observant. How do you remember such details?"

"Training. Taught myself to file information—up here." She tapped her temple.

"Rather obscure information."

"Maybe. Let's take those samples. Where should I start?"

He glanced about. "Because the light's poor, let's work as a team. We'll gather what we can tonight, enough to prove a home existed, then I'll come out at dawn and take more samples, as well as map the site."

Forty minutes later, she helped him pack up. Darcy yawned repeatedly as her SUV bucked over the moonlit roads to the rental. Dead tired, she parked in the garage and slid out of the driver's seat, ready for something to eat and some sleep.

"Go in," said Ed, "and check for messages. I'll unload."

Rio raced into the garage, her expression hopeful. "Did you find anything out there?"

Darcy weighed her words. "We collected samples but won't know anything until the lab analyzes them."

"Oh. Okay." She ducked back into the kitchen.

Ed bent closer to Darcy. "Shrewd. Give enough information to avoid suspicion but not enough to cause alarm."

"Yep." She snagged her Kelty from his hand and entered the kitchen. Bullet bounded up to Darcy, and she hugged him. "Any messages?"

"One. A man named Walt called," Rio said.

"When?" she asked, letting her backpack slip from her shoulder to the floor.

"Around five." Rio read off a pad near the telephone. "He'll call again at seven with details. The phone should ring any minute now. Are you hungry?"

"Will be after I unwind." She kicked off her hiking boots and stared at the wall clock.

Ed sauntered in. "Did Walt call?"

"At five. He's supposed to call again at seven. Help yourself to a drink." Darcy motioned to an overhead cupboard near the sink.

"Good, you have Scotch." Ed poured himself one. "One for you, Darcy?" He held up his glass.

"Sure. Neat."

He handed Darcy her Scotch, took a seat opposite her in the breakfast nook, and nursed his liquor.

Rio moved about the kitchen. The pungent smell of roasted chilies filled the room. "How about dinner, Darcy?"

"I'll eat after Walt calls, so don't wait for me."

Without asking, Rio heaped stew into a bowl, piled a plate with salad, and placed both in front of Ed. "Bread's on the table in the basket. Eat up."

"Smells delicious." He devoured his food. Twice he looked up at Darcy. "Sorry, but I'm starving."

"Don't apologize. There's nothing wrong with a healthy appetite. I had one ten minutes ago."

"What changed?" he asked.

"Walt hasn't called back." She polished off her Scotch. Over the din of utensils scraping china rose the persistent ticktock of the clock as time flitted away. The later the hour, the more troubled Darcy became. Seven fifteen came, then seven thirty.

She spooned salad onto her plate and speared a tomato. "The salad's good, Rio."

The phone rang.

Darcy leaped up so fast, she almost knocked over her chair. She ripped the receiver from the console. "McClain."

"Good, it's you," whispered a harsh voice.

At first, she didn't recognize the caller. "Who's this?"

"Silverbird."

"An—" The name died on her lips. With her back to Rio and Ed, she cupped her hand to the mouthpiece and spoke softly. "Where are you?"

"At the lab."

Darcy wanted to shout, "At the lab? Are you crazy?" but she remained silent.

"Walt got me in."

"Where is the—"

"Listen. We tried to decode the drive, but a problem came up. They know I'm here."

The fear in Andrew's voice sent a chill through her. "Leave."

"Won't be easy."

"If Walt got you in, he can get you out. Is he there?"

"Close by."

"Put him on."

"Can't."

"Look, I'm trying to help you. Put him on."

"Walt's dead."

16

*D*ead. The word swirled through Darcy's stunned brain. When Rio bent over to load the dishwasher, Darcy motioned to Ed.

He nodded. "Hey, Rio, forget the dishes. You cooked—now I'll clean."

"Thanks, but I don't mind." She rinsed a handful of flatware.

"No, go." With his hands on her shoulders, he propelled her toward the kitchen door.

"Okay, okay, we're leaving. Right, Bullet?"

He dashed from under the table, and the two disappeared into the living room.

"Are you still there?" Andrew's panicked voice resonated over the line.

"Yes. You're sure Walt's dead?"

Ed snapped his head in Darcy's direction. Water dripped from the glass in his hand and spotted the floor.

"He's dead all right," said Andrew. "Throat slashed from ear to ear. Lying in blood."

Fear spiked through her, fear for Andrew's life. "If you can't leave, is there any place you can hide?"

"I'm . . . I'm thinking. Not sure." Andrew's words rang clear, faded, and became sharp again as he moved his mouth away from the receiver, then back.

He's looking about, worried someone might be watching or approaching. Her conclusion disturbed her. She hated to ask but had to. "Where's the flash drive?"

"In a safe place."

"I have to know where."

"At Z. Someone's coming. Gotta go."

"No, Andrew. Wait. Where's the drive? It's at what?" The dial tone droned in her ear. "Dammit." She slammed down the receiver. "No flash drive. And no Walt."

"What happened?"

"He hung up. Or someone hung up for him. And I can't do a damn thing to help him unless I'm on the inside. And as awful as it sounds, if anything happens to Andrew, I may never find the drive."

"I meant to Walt."

"Sorry, Ed. How thoughtless of me." How much should she say?

"Just tell me what happened. Walt and I were only business acquaintances."

She repeated Andrew's description.

A long silence ensued.

Ed broke it. "With Walt dead, this complicates things, but we'll have to work around the problem. This leaves only his boss Norm, and convincing him won't be easy. He can be a real SOB." Ed poured himself a refill. He lifted a glass in the air.

"No thanks. Had enough." Darcy put a filter in the coffee-maker.

"What did Walt say? 'You guys have no idea what you're dealing with. Snoop around and someone'll get hurt.'"

"Something along those lines."

Neither spoke for a long time. Ed sipped his drink. Some-where between swallows he folded his hands, his index fingers extended, and tapped the tips on the edge of the table. Mentally, Darcy drowned out the steady drumming and dwelled on her predicament. Wired on caffeine, she thought until the threads of a plan slowly gelled in her recharged brain. The strategy held little appeal, but the alternatives stunk.

Ed pushed out his chair. "Instead of sitting here doing noth-ing, let's track down Norm's address, phone number—whatever we can find—and I'll start bugging him at home. Damn shame about Walt, but we still have an edge."

Darcy poured the last bit of coffee into her mug. "Brecken-ridge?"

"Yeah."

"But does this still apply with Walt dead?"

Ed nodded.

Even if blackmail helped her cause, she hated it. "Okay, come on." She walked out of the kitchen, Ed with her.

"Night, you two." Rio switched off the TV and headed down the hall.

Darcy climbed the stairs to her office, tired yet wide awake after all the coffee she'd drunk.

"If I doze off, kick me." Ed stretched out on the sofa in Darcy's office before Bullet could claim the choice spot.

Bullet nudged her as if to say, "Make him move." She patted his head. He sighed loudly, then ducked under the desk and fell asleep, draped across Darcy's feet, while she logged on. "What's Norm's full name?"

"Norman Arnold Carter. Last I heard, he lived in White Rock."

She typed in her password. "I'll start there. What department does he work in?"

"Same as Walt."

"I know, but what department did Walt work in?"

He rolled his head sideways. "Sorry, my brain's fried. CIC—Computing, Information, and Communications. Norm's head of computer security, or something along those lines. I have no idea what title he holds. He's been promoted a lot."

"I'll find out," she said, more to herself than him. She located the information and clicked on PRINT. The laserjet hummed in harmony with Ed's snores. She tapped him on the shoulder.

"Huh? What?" He raised himself on an elbow.

"Norm's info." She placed the sheet of paper on Ed's chest.

He rubbed his eyes. "I'll call from my room."

"Ring me if he agrees to help. No matter how late."

"Will do."

The instant Ed vacated the sofa bed, Bullet reclaimed his spot. Darcy let Ed out the side door, locked up, and returned to her office. Standing at the glass sliding door, she watched him cut across the enclosed courtyard to the guesthouse. He passed under the corbels that framed the portal and disappeared inside. What, no Green tonight?

Seated at her desk, she propped her feet on the edge, and reclined in her chair. In her opinion, Norm was a long shot, so she resorted to the contingency plan she'd dreamed up in the kitchen no less than thirty minutes ago. The fallback strategy was as big a gamble as Ed's blackmail idea. Norm stood to lose his job if he helped them. And few employees as tenured as he would jeopardize their livelihoods for such a foolhardy scheme.

If caught, Darcy too had a lot at stake: her PI license, a stiff fine, and maybe jail time for cracking into the lab's computers. If Walt were alive, she'd probably dismiss the possibility of any real threat to Andrew's safety, but his sudden demise, and in such a violent fashion, troubled her.

She drew her laptop closer. This wouldn't be her first break-in, but unlike times before, no one had hired her to find the weaknesses in LANL's restricted operating systems, assuming any still existed. Under fire for recent cracks into their classified databases, the top watchdogs at the nuclear weapons lab had assured the officials at CERT, the Department of Defense's computer security organization, that LANL had implemented an ironclad layer of security guaranteed to resolve the serious deficiencies in their top-secret operating systems. It didn't take long for Darcy to realize the lab's wake-up call would make her life hell.

Hours passed, and her cryptowar of secret codes and ciphers, designed to stonewall even an elite cracker or master decoder, raged on. But persistence paid off. She slipped below the lab's surveillance radar and overwhelmed the intrusion detection software to gain access to LANL's unclassified network. Before she continued, Darcy made a note of the unguarded port so she had backdoor access the next time she wanted in. If this was how the lab guarded nonsensitive material, then she had a real challenge ahead.

Midnight arrived. She finally penetrated the last firewall, jumped a digital security fence, and cracked the code that locked her out of the classified networks. Not there yet. Still, she anticipated victory, so she swallowed her last gulp of coffee in advance celebration. After all, how complicated could it be to break into the Human Resources department?

As she discovered, not difficult at all. The final hurdle required only manipulating a software glitch. Although minor, someone had overlooked the security hole. At the right time, she'd notify Norm to plug the unprotected ports, but for now . . .

Darcy poked around personnel for several minutes before she scrolled through the list of job openings not yet posted on the lab's Web site. As luck would have it, Norm had two postings—technically three with Walt dead. She skimmed the descriptions, skipped over the entry-level slots, and read the duties for codemaker, the post second in command to Walt, according to the attached organizational chart. With a three-year stint at the NSA, the most sophisticated snooping operation in the world, she qualified for the job. Even if she fell short in some areas, a few keystrokes bumped her qualifications.

Next, she inserted herself onto the payroll, then created a personnel folder. In the file she placed a resume tailored to the responsibilities for codemaker. To her record she added glowing reference letters, followed by the results of her company physical and mandatory drug test, along with a police report. When done, she double-checked the contents of her folder against those of two new hires to be certain she hadn't overlooked anything. All documents in her file appeared to be in order, so she stashed her records with the rest of the *M*s, but not under McClain.

Because her career at the FBI had brought her in contact with many government agencies and scores of state and federal employees, she played it safe and used her street moniker, Dee Miller. If anyone recognized her, she'd handle the problem then. Why draw attention by using her real name? *Real name?* The words triggered a thought. What about an ID badge? She didn't recall a form or any instructions regarding company identification.

Darcy located the document under New Employee Application Procedures. To complete the electronic hiring, all she needed was a picture. No problem. She'd scan a recent snapshot she kept in her wallet and . . .

The fine print on the form glared from the screen. Damn. She had to appear in person for her photo shoot. No exceptions. "Knew this was too easy." Last time she ran into a similar road-block, it took days to circumvent the system via the computer. This go-around, she didn't have the luxury of time. Crap, all this work, and for what? Norm had better come through.

She read on. LANL had recently issued new security proce-dures. The old badge had been replaced with an Eyedentacard, the ID embedded with the individual's biometric identity, and LANL wanted everything: finger, hand, face, retina, and voice scans. What? Heck, while they were mapping her, why not take her DNA as well?

She checked the hour in the right-hand corner of her screen—2:00 a.m. The sofa beckoned, but she wasn't done. She turned back to the monitor and wrote a program to tag the information in her folder. No matter where the documents traveled within LANL, or on any linked system, she could track her records and instantly erase them. She also added a timeline marker. After a month, the file would simply disappear unless she extended the deadline. Before she logged off, Darcy created a trapdoor, which allowed her to return undetected.

At 3:00 a.m., she put her laptop on standby and stretched out on the bed in the other room since Bullet had commandeered the daybed in her office. But sleep eluded her, her mind drifting over the day's events. At some point she must have dozed off. She sat straight up, startled to life by a cold nose on her cheek. Bullet stared back, his brown eyes pleading. He padded from the room and she tagged along. The wall clock by the backdoor read five thirty. On her way out, she grabbed bags and a flashlight.

The strong beam flitted over the outdoor staircase, the steps sheeted in ice. She climbed down cautiously to the courtyard, not as sure-footed as Bullet, who blended into the dark. While she waited for him, Darcy leaned against the wall of the house, the cold stucco jolting her awake. When he didn't return after several minutes, she stepped away from the rough exterior, flicked on her flashlight, and called out, "Come on, boy. I'm cold."

Loud growls, punctuated by snarls, drew her to a recess where the garden wall butted to the garage apartment. She flashed the beam over the area. Bullet danced about like a prize-fighter, alternating between growls and barks. A stout hedgerow separated the frenzied schnauzer from whatever he'd tracked down.

She slid her hand under her parka, her fingers poised over her Browning, and inched toward the area. The closer she came, the more excited Bullet became. The moment she flooded the cavity with light, a burly figure sprang over the four-foot hedge and darted across the icy flagstone. Green slipped and slid, along with Bullet. Each tried to avoid the other, but Bullet won.

Darcy aimed. "Stop or I'll shoot!" she shouted, but the man didn't even break stride.

Green hurled his large frame at the compound wall, locked his hands over the edge, and heaved himself up, one leg dangling on the wrong side of the fence. Bullet lunged at him. The man bellowed in pain and hit the ground. Bullet bit him again and held on. The man tried to shake free but failed. Light glinted off steel. Darcy caught sight of the Ruger and fired a warning shot as she shouted, "Drop the gun."

An agonizing cry sliced the night, followed by a thud. The Ruger discharged, and glass shattered.

The intruder scaled the wall and fell from sight. Darcy yanked open the pedestrian gate and swept the neighboring terrain with her flashlight. The powerful beam caught him as he ran down the dirt easement. She didn't pursue him. Like before, he'd probably parked at the fork in the road and would be gone by the time she got there. Besides, she thought it unwise to leave Rio and Bullet unprotected.

"Come, boy," she called, anxious to find Bullet; afraid the man may have hurt him. He broke from the shadows. "You okay, boy?" She checked him over. He tried to slip through the open gate, but she restrained him. Deep-throated growls vibrated in his chest. "Good boy. Now let's collect his gun and run some prints on Green."

17

Darcy holstered her Browning, then searched the courtyard for the Ruger.

Light flooded the compound.

Ed stumbled onto the portal. He wore pajama bottoms and a parka. "Darcy, Darcy— where are you?" His shout floated on an icy breeze. "Are you okay? I heard a gunshot."

"We had an intruder. Bullet scared him off."

Ed shuffled across the flagstone walk to where she stood. "A burglar?"

"In a manner of speaking, though I don't think he planned to steal anything."

"What do you mean?"

She gave him a brief rundown on Green. "Somewhere around here he dropped his Ruger. There." She knelt beside a trail of blood.

Ed bent down next to her. "Blood. You shot him?"

"No. Bullet bit him. Twice, I think."

Ed stood. "Be back in a sec."

Rio flung open the patio door. "What's going on?"

Bullet sprang from the shrubbery and danced around the compound, excited by the commotion.

"Rio, do me a favor. Put on coffee, and take Bullet with you."

"Sure, but what happened?"

"I'll explain later."

"Oh, okay." She opened her mouth to say something, closed it, and rushed back inside, taking Bullet with her.

A knife-like, cold wind cut through Darcy. She shifted her weight from one foot to the other. What was keeping Ed? She wanted the semiautomatic stowed in a safe place—and now—so she could go in for a hot shower and sleep. Her hand caressed the Browning, snug in its shoulder holster. Dan's words from a prior case came to mind. "If he's shot, he's pissed. Might come back armed and primed for revenge." She wondered if she'd hit him.

Daybreak grayed the black sky as Ed emerged from the house, his arms filled with collection paraphernalia. He dumped the bundle on the patio table and sorted through the pile for a container. "I thought I heard Rio." He snapped on latex gloves.

"I sent her inside to fix coffee. A diversion."

"Is this guy dangerous? Of course he is—he had a gun," Ed said. "Shouldn't we call the police?"

Maddox? No thanks, she didn't need him snooping around right now. "All in good time. By chance, are you packing?"

"I'm seldom without a firearm, but right at this moment, no." He knelt on one knee. "Can you put a light on this?" He pointed to the trail of red.

She lit the area. "I fired a warning shot but don't think I hit him. I'm sure the blood is from Bullet's bites."

"Lot of blood for dog bites." He took a sample. "I wonder how bad he's hurt."

"Can't be too bad. He escaped over the wall without a problem."

Ed snorted. "Good point."

"Heard anything from Norm?"

"No," he said without looking up. "I left messages at home and at work. He'll call—just a matter of time."

She wasn't as optimistic.

A door creaked.

Her hand closed on the Browning.

"Call for you, Ed," Rio shouted from the upstairs balcony. "Said his name's Breckenridge."

"Can't break right now. You go."

Darcy's sleepy brain woke up. "I'll be right in."

"Go." Ed waved her on. "I'll box the Ruger. Be there in a few minutes."

In her office, she scooped up the landline and punched a button on the console. "Hello." Hearing only dead air, she felt her pulse soar. He expected Ed. He'd hang up. "Don't hang up. Ed's–"

"No names," the caller said. "This isn't a secure line. Are you his friend?"

"Yes."

"Job's yours. Tuesday. Report to HR-5 at 1400." The line went dead.

Ed entered the room in a hurry. "What'd I miss?"

"Tuesday at 1400." She saluted.

"How'd you know Norm was an ex-Marine?"

"By the tone of his voice." She dropped onto the couch, elated and exhausted, but suspicious as to why Norm had capitulated this easily. She expected Ed to show surprise as well, yet he said nothing.

Pale light washed across the floor as Ed headed for the door. "Glad he came through. The sun's up. I better finish out there."

No sooner had his steps died down the hallway than Darcy's cell phone pulsed.

"Hi, sis. Vicky and I are headed to Misery Mountain in Alberta to ski. We'll be there for about a week, but still plan to come down to Taos for Christmas. I'm glad you understand. Gotta go. Running late," said Charlene in her typical rapid-fire fashion. She knew this tactic would meet with little opposition because Darcy never had the opportunity to speak.

"Wait a minute. Charlene. Listen. Can I get a word in?"

"Hurry, 'cause Vicky and I have to leave. Valet has our SUV ready."

"No, I don't understand," said Darcy, talking over Charlene.

"Thanks, sis. You're a peach. Sorry for the early call. Bye."

A dial tone droned in Darcy's ear.

She stared at the telephone, not believing Charlene had suckered her again. This time she planned to confront her sister. She dialed back. The desk clerk at the hotel in Banff said, "They just pulled away from valet parking. No ma'am, they checked out."

Rio walked into the room. She slid a tray onto the table. "Coffee?"

"Sure." Darcy counted to ten.

Silence. Rio poured coffee while Darcy fumed.

The whine of the fax machine brought life to the room.

Darcy jumped up. One look at the transmission sheet and she forgot about her conversation with Charlene. "More paperwork for Ed. I'd better deliver it." She brushed past Rio. "Save me a cup. I'll be back in a moment." She maneuvered around Bullet, planted in the doorway, and unhooked her jacket from the hall stand. Ed was still in the courtyard collecting evidence as Darcy cleared the last step on the outdoor staircase.

He stood as she approached. "I checked for footprints, but there's nothing—not even a trace of mud on the flagstone, expect for over there. Plenty of dog prints, though. Whatcha got?" He nodded to the papers in her hand.

"Testco results." She fanned the fax.

"Have you read them?"

"Not yet. Let's go in. I'm freezing."

In a makeshift office next to Dan's vacated bedroom, Ed slid into the chair behind the desk and pulled a yellow highlighter from his pen holder. He gave the marker to Darcy. "You'll need this."

She smiled. "I'm too predictable."

"On some things."

She skimmed the results. "The dark stain on the wool cap is dried blood, AB negative." She highlighted the blood type.

"Rare," said Ed. "Do you know Johnny's type?"

"No, and every time I ask Rio a question her antennae go up."

"Want me to try?"

"Might help." She flipped the page. "Hmm, interesting. The white feathers are goose down—good hunch on your part. The fiber I snagged off the flash drive"—she tossed the sheets on the desk—"is sweater fuzz. Probably Johnny's."

"You seem agitated. Something wrong?"

"Wish I had that damn flash drive." She made a fist and smacked it into the palm of her other hand. "Since I don't report to LANL until tomorrow at 1400, why don't we drive up to Los Alamos today?"

"Good idea. Maybe on the drive back we can stop at Enzo's, if you aren't completely exhausted by then."

"Sounds good."

"Have you called the police about our intruder?"

"Not yet." Nor did she intend to. Ed didn't challenge her response, so she said nothing more.

"Later today, I'll mail the evidence we collected in the arroyo." He smacked his forehead with his palm. "Shoot, I almost forgot—Dan asked me to lift that print by the garage."

"Glad you remembered. There's been a lot going on."

"No kidding." Ed collected his duffel bag, and Darcy followed him outdoors. He crouched at the edge of the gravel drive. "The print should be around here."

"There." She squatted beside him. "Big guy."

"Yeah. Size twelve, maybe."

Darcy's cell chirped, and she checked the number. "I wonder what he wants at this hour. Hi, Matt. What's up?"

"Sorry to call so early, but I thought you'd want to know right away. I have fabulous news. I know it's short notice, but the judge set a court date for the twentieth."

"I have a conflict."

Only silence at the other end.

"I mean, I'm not dropping the easement suit. I just can't be in court next week. We'll have to postpone."

"Until when?"

The heck if she knew. "I'm not sure."

"It took some finagling to put your case on the docket, especially so close to the holidays." He spoke with cold cordiality.

"I can imagine. And I appreciate your hard work."

"Appreciation won't satisfy the judge. If we ask for a continuance, she won't be as understanding the next time around."

"I'm sorry, Matt, but I'll have to take my chances."

"Very well." He was doing his best to control his temper, and she heard the anger in his voice when he said, "If you don't mind my asking, what became so important between last week and today?"

"Family matter." The excuse sounded flimsy even to her, but she couldn't say . . . murder.

18

Billowy clouds scudded across an ice-blue sky and sailed over the Jemez Mountains, just as the sun broke on the horizon, but the intense rays that snaked through the sedan's tinted windows failed to warm the frigid interior.

Darcy cranked up the heater and repositioned the vents. The hot air magnified the cobwebs netting her brain. Exhausted, she stared through the windshield at the breaking day and dwelled on the long hours squandered trying to crack LANL's databases, hours better devoted to sleep, especially since Norm had agreed to cooperate. Still, it never hurt to have a contingency plan.

Thinking of sleep reminded her of yesterday's futile visit to Los Alamos. Ed agreed the trip was pointless when he walked into Johnny's duplex, although he frittered away two hours scraping, lifting, dust-busting, and collecting. What surprised Darcy was Andrew's house. Someone had cleaned it as well. This really bothered her. And, as she stood in his foyer, she recalled Elena's parting words, "If you see Andrew again, tell him . . . tell him I love him." Darcy had forgotten to tell Andrew when she last saw him in El Mira.

She passed the east gate and cruised into Los Alamos, reliving, as she coasted along, her first visit to the Hill. Years ago, as a young GS-10 at the FBI, she had gaped in wonderment at the concrete buttresses that erupted from the mountain plateau like stone giants, the gray beasts out of place amid the towering ponderosa pines.

Today, LANL no longer intimidated her. Age certainly had a way of tempering greatness and instilling reality. Yet the sterility of the place remained: the same drab, lifeless buildings in the same vibrant landscape. A shame what people did to the land. We weren't the best stewards, before or after the Cerro Grande fire.

She parked the rental at the far end of visitors' row and walked to HR-5. Yesterday, on her way back to Taos from Los Alamos, Darcy decided to loan Ed her 4Runner and rent a compact while employed at the lab. Why draw attention to herself by sporting a vehicle with a California license? She also removed anything that identified the sedan as a rental and stowed the stickers in the glove box.

Instinctively, she shoved her hand under her jacket, expecting to touch her shoulder holster. She felt naked without her Browning. Later, if possible, she'd arrange to sneak a firearm onto the premises.

A wintry breeze skipped across the parking lot. Her stride quickened. She entered HR. The interior shouted government, from the dingy furniture to the vinyl floors to the plant-free environment.

The woman behind the reception desk greeted Darcy with, "New hire? Well, you're late. In fact, you missed morning orientation. You'll have to make it up. However, you can catch the afternoon session if you hurry. The benefits presentation started at one thirty sharp." She leaned over her desk and thrust a sheet of paper at Darcy. "As a reminder, tomorrow from eight to four is general employee training at White Rock Center. Here's a map." She ripped a second sheet from a stack.

A real sweetheart. Darcy smiled. "I am a new hire, but if you check my file you'll see I attended orientation last Monday and general employee training last Tuesday."

The woman scowled.

"My name's Dee Miller. I have an appointment with Norman Carter." Didn't anyone read anymore? To avoid exactly what she'd just been through, Darcy had made a concerted effort to complete all of the obligatory paperwork when she hacked into LANL's HR database.

The woman picked up a file sitting on her desk and sorted through the papers. Her eyebrows arched, giving her an owl-like appearance. "Then I assume you have your token card and an Eyedentacard?"

"The token yes, but no ID, which is why, I believe, Mr. Carter asked me to meet him in personnel."

The woman leveled dark eyes at Darcy. "What time was your meeting?"

Darcy leaned forward so she could read the woman's badge. "He said fourteen hundred sharp, Ms. Mathews."

She seemed offended being called by name. A skeptical look crossed her face, and the arched brows headed toward the ceiling. "One moment, please."

Darcy studied Mathews. She's wary, suspicious. What now?

The HR woman cradled her phone to her ear. "There's a Dee Miller here. She says she has an appointment with Dr. Carter at two today. Hmm. Okay. I'll tell her." She hung up. "Dr. Carter's running late. If you'll have a seat, please."

"Thank you." So it was *Dr.* Carter. She made a mental note. The tension in her stomach eased a bit. She chose a chair near the magazine rack and skimmed an article on quantum computation and cryptography, which commanded her interest for about ten minutes. She looked up to catch Mathews staring.

"Law degree from Stanford. Impressive." Mathews closed the folder.

Darcy merely smiled.

Time wore on. Boredom gave way to concern, which dissolved to apprehension. Had Norm reneged on his promise? Had someone discovered her hack and ordered HR to detain her until the authorities arrived? Why the stalling? Stay cool. "Can you please check and see how much longer Dr. Carter will be? If I have to, I'll reschedule."

Mathews whipped the receiver off her desk. "Carol, Ms. Miller . . . oh, I see. Well, no one told me." She glowered at the telephone in her hand. "Carol, Dr. Carter's secretary, will be here shortly to show you to his office."

About time. "Thank you."

In minutes, a dark-haired woman dressed in black with wire-rimmed glasses perched on her nose and lips drawn to a thin red line marched into HR. "Ms. Miller?"

Darcy stood. "Yes, ma'am."

"Carol Manchester, Dr. Carter's secretary." She extended her hand. "Sorry, but there's been a slight mix-up. Dr. Carter won't be in today. He's on vacation."

Darcy perked up. She was his secretary and no one had informed her? Funny, HR had said the same thing about Andrew Silverbird. An uneasy feeling gripped Darcy.

Carol started down the hall, and Darcy followed. "Dr. Carter called earlier. He'll be back next week. He asked me to help you settle in, but first there's the matter of a badge. How are you feeling? Much better, I hope."

The question surprised Darcy. "Much better."

"I've never had food poisoning but know people who have. Norm—Dr. Carter—should never have taken you to Mr. C's for lunch. I ate there once and never went back. Had an upset stomach all afternoon. But he seems to have a cast-iron gut. Here we are. I assume you have the required identification?"

Darcy patted her briefcase.

"Good." Carol yanked open the door and breezed in. "Sue, this is Ms. Miller, our recent California transplant."

The surprises kept coming.

"Sue will scan your retina, fingers—you name it. All necessary but painless."

The smile was in her voice, not on her face. No laugh lines there.

"When you're done with Dee, ring me." Carol whirled out of the room.

The scan session went without a hitch, but while she fed false information to Sue, Darcy wondered what Norman Carter looked like. After all, she'd apparently had lunch with him.

As soon as Sue completed the paperwork, she rang Carol's extension. This time Norm's secretary appeared promptly.

Carol chatted nonstop on their long trek through narrow corridors to a bank of elevators, the white tunnels dimly lit by ceiling lights. Every open office Darcy passed she discreetly peeked in. Every person she walked past she scrutinized. No Andrew. No Johnny.

"With Norm on vacation and Walt sick," said Carol, "we're a bit shorthanded, so I asked Sonny Barber to show you around." Carol stopped in mid-stride. "Silly me. I was about to explain, but you already know Norm is Walt's boss. You interviewed with both. Says so in your file." Carol waltzed into an elevator.

Norm must have made the notation because Darcy certainly hadn't. "It's unusual for me to confuse dates and times.

I could've sworn Dr. Carter said to meet in HR-5 today at two sharp." She acted sheepish.

"Oh, I'm sure you're right. Norm's the absentminded one."

"When did he leave on vacation?"

"Friday, around three. I should have questioned Eve when she said Norm was in a meeting." Carol paused at a glass door that opened automatically. Another corridor. More elevators. "We'll be there shortly. AI's quite a hike from HR."

Intrigued, Darcy asked, "AI as in Artificial Intelligence?"

Carol wagged a finger. "Sorry. You're right. The R&D folks are constantly correcting me. The department changed their name to AL, Artificial Life or A-Life. I keep forgetting." She wedged her foot between the elevator doors. "You'll still see AI on interoffice memos and the like because change is slow to come and costly. You know the government. Nothing moves fast. Not to mention budget cuts."

Not to mention the right hand not knowing what the left was doing. Darcy climbed aboard. "Ms. Manchester . . ."

"Carol."

"Carol, there must be a mistake. I applied for decoder in the CIC Department, not a post in AL."

Carol shrugged. "I'm never sure what those CIC guys are up to." She wrinkled her nose. "Sneaky bunch. Heck, they could be building another bomb, and I'd never know. But I never doubt the paperwork or the instructions in a file. Yours says to report to the AL lab. You're heavy in computer skills, so they must need a computer whiz more than CIC does."

The elevator landed.

"Follow me," Carol sang out.

Darcy disembarked into a luminescent white corridor, the passage wide and high enough to drive a semitruck through. Carol's voice rang in the hollow space, as Darcy inspected the spacious hallway, her eyes on the terrazzo floor, amazed at the cleanliness.

Carol marched up to a glass entrance. "Your first LANL scan. Ready?" She motioned with her hand to the biometric screen mounted on the wall.

Darcy forced a smile. "Would be easier if you showed me how the pros do it."

"I'm sure you've done this a gazillion times. Not here, but at your former employer." Carol placed her right hand over the imprint, her face close to a white circle. "Carol Manchester."

A tinny voice drifted forth. "Identity confirmed."

"Go on. Don't be bashful, Dee. In a day or two, you'll be a pro at all the checkpoints. We definitely have our share."

"Here goes." Darcy pressed her palm to the pad, aligned her right eye with the circle, and stated in a firm voice, "Dee Miller." She held her breath. Seemed an eternity before Mr. Tin's stilted reply echoed through the corridor. "Identity confirmed."

Darcy sucked in breaths of air to settle her pulse.

The automatic doors parted, and Carol breezed into a room abuzz with activity. People bustled back and forth, and equipment hummed. She ducked into the nearest office and said, "Have a seat. I'll track down Sonny." She handed Darcy an organizational chart. "While you wait, familiarize yourself with AL." She tossed a file on the desk and disappeared.

Alone, Darcy whisked her personnel file off the desk and riffled through the sheets. Every document looked identical to the ones she'd completed online until she came across an employment application. Someone had filled out the form in longhand and signed her name. Above the fake autograph was Norman Carter's sprawling but legible signature. The application had been signed today at 9:00 a.m.

A hand snatched the folder from Darcy.

She shot up, spun, and found herself eye-to-eye with a man about her height. Black collar-length hair framed a face that seldom saw the sun. He grinned as he thumbed through her file. "New hire, right? Egads. A Stanford law grad, an intelligent woman. We need more of those around here."

He stared at her as though scanning her every feature into his memory bank. "Good. Your Eyedentacard should be around your neck, clearly visible at all times. You follow orders well. Loan it out, even once, and you can kiss your LANL career goodbye. *Capiche?*" He eased his shapeless butt onto the edge of the desk. "When you're inside these walls, you belong to LANL."

"Thanks for the advice."

His bushy brows dove for the comfort of his prominent nose. "I like you. You've got spunk."

"Thanks again, Mr. . . ."

"Solomon Lee Barber at your disposal." He bowed from the waist. "Friends call me Sonny. I don't shake. Ever. So don't be offended. These"—he raised his milk-white hands in the air and wiggled his bony fingers—"are my lifeblood. No one touches them—no way, no how."

Interesting fellow. "What do you do at LANL, Sonny Lee?"

A grin lit his thin face. "I'm a member of the digerati. You?" He leaned toward her.

"Likewise."

His eyes sparkled. "Ooh, fabulous. We nerds need to stick together. We can be so misunderstood. Right, Mill?"

She nodded. It amused Darcy that he'd already nicknamed her.

He clasped those signature hands together. "Well, ready for the grand tour, Mill?"

She nodded again.

"Should we start any place in particular?"

"Does Tech 3 have a lobby? A section where everyone signs in and out? LANL does keep security logs, right?"

A quizzical expression crossed his face. "Why the interest?"

So he was the suspicious type. "I'm a stickler for protocol. I like to know exactly what's required."

The frown faded. "Oh? Okay. Good."

Sonny escorted her through the usual maze of white passageways, then in and out of several elevators. Finally, he arrived at a pair of glass doors marked LOBBY. To her, it looked more like a security post than a reception area.

"New hire, Fred," Sonny announced to the guard. "Mind if I show her the log? She wants to brush up for tomorrow's sign-in."

Fred nodded stiffly, his face expressionless and his eyes on the ID badge dangling from Darcy's neck.

Sonny carried on a monologue with the guard while she skimmed the book. In seconds, her suspicions were confirmed. Norm had signed in at 7:00 a.m. that morning but never signed out. Curiosity overtook her. She hunted through the pages for Walt's name.

"Ma'am." Fred yanked on the log.

Reluctantly, she released the book.

"If you're done," said Sonny, "we'll start the tour. Oh, and remember, no guns, cell phones, pagers, or laptops allowed in, and nothing goes out of the building. And you're subject to a physical search at any time." Sonny beamed, obviously pleased with his little speech.

"Figured as much," said Darcy. She'd left her cell phone in the rental car after reading the voluminous list of corporate policies.

"Okay, let's hit it."

They toured offices and labs, and Sonny made employee introductions. Darcy's dry eyes burned, and her head buzzed.

Nothing but a waste of precious time because it didn't bring her any closer to finding Andrew, Johnny, or the flash drive. The clock in her head ticked off the minutes. How long could she safely stay undercover at LANL?

"What do you think?" Sonny's voice snapped her to attention.

She humored him for another twenty minutes, then feigned overload.

He appeared relieved. "Come on, I'll show you your office. Here's some more advice: remember that the walls are paper thin."

She passed another Permalite station, one of a hundred she saw during the tour. "What are these wall-mounted boxes for? They're everywhere."

"Permalites are backup flashlights designed by LANL. They function on Solar Gel batteries. Don't ask me how they work—they aren't my product line. We get a lot of lightning storms that knock out the power. Permalites fill in until the backup generators kick in. You won't find them outside of LANL. They're exclusive to us. Here's your office."

Darcy crossed the threshold. The decor was standard government issue, but what sparked her curiosity sat on the desk.

Sonny stroked the twenty-two-inch monitor as if it were a favorite pet. "Finest baby in the entire universe. So far."

"So far?"

"You're a very lucky person, Dee Miller." His grin blossomed into outright glee, and his voice dropped an octave. "Not many are chosen to work on Con."

"Con? What's Con? A PC?"

"Tomorrow, you'll lay eyes on our newest wonder. Gotta run. I'm late for a meeting." He shut the door after him.

What theatrics. Darcy draped her suit jacket over the back of her chair and clicked the mouse to life. The computer prompted her for a password to log onto LANL's intranet, but she didn't have one. After a few seconds, the desktop said, "To proceed, insert Eyedentacard." The male voice startled her. On the computer's screen was a replica of her ID badge being inserted into a slot below the monitor. "Please insert now or shut down computer."

"Okay. A bit testy, aren't we?" She whisked the card from around her neck and slid it into the cavity. Immediately, a light flashed, and the PC said, "Proceed to step two: finger imprint." A new layout materialized on the screen. The diagram showed the correct placement for five fingers. She complied, irritated by the procedure. The computer beeped. "Thank you, Dee Miller. Please Proceed."

Logged on for less than five minutes, Darcy agreed with Sonny's assessment. Not only was the desktop the smartest toy in the universe, it was the fastest. Forget fiber optics—time to make way for whatever superspeed data service the lab used. She could barely keep up. Good thing too, because if they were tracking her, speed meant safety, although she doubted that thread mining in HR was as closely regulated as LANL's highly classified connections.

She accessed the company telephone directory and typed in three names—Johnny, Andrew, and Walt. No matches were found, so she dialed Sonny's extension, remembering too late that he was at a meeting. While she waited for him to return to his office, she surfed through various LANL sites and soon lost interest, so she dialed him again.

"What's up, Mill?" he said, answering on the first ring.

"A friend of mine works in T6-CIC3, but I can't find his name in the company directory. Is there another place I can check?"

"Nope. There's only one database for all ten thousand of us. Don't use nicknames."

"I'll try again. Thanks." She hadn't used nicknames. According to LANL, the employees simply didn't exist. She probed deeper. Her search led to a morgue of deleted HR files. From the menu, she clicked on Purgatory. Odd name for a file. Someone had a sense of humor. Purgatory said all three employees, Johnny Duran, Andrew Silverbird, and Walter Spears, had resigned. She scrolled through their personnel data. If the files had contained anything pertinent, the information had been purged.

On a hunch, she returned to the telephone directory and clicked on Limbo, but Dr. Norman Carter hadn't been parked there. Evidently, hell didn't exist in the world of the government and neither did heaven, which seemed equitable, and there were only two ways to leave a company: resign or get fired.

Back in HR's database of deleted files, Darcy clicked on Terminated. To her relief, Norm didn't appear on the list, but when she typed his name into Search a new file popped onto the screen. Of the eight names, she recognized four: Norm, Andrew, Johnny, and Walt.

She must have stared at the list for a long time because the PC prompted her with, "Ms. Miller, do you wish to save or close the folder?" She'd always found talking computers progressive, sometimes fun, but mostly irritating. "Please, repeat your response," said the PC.

"Close."

"Thank you," said the computer's modulated voice. "Closing folder . . . E . . . R . . . A . . . S . . . E."

19

Erased. Not terminated or resigned, but a fate far worse? No, she refused to believe they were dead. After all, two words preceded erased and terminated: *targeted for.* A sick feeling washed over her. She knew what powerful people in high places were capable of, especially if a whistleblower's information threatened their livelihood. Suddenly, the room had become hot and stuffy. She opened the door, resumed her seat, and stared at the screen, mindful not to put in for vacation while employed at LANL.

A shadow fell across the floor. Darcy swiveled in her chair. "Goodnight, Mill."

Sonny stood in the doorway, his lean body propped against the jamb, a Tumi backpack slung over his shoulder. She kept her hand on the mouse, her index finger poised to exit the program if he came any closer. "Thanks for the tour today."

He smiled. "Happy to show you around. So, are you a workaholic or a brownnoser?"

She laughed. "Neither. Started late and thought I'd put in a little OT to make a good first impression."

He shot her a quizzical look. "Don't make it a habit. You'll show up the rest of us."

"I won't. Promise." Leave, her inner voice shouted. If he stayed any longer, she'd have to log off. She checked the clock in the lower corner of the screen. One second gone, then two.

Sonny lingered. "If you like, help yourself to my CD collection."

"Thanks." Now go.

"Scan to proceed," her computer prompted.

"I better go. Don't work too late. Tomorrow's a big day."

"Oh?"

"Tomorrow, you meet Con." He touched his beret. "Later."

Again, he disappeared before she could ask, "Who or what is Con?" Didn't matter. She had more important things on her mind. Besides, she hated being baited.

She rested her fingers on the keys. The system scanned her prints into the mainframe. Although brief, Sonny's interruption had cost her, and these days time could be the enemy. Or was it her ally? It all depended on how often Big Brother spied on his drones. She counted on the fact that as a new hire with top-secret clearance, thanks to her own ingenuity, the likelihood of security tracking her whereabouts in the electronic corridors was low, at least for now. Still, it paid to have a contingency plan, especially if she wanted to dig in LANL's most restricted operating systems at any time and for as long as she wanted without risk of discovery. Three schemes came to mind.

First, she tried writing a program to hide from the intrusion detection software, but every attempt she made to circumvent identity recognition failed, so she opted for plan B.

The second strategy, to locate a workstation vacated by an employee who'd resigned or been terminated, fizzled because the minute a worker left LANL someone from IT immediately carted away the PC. A new hire either received a new computer or a purged PC reprogrammed with his or her iris and/or fingerprint scans.

Scheme three, electronically breaking into the service section at IT, required nothing short of divine intervention.

Disgusted, she pushed her chair away from the computer and glared at the monitor with disdain, which accomplished nothing. After feeling irate for a few seconds, she slid back and took a virtual tour of LANL's campus, hunting for anything with Z in the name or designation. But the computerized excursion was too streamlined to identify specific departments or outbuildings.

Regardless, she printed a locator's map of the technical areas and noted what departments scheduled a swing and/or night shift. Many employees at the lab worked flextime, coming and going at odd hours, weekdays and weekends. Not even in the dead of night would she be alone. She signed off and paced. The habit helped her concentrate.

She wanted to assume Andrew had found a hiding place, somewhere secure both day and night, but did one really exist at the lab? If so, where and how in the heck could she find his hideout with fifty tech areas to search and time a major constraint? Talk about the proverbial needle in a haystack. Cliché be damned; here the phrase definitely applied. Walt had worked in TA-3. Maybe she should start there.

She changed into running shoes and for the next hour wandered the labyrinth of passageways that comprised TA-3. It helped to have a good sense of direction, but the miles of endless white corridors made it tough to discern one from another, and all the elevators were clones.

She arrived at another unmanned security post. Biometric checkpoints at strategic locations throughout the facility eliminated the need for guards, which allowed her to move freely from one sector to the next. Funny how everyone felt more secure with technology administering security checks when in reality nothing replaced a human being. A biometric scan wouldn't be curious or suspicious of a new hire strolling the basement at this late hour dressed in business casual but wearing sneakers. However, a human might. And unlike humans, machines wouldn't question why an AL worker liked to snoop around the human genome lab or visit the cryogenics facility after work. Was it standard practice? She thought not. So in this case, electronics gave her an edge humans wouldn't.

Darcy paused in the passage. Directly above her, at ceiling height, she noticed two surveillance cameras, one aimed at her. She had the clearance to go almost anywhere, but attached to the privilege came risks, the biggest danger being memory. Every time a security plate scanned her face or read her fingerprints, or in most cases demanded voice recognition, a mainframe somewhere stored these biostatistics in a database. The key question was how often someone combed the information for violators or purged the programs.

This thought brought up another, something she'd learned her first year at the NSA. Hacking stupidity 101: never hack from home, i.e., the rental. Still, she hoped to stay well ahead of Big Brother, her former employer. Having worked for the NSA, she banked on her expertise to outsmart the feds, at least until she accomplished her goal to rescue both Johnny and Andrew.

While she stalked the halls, Darcy kept watch for fellow workers. The fewer people she met, the better. In three hours, she hid from and then tailed four men and two women in lab coats, but no one led her anywhere she thought Andrew might hide, so she left the ground levels for the basement. Perhaps she'd have better luck there.

The elevator door opened. An eerie silence hung over the lower concourse. As she stepped out, a shiver skittered along her spine. Climatically controlled. Must be fifty or so below. She sniffed the air. A hint of something caustic pricked her nostrils. The odor faded, then returned. As she snuck down the hall, the smell grew stronger. In the passage, approximately the length of a football field, she saw no place to hide or shadows to blend into. The recessed spotlights haloed the floor in soft yellow circles, then fanned out to dingy white and washed the walls in muted gray. She tiptoed forward, her eyes fixed ahead.

A wall panel broke alignment and swung outward.

Darcy squatted, startled when a woman came through the cavity into the hall. She waddled along, burdened by an armful of computer printouts and seemingly oblivious to Darcy's presence approximately twenty feet behind her.

"As soon as I dump these reports, I'm out of here." She talked into a tiny microphone strapped to the shoulder of her lab coat. "Okay. Bye."

Darcy held her breath and prayed the woman wouldn't turn around.

"Janet Murasaki," she said to a wall-mounted biometric scan, her foot tapping the floor until the door rotated out. Before the panel fully extended, Janet squeezed through the slit.

Darcy followed just as the panel was poised to close, ready with an excuse if confronted, but Janet was already halfway across the room, her head bobbing above the workstations in a large space carved into cubicles.

At the back of the floor stretched four office suites. Janet ducked into one, emerged, and entered the next until she'd visited all of them. Now with her arms empty, she stood near the far wall. Again, a panel broke alignment and Janet slipped through, seconds before the exit shut with a decisive snap, the door an integral part of the wall system.

Mindful of the time, Darcy wound a path through the cubicles to the office suites. She searched quickly and methodically, beginning with the office of Gert Alton, her name and title, Vice President of Research and Development, etched on the glass. Gert defied company policy by smoking in the building—she hid her cigarettes in her desk drawer amid a ton of mints—but Darcy found nothing pertinent to the case.

The next office belonged to Isaac Denahy, Executive Vice President of Research and Development. A collage of photographs chronicled his life: Navy Seal, Pulitzer Prize winner, father of two. But again she found nothing valuable to the investigation.

Frustrated, she hurried into the suite of Dr. Gale Clifford, who had the ambiguous title of Director. Chanel perfume hung in the air, but which one eluded Darcy. She yanked open drawers and rifled through their contents, pleased to find a current passport tucked beneath some legal papers. Darcy stuffed the document in her pocket and exited the way Janet had.

On the other side of the paneled wall, the corridor angled, sloped downward, and ended in a flight of stairs leading to a lower level. Darcy hadn't anticipated this. She looked around for an elevator but didn't see one. When she tried returning to the office suites, the wall panel wouldn't open. She had no choice but to go down.

As she meandered through the passage, the floor continued its gradual decline, and with each step the temperature seemed to drop a degree centigrade. She buttoned her jacket. The overhead lights dimmed and went out. Nightspots flared to life, the recessed cans a foot above the floor line. Their illumination cast parabolic shadows on the shiny floor. Her instinct said, "Proceed with caution."

She slowed, stopped, checked her back, and moved on. In the distance, she could barely make out an elevator. At first, Darcy thought she'd willed it to be there, but the elevator was real. She boarded. Only two buttons, both headed down. She punched the one to the bottom floor.

The elevator landed with a soft thud. She leaned out and listened, her thumb hovering over the Close button should anyone appear. Two minutes passed. No one showed up, so she made her way down the corridor until the hallway ended in a glass wall with a security plate stamped into the pane.

On guard, she marched up to the biometric scanner as if she belonged there, surprised to see no iris or retinal reader, only a fingerprint identifier. She pressed her hand to the wall imprint, and immediately the door beeped. Darcy yanked it open and darted in.

Light split the corridor. She moved toward it, putting one foot in front of the other as though testing her foothold, ready to flee if need be. Voices, audible but faint, filtered through the area. She peered around the corner and quickly pulled back into the shadows to spy on the guard at the manned station. He sat up as the double doors across from his security post swung wide and two men wheeling a gurney shuffled into the hallway. They nodded to the guard and proceeded through the lit passage. The guard fiddled with his wristwatch and sighed. He reached into a drawer and pulled out a bag of cookies. Darcy's stomach growled.

At exactly ten o'clock, the guard unclipped a metal ring from his belt and inserted a key into a wall slot mounted next to the double doors. A red header bar pulsed to life. He sauntered back to his post and stretched out.

Darcy debated her next move. She couldn't stay here all night and for nothing.

"Spence!" an angry voice yelled.

The guard bolted to his feet. "Yes, sir."

"How many times must I ask? Get someone to mop up. Now."

"Sorry, sir. I rang, but no one came."

"Ring again."

A door banged.

Spence picked up the telephone and dialed. "No, now. He's pitching a fit, and I'm tired of listening to the bastard." He slammed down the receiver, ambled to the double doors, and switched off the flashing red bar. Somewhere an elevator droned. As the sound grew louder, the guard barged through the double doors and disappeared from sight.

Darcy raced past the security station, sprinted around the corner, and crept down the hall. A gurney with a sheet draped over the top blocked her way. She crouched beside it and surveyed her surroundings. The faint but familiar odor of blood wafted from the linen. Her heart beat wildly as she separated the folds in the sheet. A large red stain had discolored the bottom half of the bed linen and soaked into the thin mattress below. She tugged a Kleenex from her pocket and blotted the circle with the tissue.

"Here," someone called out.

"What about the gurney?" another person called back.

Darcy rocked gently back and forth, ready to run. But where?

Keys jingled. "Later. Clean up this mess first. Spence, be sure to lock up."

"Yes, sir."

A door closed. A latch clanged. Silence followed.

Darcy peeked around the corner. The guard station was unattended. For a moment, she considered leaving through the double doors, but the pulsing red bar killed that idea, so she walked quickly in the direction from which she'd come, not sure how to reach the upper levels. Ahead, she spotted an elevator. She ran toward it, her brain working as rapidly as her feet, which skipped over the tiled surface. Whose blood was on the sheet?

She zipped past a lab, stopped in mid-stride, and stepped backward to read the word on the closed door: SQUID. Why would LANL research cephalopods? The minute the thought registered, she dismissed it. Dummy. SQUID was an acronym. It stood for superconducting quantum interference device, a magnetometer used by neuroscientists to measure extremely subtle changes in the human body's electromagnetic energy field. LANL was studying brainwaves, but why? Speculation fueled her curiosity. The most plausible answer: brain mapping.

20

The alarm clock tucked under her travel pillow chimed. Darcy sat up, stiff from sleeping on her office floor. The first thing she noticed was the blinking light on her telephone console, the ringer shut off to keep the phone from waking her before dawn. She tapped the message button. Sonny's voice filled the room. "Don't forget—today you meet Con."

"Better be good after all this hype." She walked away, then spun back toward the desk. Darn, how did she overlook such an important clue? She logged onto the lab's intranet and in seconds broke into their telephone records. Only one call had been placed from LANL to the Taos rental over the past few days. The call came from 5052397483. Two, three, nine. Odd, since the rest of the outgoing numbers, over two thousand on that particular day, all had prefixes of 656 to 678.

She checked the time—5:00 a.m. According to coworkers,

Sonny always arrived early, so Darcy headed for the rental car to retrieve clean clothes from the trunk, then stopped at the women's restroom to shower and dress in business casual. She made it back to her office seconds before Sonny exited the elevators.

He waved. "Hey, mornin'. If I didn't know better, I'd think you spent the night here."

Darcy laughed. "Yeah, right. Do you own a cell phone?"

"Sure, but not on me. You know we can't bring them into LANL."

"I'm asking because there's a number on my bill I can't identify. The prefix is two, three, nine."

A spark of recognition flashed in his eyes. Her hopes rose, but his comment contradicted his expression. "Doesn't sound familiar."

He's lying, but why?

Sonny instantly changed the subject. "Did you get my message about Con?"

"Forget Con and answer my question," she wanted to say, but something in his demeanor told her not to push the issue. "I did."

"Then let's go." He practically ran out of her office.

She caught up to him at the stairwell door. "We're taking the stairs?"

"Yes." Something about his demeanor put her on guard. His actions and speech, although jovial, sounded forced; yesterday they'd come naturally.

At the bottom of the stairs, he abruptly veered to the right and kept going without engaging her in conversation—also out of character.

"Next right." He passed through an automatic door, Darcy on his heels.

In a section of the AL basement new to her, Sonny cleared the automated security system, then waited for her to do the same.

"You first." He ushered her into a room.

The soft, protracted hiss of hermetic pistons whispered through the black interior, followed by a low sucking sound as the heavy metal door sealed airtight. Surrounded by darkness, Darcy recalled an incident from years ago, the event as vivid today as the experience had been then. The bullies had beaten her up for a buck in change, shoved her in the ice cream parlor's deep freeze, and locked the door. Assholes. The so-called practical joke left an indelible impression on the meek fifteen-year-old, but no one ever bullied her again, at least not physically.

Sonny grabbed her arm.

She flinched, aware of his presence but unprepared for his touch.

"Wait for the lights."

Overhead, bulbs flickered to life, their amber glow warm yet insufficient to chase the chilly bite that engulfed her. She crossed her arms and rubbed her shoulders.

"Climatically controlled," he said. "The same day those lucky bastards in nuclear fusion got new digs, A-Life moved to the bowels of the basement. I took it as a demotion. Would you agree?"

She grunted. "What's the temperature in here?"

"Thirty-nine. Want my jacket?"

"No, I'm okay. Why so cold?"

"Research labs. I can't tell you anything more because you don't have the proper security clearance. Yet."

Yet? The word piqued her curiosity.

Darcy tagged along behind Sonny as he moved from one passage and into another, all of them cold and sterile and the air tainted with antiseptic smells. No different from a hospital. Bad memories of her parents' charred bodies and the stench of singed hair flooded back to her. But thoughts of them flitted away when she entered a sparsely furnished conference room, the area barely large enough to hold six chairs and an oak table, the top scarred and stained. Brown and beige abounded. On the wall hung a solitary black-and-white John McCarthy quote framed in red metal: "To succeed, artificial intelligence needs 1.7 Einsteins, two Maxwells, five Faradays, and .3 Manhattan Projects."

At one end of the table sat a coffeepot, the red light aglow, and a tray with cups, stirrers, cream, and sugar. Sonny gravitated toward it. "How can our government squander tax dollars on senseless programs but can't buy decent coffee machines? Or coffee. Want a cup?"

"Thanks. Black."

"Gert asked to see you before we meet Con."

Darcy's guard went up. Not once had Sonny mentioned that little detail on the long hike from upstairs to the subterranean level. An oversight or intentional? If intentional, why? Deviating from the original plan sparked suspicion and concern. Were they on to her?

"Just protocol," said Sonny. "You need the right clearance."

"For what?"

"To meet Con." He held up his hand. "No questions. You don't have the right clearance."

All this BS. Darcy hated it. She checked the time. This was what she disliked about undercover work—playing games. Instead of sitting here, she should be searching for Johnny, Andrew, and the missing flash drive.

A thin man entered the room with the energy of a whirlwind. Tall, nerdy, his bifocals sitting low on a bulbous nose, he leveled black eyes at Darcy as though he'd never seen a woman. "Who are you?"

His bluntness amused her. "Dee Miller." She extended her hand.

He ignored the offer. "Oh, the new hire."

"And you are?"

"Galvin Perry, the chief cybernetic scientist on the team." He thrust out his chest, a broad smile plastered on his gaunt, ashen face. "I invented Con."

"Great. Then tell me: Who or what is Con?"

"You'll find out soon enough. Sonny, Gert's running late." Perry dropped his attaché case on the floor and walked over to the coffeepot. "God-awful stuff, this company coffee. Taste's worse than charred mud, but better than nothing."

He carried his cup to the table and opened his laptop. The screen saver was Perry clad in red shorts and a floral shirt with a fruit drink in his hand, a little umbrella hanging off the rim. She sensed an egotist. And he's in charge of LANL's premier AL program? She toyed with the idea of Perry as Walt's killer. He had the right attitude—nasty.

Footsteps sounded in the hall.

Sonny sat up.

A woman barged through the doorway—tall, big boned, and with dark hair so short it bordered on a crew cut. Her keen brown eyes surveyed the gathering. "Good, you're all here. You must be Dee Miller. I'm Gert Alton."

Darcy shook the VP's hand, the woman's grip a bone-cruncher. She sized up Gert. Strong and large, she could have grabbed the short, stocky Walt from behind, slid a knife under his double chin, and slit his throat from ear to ear. She looked as if she had to the strength to do so.

"Since Walt and Norm are on vacation, I'm filling in." Gert plopped her healthy frame into an overstuffed chair. "Dee, on the way down, you probably saw Sonny use a blue Eyedentacard rather than the green one issued by HR."

Wary, she said, "Yes."

"On the blue IDs, in place of your picture, there's a wafer-thin computer chip. It stores your biometrics. This new badge, along with a password, will get you into the lower levels."

Darcy feigned puzzlement. "I thought I already had access to the lower levels."

"Not this low." Gert handed the new ID and a piece of paper to Sonny, who passed both to Darcy.

Gert didn't explain why Darcy needed access to the lowest levels or what was down there, and she didn't ask. She set the blue Eyedentacard on the table and stared at the six-digit code written on the slip of paper.

"Memorize your password before you leave this room, then destroy the sheet." Every word Gert spoke sounded like an order. "On the way back up, Sonny will show you when to use the card."

"Is the clearance for all labs?" asked Sonny.

Intrigued, Darcy perked up.

Gert's head bobbed. "Yes. She has identical clearance. Now, pass your green badge to me."

The second the old badge landed in Gert's hand, she fed the ID into a handheld shredder. The machine whined but didn't spit out the plastic confetti. "It's official. Welcome to the A-Life team, Dee. This will probably be boring for you, but bear with us. I need a status report from Sonny."

Darcy half listened, her thoughts on the lowest levels. Maybe Andrew was hiding there.

"Monday, I called the Santa Fe Institute," said Sonny as he scanned his notes. "They said the neuromolecular computer project has entered stage four."

Gert slapped the table. "Terrific news! Imagine the impact."

Darcy straightened up in her seat. The impact may have been lost on her, but not the mention of the institute. She leaned sideways to read over Sonny's shoulder. Her eyes locked on the acronym SFI/AIL printed in red on his notepad.

"Do you really believe them?" said Perry. "I mean, stage four? Those a-holes are bluffing. I wouldn't give their update an ounce of credence. No wonder there's war between the Santa Fe Institute and us." Perry's words detonated a heated discussion.

"Enough." Gert put an end to the verbal sparring, and the status report proceeded in a more civilized tone.

Darcy's stomach growled and flipped. With nothing to eat since lunch yesterday, anything looked good to her, even the mints she clawed out of her pocket. She tossed three into her mouth. She felt eyes upon her and looked sideways at Perry. Those black globes drilled holes in her. What was his problem? He stared at her as if she'd interrupted his life. She ignored him and pretended to jot down notes.

Perry wandered to the end of the table to refill his mug. Gert scowled, obviously displeased with the distraction. On his way back, he bent forward to pick something off the floor, or so Darcy thought. Instead, he tucked a note between her thigh and the chair, fingernails raking her pants in the process. She recoiled, glad she hadn't worn a dress. For a second, she debated retrieving the note or leaving it concealed under her leg until the meeting ended.

A harsh cough came from Perry. She gazed at him. He flexed his hands and cracked his knuckles but kept his eyes on her. Sonny and Gert, busy analyzing a chart, seemed oblivious to the exchange, so Darcy read the note: "Johnny, Andy, Walt, Norm. Don't make the fifth . . . Darcy."

A chill ripped through her, triggering a charge of sensations. The feelings tumbled over one another, coming at an uncontrollable speed: excitement, apprehension, curiosity, and anger. To her, Perry's warning said, "You're on the right track." It also told her the four were probably dead, if she trusted the note's author. But what stunned her the most? He knew her real name. How? Would he blow her cover? Was he the killer?

Darcy slid the note into her pocket and suppressed the overwhelming urge to confront him. The warning certainly ratcheted up her heartbeat, but the telltale sign of worry surfaced on her hands. She wiped them on her pants, soaking up the perspiration that beaded on her palms.

"Meeting adjourned," said Gert. "Dee, have you memorized your password? If yes . . ." Gert held out her hand.

Darcy had, so she handed over the sheet of paper.

"Dee, any questions before we break up?"

It took a second for Darcy to drag her brain from memorization of the password to the VP's question. "Pardon my ignorance, Ms. Alton."

"Call me Gert."

"I must've missed something during the update. Exactly what are my job responsibilities? I applied for a position in CIC, but find myself assigned to AL."

"Because," said Gert as she crammed a manila folder into her briefcase, "we need your computer expertise more than CIC does. As for duties, Galvin will brief you."

Darcy held up her finger. "Two questions, if I may."

An exasperated expression crossed Gert's face. "Yes?"

"What is the AL project, and does it have a name?"

Gert folded her hands. "Of course. Let me give you a quick overview. We're an elite team of scientists recruited from various think tanks around the nation. We've assembled at LANL because the lab offers an environment critical to achieving our goals."

Nothing the VP had just said answered either question. "But what are the team's goals?"

"As I said, Galvin will brief you on the charter of the bionics team as soon as we're done. As for the name, we coined our project Brainwash."

21

*B*rainwash!

An electrical charge skittered along Darcy's spine. The message on Johnny's computer screen read "Andrew's next," signed by Brainwash. Her mind raced at warp speed. Could Perry also be responsible for Johnny's and Andrew's disappearance? She sat motionless as Gert, Perry, and Sonny filed from the conference room. Could one of them have written the message?

"Well, are you coming, or do you intend to sit there all day?" said Perry from the hallway.

Darcy packed up, then crowded into the service elevator with Sonny and Perry.

"Your passkey." Perry held out his hand. "I'll show you how to use it." He inserted her blue Eyedentacard into the digital numeric pad. "Now, punch in your access code." The two turned their backs. "Lot of people around here laugh about guarding their passwords," said Perry, "but keeping your code secret is imperative."

The scanner sucked in Darcy's badge, computed her biometrics, then spit out her ID. She clipped the badge to her lapel as required by company policy.

The elevator doors closed with a decided thunk, and Sonny pressed the button for the basement. The steel box vibrated as it descended, landing minutes later with a jolt. The doors creaked open.

Perry exited in a hurry, as though late for an appointment. Darcy studied her surroundings. She stood in the same corridor as she had the night before when she stole past the SQUID lab. The hallway angled, and the glass enclosure came into view. Bright fluorescent lights illuminated the way, their dazzling glow reflected in the stainless steel walls. The sharp bite of cleanser choked the air. She sneezed.

Puzzled by how she'd gained access to this level with her green ID, she said, "So only blues are allowed this low?"

"No. Green will get you here, but no lower." Perry stopped at another scanner, set his briefcase on the concrete floor, and slapped both hands on the biometric plate. After the disc read his bios, he moved aside. Sonny repeated the procedure. Next, Darcy. The entrance glided into the wall casement, and Perry headed forward.

"Speed it up," he ordered.

Sonny mouthed the word "Asshole."

"Is he always this rude?" she asked in a low voice.

"Yes," said Sonny, "perpetually in a state of nastiness."

Perry waved them on. "Hurry. We've a lot to cover."

Two checkpoints beyond the SQUID lab, Perry said, "We're

about to enter one of our highest security areas—off-limits to all but those with blue badges." He sauntered up to a manned guard post and patted the ID badge clipped to his collar. He signed in and passed the log to Sonny.

The guard's hand dove under the desk. "They're waiting."

"Thanks." Perry motioned to Darcy to sign in.

She scribbled her name, illegible on purpose. "Don't you ever get lost around here?" She tried to sound casual, but inside her tension built. Her heart fluttered, then settled.

"Not anymore. Built-in GPS." Sonny tapped his temple with his finger.

"I wonder about you."

He smiled. "You should. Everyone on the Hill is nuts. Otherwise, why work here?"

Perry paused outside a metal door with the letters RDNA stenciled on it. After the bioplate confirmed his identity, the partition slid open. Beyond stretched a wall of office suites. Perry entered one. He set his laptop on the desk and dropped his briefcase on the floor. Darcy poked her head into the room. Awards and degrees, all framed and matted in black, cluttered the area behind his desk. No wonder Perry sported an ego the size of Texas; he had the credentials to back his accomplishments. Still, arrogance was an ugly trait.

"Come on," said Perry as he barged past Sonny. "I assume you're familiar with clean room procedure, Dee?"

She ignored the sarcasm. "I am."

Perry marched through an archway and pointed to a door marked WOMEN'S LOCKERS. "In there. The instructions are on the wall. And make damn sure you don't forget to strap on your antistatic wristbands, or the wrath of Id will befall you." He disappeared into the men's lockers.

"Who?"

"Id," said Sonny. "Isaac Denahy, God of A-Life and top dog."

"Higher than Gert?" she asked as a matter of conversation, since she already knew Id's title.

"Much higher. Gotta go. I shouldn't keep Perry waiting."

Darcy snickered. She pushed through the doors, located an empty locker, and hung up her jacket. Gowned in scrubs, her head covered, and padded booties over her stocking feet, she stuffed a pair of latex gloves into her pocket and took a surgical mask from the stack in a nearby bin.

She didn't even glance at the instruction plaque mounted on the wall until it came to strapping on the antistatic wrist-bands. With them in place, she adjusted the Velcro straps, then looped the grounding wire through tabs sewn into her pants. What a process. She snapped on gloves and used her elbow to punch the metal button that protruded from the wall. The doors fanned wide open.

In the adjoining room Sonny and Perry loitered, engaged in conversation with an imposing man decked out in all black. Sonny mouthed the word "Id" to Darcy, who listened with curiosity and admiration as the AL luminary spouted scientific jargon. The technical terms made no sense to her, but they must've to Perry, who responded in like fashion to the founding father of artificial intelligence.

Without facing her, Isaac said, "Join us, Dee."

Big and strong. Maybe he'd killed Walt?

"Spin." Isaac drew a circle in the air with his finger.

Darcy spun like a top.

"Gowned, gloved, and with wristbands. Good. Let's go."

The men led the way.

Before them stretched a glass causeway. Behind the transparent walls, lab techs bustled back and forth. Darcy couldn't tell men from women with everyone cloaked in white and their faces concealed by surgical masks.

"Clean rooms," said Perry in a caustic tone.

"Cleaner than any OR in the nation," Sonny said. "I'd rather be operated on in there than in a hospital. Chances of catching an infection are nil." He made a zero with his fingers.

Darcy stared through the glass. "What are they working on?"

"Robotic software," said Isaac.

She studied the workers cloistered inside. Since when did software production require test tubes? A gowned worker shifted his gaze from a centrifuge to Darcy. His eyes smiled, but his expression evaporated so fast, she wondered if she'd imagined it. A hand closed on her shoulder.

"Come on." Perry ushered Darcy into an adjacent lab with padded walls. The door snapped shut, the noise remarkably close to the clang of a freezer door.

Isaac nodded, the gesture stiff and rehearsed. "If you'll excuse us, we have a matter to attend to. Be back in a few minutes."

Left alone, Darcy toured the lab. There wasn't much to see—workbenches and stools in an otherwise bare room. She inspected the cushioned walls; a blue, nubby fabric stretched taut over spongy foam.

A soft hiss.

Instinctively, she reached for her 9 millimeter, the habit ingrained, but her fingers closed on flesh, not steel. Only once had she defied bureau regulations and not carried a firearm. The mistake had almost cost Darcy her life.

She saw nothing to concern her, so she went back to examining the wall. Her fingers probed the weave, searching for the slightest change in texture, anything indicative of a hidden camera or a two-way mirror.

Another hiss followed by a low vibration, then silence.

Darcy sensed a change in the atmosphere and sniffed the dry air.

"Dehumidifiers," said a deep voice.

She jumped and whirled.

A man stood near the entrance to the lab, his legs apart, arms at his side, black hair plastered to his head, and his dark eyes unblinking. He wore a gray jumpsuit and gray combat boots.

"The hisses are dehumidifiers. They suck every ounce of moisture from the air."

Something about the way he pronounced the word "suck" sent a chill through her.

"Yes, cold in here," he said.

He must've seen her shiver.

"I forget my manners. Glad to meet you. Everyone needs a friend."

She thought the statement odd, his familiarity premature, but she said, "True. My name's—"

"Dee Miller."

She recovered from the surprise and asked, "And you are?" But she'd already made the connection.

He walked toward her, his stride stiff and deliberate. He stuck out a gloved hand. She grasped it, the material soft as chamois and the palm beneath as pliable as real flesh. She expected metal, so this amazed her. "Am I right to assume . . ."

"You are. I'm Perry's brainchild . . . Con."

22

Darcy stared in wonderment at Perry's creation. Bionics had come a long way since the industrial automatons she knew as robots. Sleek, tall, lifelike—Con reminded her a lot of Isaac Denahy, only with hair. "Pardon my crassness, but do you mind if I take a closer look?" What a dumb question. He was a machine. However, something about him commanded respect.

"What do you mean by a closer look?"

"Can I touch you?" For a second, Darcy swore she saw his pupils constrict, then dilate. She discounted the possibility as ludicrous.

"Yes, but I warn you, I am not like most robots."

She clasped her hands together, delighted and fascinated by Perry's creation. "I can see that. Walk over there, if you will."

He moved with a soft swishing sound. Then why hadn't she heard him enter the room? "Come back," she said.

He stopped a few feet from her. "You may examine me now."

She chuckled, amused by his formal, refined speech. She detected a slight British inflection like Isaac's.

"I am more like Id than Dr. Perry."

His statement surprised her. Be serious. He couldn't read her mind. He was a machine. Some systems analyst programmed him.

She circled Con, touched his arms, and let her fingers roam his broad shoulders. He felt real, his muscles firm, bone hard, and tissues soft. She studied his face; his eyes were unblinking, focused straight ahead. She'd never seen an android like him.

"I am not an android, Dee. I am a humanoid."

She jerked her hand away and stepped backward.

He laughed, a strange, mechanical chuckle. "Don't be alarmed. We both know I can't read thoughts. I have been programmed to respond."

"Of course you're programmed. What a fool I am." Why name him Con when Perry was such an egotist? Why not name his invention after himself?

"Because Con is short for contrary."

Now this was too much of a coincidence. Darcy's guard went up.

"Everyone wants to know, so I knew you would ask."

Made sense—sequential programming, just like a flow chart.

Con smiled, an odd, twisted expression that made her even more suspicious. How could a robot smile?

"You may return to examine me."

He didn't have to coax her. Awestruck, she touched his cheek, the skin warm. The sensation puzzled yet intrigued her. Some form of new material? She noticed moisture on his lips and traced a finger over them. Wet? How could this be? But his flesh felt like the genuine article. Her gaze traveled to a hairline scar at the base of his neck. A skin graft? Not likely.

On tiptoe, she ran her fingertips over his prominent cheek-bones, then over his strong, angular jaw to the scar. When she reached his collarbones, his body warmth dipped to a chill as nippy as the air in the room. Baffled, she walked her fingers up and down his face and neck, confirming the temperature change but not believing it.

She touched his cheek and said, "Con, why are you warm here"—she then placed her palm on his chest—"but cold here?"

"It's your hands, Dee."

Yeah, right. Darcy locked eyes with him.

"Are you done inspecting me?"

The stare he gave made her blush. Embarrassed, she withdrew her hand, all the while reminding herself he was only a machine. "You really didn't answer my question."

"You didn't answer mine. Are you done inspecting me?"

"Yes." She backed up.

He touched his neck, drawing attention to a black wire that protruded from his collarless jumpsuit.

"No. Wait," she said.

"Yes or no?"

"No," she answered, her eyes trained on the wire. The find enticed her to investigate. She slid his jumpsuit zipper down a few inches and gaped in astonishment at the mass of black curls covering his muscular chest. Half-warm, half-cold, wet lips, hairy chest—nothing like any robot she'd ever seen or felt.

"I think of myself as a creation, Dee. Not an invention. Machines are inventions."

Stunned, Darcy clapped a hand over her mouth and retreated, her eyes glued to Con's face, waiting for a reaction, but he gave none other than to say, "Are you done?"

"No." She fumbled with the zipper on his suit, prepared to close it, when she noticed a tattoo on his stomach; the discovery too intriguing to pass up. She bent forward, her nose inches from his body. He smelled of baby powder and plastic. Her eyes locked on the two lines etched below a perfect navel. "Con, property of SFI/AIL and LANL," she whispered.

Just as softly, he said, "Please, go no further, Dee."

She slowly raised her head and made eye contact.

He looked back. "I am equipped with biosensors. You might trigger a reaction you are incapable of countering. Do you understand?"

She laughed. "Been there a few times myself." Curiosity consumed her, but propriety won; she zipped him up.

"Really, Miller. Whatever happened to common decency?" Perry charged into the room.

Mortified, Darcy forced a smile. Behind him trailed Isaac and Sonny.

"A clinical appraisal, nothing more. He's so lifelike," she added.

"I'm pretty lifelike myself," said Perry, "but you didn't undress me when we met."

She glowered at him.

"Because you, Perry," Isaac said, "aren't as handsome or as well built as our man Con. Right, Dee?"

Perry shrugged off the comment, as did Darcy. "Why'd you name him Con?" she asked.

"Because"—Perry studied his nails—"contrary to the bets everyone placed, I succeeded. And you, Ms. Miller, just had the privilege of exploring my finest creation."

Egomaniac. "Who programmed him and chose his voice?"

Perry bowed to Isaac. "There, Id contributed."

"His voice surprised me. I expected a modulated tone like most bionic inventions."

Perry scoffed. "No way. We've always envisioned Con as a replica of ourselves. Right, Isaac?"

"True. Aren't all creators the same?"

"Why the resemblance to Id rather than you, Perry?"

"I'm better looking," Isaac answered.

Perry frowned in disapproval. "Fun's over. Room 4. We'll meet you there, Dee."

Con, escorted by Isaac and Perry, departed through one exit, and Sonny and Darcy the other.

"A setup, right?" Darcy asked.

Sonny acted disgusted. "Grown men acting like kids. They enjoyed a vicarious thrill at your expense. I wanted to warn you, but Perry has a vindictive streak. Cross him, and you're dead politically."

Vindictive streak? She pictured Perry with a skinny arm clutched around Walt's pudgy neck and a knife in the other hand. Nah. The man has trouble lifting his laptop, never mind slitting someone's throat.

Sonny meandered on in silence, Darcy beside him, thankful for a quiet moment to speculate on the potential link between the stolen flash drive and Con, both the property of SFI/AIL. But what was so important that Johnny risked his life to download it? Could Con be involved? If so, had someone programmed the humanoid to kill?

Her thoughts drifted from the missing drive to the evidence she and Ed had discovered in the arroyo. Surely, he had those results by now. She'd phone at noon.

"Hey, Mill. Lab 4's up ahead." Sonny motioned for her to hurry up.

"Tell me this isn't another meeting. Doesn't anyone work around here?"

"Quit complaining. You had your hands-on session." The old Sonny had returned. She punched him in the arm.

Perry and Isaac entered the room and took seats at a long workbench. The update dragged into an algorithmic hour mired in the mathematically oriented science of control feedback therapy. If she asked a question, the three neatly sidestepped her inquiry. Dying to leave, she woke up when Perry said, "Now, for Dee's assignment. We need you to program Alt for extremely low-level intelligent behavior."

Her shoulders fell. Boring. "Does each behavior have its own control program?"

"Yes," Isaac answered for Perry.

"Is Alt equipped with sensors?"

"Spring-based sensors," said Sonny, completing a computation on his pocket calculator.

"Which means Alt can feel a collision, which should trigger a behavioral response?"

"Correct. Very good." Perry's ruddy face lit up like a Christmas bulb.

Her question obviously pleased him. "Should I do only the basics, such as lift front leg, walk forward?"

Perry nodded. She jotted notes and feigned interest, until he concluded with, "The meeting's over."

Relieved, Darcy started collecting her belongings. Isaac and Perry remained seated, two neuroscience powerhouses swapping test results on cell studies they'd done using the conductive material, indium tin oxide (ITO).

Disinterested, she rushed into the corridor and made a beeline for the restrooms. Just outside the door, she froze in mid-step. Her thoughts tripped over each other, the puzzle still a jumble of pieces, but quickly falling into place. SQUID lab. Brain mapping. Biosensors. ITO. Sounded as though the bionics team was developing a semiartificial neural network with the capacity and interconnectedness of a human brain? A brain fashioned from biochips, chips forged from living cells . . . Con. The assumption jolted her.

"Hey, earth to Dee," said Sonny. "Where are you today?"

She wanted desperately to be alone, to have some peace to

think through the questions swirling in her brain. The buzz in her head blurred Sonny's words. "What did you say?"

"Nothing. Come on. Bet you're eager to write those programs for Perry." Sonny punched the call button for the elevator. On the ride up, he kept Gert's order to acquaint Darcy with the new Eyedentacard. Not once, but three times, he walked her through the security procedure on the jaunt from the basement to the upper-level office suites. "Last one to the top."

"About time. Wonder if I'll ever get use to all this security."

"It becomes second nature. Any plans for lunch?"

"Meeting an old friend."

He acted dejected.

"Will you take a rain check?"

He brightened. "You're on. Later." Sonny wandered toward his office.

In the lobby, Darcy signed out and drove to the neighboring suburb of White Rock. Snow powdered the highway. She cruised up Longview, parked in the deserted lot behind Maxine's restaurant, the establishment closed until 5:00 p.m., and waited.

Certain she hadn't been tailed, Darcy locked the rental car and walked briskly across the main road to Fred's, open twenty-four hours. A crowd hovered inside the entrance. Hungry customers studied menus and talked about the lunch specials scribbled on the blackboard. Familiar with the layout, thanks to a virtual tour, she headed straight for the restrooms diagonal to the entry and dropped several quarters into the pay phone, probably one of the last ones in existence.

"Hello." Ed answered his cell on the first ring.

"Hi."

"Hey, hi. Didn't recognize the number."

"Pay phone. Conserving my cell phone battery."

"I'm glad you called." He sounded excited. "You had us

worried the other night when you didn't come back. Rio stayed up until one. Everything okay up there?"

"Moving slower than I'd like."

"Any sign of Andrew?" he asked in a low voice.

"No, which isn't good. Where's Rio? I expected her to answer the phone."

"Resting. She feels good one minute, punk the next. She's happy one hour and crying the next. Spends a lot of time in the bathroom."

"Did you get the Testco results?" She wanted to discuss business and return to the lab before the forecasted snowstorm hit.

"Got them right here." Papers rustled. "We can't nail down the exact date, but the evidence confirmed Johnny was in the arroyo. Let's start with the shoe print and the partial lifted from the area. By the way, the partial matched the complete print. They're Johnny's."

She opened a small pad. "How do you know?"

"I showed the photos to Rio. I can't believe she had a pair of Johnny's Reeboks in her suitcase. Bought them as a gift, a present she never gave. The style's a favorite of his. The new treads matched our impressions, and they're the right size too."

She felt sad for Rio. "Is she okay?"

"We had a long talk. She cried, and I consoled her. I think she realizes he's gone."

"Whoa. We aren't sure yet."

"The blood I scraped off the rock—AB negative. Same blood type as Johnny's, according to Rio."

"Is she sure? I don't even know Charlene's, and she's my sister."

"He gave blood on a regular basis, at Holy Cross in town. And AB negative matched the dark stain on the wool cap."

"I remember." Bad news, but not conclusive. "Does Rio know all this?"

"About the shoe prints, yes. But the blood work, no. I told her I needed Johnny's blood type for my logs."

"Good. Go on."

"The lab also found traces of AB negative in the soil we collected."

She closed her eyes and pictured the crime scene. "From what area?"

"Near the sagebrush where Bullet found the hat. Art, a forensics guy at Testco, said the hair fibers taken from the cap were direct matches to the two we collected in the soil. Both samples had the follicles intact, so both were ripped out."

She swallowed hard. "Johnny's?"

"Yes, Johnny's."

Her spirit deflated, she asked, "And what about the syringe?"

"Not much news there. A custom design, but no one knows what the hypodermic is for. They did find one fingerprint."

Her spirits lifted.

"Unfortunately, badly smudged and useless. Wish I had better news."

She inhaled deeply and blew out a lungful. "What about the swatch of blue?"

"Gore-Tex, which adds up since we already know the feathers snagged on the sagebrush were goose down."

"And the parka—what make?"

"L.L.Bean, a recent purchase according to Rio."

Darcy rubbed her aching temples, the prelude to a bad headache. After weeks of denial, now she had to face facts. "He may still be alive." Her comment lacked conviction. "What about the footprint you lifted for Dan? The one near the driveway?"

"Hold on. The report came a few minutes ago."

She listened to silence, an emptiness grinding in her stomach.

Ed came back on. "The tread's unique. Got a pen? You might make a note of the pattern."

She titled the page Green Foot. "Go ahead."

"Two large XXs, four small x's in the center, then two large XXs."

"Interesting. What about the Ruger?"

"On the gun, nothing, but the blood trail he left is o positive."

She remembered the bloodstained tissue locked in her desk. With all the lab facilities at LANL, she had decided to test it herself rather than mail it to Testco.

At the other end of the line, Ed cleared his throat. "Excuse me. I think I caught a cold. Now, about the soil samples from the Duran property . . . a home once sat on the site. And I visited the county files, and no warranty deed's recorded."

"Doesn't surprise me. Any other messages?"

"Matt called. Something about a new court date." He rattled off a telephone number. "No other calls."

"Thanks. Gotta run."

"No, wait. Remember the silver wire snagged with brown hair, the evidence you found in the drain trap at Enzo's house? The brown hair belongs to Johnny. The silver wire is steel wool, with traces of cleanser on both."

The news wasn't worth holding the line for. "That's not much help. Anything else?"

"What's your blood type?"

"AB positive. Why?"

"I found a metal strip embedded in the shag carpet that came from the trash heap in the arroyo. AB positive is on it."

"Probably mine. Scratched my hand gathering feathers. Anything else?"

"We're done for now. Be careful."

Worried about the approaching weather, Darcy ordered food to go and hurried to the rental car.

In the blowing snow, she gassed up on the outskirts of town, topping off the tank, then inched cautiously toward Los

Alamos, the road treacherous and encased in black ice. Preoccupied with the investigation, she ignored the distant drone of an engine until it grew to a loud rumble. She glanced in her rearview mirror, but white enveloped the car, the falling snow so thick it obliterated the mountains and mesas. In front of her, the skies began to clear. Behind her, the vibration built to a thunderous din.

Out of the haze shot an army Black Hawk. The aircraft swooped low, engine roaring as it flew overhead. The pilot looped in a wide arc, hovered for a few seconds, and bore down on her, the helicopter's black body rocking gently from side to side as it rode the current.

A flash of yellow distracted her.

A white pickup with pulsing amber lights and "Wide Load" across the top of the cab zoomed past Darcy. The driver signaled as he pulled into the slow lane ahead of her. After the white truck, a Jeep broke from the gloom, its headlights reflected in her side mirrors. The vehicle blew by, far exceeding the seventy-mile-per-hour speed limit, and veered in front of Darcy. No license plate, only a shiny red, white, and blue vector decal in his hatch window. The Jeep braked and fell behind the white pickup. Darcy reduced her speed, hanging back.

In minutes, a large silver mass emerged from the fog. A tractor-trailer lumbered up the incline, nosed by on her left, and signaled to move into the slow lane. She eased off the pedal and hit her high beams, telling the big rig driver to move over. He too had the same shiny NASA vector decal posted on the cargo door of his semi. Escorted by the white pickup and the Jeep, the tractor-trailer trudged up the hill toward Los Alamos.

The smell of gasoline permeated the rental. Darcy dismissed the odor, her eyes fixed on the fleet of government vehicles as they exited the highway. The stench inside the car intensified, made worse by hot air spewing from the heater vents. Still, she ignored it. Curious as to where the convoy was going, she sped up to keep the Jeep in sight. The driver climbed the grade to S-site, the tech area closed after the detonation of the first nuclear device. He rounded the curve in the road, disappearing from view.

Darcy accelerated. She wheeled around the corner, intent on catching up, yet worried about the road conditions. The rental sputtered and bucked. The smell pervaded the interior. Her gaze darted to the fuel gauge, the needle stuck on empty. The car coasted down the slight decline, rolled over a dip in the road, and died.

23

"Crap." Darcy whomped the dashboard with her fist. No gas? No way. She'd just refueled and reset the odometer. The gauge read fourteen miles. She flipped open her cell phone cover.

"Barber," Sonny answered on the first ring.

"It's Mill. I'm in White Rock with car trouble."

Keys jingled at Sonny's end of the line. "Where in White Rock? I'll come get you."

"No, that's okay. I broke down near a gas station and had the car towed. The mechanic's working on the problem now. If anyone asks, I'll be in the office as soon as it's fixed."

"You sure? I mean, I can zip over and bring you back when the work's done."

"Thanks, but the mechanic said it was minor. Shouldn't take long. Besides, why go out in this weather if you don't have to?"

"Good point. Nasty out there. Be careful." Sonny hung up.

A loud rumble shattered the stillness.

Darcy peered through the windshield into a milky gray sky. Barely visible in the thick cloud cover, a Black Hawk hovered. The helicopter whirled overhead, rotor blades slicing the soupy heavens. She expected the pilot to conduct a flyover, but he proceeded on, vanishing into a thick ceiling of clouds.

She flung open the car door, yanked her laundry bag from the trunk, and hauled it into the backseat. Changing in tight quarters took the skill of an acrobat, but the thought of dressing outdoors held no appeal. She wouldn't get far in this weather in her current attire, not to mention she'd ruin an expensive pair of shoes, so she stripped off her good clothes and layered on everything in her bag, including three pairs of socks, which made it hard to cram her feet into her hiking boots. She stuffed her cell phone in her Kelty and abandoned the rental.

Soft flakes specked her sweater and dotted her pants. In seconds, the snow beaded into tiny drops. The wind kicked up. Darcy shouldered her backpack and ran to the timberline. Deep in a stand of ponderosas, she located a trail that paralleled the dirt road and trekked down it toward who knew where or what. The stench of diesel clung to the frosty air, the only evidence the convoy had passed this way.

Approximately a mile in, the muddy easement converted to shiny pavement, the three-lane blacktop sheeted in ice. Why would anyone start or end the asphalt here unless they wanted to conceal the access from the main highway? Feeling vulnerable in the open, especially without a firearm, Darcy dove back into the forest and hiked on.

A hogback rose on the horizon. Keeping it in sight, she trooped toward the outcropping of rocks and scaled them to survey the valley below. Less than a half mile away, a series of metal rooftops jutted above the canopy. She skidded down the last stretch of embankment and jogged in their direction, her footfalls muffled by a thick layer of dead needles strewn across the canyon floor. Snow fell heavy and fast, the flakes carried on a pine-scented breeze. Her steady jog dropped to a walk as she slowed to check her position with a compass. Her father had taught her to read one; memories of him warmed her.

Somewhere, an engine roared to life.

The sound grew louder as she pressed deeper into the piney woods. Ahead, blues and grays peeked through the foliage. Cautious, she darted from one huge pine to the next, using the trees as her camouflage until she reached the forest edge.

Several yards from where she crouched sprawled a gray structure with a blue metal roof. From the photographs she'd seen over the years, not one of those pictures resembled the S-site that unfolded before her now; the building was all new construction, right down to the last nail. "Abandoned site, my ass."

Prostrate, Darcy crawled into the bushes that rimmed the shipping yard. Broken limbs gouged her arms and neck. She made her way to the back of the hedgerow and panned the area with binoculars. Two silver tractor-trailers were parked at the loading dock, along with the white pickup and the Jeep. She wanted a closer look at the vehicles but didn't stand a chance, for a twelve-foot-high chain-link fence capped with razor wire surrounded the entire arena, and guards manned the security post at the main gates. An unsettling thought pricked at her. Where were the surveillance cameras? She craned her neck and scanned the adjacent trees, but saw none. Still, the possibility of their presence disturbed her.

Loud voices filtered up to Darcy, but no one appeared in the yard below. The minutes ticked by. A damp cold seeped from the frigid ground into her stiff body. Snow dusted her pant legs. She removed a small tarp from her Kelty and positioned it beneath her. The last thing she needed was a chest cold.

A shout rang out.

Three men shuffled onto the dock, two in white uniforms and a third in jeans and a leather jacket. She trained her binoculars on them. The man in jeans Darcy tagged as J. He threw the latch on one of the semis, barked an order, and raised the rig's door. The two in white scurried onto the platform. They flicked their spent cigarettes at the fence. The electrified chain link spit, then ejected the charred butts into the snow. The unloading began.

As the men wheeled box after box from the cargo compartment, J ticked off the deliveries on a clipboard. Darcy zoomed in on a carton sitting near the open bay. She sized up the cardboard boxes—about five feet wide and eight feet long. Whatever they contained must've been light, because the men loaded each without a struggle, but what she didn't understand was why they moved the boxes on a gurney rather than with a dolly.

"One down, one to go," J bellowed as he threw open the cargo doors to the second Peterbilt truck.

Riveted, Darcy hoped something, anything, might give her a clue as to the boxes' contents, but nothing did, so she shifted her focus from the cartons to the workers. One man in particular, the shortest in the group, whom she labeled Shorty, looked familiar. Her lens roamed his face and the features of the others. Uncanny how she recognized them all, but their names escaped her.

Glass shattered.

Darcy flinched but kept her binoculars fixed on the loading dock. J pivoted. Shorty, his back to the supervisor, bent down to examine the broken box. J chopped him across the base of the skull, and Shorty hit the concrete platform with a sickening thud.

Darcy winced.

The worker rose to his feet, a peculiar smile painted on his lips. J massaged his hand. Pain contorted his face. "Little good that did," he yelled. "Back to work. Be more careful."

The smile, the supervisor's reaction—both confused her.

A white cloud obscured her vision. Damn, her binoculars had fogged. She wiped them with a gloved hand. Through smeared lenses, she watched J drag the split carton to the edge of the dock and shove it off. Glass crashed as the box landed in a Dumpster marked Recycle and fell apart. She zoomed in for a closer look. Nothing more than a heap of tempered glass and cardboard. The workers carted the last of the boxes into the building, and J locked up. An eerie silence gripped the yard.

After a long while, Darcy lowered her binoculars and wiped condensation from her eyes. Her teeth chattered. The tightness in her chest became a major distraction. She wrung her hands, but nothing restored her circulation. Her entire body was numb.

The sky grayed; another snowstorm was headed her way.

She pushed back the layers of wool that concealed her watch: three hours to dusk. Too long to wait and too hard to stay alert when cold consumed her thoughts, so she backed out of the blind, knocking the branch above her as she snaked free. Snow cascaded onto her head. She brushed the flakes from her face, crammed the tarp into her backpack, and ran for the forest.

Her joints ached from the cold, and her stomach growled. The latter spurred her on. She cut through the underbrush at a hasty clip, eager to return to the rental car for her belongings before she trekked up the hill to the lab. Yards ahead, the blue sedan burst from a sea of white. She rushed toward the rental.

A flash of green grabbed her attention. A figure darted through the trees.

Darcy dropped to a squat. If it weren't for the snow blanketing the forest, she might not have seen Green. Here, his emerald green jacket blended in well with the dense ponderosa pines, making it harder to pick him out than among the olive-green of Taos.

Motionless, Green rested against the trunk of a tree, his binoculars pointed at her rental. After a few minutes of prowling the shadows with his oculars, he broke from his camouflage and crossed the meadow to her sedan, his movements rigid and cautious. He skirted the car, a Ruger clutched in his bandaged hand.

Darn, she'd forgotten to lock the trunk. He sprang the lid, leaned in, then backed away from the car.

Her phone vibrated. Not now.

When she zeroed in on Green again, he'd retreated into the woods. She waited for an engine to start, but only silence ensued, so she backtracked to the paved road and headed in the opposite direction, putting distance between her and him.

Her phone pulsated again. "What's up, Ed?"

"Been trying to reach you," he blurted. "The prints off the Ruger . . ."

She smiled, her spirits high. What timing!

"They belong to Charleton Cain."

Her grin sagged. "The name means nothing."

"Cain died sixteen years ago. Murdered."

24

The prints belong to a dead man?" She heard the disbelief in her voice. "That raises some interesting possibilities. Any details?"

"Not yet, but I have someone at Dan's working on it."

"Good." All the while she listened, Darcy slowly pivoted, her eyes scanning the woods for any sign of Green/Cain.

"I also called to tell you I've been summoned home. Boss's orders."

"When?"

"Thursday morning."

Plenty of time for Ed to check the car to see if anyone had tampered with the fuel tank. "Now that you're on the line, the rental broke down and left me stranded."

"I'll pick you up."

"Let's meet somewhere." She pictured the map of the

technical areas she'd downloaded from LANL's Web site. The bioscience facility, with its remote location, was also under construction, and the workers quit early in the winter. She gave Ed directions, rattled off a list of items to bring, and advised him to dress warm. "We'll be outdoors for a couple of hours."

"See you soon."

Darcy cocked her head, straining to hear, the ethereal stillness disconcerting. All around her gleamed white, except for beneath her feet where the forest of dead pine needles was awash in dappled light. Above, the sun's rays paled as the approaching snowstorm darkened the afternoon sky. A stiff breeze rustled the rice grass and clinked icicles suspended from a young pine. The wind died, and the dense silence returned. She moved on.

Avoiding Green/Cain forced her down a dirt easement, the farm road mired in slush and soggy clay. Ice filmed the potholes, and frozen weeds crunched beneath her boots as she trekked through the murkiness that shrouded the cornfield. Another yard or so to the main highway. Her stride quickened.

A hundred headlights shone through the haze like fireflies on a runway dusted in white as Darcy broke from the forest and stepped onto the paved road that led to the Hill. She hiked up the incline at a steady pace but soon increased to a full-out run, eager to escape the cold and reach cover before the snowfall broke. Despite the inclement weather, she passed several joggers on the well-traveled route to and from the lab. No one slowed or looked twice as she raced up the shoulder to Jemez Road and over Omega Bridge, circumventing parked cars and negotiating the crowded streets that linked the network of buildings.

The bioscience lab was wrapped on two sides by heavy tree cover and butted to a forested canyon; the area as secluded as possible on a campus of ten thousand. She sprinted to the back of the structure and surveyed the tree line. Purple shadows mottled the edges of the empty parking lot

Seeing no sign of life in or around the building, she staggered forward, winded by the altitude, her throat burning from the frigid air. After a short break, she took shelter alongside an unfinished retaining wall and watched traffic zip by on Diamond Drive. A brisk wind blew snowflakes in her direction. Seconds passed like hours. Numb, her face smarted from the cold, and her feet felt like two bricks, no life left in them. She shoved her hands under her armpits. "Hur . . . ry, Ed." Her teeth chattered.

Darcy's 4Runner swerved around the corner and slid to a stop next to the building. She hopped the low wall and sprinted to her vehicle, glad to escape the cold. Nestled in the passenger's seat with a blanket over her legs and hot air blasting from the heater vents, she gratefully accepted the thermos Ed handed her. Other than a quick greeting and the words "hot stew," he said nothing while she downed the chunky beef and vegetable meal in a matter of minutes. She swallowed, "Thanks."

"Coffee?" He poured a cup. "Careful. It's hot."

She felt the chill slowly flee her body. "Sorry to drag you out in this mess."

"No problem." He motioned to the hatch. "Brought everything on your list. I'll park by the trees to give you some privacy."

He backed her Toyota to the canyon and took a walk while she stripped to her thermals and layered on wool and fleece. She longed for a hot shower, but for now, clean clothes would do.

She leaned over the seat to retrieve a metal case. It housed her Browning. On the sponge lining next to the firearm sat three magazines. She picked up the 9 millimeter, ejected the cartridge, and inspected the chamber. Empty. She loaded the magazines. She stuffed one in the waistband of her pants, pocketed the second, and inserted the third into the grip. The minute she strapped on her shoulder holster, she felt whole again.

"Come on, Ed," Darcy shouted out the window as she switched on the wiper blades.

He dove into the passenger's seat of the SUV. After the windshield cleared of snow, she shifted into gear and headed back down the hill.

Dragging Ed along had seemed like a good idea. Now she had serious doubts. Whatever the goings-on at S-site, they spelled danger. Risking her life was one thing, but she had no right to jeopardize his. On the other hand, he might come in handy on the return visit.

"Do you mind bringing me up to date?" he asked.

She filled him in, ending with, "A question for you. With Walt and possibly Norm dead, what was their connection to Breckenridge?"

"Walt and Norm were lovers."

"Oh, really?" The statement surprised her. "You sure?"

"Caught in the act at a ski lodge in Breckenridge."

Darcy hated blackmail and emotional blackmail even more. "By you?"

"Hey, I'm not proud about using them . . . I did it as a favor for Dan, so let's change the subject. Tell me what happened to the rental car?"

She began with her gas-up in White Rock and finished with, "You paged me."

"How far are we from the car?"

"Close, but Cain's a problem."

"The gas issue sounds suspicious."

"I agree. I'd like you to take a look at the car, but first let's concentrate on S-site. Ed, maybe you should—"

"No, I won't stay behind."

Darcy steered onto the dirt easement that led to the cornfield and rode the grassy shoulder to the end of the road, the center a giant mud puddle. She nosed the 4Runner into a thick stand of dried stalks and squeezed out of the driver's door.

Ed met her at the hatch. "Be dark soon."

She nodded, busy sorting through the items he'd brought so she could replenish her supplies. Ready, she fell in step beside him, the wet leaves silent beneath her feet and soaked under a layer of snow. Every shadow demanded scrutiny, and the occasional sound, exploration.

"Are you worried about patrols from S-site?" said Ed in a low voice.

"No." She'd dismissed the idea of patrols. Why police the forest when an impenetrable fortress of concrete and steel protected the real prize? "Keep an eye out for Cain."

Several yards up the path she'd bushwhacked earlier, Darcy cupped binoculars to her eyes.

Ed did the same. "There's something blue among the trees."

"Rooftops to S-site. Come on. We're almost there."

The wind shifted direction.

"Voices," Darcy said. Her eyes probed the gray fog that hung over the valley floor.

"I hear them too," he whispered. "They're rather loud for anyone playing it low-key."

"Overconfident, perhaps?" She eyed the brush and listened. Only silence. She motioned him forward.

Within less than a yard of the site, the nebulous shadows dissolved to black as the last shades of day dwindled to night. She paused and waited for the moon to clear the canopy.

A burst of glaring light illuminated the canyon floor.

Ed squeezed her shoulder. "Fire?"

"No." She darted from the forest edge and sidled along the hedgerow where she'd hid hours earlier. Below, the enclosed yard was aflame with brilliant light.

"Place is lit up like a ball field," said Ed, his breath warm on her cheek.

Engines roared, and diesel fouled the air.

"A 3406," she said.

"What's a 3406?"

"A big sucking diesel engine. Come on."

Darcy stuck close to the shrubs, the hedge aglow from the floodlights, and crept to a stand of evergreens. She gestured for Ed to scoot into the tunnel she'd cored hours ago. While he crammed his frame into the bushes, she panned the timberline with night vision binoculars. Nothing moved. She clawed a new hole among the shrubs and crawled in, her belly raking the frozen ground, until she emerged from the scrub alongside him.

"You can see everything," he whispered.

No kidding. Any closer and the dock workers could have read her thoughts. The yard sizzled with enough voltage to illuminate a city, and the frosty air buzzed with excitement as a boisterous group near the front gate tossed horseshoes at a stake. The men laughed and cheered. In contrast, others chain-smoked and paced the platform, their half-spent cigarettes discarded in the snowdrifts that girded the side wall. Darcy searched but didn't see J in the crowd.

"Incoming!" someone shouted.

The buzz from the concrete arena built to a clamor. Men pitched horseshoes aside, ground out cigarettes, and snapped to attention. In the distance, the roar of engines blasted the night. Darcy's pulse spiked.

Brakes hissed and screeched.

Ed gave a thumbs-up. "Can we get closer?"

Darcy wiggled out of the cavity, and he followed.

"Is the entire facility fenced?" he said.

She snorted softly. "Twenty-foot Cyclone barbed wire capped in razor wire. Electrified too."

"So we can't get closer?"

"No, but the angle's better from the other side. We might see more." Darcy started up the west slope.

"Why west?"

"Quicker to go south, but we'd have to pass the front gates."

"Seen any dogs?"

She shook her head. "Not yet."

"Do you think there might be a way in?"

Brave fellow. "Maybe, but the question is, could we get out?" She pictured herself dashing through the woods to the break in the easement where the dirt met pavement. The trucks braked at the junction to roll over the bump in the grade. If she slid under a big rig, wrapped her arms and legs around the axle, and rode into the compound . . . the idea translated to a suicide mission. No way, not this soon in the investigation. Darcy slipped into the forest, Ed at her heels.

She skirted the front of the site and approached from the opposite direction. Now, she was directly across from her previous hiding place and had a ringside seat on the action. Hunkered down in a blind of junipers, she communicated with Ed through gestures and touches. He tapped her knee. J appeared on the loading dock, but no sign of Shorty.

"Aames!" J shouted as he mingled with the workers. "Drag your sorry ass over here and help this poor bastard load the last two."

"Dented one, sir," someone yelled.

J marched across the platform to a steel gurney. On it rested a cardboard box approximately eight feet in length and five feet wide, the same size she'd seen during her earlier stakeout of the yard. Heavy plastic straps held the corners in place. J slit the restraints with box cutters, then Aames took one end of the long lid, J the other, and both lifted at once. Inside was a Styrofoam container approximately the same length as the cardboard box. J removed the foam lid and tossed it on the dock.

Darcy zoomed in on the gurney and held her breath, but exhilaration dissolved to disappointment when she had her first look at the contents. Lying in a molded bed of Styrofoam rested a glass or Plexiglas box; she couldn't tell which from this distance. At one end of the transparent container was a circular metal plate with wire prongs jutting from the steel. Engrossed, she ignored Ed's touch until he rapped harder.

Headlights lit the shrubs. Brakes whined, and a semi chugged to a halt outside the front gates. On his tail came another big rig. The driver of the first truck swung onto the running board and spouted a number to the sentry, who repeated the code into his cell phone. After a pause, a loud beep sounded, and the automatic gates cranked open. Six men in camouflage broke from the shadows in the yard. Each brandished an Uzi.

The first driver made a wide U-turn inside the massive concrete pit, then backed his rig to the platform. Darcy panned the trailer, but the only identifier on the silver body was the letter *S*. She scanned the dock. J stood by while four workers rushed toward the truck. Metal struck metal as the driver flung open the cargo compartment. Fog billowed from the refrigerated interior. When the veil cleared, one worker after another filed into the back of the rig, and one by one containers equipped with casters glided out and onto the dock. In all, they unloaded twelve aluminum receptacles that looked like food storage boxes—the kind used by the airlines, only taller and longer.

The delivery over, shouts filled the night air, followed by racing engines. The automatic gates parted, and the caravan of trucks filed through on their way down the lane to the main highway. Armed patrols guarded the yawning exit until the gates banged shut.

Darcy felt a sharp jab in the shoulder. Startled, she stifled a cry.

Ed's hand shot out; his finger pointed at the tree line.

She scooped up her night vision binoculars and tracked the

unidentified target as he migrated from detection to recognition range, the ambient light working in her favor. He vanished for a moment, but soon the image intensifier picked him up. From experience, she knew that if her infrared illuminator caught him, he lurked within a hundred yards. This was no threat; she'd outrun him if she had to. But what about Ed? She zoomed in for a close-up. Damn. Cain. What a nuisance he was, especially for a dead man.

For a long time, Cain hovered at the shadow's edge before he sprinted across the paved road, a blind spot for those in the yard. Binoculars dangled from his neck. Had he seen her? She touched Ed's arm. He nodded. She put a finger to her lips, abandoned her cover among the shrubs, and retraced a path to the front of S-site, again giving the building a wide birth as she traipsed through the underbrush. Since Cain avoided those in the yard, he wasn't likely one of them—just intent on snooping like she'd done for the past few hours. Darcy glanced over her shoulder to be sure Ed was close.

Rapid footfalls advanced. The heavy pounding grew louder as Cain drew near. The hairs on her neck bristled. She froze. Ed bumped into her. While stationary, she timed the advancing drum of the feet. So, Cain had seen them. She waved Ed forward, and he took the lead.

Without a prompt from her, he veered sharply to the right, circumventing the trail to the cornfield. She placed a hand over her breast pocket, the compass securely in place. She'd need it if Cain forced her too far into the woods. Ed slowed. Darcy looked back. A yard or two behind, a figure emerged from the trees. She faced forward, in time to duck under a low-hanging limb before it smacked her in the head.

The footfalls were closing in fast.

Ed broke into a run. Darcy kept up as Cain drove them deeper into the forest. Her knees pumping high and her breathing labored, she flew through the woods, her lungs burning. She saw the ravine, but too late. Her boot clipped the rim of the arroyo and over she went, tumbling headlong to the bottom, but she recovered quickly. Ed landed beside her. He rocked forward and stood.

Darcy sized up the situation. The arroyo provided protection, but the uneven terrain would slow them down. To the south lay the cornfield and safety—if she reached the 4Runner without intercepting Cain. She gambled and headed north, staying, for the time being, in the ravine.

For a long stretch, the wide gorge allowed Ed to walk abreast of her. She shot him sidelong glances, studying his face and actions for any signs of fatigue or dehydration. Although panting sporadically, he acted alert and maintained the pace. She surveyed the ridges. Shadows danced off the walls. Above, a full moon burned bright, and the sky sparkled with stars.

The arroyo narrowed. Darcy overtook Ed. Her eyes on the rim line, she squinted at every piñon that clung to the eroded bank, for it provided a potential shield for Cain. Is this how Johnny had felt? Hunted? Insane with fear, scurrying like a rat through this clay labyrinth, and wondering if—or knowing that—death waited at the end of the dark maze?

Ed faltered. "Can we rest for a second?"

Bad idea, but she said, "For a few seconds."

He slid out of his JanSport, grabbed a handful of snow, and ate it.

She stepped forward to stop him. "Don't eat anymore."

"I'm thirsty."

"If you do, you'll lower your body temperature and increase your chances of dehydration."

"I know, but I'm out of water."

"There's some in my side pocket. Drink slowly."

He removed two bottles and offered her one.

"No, thanks. I'm fine for now."

Between sips, he said, "Must be . . . the altitude." He recapped the bottle. "Okay, let's go."

"You sure?"

He nodded.

Darcy went first. Unlike the dry slope she'd fallen down earlier, the walls along this stretch were slick from melted snow. "Soon as we find a dry spot, we'll climb out."

"Good idea," said Ed. "I feel like a trapped rat."

A breeze picked up and played tricks; it rustled limbs and tossed shadows about. When the gentle wind died, the moon toyed with her senses, hiding behind clouds, then emerging in its brilliant glory.

She rounded a bend. "This looks like as good a place as any."

"I'm right behind you."

She scrambled up the bank. Ed seized hold of a tree root and hoisted himself out of the shallow section of the arroyo. Hunkered down in the bushes with binoculars cupped to her eyes, Darcy searched the forest floor, hardly believing she saw movement in her peripheral vision. She yanked Ed to the ground.

Hidden in the undergrowth, she watched Cain split from the cover of a ponderosa, his footsteps light but audible. With Ed prone beside her, Darcy raised herself on her elbows, high enough to see Cain squatting about two yards from her, his face partially obscured by binoculars. After a few seconds, he stood, then jogged to the ravine and slid from sight. A soft sucking noise rose from the arroyo as he trudged up the muddy gorge. As soon as the sound died, Darcy signaled Ed to get moving.

She turned inland and angled across the forest to put as much distance between her and Cain as possible. It crossed her mind to check her compass, but if her pace slowed he might gain on them, so she kept going and motioned to Ed to do the same.

She tore through a stand of young pines into a clearing and broke stride within feet of a gaping arroyo; the drop a good thirty feet or more. Moonlight reflected off the slippery bank and streamed up the opposite wall, which appeared dry. Before Darcy decided on her next move, a spidery silhouette inched up the gully. Tall and thin, Cain grew in stature as he stumbled around the corner and stopped just below where Darcy stood frozen on the ridge. The pale shaft of his flashlight, low on battery power, washed over the basin.

"Any sign of him?" Ed whispered as he reached her side. The question sounded like a scream in the dead silence of night.

Cain jerked frantically from side to side, trying to pinpoint the location of the voice, his Ruger in one hand and flashlight in the other. The beam blinded Darcy.

"Duck!" Ed shouted.

A shot rang out.

She braced for the hit, but felt nothing. When her vision adjusted to the sudden darkness, she was stunned to see Ed in the arroyo, standing over an unconscious Cain.

"He's out cold but has a pulse," Ed called up to her.

"Stay there. I'm coming down." She hit feet first. "What happened?"

"I shot him. I had to. He could've killed you. Besides it was my fault for blurting out that stupid question. As soon as he shone his flashlight on you and aimed, I shot him in the shoulder, slid down, and whacked him in the neck."

Darcy gawked at the fistful of firepower in Ed's hand. More gun than any person needed. "You're packing a lot of hardware, aren't you?"

He smiled.

No wonder he's exhausted, hauling that cannon around. She examined Cain. "Flesh wound. He's out cold but has a strong pulse. Let's go. I've had enough of him for one night."

"You think he'll recover and come after us?"

"Let's not hang around to find out." She cradled the compass in her palm. The luminous dials sparkled in the nocturnal light. "I should have used this earlier. Seems we looped back on our own trail, which is why we ran into him rather than getting away. I don't want to make the same mistake twice." With Cain out of commission, Darcy decided to stay in the arroyo. She took off at a fast pace, and Ed matched her speed.

A mile up the ravine, she paused to collect her bearings. "Good, we're close to the fork."

At the junction, she hung a right and headed northwest at a good clip. The arroyo narrowed for a stretch, then opened up and branched again. She maintained course. The moon deserted her, so she fished out her penlight and flicked the strong beam over the arroyo floor, surprised by the river of muck that spread out ahead. "Hey, Ed, check this out."

He arrived beside her. "Mud?" He sounded incredulous.

"Mud." She stuck her boot into the sludge to gauge the depth. The impression filled quickly. "A whole lot of mud. An inch thick, maybe thicker. But we haven't had enough snow or rain to create this much mess. Let's head up."

"Wait." He held out his hand. "Lend me your binoculars."

She handed him her night vision lenses.

"Looks like fog up there." He frowned. "But the conditions aren't right for fog. And there's something shiny below the haze, but I can't make it out."

She stared up the arroyo. Light reflected off a polished surface. "Do you think we can walk that far in this quagmire?"

"I'm game. Looks drier over there." He treaded across the arroyo to the opposite side.

Halfway there, Darcy lost her balance and pitched forward. Ed's arm shot out. She latched hold of him to steady herself.

"Thanks. The thought of landing in something cold when I'm already freezing . . ." She shuddered.

"Know how you feel. Half-frozen myself—no feeling in my hands or feet. Careful. The entire area's socked in. This is very strange."

Darcy inched forward as if in slow motion, testing every footfall. In front of her, Ed slipped into the veil that cloaked the arroyo and was obliterated from view. She stifled the urge to call to him. One mistake tonight was one too many. Who knew if Cain lurked nearby?

She lifted her leg. Gray ooze coated her pant leg, the river of muck now calf high. She trekked on. The toe of her boot stubbed something hard, unexpected in this sea of mud. She tripped and fell. Pain shot up her leg.

"Darcy?" Ed called to her in a low voice.

She yanked off her glove and ran her fingers over concrete, the surface wet yet warm.

"Darcy?"

"Here. You won't believe this," she said in a soft voice, "but the arroyo's paved, at least where I am."

Dim light pierced the fog, and Ed appeared. He shone his flashlight over the slab.

"The concrete's warm." She patted the pavement.

"You're kidding. It's winter." He touched the cement. "You're right. Hey, isn't it against the law to alter an arroyo?"

"As in pave it? Yes, but the government's above the law."

"Oh, yeah. I forgot. Now this is really strange. The fog's lifting. Let's wait and see if the area clears completely."

He passed the time walking in a circle to stay warm while Darcy massaged her hands to restore circulation.

The fog thinned, and moonlight penetrated the evaporating haze; white gave way to blurred images, which slowly sharpened to contrasts of black and gray. Awestruck, Darcy gaped at the massive concrete shelf on which she stood, the first in a series of ten immense spillways that rose high above her. She walked off the area. Each shelf measured approximately thirty feet deep by thirty wide, and four feet high.

When she climbed to the top spillway, she was astounded by the depth and breadth of the giant concrete amphitheater, for that's what the arena resembled. Beyond the massive platform stretched a manmade culvert, the clay banks over forty feet high and the bed over a hundred feet wide. At either end, the channel fed into a wide arroyo, the spillways designed to break the flow of water. But why? To accommodate flash flooding? Unlikely. There wasn't enough rainfall or snow in this region to warrant a labor of such magnitude.

From across the way, Ed waved. He motioned to a circular drainage pipe jutting from a concrete wall, the opening capped with a metal grate. "What do you think? Maybe twenty feet in diameter?" he said as she joined him.

"Good guess." She inspected the bars. "Heavy gauge steel, the horizontals and verticals welded."

"They'd be impervious unless you brought a blow torch."

She rested her forehead against the grate.

"What do you see?"

"Nothing. I'm listening."

Ed placed his ear to the opening. "I don't hear anything."

"There."

"Oh. Sounds like . . . gushing water."

She shoved him. "Run!"

He stumbled, regained his balance, and fled. Clear of the drain, she slammed him against the wall.

"What—in the—hell?" he sputtered.

A powerful roar.

Water gushed from the pipe in tsunami waves, pummeling

concrete and crashing into walls as the flood rushed toward the spillways and swamped the arroyo, churning up rock and mud with hurricane force.

25

The flood dwindled to a constant stream.

"Whew. You . . . you saved my life," said Ed.

Darcy punched him gently in the shoulder. "Heck, you would've done the same for me." Not being someone who accepted compliments well, she changed topics. "We should take some water samples."

"Definitely." He gathered the empty water bottles from their packs and held one under the trickle that splashed from the culvert pipe until the container filled. He carried another to a slight dip in the asphalt and with the cap scooped liquid into the bottle.

"Why two samples?"

"The big gusher looked grayish-white but cleared up the longer the water ran. Have you ever backwashed a pool?"

"Sure. I see what you mean. The initial surge appeared cloudy, like a combination of water and diatomaceous earth."

"Right." Ed raked the cap over the concrete, collecting the last dribble from the puddle. "But I don't believe the white residue is DE. At least not the kind of powder used in pool filters."

"Then what?"

"Not sure. Let's have Testco tell us." He labeled the bottles while she explored the area with her night vision oculars.

"Worried about Cain?" said Ed.

"Never stopped worrying," said Darcy, without lowering her binoculars. "Standing here in the moonlight, we might as well have bull's-eyes painted on us."

"Your analogy hits a bit too close to home." He shouldered his backpack. "North?"

"North." She jumped from the massive slab to the arroyo floor. "Ground's dry along this stretch. The culvert must only drain to the south." She scouted the woods.

"See anything?" he asked in a low voice.

"No."

He walked ahead. "What about checking your rental car?"

"It'll have to wait."

"There's still time tomorrow." He fell silent.

Darcy scrutinized the shadows, attuned to every sound, alert to every movement.

About five miles up the trail, Ed took a water break. "Ever kill anyone?"

The question surprised her. "No," she lied, not in the mood for the litany of questions guaranteed to ensue. "The cornfield's coming up."

"I'm beat. Feel like I ran a marathon."

"I can relate."

The rest of the trip they made in silence, Darcy happy to see her 4Runner. She disarmed the antitheft system and packed their gear in the rear compartment.

Ed leaned against the vehicle and yawned. "All I want is a hot shower and sleep."

"Ditto." Darcy practically threw herself behind the wheel.

He jumped into the passenger's seat. "Where'd you crash last night?"

"On the floor in my office. Showered in the women's restroom. Can't wait to sleep in a bed tonight."

"I bet." He sunk low in the seat and closed his eyes.

The Toyota bucked and bounced over the uneven road until they reached the main highway. On level ground the tires spit gravel, the rocks sheared off the treads by the rough pavement. They clanged through the wheel wells and shot out the back of the vehicle. When the clattering died, the only sound in the warm cab was hot air whooshing from the vents. With traffic light at such a late hour and the road conditions greatly improved, Darcy made the drive from Los Alamos to the Talpa rental in record time, pulling into the winding lane shortly before 11:00 p.m. The minute she parked outside the garage, Ed began unloading their backpacks.

The portal light came on, and Rio stepped onto the porch with Bullet.

"Hey, big guy," Darcy said as Bullet raced up to her. She showered him with affection. "Any messages?" she called to Rio.

"Matt said there's still time to make your court date, which is 9:00 a.m. tomorrow."

Tomorrow? Her mind juggled schedules and responsibilities. The blur in her brain grew darker and thicker. Right now, so many other issues seemed more important than securing an easement for her land, like food for starters.

Ed held the door, and everyone filed into the house. Rio fixed Reuben sandwiches, hot off the kitchen grill. Between bites, Darcy forced herself to join the lively conversation, but after a while Ed and Rio's banter grated on her sleep-deprived nerves. So shortly after dinner, she retired with a warm brandy and sat in bed to savor the liqueur. The last, healthy swallow burned on the way down. Finished, she snuggled up to Bullet, already fast sleep, and stroked his fur. His presence alone had a calming effect on her.

*   *   *

Sometime in the hours before dawn, Darcy woke with a start. She sat bolt upright and listened, but only silence filled the house. Bullet groaned his disapproval at being wakened. He shifted positions and drifted back to sleep. Darcy stared at the clock. An hour later, she was still awake. How she envied Bullet, snoring like a freight train chugging up an incline. Eventually, she must've dozed off, because the next time she woke the red LED said 5:00 a.m.

Showered and dressed, she packed additional clothing, then headed downstairs to replenish her food supplies with the idea she might be at LANL for a much longer stay. In the kitchen, Rio added several sandwiches and three thermoses to the dry goods collection Darcy had already amassed on the counter. "Two hot soups and one espresso, in case you need a charge later."

"Need the charge now. Slept like heck."

Rio poured coffee into a mug and handed it to Darcy. "So no court today?"

Darcy shook her head.

"I reserved another rental car," said Rio, "but it won't be available until later this afternoon. Too late for work this morning. They're running low on vehicles with the holidays."

"Figured as much, so I'll have to take my 4Runner."

She made the drive to the lab in under an hour, cleared

security, and hurried up the stairs to her office. After two cups of Rio's espresso, Darcy felt ready to tackle her first assignment as computer expert on the AL project. "This will be a tough one," Sonny had warned her, but he was wrong. On only four hours of sleep, she'd found it harder to drag herself from a warm bed than to program Alt the gnatrobot for low-level intelligent behavior.

Done wiring Alt, she saved its bug brains and spent the next hour engaged in a tedious session of identity theft. After a long while, she finally located a glitch in LANL's software, a hiccup that gave her access to the lab's restricted database. Nothing was perfect, not even biometrics. She stole what she needed from Gale Clifford's file and logged off seconds before the shuffle of lazy feet sounded in the corridor outside her office.

A knock, then Sonny burst in. "You're here. Good. Gert'll be ecstatic. You should have seen her face yesterday when she couldn't find you. She hardly ever shows up in our area. Beneath her, I guess. She must have wanted something important."

Darcy typed "Dee Miller" on the bottom of the report, loaded paper into the laserjet, and hit Print. "What'd you tell her?"

"The truth. Your car broke down."

The printer purred as it spit out pages. "Was she mad?"

"Pissed, but she won't be if you meet your deadline, which doesn't seem likely."

"Oh? Why not?"

He rapped his wristwatch. "Because it's nine now, and our meeting's at ten. Think you can knock out the report in an hour? No way. My first assignment wasn't one tenth as difficult as yours, and the project ate up a week."

"Hmm." She collated the printed sheets and stapled them. "Here's your copy of the report."

His jaw dropped. "No frickin'-ass way." He skimmed the

data. "Hey, good stuff, Mill. Damn good. You're a smart chick. Did you know that?"

"Do now," she said in a deadpan way.

He roared with laughter. "Stick with me. Together, we'll go far in this organization."

She punched him gently in the shoulder. "You're on. Okay, clear out. I have less than an hour to run copies."

He saluted. "Yes, ma'am. Should I close the door?"

"Please."

Alone, Darcy logged on to a weather Web site to check the climatic conditions for the Los Alamos area. Ed had been right. From everything she read, all environmental factors mitigated against fog at S-site—yesterday, today, or even in the coming month. So what caused the thick veil? Steam? Unlikely. And why was the concrete warm? Hot water? She moved to her next mind twister.

Curious as to when and why the government had revamped the abandoned plutonium site, she rooted around in LANL's archives but discovered nothing helpful regarding S-site, so she scrolled through the list of files on her screen and clicked on Menu.

A map of the lab spread across the monitor. "Darn computer. Menu, not map." The date in the lower right-hand corner of the diagram caught her eye; this version was more current than the one she'd copied during her virtual tour. She printed the updated map and snatched the page off the laserjet, the paper still warm to the touch. The two versions appeared identical. She double-clicked on the site location, and the words leaped off the screen: "TA-88, acquired 1943 by War Department. Renamed S-site 1950. Closed 1980. Reopened 1985 as Z-site. Home to the new Nuclear Weapons Facility."

Andrew had hidden the flash drive at Z. A tremor coursed through her—not excitement, but anxiety, the magnitude of which overwhelmed her. Z wasn't a department, but a facility—a damn big one with maximum security. Her stomach churned as the words tripped through her brain: Z-site. Flash drive. G-cell.

She started a new search. The current probe gave her an in-depth description of G-cell, LANL's supercomputer, but didn't answer her question. Okay, okay, so this baby can perform a brute-force attack in seconds. Great, but *where* is it? The computer had to be inside Z.

The phone rang, the shrill noise startling her.

"Dee . . . Miller," she answered.

"You don't sound sure." Gert's booming voice made Darcy sit up.

"Sorry, Mrs. Alton. I had my mind on the Alt report." The name prompted her to wonder if the team had named their mechanical wonder after the VP.

"The meeting's off," said Gert.

Darcy glared at the stack of documents arranged neatly on her desk. Wonderful. All that work for nothing.

"Find Sonny, and both of you report to Perry at ten." She hung up.

Darcy logged off and poked her head into Sonny's office, but the room was empty, so she sat at his desk to wait. From the corner of a manila folder protruded an old issue of *Comp-Expert*. She flipped through the computer journal. Bored, she tossed the magazine aside, her eyes drawn to the tab on the folder next to the telephone. She picked it up.

Facing the door to watch for Sonny, she skimmed the articles sandwiched inside the file. "The Vatican bans human cloning." "Does a human clone have a soul?" "Is it possible to clone the dead?" "Set up your own cloning lab." "Clone a child to harvest its organs." The list continued, each title more intriguing than the last. Darcy saw Sonny in a new light. She closed the folder and opened the magazine.

"Find something interesting?"

She remained seated. "Yeah, an old issue of *CompExpert*. I had a chance to read the editorials, especially the one about the guy who built his own computer."

He snorted his laugh. "Yeah. Almost busted a gut when I read that one." A frown creased his forehead.

She pitched the magazine on the desk. It landed with a soft whack. "Gert called off the meeting. She wants us to report to Perry at ten."

His gaze darted to the desk. "Meet you at the elevators at ten."

"Got a better idea. See you down there."

"Okay. Later." Sonny shut his door.

Darcy walked into her office, unlocked her briefcase, and removed a small envelope. Logged on to the intranet, she found what she wanted in LANL's digital morgue of healthcare data. She already knew Johnny's blood type, AB negative. Now, she needed the others. But why erase a person's employment history but not his medical file? Either sloppy bookkeeping or a serious oversight, especially if there was a murder investigation.

When she had all four blood types, Darcy closed the program, clicked on Search, and typed in "Blood Lab." She found eight locations total, six in her building alone. The nearest one, a floor down, had low-level security—no ID badge or password required. Located next door to the lab was a clean room, which meant lockers. Perfect.

On the lower level, Darcy checked the glass inset in the stairwell door before she entered the hall and ducked into the women's locker room. Gowned and with a surgical mask hiding most of her face, she snapped on gloves and rushed into the blood lab next door.

Using forceps, she transferred the bloodstained tissue from the envelope to a clean petri dish and poured saline over it.

Red blood cells leached into the liquid, tingeing the water a bright pink. She discarded the soggy tissue, then added blood typing solution. The coagulated cells turned milky white. The hemoglobin in the dish matched Walt's.

A creak alerted her.

She stood abruptly. Her stool toppled and crashed to the floor. The half-open door started to close, the hydraulic hinges emitting a low hiss as the door slowly sealed. She ran to the exit and burst into the corridor, but saw no one. An uneasy feeling gripped her.

She returned to the lab to clean up. Someone had entered but left without a word. Perry? No, he'd demand an explanation. Sonny? He'd strike up a conversation.

Whoosh. Darcy jumped, then recognized the noise. The central air/vac unit had switched on. Hastily, she wiped the bench top clean, replaced the saline bottle, and double-checked her work area. The wall clock read ten.

Already late for her meeting with Perry, Darcy scurried into the locker room to change. She bypassed the quickest route to his office in favor of the safest. At the bottom of the staircase two levels down, she sailed into the hallway, surprised to see Perry and Sonny loitering beside a cart parked by the elevators. Sonny smiled when he saw her. Perry glowered. Hands on his hips, he shouted, "You're late, Miller. A whole fifteen minutes late."

Big deal. "Sorry."

"So much for warming up the buggy. Waiting for you, the engine almost overheated." Perry took the wheel of a modified golf cart. He rammed a key into the ignition, and the engine puttered to life, the drone loud in the hollow tunnel.

Grabbing hold of the crash bar, Darcy swung herself into the seat next to Sonny as Perry floored the accelerator. The tires squealed as the cart lurched forward. She held on. At the only manned checkpoint along the route, Darcy expected Perry to park and ride the elevator to his subterranean office, but he waved to the guard and drove on without showing ID.

"I've never been in this area," she said, managing to curb her curiosity and excitement.

"And you never will without me or a higher up," said Perry as the corridor ended. He braked.

Darcy scrutinized her surroundings: a wall ahead, a wall to her right, labs to the left, and everything stone white. Perry reached for the remote attached to the console and pressed a button. The wall parted. Before the panels completely separated, he gunned the engine and zipped through the break. Behind them, the partitions ground to a halt, then started to close. He switched on his headlamps, throttled back the engine, and cruised around a corner, the passage black and cold. The grade changed as he guided the buggy deeper into the earth. Spotlights flared to life.

"Floor sensors," said Sonny. He sat sideways, his arms crossed, and said nothing more.

His behavior concerned her.

She rode in silence, pondering how Perry knew her real name, and what he planned to do with the information, especially since she had no idea where he was taking her or why.

The descent leveled out, and the cart slowed. Sonny barely moved, his slender frame rocked gently by the rough idle of the engine.

Worried, she placed a hand on his shoulder. "You okay?"

Although whispered, her question drew an immediate reaction from Perry. "What's wrong?"

"Had sausage for breakfast"—Sonny stifled a belch—"didn't sit well. I'll be fine once we stop moving."

Unconvinced, she kept a watchful eye on him. "Hey, Perry, at the risk of sounding rude, where in the hell are we headed?"

"Maximum security." He braked, jumped out, and walked

up to a minicomputer built into the wall. He ran his badge through the computerized reader and returned to the cart.

"Maximum security, as in prison?" She kept a jovial tone to her voice.

Sonny sat upright, his eyes wide.

His gaze unwavering, Perry said, "Good correlation, Miller, but even if I told you, the name wouldn't mean anything."

"Try me."

"Hang on. If I screw this up, I'm dead." He donned tinted goggles and handed a pair to her and another to Sonny. The cart inched forward, gliding through the cavity in the breaking walls and into a cavernous room flooded in blinding light. Above the earsplitting din of machinery hard at work, Perry's harsh voice rang out clearly, "Dee Miller, welcome to . . . Z-site."

26

Z-site. Darcy's heart drummed against her ribs. Finally.

In front of her sprawled a bank of service elevators. The double-wide doors resembled garage bays, their exteriors finished to match the walls. The polished glossy white surface reflected the strong halogens, tossing the light at the fleet of stainless steel motorized carts ready to board the elevators.

"Where's the site? All I see are elevators. All I hear are generators."

"Z-site is a building," said Sonny. "A very big building. We're in the basement."

A very big building. Great. Now her cliché of a needle in a haystack had become reality.

Perry shifted into gear and coasted to a wide yellow stripe on the floor where he sat until the bay doors separated. "Glad these babies run on batteries—otherwise we'd all die from carbon monoxide fumes." He parked in the center of the huge elevator. The ride was so smooth, Darcy barely detected movement. A level up, the doors opened, and Perry cruised toward one of the manned security stations. As bad as tollgates.

After he'd been bio-IDed, the guard waved Perry on. He found an empty spot in the subterranean parking lot and killed the engine. "Keep your Eyedentacard handy. Lots of checkpoints."

"Yeah," said Sonny. "And you thought TA-3 went overboard. You ain't seen nothin' yet."

"What's the site protecting? Plutonium?" Darcy managed a laugh.

"Not anymore," said Perry, no humor in his voice.

Both men stepped aside and let her clear security first. Suspicious, Darcy presented her ID to the guard and watched warily as he typed her employee number into the computer.

"Confirmed," the machine responded in a mechanical tone.

"Now the scans," said the guard.

Her eyes aligned with the circles on the wall sensor and hands pressed to the plate, she prayed all would go well. If not, she had no contingency plan.

"Biometrics validated." The guard ushered her forward.

Relieved, she waited while the men completed the process.

After being cleared, Perry crossed the underground lot to a glass-enclosed building. Another elevator, another level—this ride was also a floor up. More security. The sign mounted above the station said WOMEN/RIGHT, MEN/LEFT.

Her turn came. She unbuttoned her jacket and prepared for a strip search, but the beefy female guard said, "Through there. Proceed slowly." She pointed to a glass tunnel.

Fascinated, Darcy watched the motorized floor inch along. The dual-paned walls on both sides of her flashed a lime green. The color intensified as she reached the center. At the other end, the glass door opened automatically, and a second guard waved her toward the exit.

"Here she is," said Perry.

Sonny looked relieved. "This way." He motioned to a gray concrete stairwell.

"What, no elevator? I feel cheated," she said to help ease the tension knotting her stomach. She felt completely boxed in, almost like being in prison.

"We aren't going far. Besides, Sonny isn't up to the ride," said Perry, a hint of disdain in his voice.

Darcy placed her hand on the cold pipe railing and ascended. The astringent odor of cleaning solvents clung to the chilly air. She reached the concrete landing first, followed by Perry. "Women's lockers are in there," he said before disappearing into the men's room with Sonny.

Darcy lingered in the hallway. She removed her shoe and pretended to examine the heel. Her head slightly bowed, she surveyed the ceiling. Surveillance cameras. She timed their pans, replaced her shoe, and entered the locker room.

Gowned, gloved, and masked, she pushed open an adjoining door with her shoulder and found herself in a clean room, or so the sign said. However, the space reminded her more of a workshop than a laboratory, each station dedicated to a specific product.

"There you are!" Perry's voice boomed.

She walked up to the nearest workstation and fingered a pair of glasses lying on the table. "What are these for?" She stalled for time, waiting for Sonny to arrive.

"Optivision goggles, the latest in night vision wear. They've never performed well. Strong moonlight causes visual distortion, making it difficult to track body heat, but with them off you can't track a damn thing."

"And this?" She picked up a helmet of molded aluminum.

"Go ahead. Try it on. I'd love to see what you're thinking, Dee Miller." He crossed the lab to where she stood. "The helmet reads thoughts. Only repetitious thoughts, but one day . . ."

Jerk, she thought as she replaced the head shield.

"I had a hunch you wouldn't be enthused." He stood so close she felt his breath on her cheek.

"Try this thought, Perry. The note you gave me . . . who's Darcy?" She braced for a reaction, especially a physical backlash, but he disappointed her.

A blank expression on his face, he said, "You ask a lot of questions . . . for a girl."

"Where's Sonny?"

"In the john. We're moving to the next lab." Perry maneuvered around the workstations and into an adjacent room.

Darcy entered after him, her guard up. He led her to the center of the lab.

Tables arranged in horizontal rows occupied the entire space. On them sat a multitude of small wooden boxes approximately three inches square. Glass domes covered the tops of each one.

"Remember Alt?" he asked.

"Sure, the gnatrobot I programmed for low-level intelligent behavior. I remember him on paper, but I haven't seen the real thing."

"You're about to catch your handiwork in the flesh, so to speak. Take off the surgical mask. You don't need it in here."

"Why would I need it at all? These are machines, right?" She let the mask dangle around her neck.

"In manner of speaking."

Which meant what? Darcy glanced about. "Shouldn't we wait for Sonny?"

Perry screwed up his face. "No. The man has the constitution of a . . . forget him."

Darcy didn't want to forget him. She trusted Sonny.

Perry gently lifted one of the glass domes as though he expected the glass to break merely from handling it. Using tweezers, he plucked a black object off the felt interior. "There are a dozen Alts to a box. Hold out your hand. Unless you're squeamish about bugs, which I doubt." He placed the gnat in her palm. "Careful. They're fragile. Each cost over a hundred thou."

"A hundred thousand dollars?"

"You heard right. These were our first prototypes. Almost broke our budget. We had no idea what we were up against. But that's history."

Fixated on the gnat, Darcy scrutinized every aspect of the creature. "He's so tiny—smaller than half a grain of rice."

"One millimeter, carved from a single crumb of silicon—brains, motor, and all."

She prodded the bot with her fingernail. "What's his purpose?"

"He's equipped with nanoscalpels—micro-surgical teeth. I'll put him under the scope." He flipped the bot over and tweezed it onto a glass slide. "See the teeth? They're razor sharp. And check out the legs. See the serrations?"

"Uh-huh."

"Someday, the next generation of these babies will crawl into your eyeball or your arteries to perform surgery."

"Fascinating prospect."

He scoffed. "The thought disgusts most people. I figured you'd find it intriguing, though. Of course, if the inventor has his way, these bots will also clean your carpet, carrying off the dirt speck by speck, or swarm the exterior of your house, covering your digs in a coat of elastomeric paint."

"Are you serious?"

"Dead serious."

"So they're programmed to do good tasks."

He looked skeptical. "What do you mean?"

She shrugged. "Can you program them to kill?"

Perry's eyes narrowed. "Why would we?"

Why indeed? "Are they difficult to mass produce?"

"They are now, but someday they'll self-replicate."

Self-replicate? That tidbit fascinated her. "Are you the inventor?"

He hesitated. "I played a part."

Modesty from Perry? A first. "This is cool. Really cool."

Perry smiled. "Ready to see the bugger in action?"

"You bet."

He laughed. "You sound like a kid with a new toy." He pulled out a stylus, the probe as thin as fine-gauge wire. "Okay, hand him over."

She hated to give the gnat back.

Perry flipped the bot. Using the stylus, he pressed a membrane switch on its belly and placed the wafer-thin bug on the table. "The next generation is remote activated."

"He moved." Darcy rubbed her hands together, delighted.

"I hope so."

The bot crawled across the surface, black wired legs scrambling along. "Zinc-oxide slivers," she whispered, "thinner than a human hair, gearless, jointless, piezoelectric limbs."

"You've got a great memory."

"Only project I've worked on, so why wouldn't I remember?"

"Watch." He headed toward the back of the room. "Go to the second row. Those are our next generation. The remote-activated gnats. Lift the tops on about ten boxes, then stand back." He scooped a small remote off the tabletop.

She removed the lids. Gnats swarmed from the containers like airborne dust. They alighted on desktops and equipment, teetering and poised for flight. Then one by one, they soared into the air, filling the room with soft whirring sounds.

"How cool!" said Darcy.

"Old technology," said Perry. "The next generation, our 220s, are 200 billionths of a meter."

"Wow, two thousand times smaller than the shaft of a human hair. Unbelievable."

Perry tapped his remote. All but a few gnats returned to their boxes. "Help me corral the rest of these pesky pets, and I'll brief you on your next assignment."

Darcy noticed a larger domed box sitting nearby. "What's in there?"

"Really old technology—gnat scouts. Take a look if you're interested."

She lifted the dome. Four red bots that resembled ladybugs sat on a blue cushion. "What type of scouting?" Reconnaissance, perhaps?

"The exploratory type. But forget gnatrobots—they're child's play compared to what's in store."

Excited to move on to the next discovery, Darcy collected the remaining gnats and placed them in their boxes. She loitered over the containers, marveling at the creatures.

Perry tapped her arm. She tensed under his touch. "Can't wait to show you our prototype workshop." He crossed the room to a swinging door and pushed it wide open with his foot. As in the last lab, the tables were arranged classroom style in long horizontal rows, but on these sat robotic heads shaped like those of humans, only with no identifying features such as eyes, noses, or mouths. Darcy counted forty in all.

"Artificial heads. Don't tell me . . . my next assignment is to program them for medium-level intelligence."

Perry snorted. "Hardly. You might be a brilliant computer scientist, Miller, but no single person at Z-site had, or has, the ability to program these prototypes. Besides, they're already programmed, and the work took a team led by a genius to do the job."

"You?"

"And Id." He sounded as though he hated to admit the truth.

"Interesting. What are they?" She waved a hand toward the forty.

"Grab a stool. I'll show you."

"In a minute." She leaned closer, her eyes riveted to the human-like forms.

A click broke the silence. An oval display lit up the front of the head, and a human face spread across the screen.

"What turned it on?"

"Body heat. Yours, Dee," The animated lips on the screen formed the words.

After her encounter with Con, not much astonished her. At least he called her Dee, not Darcy, and Perry had called her Miller, not McClain. Why was he playing mind games with her? To control or scare her?

"Body heat. Really?" she asked. "You programmed my name into the system, right?"

Perry smiled. "Not exactly."

"Are you saying he recognized me?"

"I recognize everyone," said the robotic head. His eyes shifted in Perry's direction. "Hello, Perry. Have you seen Isaac today, or Gert? I have a problem I must discuss."

"Later," said Perry.

Thrilled, Darcy gazed into the animated eyes on the screen. "What's your name?"

"Stork."

"How many babies have you brought into the world?"

Amused, Perry said, "Now you've started something."

"I only deal with data, Dee, and the facts state that storks do not deliver babies. If you can be more specific, we can discuss birds, babies, or the conception of babies."

"If you're a data robot, tell me . . . what's Con?"

"No!" Perry shouted as he sprang off his stool.

"Con is a humanoid with telepathic capa-bil-ities," the head said as Perry jumped between it and Darcy.

"You're treading on dangerous ground, Miller. Now stop. You've asked enough questions."

Stork said something garbled before he shut down.

"Don't do that again," said Perry, his tone threatening.

"Do what? Ask a question? If I have the clearance, why not?"

Those hard eyes of his softened, and in an uncharacteristically pleasant voice he said, "Sorry, I overreacted."

His over-the-top reaction didn't amaze her as much as his apology. Perry, sorry? She decided to take advantage of this lapse in nastiness. "I do have another question."

Perry eyed her with skepticism. "What?"

"A while back, I noticed a lab named SQUID."

"So."

"Sounds like LANL is brain mapping."

"Let's cut to the chase. Yes, the SQUID team is mapping the human brain so they can replicate its neural pattern on a computer chip, which will become the master neural network for our next generation of cognitive computers."

Ambitious, but it explained a lot of what she'd just seen. "You're saying my next computer will have the ability to think like the machines I just saw?"

"Yep, they'll think like you." He snickered. "Well, maybe not just like you. Enough questions. Come on. One more stop before we call it a day."

Angry one minute, solicitous the next. Why? "Where are we going?"

"The AL lab for your next assignment."

"Thought we handled all AL functions at Tech 3."

"All depends upon program sensitivity. And Walt's project is top secret."

Walt? Darcy's heart skipped a beat. Maybe Andrew had hidden the drive in the AL lab? After her pulse settled to near normal, she asked in as disinterested a tone as possible, "Does my new assignment have anything to do with Walt's project?"

"Everything, which is why I showed you the heads. You'll understand once you review Gert's instructions. Through here." Perry strolled out of the lab and down the hall to a bioscan. He inserted his Eyedentacard and punched in his cipher code. "Walt had a deadline, but he's been sick."

Dead was about as sick as you could get.

"Gert wants you to keep his deadline."

"When do you expect him back?"

"According to HR, it'll be a while," he said.

Guess so. Tough to return to work with a slit throat.

"Someone mentioned cancer." Perry avoided eye contact.

As good a lie as any. "What's Gert's deadline?"

"Monday noon. Here we are. Try your ID—make sure everything's in order since you'll be working here until Walt returns."

A job for life—wonderful. Darcy slid her Eyedentacard into the wall slot, tapped in her access code, and waited for the customary click. The plate on the door read BIOLAB, but Walt's scientific research had nothing to do with chemicals, drugs, or anything biological.

Eight high-resolution black-and-white terminals ate up most of the room, the CRT glow bright enough to read by. On the wall above the big-screens hung a neon orange banner that read WALT'S GARAGE.

She saw movement near the ceiling. A surveillance camera painted white to blend in with the wall tracked her every move.

"You should be in your element with all of these computers. Excuse the pinup girls."

Darcy gave Walt's gals a cursory appraisal. "He has good taste."

Perry wrinkled his nose. "Whatever. So there's no misunderstanding, you have limited access to Z-site, which means you stay here. No wandering the halls. The bathroom's in there."

She poked her head into the powder room. "Any other orders?"

"Flex hours don't apply. You leave promptly at four thirty. At four twenty, dial 888. The guard at the main security station will arrange for an escort to Tech 3. For now, Sonny or I will fill in."

"Four thirty? Too bad. I do my best work at night."

"Not here. You start at seven thirty. Got a problem with that? Tell me now." His nasty tone had returned.

"No, no problem at all, but all these rules and regulations make me feel like I'm in prison."

"Can't be helped." He crossed to the desk and thumped a paper binder with his palm. "Your assignment. Call Gert if you have questions."

Eager for him to leave, she switched off the lights. "I work best in the dark."

"No matter—dark or light, the cameras can still see you."

Bad news, but she said, "Doesn't bother me."

Perry drifted toward the exit, hesitated as though he had something to say, then left in a hurry.

Odd guy. Darcy locked the door and started her search for the flash drive. She hunted through the desk drawers, bathroom cabinets, even inside the toilet tank, but found nothing. At LANL everything was stored on the central computer. Now that gave her an idea.

She pulled a chair to one of the terminals. A sticker on the keyboard read "Big Brother's Watching." After logging on, she typed in her password and keyed in Walt's department code, the alphabetic/numeric PIN stamped on the assignment binder supplied by Gert. Darcy tapped ENTER, only to be greeted by a second level of security asking for another PIN, also courtesy of Gert.

Finally connected, Darcy surfed through an ocean of AL programs, all supervised by Walt over the past several years: scores upon scores of files beginning with AL-1neural and ending who knows where. Random skimming of the text in each file ate up an inordinate amount of time and revealed nothing, so at AL-4000neural she switched to a different approach.

From her recent research on Walt's background, Darcy knew he'd joined LANL's AL team in 1980. Five years later, Los Alamos collaborated with the Santa Fe Institute, also active in the AI/ AL field. For every LANL file, there existed a corresponding SFI file. Most folder designations in the institute's annals duplicated the indexes in the lab's archives, but not always, so she printed a hard copy of the first 4,000 LANL files and compared them against the first 4,000 files in the SFI's database.

She opened SFI-183neural-4. LANL had a corresponding file, but minus the 4. The data in both text files was the same with the exception of the last sentence in the LANL file: "I don't believe the SFI team has achieved stage four of the AL program." Dr. Galvin Perry, MD, had signed the statement. Another dead end, but her search continued.

She returned to her earlier method of scanning the text in a random sampling of files. After two hours of wading through scientific jargon, endless algorithms, and first-order predicate calculus, her brain shouted overload, and her stinging eyes begged for a reprieve. The computer clock said 3:00 p.m. The time reminded her of Gert's assignment.

Brain weary, Darcy padded into the bathroom to splash cold water on her face. Spidery red lines webbed the whites of her eyes. She dried her face and hands.

An electronic squawk blasted away the silence.

Darcy ran back into the computer room. A second squawk

sounded. The terminal flashed red, black, red. Darcy attacked the board with lightning key click speed.

"Please follow proper shutdown procedures," the display pulsed.

Of the three choices, Suspend, Shutdown, or Proceed, she placed the cursor on Proceed and right clicked the mouse. The workstation returned to the AL program, but the original menu didn't reappear. In its place was a continuance of the SFI index starting with 4,001.

"Darn machines." Frustrated, Darcy opened Gert's binder and speed-read her instructions aloud. "Locate the electronic bug in the data robot's circuitry and re-indoctrinate." Peculiar word, "re-indoctrinate." She read on. "Next, reprogram the gnatrobots for Level 1 biological vision." Both jobs sounded tedious. She perused Gert's troubleshooting suggestions, then took a few minutes to contemplate a suitable fix for the software problems.

Bored, Darcy alternated between robotic glitch repair and comparison of the SFI/LANL files. She clicked on Next. SFI-5001 topped the screen. She scrolled through the list and saw nothing out of the ordinary until the next bank of numbers flashed on the monitor. SFI-5999-G-cell leaped from the blurry list. She wiped her damp palms on her scrubs, opened the file, and devoured every word of the two-page document. Big deal—another Id invention, but not the information she needed.

The computer clock reminded her of Gert's assignment.

Darcy tore a page from the VP's instructions and clipped the sheet to the holder on the terminal. Gert's recommendation for repairing the robot's circuitry sounded reasonable, so Darcy started there. She worked on the project for another twenty minutes, then returned to her comparison of the LANL/SFI files.

The 6,000 block of SFI files jumped onto the screen. It took a second to zero in on SFI-6005-G-celldem. LANL didn't have a corresponding file, plus the size raised a red flag: 1 KB. She opened it. The one-line message said, "Sent to DEM December 16 at 8:12 p.m.," approximately ten minutes before to her telephone conversation with Andrew at the Talpa rental. But sent where? How? Could DEM be Darcy Elizabeth McClain? Maybe.

She punched up a LANL phone list. Four DMs on the directory, but no DEM. *Sent to* DEM. Of course, her e-mail address. Instinctively, she reached for her mobile, then remembered cell phones weren't allowed in the buildings. She debated calling Dan's agency on her office landline, but doubted LANL's digital security would root out one California contact from a myriad of West Coast numbers—and definitely not immediately. However, to make it harder for Big Brother to do his job, Darcy routed the call through her office computer in San Francisco, which in turn dialed Rita's cell.

"Hello," Dan's bookkeeper answered, her voice leery.

"Hi, RC." Darcy used Rita's nickname so she could immediately identify the caller.

"Hey, hi."

"No names," Darcy whispered, her eyes on the surveillance camera as the lens arced toward the door, away from where she sat at the computers. "Check two things, e-mail and snail mail."

"Got the snail," said Rita, who house-sat whenever Darcy traveled. "Box is filled to the brim." Darcy heard a thud. "You should talk to Charlene. Catalogs galore." Papers rustled. "Whatcha looking for?"

"Small package. Flash drive," Darcy said in a low tone, as the camera headed her way.

"Postmarked from your location?"

What a smart woman not to mention the state. "Should be."

"You've got a padded envelope here. Official-looking. Government."

Darcy's heart thudded wildly. "Mailed when?"

"December 18 from a town near you."

Had the envelope been sent by Andrew or smuggled out by a fellow employee? "Are you near a PC?"

"When aren't I? Hold on." The sound of fingers typing at rapid speed filtered over the line. "Business e-mail or personal?"

"Business."

"Only one from your area. Received December 16 at 8:12 p.m. I'd read the message but—"

She noted the time in the corner of her computer screen and cut Rita off. "Don't bother. I can't stay on any longer. I'll touch base later."

"Even if I opened the e-mail, I don't think it'd matter."

"What do you mean?"

"The subject line states, "Text Encrypted.'"

27

Rita's news thrilled yet troubled Darcy. Johnny's flash drive might be safe, but Andrew had compromised her cover, perhaps even endangered her life. She considered erasing his electronic footprints as well as any traces of his e-mail, but with all data stored on a central file server and knowing LANL monitored e-mail, it was too risky. Bad enough that the same scenario played out in her mind every time she logged on, for Darcy knew the instant she connected to the lab's network her every move was automatically tracked byte by byte until the session ended. No doubt about it: her butt was on the hot seat, and the clock was ticking. The longer she stayed, electronically or physically, the more likely the top brass would catch her.

Pessimistic about her progress in the case, she shrugged off the hint of self-pity, filled the printer's paper tray with bond, and worked in earnest to finish Gert's assignment. At four twenty precisely, Darcy printed her report and dialed the main security station.

"Hold," said the guard, "while I contact Mr. Perry or Mr. Barber."

She held . . . and held. Why would Andrew mail the drive, then risk e-mailing her? Afraid someone might intercept the package and steal it? The guard came on the line. "Call you back."

"What about Mrs. Alton?"

"Sorry, she's unavailable."

"Fine. Ring me when someone's free."

He mumbled a reply, an answer that didn't register, because the telephone number on her console had her full attention. According to caller ID, the prefix for the security station started with 239, as did Gert's office number. She redialed the guard.

"No luck yet," he answered.

"Have a question for you. What's the telephone number here?"

"Isn't there a sticker on your console?"

"No,' she fibbed.

He sighed. "5052397483."

Her heart flipped. "Thanks." Andrew had called from Walt's office, but the clue was useless now that she had Johnny's flash drive. However, it raised another question. Why did Sonny lie about the telephone prefix?

Four-thirty came and went.

She dialed Sonny direct, then Perry, but their lines at Tech 3 rang incessantly. They must still be at Z. She phoned the guard.

"I paged, but no one yet," he said.

She leaned back in the swivel chair, propped up her feet, and made herself comfortable. Her stomach growled. Details of the investigation crowded into her brain. SFI-6005-G-celldem, the file created December 16 at 8:10 p.m. Minutes later, Andrew had sent her an e-mail. At eight twenty, he'd called the house in Talpa. On December eighteenth, he'd mailed the flash drive. This made sense, the eighteenth being the first business day of the week. He'd probably packaged the drive and put the padded envelope in LANL's outgoing mail.

She mulled over her conversations with Andrew. Had he fed her a clue, something she'd overlooked? What about the encrypted e-mail? At the first opportunity, she'd retrieve the message, then decrypt it. And she had to get Johnny's USB.

Tired of waiting, Darcy switched on the lights and nonchalantly headed for the bathroom. The camera's probing eye followed her. The lens reached mid-arc. Inside the bathroom, she counted down the seconds until the camera stopped panning and started back. Out of range, she rushed to the outer door, slipped out, and strolled down the hallway, dodging the electronic eyes installed at strategic locations. She wondered how long she could enjoy this freedom before someone noticed her missing from Walt's lab.

She turned the corner. Caught in an inquisitive viewfinder, she crouched and adjusted her foot covering, her face pointed toward the floor. When the camera's eye panned in the opposite direction, she raced through the corridor to an unmarked door and knocked, but no one answered, so she slid her Eyedentacard into the slot above the chrome handle and keyed in her code.

A low buzz greeted her.

Inside, she quickly scanned the area, assessing the equipment and scrutinizing the rows of stainless steel tables. Familiar with laboratories from previous investigations, she concluded that none of the material appeared transmissible, but to be safe, she put on a surgical mask and snapped on latex gloves.

Clusters of vials, petri dishes, and cups, each grouping covered with a glass top, cluttered every workbench. She moved from one collection to the next: some green, others red, a dozen yellow, and many orange. The significance of the colors was lost on her, but she definitely understood the importance of the words written across the glass covers: "stem cells," "hybrid nerve cells," and "neural cells charged with NGF" (nerve growth factor).

On the next tabletops, she discovered row upon row of neural chips, living cells growing and thriving on the semi-conducting compound indium tin oxide. Quite a feat. From the journals Darcy had read, in most test cases the cells grew but never thrived. At a certain stage in their growth, the cells migrated off the ITO. So LANL had *succeeded* in growing human cells on a silicon chip.

When Perry answered her question about the SQUID lab, he made it sound as if LANL's mind machines were in the developmental stage, but what she saw dispelled that theory. The team had, in her estimation, accomplished their goal and moved to the next stage: implementation.

A lab log propped on a wooden stand confirmed her conclusion. Spellbound, she leafed through the records. Con and the computer heads in the prototype lab . . . now their intelligence made perfect sense. LANL had equipped them with the latest in brain technology. Wait a minute. No wonder the workers on the dock at Z-site all looked familiar; all of them were humanoids, or robots, every darn one—except perhaps for J.

Darcy wandered past a long table, the section dedicated to neural chips, and studied the labels on the glass tops. The words "Blood type o" jumped out at her. She retraced her steps. Why hadn't the cell cultures been sorted in the usual fashion according to species such as sheep, mouse, or human as in most labs? Instead they'd been categorized by race and blood type. And why were the majority of the cell cultures from Hispanics with a blood type o?

An uneasiness washed over her—an excitement brought

on by discovery but tempered with a chill. Not only had LANL successfully manufactured human computer chips, but it also seemed they were harvesting them in vast quantities. But why use this particular method of cell culturing? Why blood type O? And why such a large Hispanic contribution to the program rather than a cross-section of races? Pondering these questions, she slipped out of the lab.

She spotted movement near the ceiling.

She sprinted to a nearby stairwell, narrowly escaping capture by the electronic eye as the camera drifted toward her. On Level 2, she cracked open the hallway door. To her astonishment, Sonny strolled by. He sauntered up to a security checkpoint and slapped his ID on the counter.

The uniformed guard inserted the badge into a bioreader and squinted at the monitor sitting alongside a panel of TV screens. "Where are you headed?" He handed back Sonny's card.

"Cloning."

"What's going on there?"

"Same old crap. See ya, Mike."

As soon as Sonny disappeared around the corner, Darcy breezed through the stairwell door and marched up to Mike, her hand extended and Eyedentacard between her fingers.

The guard smiled. "You've done this a few times."

"Yes, but on a different shift."

"All clear," said Mike after he fed her badge into the bioidentifier.

Darcy pocketed her card and suppressed the impulse to run after Sonny.

"There must be a convention going on in cloning. Gert, Isaac, Perry, Sonny . . . now you."

"Sonny? Wish I'd known. I could've saved myself the errand."

Mike pointed down the hall. "You missed him by a second."

"Where'd he go in cloning?"

"B3."

Out of eyeshot of Mike, Darcy jogged past a series of labs until she located B3, but Sonny wasn't there. Shelves laden with glass jars lined one wall, the containers stacked three to four deep and crammed together. Equipment crowded the workbenches. The room looked more like a storage area than a lab.

Loud voices.

Darcy squeezed behind the shelves of quart jars. Blobs of flesh swam in the cloudy liquid, and the faint odor of formaldehyde wafted from the sealed lids. She pinched her nostrils and breathed through her mouth.

Gert stormed into the room, her large frame magnified yet blurred as she walked past the liquid-filled jars. Darcy shifted positions to find a slit between the glass containers and pressed her chin to the shelf, careful not to bump anything. She didn't see Sonny enter, but there he stood, his shoulder against the wall, his eyes red and swollen, and his nose crimson. Across from him, Gert's ample frame hugged a lab stool.

Sonny hung his head and swayed from side to side. "You promised."

"I promised nothing," said Gert in a low, controlled voice. "You knew the risks. We discussed them at length. The team tried. I tried. Everything failed. No one's to blame." Gert crossed her arms and a defiant look creased her face. "Remember, timing is crucial because the donor cell must have an intact membrane around its DNA. That membrane starts to degrade immediately after death. The sooner we harvest it, the better our chances of success."

"So we waited too long."

"No," said Gert, "we didn't wait too long. You did everything right. Isaac did everything right. We all tried, Sonny."

"Not one," he blurted, "not one damn embryo made it to maturity. Why?"

"If we knew . . ."

"I failed them. Donna. Emma." Sonny slid down the door frame and squatted.

Empathy swelled Darcy's heart. As far as death went, she'd been there and could certainly identify with Sonny's excruciating pain, a numbing void that suffocated all the senses.

"Life's cruel. I know." Gert sounded remorseful.

Isaac walked in. "Am I interrupting?"

"No, stay." Gert ushered him forward. "I'm afraid our latest grouping of cloned embryos won't see maturity."

"Sorry," said Isaac, placing his hand on Sonny's shoulder. "Are you okay?"

Sonny looked up.

"Must be the day for bad news," Isaac added.

"Oh?" Gert's officious tone returned.

"The government yanked funding for the retinal project."

Gert slapped the bench top. "Dammit! Blasted assholes. Id, I don't know what to say."

"Why would you care?" Sonny asked Isaac.

"Early onset macular degeneration. It's been my enemy for a long time."

"MD? How bad?"

"The clock's ticking. Will certainly cut my career short."

Sonny rose slowly. "That's terrible news. We can't afford to lose you. You're the best damn scientist in the business."

"I'm not blind yet. And I'm not done fighting. Funding or no funding, I'll find a way to keep the retinal program alive. Have faith, Sonny. At least, the cloning project isn't at stake." Isaac started for the door.

"Wait." Gert raked her fingers through her short hair. "I didn't plan to say anything until our next staff meeting, but the cloning project's on hold. There's been an appropriations mix-up."

Sonny went pale. "On hold. You mean killed." He staggered toward the door.

"No, wait." Isaac started after Sonny.

"Let him go," said Gert.

The door closed with a bang. Darcy used the clamor to change positions, the ache in her back and legs tolerable but distracting.

Gert folded her hands. "We have other problems."

"Such as?" asked Isaac.

"The new engineer you hired."

"What's she done now?"

"She's been experimenting with Con's wiring. I busted my ass designing his neural network, and I'm not about to let some flunky short-circuit his solenoids because the bitch thinks she's the next Id."

"I'll handle her, okay?"

"Okay. The next problem's Otto."

"What about him?"

"He screwed up royally. Seems he had a hard time controlling our whiz kid. Johnny kicked the syringe of out of his hand and it landed somewhere in an arroyo."

Darcy tried to concentrate on Gert's words, but the mention of Johnny's name dragged Darcy back to the day she found the USB in the arroyo on her land. Could the syringe she'd found and shown Ed be the same one Gert referred to now?

"I wish I'd known sooner," said Isaac. "The chances of finding the damn thing now are slim." He shrugged. "On the other hand, why would anyone search the area?"

"Some hiker, maybe?"

"The land's private property, and the owner lives out of state."

"Horseback riders?"

Isaac shook his head. "Most don't ride the arroyos. Terrain's too uneven. Besides, if anyone finds it, they won't have a clue what it is anyway."

Gert looked skeptical.

"Is something else bothering you?" Isaac asked.

"Yeah, the Miller gal."

Darcy's pulse sped up. She tried to breathe slow and steady.

"What about her? She seems competent, especially after Walt, and her background check came back clean."

"Call it what you choose—suspicion, feminine intuition. Just watch her."

"You haven't said why."

"I don't trust her."

Isaac blew air through his nostrils. "Then why does she have top-secret clearance?"

"Norm set up her clearance not me, which is why I'm concerned."

He threw his hands into the air. "So play it safe. Limit her access to less sensitive areas. Start by putting Z-site off-limits."

Gert glared at him. "If we limit her, who will do Walt's job?"

Isaac shrugged, then walked out.

Long after his departure, Gert remained seated, her eyes on the far wall. At last, the VP stood. She buttoned her jacket and went through a drawn-out exercise of inhaling and exhaling as though she needed the workout to face the outside world. A painful five minutes later, Darcy breathed a sigh of relief as the lab door closed after Gert's departure.

Darcy squeezed from her hiding place. The room had three exits: one to the hallway, the other Gert left by, and a third marked B4. She opened B4 and cut through the lab to B5 but saw no one. She had to find Sonny—and soon.

In B5, she donned a fresh surgical mask before she stepped into the hall. Her head low, as if in thought, Darcy approached the security camera mounted at the end of the passage. The lens arced her way. To avoid detection, she barged into the first restroom she saw and checked under the stall doors for feet. Her watch read 6:00 p.m. Where in the hell was Sonny?

The door swung open.

"Sonny."

He gaped. "Mill? What are you doing in here?"

"Looking for you. I've been calling, but no one's around to take me back to Tech 3."

"Perry's furious. He has Mike gunning for you."

She linked her arm though his. "What's wrong?"

"It's personal."

"Talk to me."

He broke into a sob. "Two years ago, but the accident's as vivid as last night. I drove like a wild man: four-way flashers, horn honking, running red lights. My baby girl's lifeless body was sprawled on a gurney. *Gone. Dead.* The words severed my heart. Donna, my wife, told me not to let Emma climb trees. Never forgiven myself and never will."

Afraid Perry or Mike might barge into the bathroom at any moment, Darcy tugged gently on Sonny's arm. "Come on. Let's find some place more private."

A few labs away from the restrooms, Sonny pulled out his ID and slid it into a keypad. The door closed behind Darcy with a soft, decisive thump. She immediately noticed the ceiling-mounted camera. So much for privacy.

She hated playing games, especially messing with people's feelings, but dammit, she had no choice. The case had dragged on too long without any results. "I hate to ask at a time like this, but I need a favor—a big favor." When the electronic eye burned red in her peripheral vision, she turned her back to the lens making it harder to recognize her, then swiped off the light switches. "Any audio in here?"

"I don't know. Why?" He slumped against the wall.

"Because I wouldn't want anyone to hear me bribe you."

"What's going on?"

"I told you. I need a favor."

"You said a big favor."

Time was running out. Make your point McClain. "John Horton's a good friend of mine."

Sonny grabbed her arm and drew her close. "You know the chair of the appropriations committee?"

"He isn't the chair yet, but he will be soon."

His grip tightened.

"I hate bribes, Sonny, but we both have a lot at stake." The two of them stood so close that her breath bounced off his chest.

"I don't know what you mean." He released his hold.

"No games, okay? There isn't time. Help me, and you can talk to Horton. I'll arrange a meeting."

A long pause ensued. "And what's the favor?"

"Access to *all* of Z's off-limit sites."

He paused. "Why?"

"Johnny, Andrew, Walt, Norm."

His cheek brushed hers. "Do you know what you're asking? They'll kill you."

"They who?"

"Can't let you do it, Mill."

"Not even for Emma?"

He recoiled. "That's a cheap shot, Mill."

"Sorry, but I'm desperate."

"I loved—I love her."

His voice, heavy with sorrow, triggered bad memories for Darcy. For a few seconds, she drifted back in time to when she was broken by grief, with no one to comfort her while she waited for news of her parents' fates.

A soft sob came from Sonny. "Still hurts."

"I know." She hugged him, his pain hers. "My parents died years ago, but it feels like yesterday."

"When do you need this favor?"

"Now. Time's running out."

"Follow me." He opened the door and headed in the opposite direction from which he'd come. He passed a stairwell and kept going. His pace picked up, and she quickened her stride. He ducked through several labs and into another corridor, almost breaking into a run as he neared Walt's workshop. "Go straight to the bathroom."

Darcy did as instructed. Sonny shut the door behind them, switched on the light, and removed the lid on the toilet tank. A loud snap broke the silence.

"What'd you do?"

"Disabled the flapper. Play along." Sonny stumbled across Walt's dark lab to the nearest telephone and dialed. "Perry, it's Sonny. Yeah, I found her. In the bathroom. The toilet in Walt's joint is broken, so she used B1's. She did call, but no one showed up to escort her back." After a pause, he said, "Calls checked out? Good. No problem." He hung up. "Let's leave."

At the first elevator he came to, Sonny punched the call button. When it arrived, he jammed his foot between the doors and said, "Get in. If the doors start to close, keep them open."

The seconds ticked by.

The doors moved. She whacked the Open button. With a shudder the doors parted, and Sonny burst in.

"Audio?" she asked as the elevator rode to the lower floors.

"Not in here."

"What was that about?"

"Timing the cameras," he said without taking his eyes off his watch. "It'll come in handy later."

"You've done this before."

"Often enough to get fired, but they haven't caught me yet."

She didn't ask why he timed the cameras, because she didn't care to know.

The elevator stopped.

"Wait." He placed a finger to his lips and leaned out. "Okay."

The first stairwell Sonny came to, he smacked his Eyedentacard to the faceplate on the door and yanked it open. "You go first."

She entered, not at all surprised to see stairs below but none above.

At the bottom of the staircase, Sonny checked his watch. "We've got an hour to kill."

"Before what?"

"The shift change for the guards. The one who's on now is too suspicious. We can't afford a snoop."

Darcy sat on the step beside Sonny. "When does Z-site shut down for the day?"

"It never does."

"Then why the requirement to leave at four thirty?"

"Gert's edict. Listen carefully." He pulled a small pad and pencil from his scrubs. "We're here, and the guard station's there. I'll distract him. When I do, immediately head along this section of corridor to an elevator and wait inside, okay?"

She nodded.

On a clean sheet, he drew a series of boxes. "Below this level is the final floor, fondly known as hell. You can't get any more subterranean. Windowless, but not hot by any means. The temp's forty or lower. I'll take you as far as hell's gate. From there, you're on your own."

"What kind of security are we talking?"

He held up his hand to silence her. "This is the main computer room." He marked an *X* on the page. "With your expertise, you'll need ten minutes tops to override the electronic doors that separate you from whatever you're after. Use these access codes to jump the firewalls." He jotted a series of numbers and letters on the page. "Once you're in, this password will override the door locks." He circled one of the numbers.

"Okay," she said, but doubts surfaced. His instructions may have sounded complicated to someone else, but to Darcy they sounded too damn easy. She suspected a trap.

"Even though you've bypassed the locks, you'll need your Eyedentacard and your body to access the inner labs."

"Body? As in biometrics?"

"Yes. The readers will demand everything."

"Doesn't sound like anything I can't handle. What's the catch?" she asked with forced humor.

He faced her, his expression serious. "Time. The clock's ticking the minute you penetrate a firewall. Everything and everyone is monitored. There are computer checks, audio, surveillance cameras, security to the hilt. Getting in is easy." He gave her the map. "It's getting out."

She swallowed, but no moisture soothed her dry mouth. "What are my chances?"

Sonny formed a circle with his fingers. "Zero."

28

Zero. The gravity of Sonny's word sank in.

The constant ticktock of a clock buried deep in the crevices of her brain picked up tempo, and the subtle click that reverberated in her ears became a steady pounding, like the thud of heavy footfalls on pavement, a sound familiar to Darcy as a runner. And in its own way, the quest to find Johnny had become a marathon—one she vowed to win.

She spent the next few minutes contemplating the professional risks of her decision: jailed, license yanked, her reputation ruined. Why was she here? Because of Rio's connection to Randolph? Because every baby deserved a father? Or because four people might be dead and someone had to pay? All noble reasons, but she had a lot riding on her decision, so the whys persisted.

Her arms wrapped around her knees, Darcy stared at the mottled concrete floor. Years ago, decisions seemed easy. The bureau had taught her to identify the problem, find a solution, then execute it. But for the first time in a long while, she weighed the stakes emotionally, not analytically. Breaching lab security had triggered a flood of uncertainty—not about the dangers as much as about her obligation to Charlene and the impact Darcy's death might have on her sister. Could she cope with another loss? Neither had dealt well with her parents' deaths.

Nagging guilt churned inside her. She'd failed as a sister and as a parent. Now she had a chance to set things right—if she didn't die first. It had been ages since Darcy said, "I love you"—to Charlene or to anyone. This trip should have been their time to bond and repair the rift between them. She thought of Vicky, and anger tainted her guilt.

"Here's the plan," said Sonny, cutting into Darcy's thoughts. "When I lean across the desk to sign the log book, I'll knock Ben's pen to the floor. He'll bend down, and you'll go."

"Okay."

"We leave in"—he looked at his watch—"twelve minutes."

A gnawing sensation distracted her. Her stomach growled. She couldn't recall her last meal. Oh yeah, she'd raided the vending machine, but that didn't qualify. She unfolded Sonny's map with its four large squares surrounded by a dozen smaller ones with an X inked in one—the computer room. "These four in the middle? What are they?"

"Don't know. I've never been in them. I don't have the clearance. I'm only familiar with this lab, the one with the blue door."

"Why blue?"

He shrugged. "Don't know."

"What's in there?"

"The gate to hell."

Not in the mood for cryptic answers, she asked, "Would you mind being more specific?"

"I don't think you want to know." He turned away.

Great. She wished he'd said something sooner, but it really didn't change anything; she was already committed. "You said Z-site never sleeps. If that's the case, how do I sneak into the computer room undetected?"

"I meant the R&D labs. They run three shifts, but the computer folks knock off at five sharp. Any more questions?"

"No." She removed the foot coverings on her flats, stuffed her shoes in her pockets, and replaced the padded foot guards.

"Oh, I almost forgot."

Darcy glanced sideways at him. "I don't like the sound of that oh."

"The biometric scans . . . make damn sure you obey protocol. If you screw up even once, an alarm sounds. These aren't as forgiving as those in Tech 3."

"Glad you remembered that little detail. It might save my butt."

He frowned. "Are you okay? You look pale."

"The lighting's bad in here." Don't drag this out, her brain shouted.

"Let's go." He steered her into the deserted corridor outside the stairwell and motioned to an intersecting hallway. "Don't take your eyes off me."

An adrenaline charge coursed through her, a spark of adventure tempered by danger. He put a finger to his lips and walked away.

The armed sentry stood as Sonny neared the security post. "Evening, Mr. Barber. Whatcha doing here so late?"

"Playing errand boy, Ben." Sonny handed his Eyedentacard to the guard, who fed it into an ID reader.

"Sign in."

Sonny reached forward to pick up the pen but dropped it in the process. The ballpoint rattled across the tabletop, then the clatter died.

"Caught it. Good reflexes, huh?" Ben smiled.

Darcy's shoulders sagged. What now?

A persistent buzz, followed by a red light, pulsed at the base of Ben's computer terminal.

Sonny leaned closer. "Anything wrong?"

"Not really. Alton implemented new security measures."

"Oh? What kind of measures?"

"For one, you gotta call ahead, let the lab know you're coming. Where you going?"

Sonny held up a sheet of paper. "The note says, 'Pick up SFG file from genetics, deliver to Perry's office.' I don't plan to visit any labs. Too late in the day, and I'm more interested in a beer and dinner."

"I hear you. Here's your badge." The guard turned back to his computer.

Sonny dropped his ID. It hit the table and fell off the edge. "Damn. Sorry, Ben."

"No problem." The guard stooped to pick up the badge.

Darcy clasped her hands over her pockets to keep her shoes from falling out and dashed for the elevators.

"Can you see it on your side?" asked Ben.

A telephone's shrill ring bounced off the walls.

Darcy dodged into the elevator. Hurry, Sonny. But as the seconds dragged, it became apparent something was wrong. Had he chickened out? Or led her into a trap? Leery, she looked into the hall. The guard had vacated his post, and Sonny was nowhere in sight. Feeling apprehensive, she tapped the button. The elevator doors closed.

So Gert had implemented new security measures. Could Darcy be the reason?

The ride to the subbasement ended with a soft jolt. Darcy checked the hallway before leaving the elevator. No guard on duty, but cameras were mounted at either end of the passage;

one was guaranteed to snap her, so she timed the electronic eyes so she could to evade one while the other filmed her back. Since all employees wore regulation blue scrubs, it would be hard to identify her from behind. The map in her pocket crackled; the noise sounded as loud as a gunshot. She froze and waited. Only silence. She walked on.

If Sonny had set a trap, did she dare trust the diagram he'd given her? The whole idea of coming down here was ludicrous, downright dangerous, especially unarmed and with no action plan.

Ahead, a familiar gray-white light spilled from under a door. She gravitated toward the soft illumination. The low, monotonous drone of equipment fans filtered into the hallway. The computer room.

Hesitant, Darcy eyed the wall pad. The instant she made contact with the biometric scan, the countdown would begin. Go slow. Remember, no mistakes. Sweat beaded on her palms. She wiped them on her scrubs and swallowed, but it did nothing to relieve the lump in her throat. Her hand shook as she inserted her Eyedentacard into the bioreader.

"Confirm identification, please," the mechanical voice said from the flat plate.

She pressed her fingers to the pad. No turning back now. The finality of the situation registered as her stomach flipped, but any fear quickly dissipated as adrenaline surged through her, the heady sensation accompanied by a false sense of invincibility.

A click.

Darcy crossed the lab to the desk. Seated at a monitor, she pulled the keyboard closer and typed in Sonny's codes. The rapid key clicks drowned out the hum of equipment. The random alphanumeric passwords helped her jump the firewalls and immediately override the electronic doors, or so the program said. The true test would come later.

"With your expertise, you'll need ten minutes tops . . ." Sonny had assured her. Darcy signed off in six.

She left the computer room and weaved her way through a maze of white hallways. In her ears, an illusory ticktock struck off the seconds to discovery. The ticking clock mimicked her erratic heartbeat. Whenever possible, she kept her back to the surveillance cameras and walked casually through the corridors, her padded feet noiseless on the tile.

"If you're out there watching, Gert," Darcy whispered, "I bet you're cackling at my boldness, or my stupidity."

Light washed the floor, and Darcy looked up. At the end of the hall loomed security, the post sandwiched between S1 and S2. Both labs faced the blue door, exactly as Sonny had drawn them on his map. The doubts about him that pricked the corners of her mind eased a little; so far, he hadn't let her down.

As she drew near the guard station, the faint scent of cheap aftershave floated on the dry air. Outside S2, the lab closest to her, she spotted a water fountain. The urge to sneak a drink overwhelmed her, but it was too close to the security post. She ducked into a janitor's closet, the tight recess almost too small to hold her along with the stored cleaning supplies, and left the door cracked open an inch so she could check her surroundings. From what she saw, the only obstacle between her and the inner labs was the guard. And now that she'd overridden the firewalls, only God knew how long she had before someone searched for her. She had to think of a plan to outsmart him, and fast.

Loud, cheerful voices floated down the hallway.

"Evening, Dr. Perry."

So this was where Perry hung out.

"Been quiet around here?"

"Yes, sir," said the guard. "Not a peep, except for Gert and Isaac coming by."

"See ya tomorrow, Robby."

"'Night, sir."

A long hush.

Darcy scurried out of the janitor's closet and crept along the wall. Robby's abrasive tone as he spoke on the phone interrupted the quiet. She poked her head around the corner. The guard had his back to her, the telephone receiver planted to his ear as he swapped football scores. She tiptoed to S2 and skimmed the security procedures stenciled on the lab door. On purpose, she completed steps one and two but omitted three. The breach in protocol triggered a high-pitched blast.

"What the shit?" shouted Robby.

Darcy ran back to the janitor's closet and slid inside like a first-base man, but she misjudged the distance and smacked her head on a shelf. Pain shot through her temples. She clapped a hand over her mouth to stifle a groan.

Leather soles slapped the tiled floor, and khaki pant legs ran past her hiding place. The running stopped. Shortly thereafter, the alarm died and again brown loafers passed within inches of her blind. Darcy tensed.

"Yes, I'm checking things out," said Robby. "Yes, it's S2 again. I know someone had to trip the alarm, but there's no one here. I've been on shift since seven and have only seen you, Isaac, and uh, Perry. I'm standing in front of the door right now. Okay. Sure, I'll call for backup." He sighed. "Bitch thinks I can't handle my job. I'll show her. Screw backup—I'll investigate myself. Step one . . ." Robby read aloud as he followed the instructions posted on the door.

As soon as he entered Lab S2, Darcy shot into action. She flew by the empty guard station and up to the blue door. Hurry. Hurry. No, slow down. Stick to the protocol. Between steps, she cursed softly, gritted her teeth, and glanced furtively over her shoulder, frantic for the system to respond. Her heart hammered.

"Identity confirmed."

She yanked on the handle, but the blue door wouldn't budge. Why wouldn't it open?

Behind her came a soft whoosh: the hydraulic door to S2. Robby was coming back.

Her heartbeat spiked. Hurry!

A familiar click.

Darcy exhaled through her mouth, wrenched open the heavy blue door, and dove in. The door closed slowly and silently behind her. She leaned against the wall and inhaled long and deep until her heart rhythm leveled out.

"I'm in."

29

Unsure of her surroundings, Darcy waited until her eyes adjusted to the dark before she proceeded down the corridor. The blackness mystified her; Sonny said Z-site ran three shifts, so where was everyone? After standing in the murky passage for a while, she felt the temperature drop to near freezing. A shiver pricked the hairs on her neck. Air hissed from the overhead vents, the promise of heat welcoming, but instead the ventilation system blew cold air.

Loud voices penetrated from the other side of the blue door. Darcy pressed her ear to cold steel to listen. Sounded like Robby and another man. From what she heard, they planned to conduct a thorough search of the area. Time to move on. Their muffled voices faded as she started down the hallway, with no idea where the passage led.

She hadn't gone far when light splashed across her path,

the sudden illumination startling. She swept the hallway with a wary gaze. The bright glow radiated from a string of recessed halogens installed along the baseboard, their brilliance tripped by motion sensors. At the corner, she checked her back. Behind her, the spotlights dulled, then died, plunging the corridor in blackness.

Since Sonny knew nothing about hell—or so he said—she had no map, leaving her to scurry aimlessly through the dismal labyrinth until she stumbled upon something important. Another corner, another glance back. This time she imagined Gert hot on her trail, but no one gave chase.

She sniffed the sterile, ionic air. Tension built inside her. Too easy. The words blared in her head. She spun. Walls surrounded her. Thinking these panels might operate automatically like those on the upper floors, she raked a fingernail over the smooth surface, hunting for a crack, any place to insert her ID, but the finish felt smooth and seamless.

A red flash startled her.

Darcy whirled, and her heart leaped.

The red light pulsed again.

The red glare came from an emergency exit at the end of the passage. She walked toward the light. Through the glass inset, she saw a stairwell that only wound down. She wondered why nothing ever seemed to go up. Below the small window was a warning: "If opened an alarm will sound." But what captured her attention was the floor plan engraved in the metal door. Meant to indicate an escape route, the tiered layout showed three floors: offices on the current level, labs a level down, and a cellar designated only subbasements. How deep had the government excavated? No wonder Sonny referred to the area as hell. But how do I get into hell?

Absorbed in memorizing the diagrams, she forgot about Robby until in his gravelly tone he said, "Jack, down here."

"Damn, it's cold in this joint," said Jack. "I haven't been down here in ages. Don't even know my way around anymore. You really think there's an intruder?"

"Nope. The old bat's paranoid."

Darcy broke into a jog, her stocking feet noiseless on the hard floor. She looked from side to side, hunting for a hiding place in this long hall of nothingness. Where were these offices? She spotted an elevator and sprinted toward it. A sign beside the keypad read "Follow instructions in precise order." Fifteen steps! She gasped. Calm down. Go slow. She groped for her Eyedentacard, dropped it, and stooped to retrieve the ID.

"You hear something?" Robby's voice echoed dangerously close.

"Nope," said Jack.

Darcy was about to feed her ID into the reader when Robby's laughter shattered her concentration, so she abandoned her attempt to access the elevator and fled, horrified when the corridor abruptly ended. She spun, ready to face the guards. That's when she saw the light, a yellow bar several feet wide at the base of the wall. The offices? She bent down.

A soft breeze caressed her face. She clawed the glossy panels with her numb fingers until her thumbnail snagged the port. She rammed her Eyedentacard into the vertical recess.

"Okay, Robby, where's this intruder you promised?"

Darcy shifted her weight from one foot to the other. Come on. Open. Hurry.

"Told you, the old broad's batty," Robby said, chewing his words.

The wall panels slowly broke apart.

"Hear that?"

"I said no, there's no intruder," Robby said.

Inside the office area, Darcy pumped the close button. The wall partitions sealed silently, and small, recessed spots shone from above, providing enough light to guide her way but not enough to read by. Eight glass-enclosed suites occupied the space, four on either side with a hall through the center. All had names stenciled on the entrances, and all had concrete floors stained maroon, but despite the warm color, the floor was cold and damp beneath her feet.

At the end of the hall, a red EXIT sign burned. Two ways in and two ways out. Good. Darcy hated feeling trapped. It was the same claustrophobic feeling she had when parking in an underground garage in California. Only took one earthquake to imprint a certain brand of fear, and she'd certainly experienced her share living in San Francisco.

She began with Gert's suite, the office cluttered with furniture and boxes, the large ones empty, the smaller ones filled with books, office supplies, and computer paper. Darcy searched quickly, hunting for anything with Johnny's or Andrew's name. Beside the telephone console sat a plastic file box. She opened the lid and thumbed through the DVDs but resisted the urge to peek at the data—too dangerous and no time.

She shut the file and sifted through interoffice memos and outside correspondence. On the last stack she found a letter penned by Brian Steele, the charismatic but brutally ruthless chairman of the United States Senate Committee on Appropriations. Darcy had met him once at a Department of Defense dinner. He either made dreams come true, or he killed them, a god in his own distorted way. Her friend John Horton, the soon-to-be new chair, distrusted him. Ousted by a power play, Steele planned to retire from public life, or so the rumors went, but Darcy never believed Beltway gossip. He wouldn't go without a fight. She skimmed the text of the letter, which outlined a deadline set by Steele and missed by Gert. Steele's tone was accusatory, Gert's attached response apologetic.

Darcy browsed another pile of mail. The initials DARPA,

subheaded by TNP, jumped off the page. She speed-read the memo. "Brainwash is a Tactical Nanotechnology Program funded by the Defense Advanced Research Projects Agency." No surprise there. "This is a high-risk, high-payoff military project . . ." She turned the page. Someone had used a Sharpie to black out the rest of the paragraphs. As chairman for the Appropriations Committee, Brian Steele had signed the document.

She leafed through the "TNP Mission Statement," set the pages aside, and picked up a stack of stapled reports. Puzzled by the content, but with no time to read each report in detail, she flipped to the summary.

Supposedly, Z-site had two major projects in the works: Brainwash and Nanostart. However, only Brainwash had been sanctioned by Congress and therefore had open status. Both projects were long-term programs that required massive funding and a steady cash flow to keep them afloat. Who better to sponsor such mammoth undertakings than the US government? But why duplicate efforts by running identical programs? Why not kill one? And, why would Gert siphon money off Brainwash to fund Nanostart?

Darcy found her answer buried in a stack of computer-generated files marked D1—code for destroy, priority one. True, Brainwash and Nanostart were identical in objectives, but the clinical data in Brainwash contradicted the clinical results in Nanostart. The former was an abysmal failure while the latter a revolutionary success, contradicting everything Darcy knew or had been told about the Brainwash program. And from what she read here, for years, Gert had fed false information to Steele, claiming major setbacks, when in reality the Brainwash team had had phenomenal success, even making history with their accomplishments. Whenever Steele thought Brainwash was faltering, he'd pump more money into the program, not knowing that the large cash infusions were being diverted.

Gert's only concern now was how to keep Steele in office and get rid of the newly appointed Horton without raising suspicion.

Finding nothing else of interest, Darcy dumped the documents in Gert's mail basket and rifled through the drawers. Then she searched Isaac's suite and Perry's. Both were futile searches, so she entered Gale Clifford's office with no expectations and went straight to the desktop, a Dell PC and a flat screen. She touched the mouse. A warning in bright red filled the monitor: "Station 441. Equipped with Level 12 Security."

"Wonder what Level 12 buys me." She tapped the Enter key.

"Verify identity, please." A stilted, automated voice resonated from the computer. "Insert cryptocard."

Darcy pulled out the fake Eyedentacard she'd made with Clifford's digitized image on it and slid the card into the workstation. If the PC demanded a biometric search, then she could go no further. Stealing a person's picture was one thing, but lifting bios was impossible. She waited while the server conducted a one-on-one search of the director's facial signature against the thousands of templates stored in the lab's central database. She drummed her fingers on her thigh. The tightness in her chest returned.

"Verification Confirmed."

She patted herself on the shoulder, a cocky gesture that proved premature.

"Password, please."

Crap. A public key. She checked the time. She stood a good chance of cracking the encrypted PIN by systematically trying all possibilities, but if she took too long someone might catch her in the middle of the attack. Her fingers assaulted the board, typing with rapid fire. The clatter sounded like a muted Uzi, an image which fueled the lightning speed of her keystrokes. She punched ENTER.

"Access Denied" burst onto the display. The constriction in

her chest intensified as the seconds ticked away. With the back of her wrist, she swiped at a strand of hair that fell across her cheek. Beads of perspiration rolled from beneath the disposable head guard and trickled down her face. Her optimism faded. On a hunch, she keyed the last password into the system.

"Access Confirmed" flashed on the monitor. She had cracked Clifford's personal access code, the first four digits of her social security number. A stupid mistake. Or was it?

Too easy. The words nagged her as she scrolled through the list of files on the screen. Sonny said hell had bioscans everywhere. Could they already be tracking her? She dragged her attention back to the documents on the monitor and bypassed those with the word "project" in them. After every dozen or so, she checked the time.

A file saved as Watchlist demanded her attention. She double-clicked on it and speed-read Gert's interoffice memo, copied to Isaac and Clifford. Why not Perry? The question popped into her mind as she scrolled to the next memo, where she noticed Perry's name, Deputy Sheriff Ronald Maddox, and—even more disturbing—Dee Miller, her undercover moniker. According to the memo, all three were slated for termination. Equally as enlightening, Maddox bore the title Head of Security for Z-site.

A line at the bottom of the page caught her eye: "Reference 8311TC." She clicked on the electronic address. The words on the screen sent a chill through her: "Termination Completed." She scrolled through the list of eight—four unknown and Johnny, Andrew, Walt, and Norm. For weeks she'd clung to the hope of finding them alive even though the evidence haunted her. They could still be alive. After all, words on a computer screen were not proof, but if they were dead, she could leave if only she knew how to get out of hell.

She opened a file labeled Prototypes. According to the main page, Enzo Duran had designed the Excel spreadsheet. His title was BP Project Recruiter. The subheadings strewn across the top read Name, Blood Type, Status, and Results. Below the Name caption, Enzo had typed two hundred entries. They started with BP001 and ended with BP200. All were blood type o negative, except for two o positive. She skimmed the data under Status and Results, the alphanumeric combinations a struggle to decipher.

Preoccupied, she dismissed a subtle click as ambient noise emitted by the hard drive, but the second click, followed by Robby's voice, rocketed her off the chair. She whomped the CTRL and w keys simultaneously. The screen cleared. Plastered to the floor, Darcy peeked from the bottom of the doorjamb.

Jack loitered in the hall. Next to him hovered Robby.

"What did the memory log tell you?" asked Robby.

"That no one entered E-sector in the past five hours." Jack walked past Clifford's doorway, inches from Darcy.

"You sure? No one in five hours?"

"No one according to the system."

"Yep, she's batty. There's no intruder. But since we're here, you take those four, and I'll take these four. Be quick. I'm starving."

Robby strolled into the offices on the right while Jack took the ones on the left.

Darcy slithered across the cold floor to Gert's suite and crouched behind one of the tall boxes stacked in the corner of the office. Hunkered down in the tiny space with her shoulders hunched forward and her arms pinned to her chest, she listened for footsteps, but her loud heartbeats drowned out most sounds. She waited, her breathing shallow.

"Shit."

The hair on her neck bristled. Jack stood within a foot of her. She braced herself for discovery and her next move once they found her.

"You okay?" asked Robby.

"Almost fell over these damn boxes. How come maintenance hasn't hauled them off? Empty, aren't they"

"Far as I know. Alton unpacked last week."

"Nothing in this one. Should I check 'em all?"

Sweat trickled off Darcy's nose.

"Well?"

Something brushed the box. She froze and held her breath.

"Nah—why bother? Told ya, the old bag's paranoid. Hell, security is so damn tight down here, no way anyone's going to breach the system. I've been complaining for months. There's a short in the damn door, but no one can even call a repairman? Let's go. My gut's grinding."

"Maybe I should stay, look some more."

"Why don't we eat first, then come back and tear the whole damn place apart."

The moment Robby and Jack left the office area, Darcy slipped out of Gert's suite, ducked through the nearest exit into the hallway, and watched the guards meander down the corridor. Since they knew their way around hell and she was clueless, she tailed them to the elevators where the two milled about, debating whether to wait or take the fire escape.

"Damn things sure are slow. Let's take the stairs."

The minute the guards stepped into the stairwell, Darcy wedged her foot in the crack of the closing door and paused on the landing until their voices faded. She leaned over the railing. Below, their heads dropped from view, and their muffled footsteps died. She wanted to put distance between herself and the men but not lose them.

A level down, the stairs ended in a small anteroom with glass on three sides. One transparent panel sported a large red circle with "Level 12 Security" stenciled in the center. She took out her Eyedentacard and Gale's ID. If her badge didn't work on Level 12, then she prayed Gale's would, provided the scanner didn't require bios. But the second Darcy's card touched the biolock the reader responded, and she slipped in, confused to find herself in a locker room. She must've taken a wrong turn, but how? With nowhere else to go, she threaded her way through the aisles and maneuvered around benches to an automatic door with red lettering. The caution read "Warning. You are about to enter a sterile zone. Gown up and follow strict protocol."

She backed away from the motorized doors to read the list of instructions on the wall-mounted plaque. One point in particular struck home, an innocuous detail she might've easily overlooked. What difference did it make if she wore white scrubs or her current blues? Probably some pointless government policy.

Regardless, she traded her blues for whites and snagged a lab coat off one of the hooks. It felt good to be warm again: the chilly environment was a constant distraction. After she slipped on clean foot coverings and a surgical mask, she stuffed the soiled blues in a trash can and dumped her flats in an empty locker—as though she'd even consider returning to claim them.

Back at the sliding doors, Darcy kept Gale's fake ID handy but tried her own Eyedentacard first, relieved when the glass receded quietly into a cavity. Okay, so she still had the clearance to go anywhere she wanted, but where did she want to go?

She entered another of LANL's endless white passages. This one had a series of swinging doors spaced approximately twenty feet apart, each similar in design to the entrance to an operating room. She snuck into one. The area reminded her more of an examination area than an OR.

An engine droned.

Darcy nudged open the door. An empty cart sat less than ten feet away. Unlike the golf vehicle she'd ridden in with Perry, this one had a long cargo bed with a canvas tarp cinched tight across the top.

Garbled voices.

Denahy passed by in his signature black scrubs, his coffee mug in hand.

"Isaac, wait," someone shouted. "Need your Hancock on a PO."

"Can't Gert sign?"

"For over half a mil?"

"Give me a sec." He lowered the tailgate of the cart before walking off.

The second Isaac turned the corner, Darcy ran to the vehicle. Without a second thought, she wiggled under the tarp and crawled up the cargo section toward the cab. New plastic burned her throat and made her eyes smart, the odor nauseating. She probed the darkness with her hands. Vertical ridges slatted the length of the metal bed. Her leg rested on one, the hard steel biting into her flesh.

"Thanks again, Isaac," said the voice.

Darcy stiffened.

"Sure. See ya."

The vehicle's engine started, died, and fired anew. Denahy swore. The cart moved forward and settled to a steady speed. The gentle rocking soothed Darcy's frazzled nerves. She swallowed, her mouth parched from the dry air circulating through the basement. The cart rumbled on.

"Isaac, stop." Gert's masculine voice blasted through the monotonous drone.

The vehicle braked abruptly.

Darcy's head hit metal. She winced.

"Did you find our intruder?" Sarcasm rang in Isaac's voice.

"No, but if we don't find the person soon, I'm pulling the plug on all new hires."

"As in deactivating their biobadges?"

"Precisely. Then I'm sending security to round them up."

Not the news Darcy wanted to hear.

A long silence followed.

"Any news on Horton?" asked Isaac.

"The accident has been arranged."

A sick feeling gripped Darcy's stomach. Trapped in here, she couldn't even warn him.

"Now, about Steele's visit . . ." said Gert.

The cart leaned to one side as someone climbed aboard—most likely Gert.

"I'm listening," said Isaac, waiting for her to continue her sentence.

Gert didn't answer. "Where're you headed?"

"The cryotorium."

The word sparked Darcy's curiosity.

"I don't want any mention of Con IV to Steele. If he has even an inkling . . ." said Gert as the cart started to move again.

"I know. I'm head of the project, remember? When does he arrive?"

Brian Steele? Arriving here? Interesting.

"Nine sharp," said Gert, "and this time make an effort to show up for the meeting. At this stage, we can't afford to blow it."

"Did you flag me down for this?"

"I flagged you down because you have a knack for avoiding messes, not facing them. I just hope nothing comes up while Steele's here, like that blasted Duran mess."

Isaac swore. "Forget Duran and let's move on."

"Or the time the Japanese tried to steal our secrets."

"I fixed that too, remember? No unauthorized persons will get into our buildings or databases again."

Gert snorted. "On another subject, convincing Brian to fork over more money when we've met our goal is dangerous."

"Why? We've done it a million times before," said Isaac. "Besides, if I recall correctly, only the two of us are clued in this time, so there shouldn't be any leaks. If there are, either you screwed up or I did, and I don't plan to be the one."

Gert snapped back, "Neither do I."

30

The cart undulated as Gert clambered out of the idling vehicle. "Remember, don't stick me with Steele. Be there. Oh, we changed conference . . ."

Darcy strained to hear the rest of the sentence, but tires squealed as the cart sped off. Minutes later, the vehicle came to a sudden stop.

"Hey, Luke, got them ready?" Isaac shouted.

"You in a hurry?" Luke yelled back. "Thought I'd drive over, give you a hand unloading."

"Why not? I never cared much for Gert's dog and pony shows."

"What?"

"Nothing. Let's load."

Load? Darcy's hand flew to her chest, as though to silence her throbbing heart. She wiggled over the metal ridges to the far corner of the truck bed and curled into a tight ball, her body buried in the darkness.

Footsteps, one pair heavier than the other, trooped down the side of the cart to the rear compartment. Someone lifted the edge of the tarp, and light stabbed Darcy's black world. "Should I yank the cover back?"

"No," said Isaac. "Leave the tailgate down and tie off your end. We'll slide them in."

Silence.

A powerful urge to crawl out and hide somewhere safer engulfed her, but where? Besides, if she planned to breach the lowest levels of hell, what better way than to hitch a ride with Isaac? Or so she hoped.

Steel clanged. Casters rattled over tile.

Gurneys? With her cheek pressed to the truck bed, Darcy stared at the open tailgate, not knowing what to expect next. Faint light invaded the cargo space. It vanished, blocked by something dark, its shape and size indiscernible.

"Slide yours in first. Right side." Isaac's voice echoed through the cavity. "Want some help? Aligning the stretcher with the runners can be tricky."

Metal struck metal, the sharp sound deafening. A black form was launched into the space alongside Darcy, forcing her to scoot to the left, but not for long. Another mass shot in, sandwiching her between the two forms, so close her shoulders pressed against both. The flap fell into place, and someone tied off the tarp, leaving a hairline of light across the rear of the bed.

"Ready to roll?" asked Isaac.

"Want me to shut the tailgate?"

"No, it'll drain better open. One's frozen."

"Good point," said Luke.

Drain? Frozen? Darcy shuddered.

A slight jolt rocked the cart as the vehicle surged forward. Panic swept over her. Was this how it felt to be buried alive? She lay there in the blackness, feeling drained of emotion and exhausted. No sleep and nothing to eat for an entire day, functioning on sheer adrenaline and the will to find Johnny; everything had taken its toll.

She prodded the form to her left; it felt icy-cold and hard. Then the one to her right, which was soft and warm. Both were encased in rubber. Body bags? Condensation dampened her scrubs. Was the warm one a fresh kill? The thought alarmed her. She detected no odors from the forms, just a faint, sweet fragrance when Isaac pushed his stretcher into the truck bed. She prayed the scent was his aftershave and hadn't come from the lifeless figure beside her.

Darcy flashed on a disturbing realization and recoiled. Days ago, while surfing LANL's intranet, she'd read an article on the lab's role in germ warfare. What if . . . ? No. But the ugly possibilities persisted. Grotesque pictures loomed in her mind's eye: people infected with smallpox, anthrax, or much worse, DLZ, a mutated strain of a virus grown by her own government to wage war on bioterrorism. The viral permutation was guaranteed to kill within hours of exposure, the airborne virus so potent, breathing alone proved fatal.

She dug in her pockets for soiled gloves, then remembered she'd tossed them in the trash, so she rubbed her hands on her scrubs bottoms, yanked the surgical mask from around her neck, and slapped it over her mouth and nose. To keep from touching the forms, she crossed her arms tightly across her chest. Fear coursed through her. She wiggled toward the tailgate, which took acrobatic skill, and gulped fresh air.

The cart stopped. The men's voices rose and died. Silence.

She poked her head out the open gate. Certain she was alone, Darcy squirmed from the cart and crouched beside the bumper. Isaac had parked across from a glass-enclosed laboratory. She waited and watched. When no one showed, she dashed to a door marked CRYOGENICS and thrust her ID into the key slot, hoping Gert hadn't pulled the plug on new hires, for Darcy doubted that Gale's fake credentials, without the bios, would admit her to this level.

A metallic click.

Inside, light gleamed off the tiled walls and reflected off the stainless steel tanks lined up against the back wall, the containers similar in design to common thermos bottles, only much larger in size. In front of them smaller bottles were housed. These she recognized from chemistry class—Dewar flasks—vessels with double walls of silvered glass designed to hold various gases. She examined them. Each had a tag: liquid air, fluorine, oxygen, nitrogen, hydrogen, and helium.

The larger area narrowed into an anteroom covered with hazard and safety warnings. Darcy stole past a wall decked with face shields and wraparound goggles to bins piled high with chrome leather gloves, the kind welders wore, and plastic crates stuffed with ankle-high leather footwear. All gear required to protect a person handling liquid coolants.

Fascinated, she weaved a path through the cryolab to an aisle of controlled rate freezers, each equipped with its own computer. She stopped at the last one. According to the technical data on the box's display, the ice chests stored blood or tissue cultures. Freezeware, a cryocontrol software program, maintained the optimum conditions for the CryoChests, the freezers' brand name.

She moved from the ice chests to the sinks, each filled with pink water. Her empty stomach flipped, the faint raspberry odor nauseating. Virkon. In the multipurpose disinfectant, lab equipment soaked.

Behind the sinks stretched a wall of glass doors, similar to the freezer section in a grocery store. She walked up to one, the frosty white front icy to the touch. A plastic holder dangled from the door rack. The card inside the pouch read "Case 222. Reference #42202." She tried the handle. Locked. She inserted her ID into the access port. Nothing. Next she tried Clifford's. Still nothing. Probably computer controlled like everything else in the lab.

Across from the freezer section stood several refrigerator boxes equipped with heavy-duty casters, the long silver cartons identical to the ones unloaded by J and his crew at Z-site. She lifted the lid on one. Ice sheeted the inside, and from one corner a congealed red substance shone brightly against the white interior. Looked like fresh blood. When she'd seen these boxes on the loading dock, they reminded her of aluminum food storage containers, the kind used by the airlines. Now they reminded her of silver coffins.

Voices floated from somewhere within the room. Advancing footsteps headed in her direction. She sought cover behind an upright freezer.

Isaac and another man ambled into view. Each pushed a gurney with a body bag strapped to it and wheeled the stretchers across the cryolab into an adjacent room. With both men now out of sight, Darcy crept quietly across the lab to the doorway and peeked in. A huge piece of equipment dominated the area, its metal feet bolted to the concrete floor. Beside it, the men had parked their gurneys.

"I like your idea, my friend," said Isaac stripping off his gloves. "What do you have?"

"Scotch, bourbon, maybe some rum. Let's mosey over and take a look."

"Might be gone a while. We'd better shut down." Isaac locked up with his biocard.

Darcy waited. The minutes passed. When the men didn't

reappear, she slid from her hideout and crossed the lab to the gurneys, passing the enormous machine anchored in the center of the room.

Not knowing what the bags contained, she put on goggles and a face shield as well as leather gloves over latex. She examined the cold body bag first. Condensation beaded on the rubberized exterior, and a steady stream of liquid trickled off the gurney onto the concrete floor. She yanked on the zipper.

A milky white fluid poured out and splashed in all directions. Something slapped her. A cry rose in her throat. She clamped her lips shut, her muffled scream imploding. An arm jutted from the bag, the bloated skin grayish-white. She squeezed the forearm. The surface had thawed, but close to the bone, the flesh remained as hard as rock.

She peeled back the rubber sack and braced for the truth. Air hissed from her nose as relief coursed over her. Walt was laid out on the gurney, his swollen frame a dingy white and his beefy throat slashed from ear to ear, the nasty gash colorless. What an awful way to die. She eyed the other bag. If one contained a dead body, good guess the other did as well. She prayed it wasn't Johnny.

Her stomach knotted as she unzipped the bag. Puzzled by the presence of an inner flap, she examined the design more closely. A body bag within a body bag? She'd never seen one constructed like this. Inside the interior bag, liquid sloshed back and forth. She stood to one side, leaned over the gurney, and tugged on the zipper. Blood gushed out. Red splattered the floor, specked her pant legs, and soaked into her foot coverings.

"Crap." She ran to the sink, grabbed the hose, and sprayed down the bloody trail she'd left on the lab floor, as well as the pool of red beneath the gurney.

Whoosh.

She whirled around. The central cooling system had kicked

on. A long hiss followed as the HEPA filtration units sucked moisture from the already dry air.

In a cabinet, she found clean foot guards. With three on each foot and fresh latex gloves, she returned to the gurneys. This time she stood clear of the zippered opening and freed the body from its rubberized grave.

"Oh my God! No!"

Darcy staggered backward, eyes fixed on his ghostly features. Her stomach roiled. The urge to vomit overwhelmed her. She clapped a hand over her mouth. Weak in the knees and her feet as heavy as lead, she fell against the wall for support. She anticipated a gory discovery, but never expected to see . . . Sonny.

31

Shocked by Sonny's brutal murder, Darcy paused to collect herself. Although she hadn't known him long, she'd grown fond of Sonny, and no one deserved to die like this. Her emotions steeled by anger, she examined his body. After several minutes it became obvious something was wrong.

Darcy shoved her hand under his head. The instant she touched his skull, she had her answer. A huge lump the size of her palm protruded from the base of his neck. She rolled him over. No signs of lividity. Damn. He'd been murdered within the past half hour while she hid in the cart. The killer must've knocked him out, stuffed him in a body bag, then slit his throat, which accounted for the huge amount of blood, the reason the murderer double bagged Sonny. The killer had just upped the stakes. Now she definitely wanted justice.

Sad and feeling guilty, Darcy quickly hosed Sonny's blood

down the drain, mindful that at any minute Isaac and Luke could return. And she wanted a good look at the machine in the other lab before they showed up.

She skirted the monstrous contraption, the entire unit fabricated from sheet metal. Rectangular and approximately twenty feet in length, the long metal box had a conveyor belt at one end and a chrome cylinder at the other. She leaned inside the steel tube, the cavity wide enough to fit a person, but couldn't identify the machine's purpose. Why house something like this in a cryolab? Stranger still, it looked vaguely familiar.

She paused at the belt feeder and stuck her head into the dark tunnel. A powerful blast of bleach assaulted her. Her nostrils tingled, and her eyes smarted. She backed away. Light danced off something glossy. The glint came from a laminated card fastened high on the machine's hood. She climbed onto one of the shrouds and skimmed the operating instructions.

No wonder she recognized the machine. At her first summer job at Jason's Frozen Foods, he'd owned a quick-freezing tunnel exactly like this one. The conveyor belt fed the plastic-wrapped meals into a section called the precool stage, where they were fanned with nitrogen gas. From there, the food moved to the freeze zone, where liquid nitrogen flash froze the meals. Lastly, the meals traveled to a postcool section to process them for boxing and shipping. Surely, LANL wasn't in the frozen foods business, so why own one of these?

Darcy scanned the lab. Opposite the machine a large chrome cap projected from the wall; circular in design and about three feet in diameter and two feet off the ground. Curious, she yanked it open. A metal ladder fastened to the interior wall spiraled into a black abyss. She hunted for a Permalite but couldn't find one, so she climbed in without it and closed the portal door after her in case Id returned and noticed the cap open.

As she descended, recessed spots guided her way. Several feet in, the underground passage curved to the right, and the cool, dry air trapped in the channel turned damp and musty. The stagnant humidity seemed unusual in this arid climate, even in winter. At the bottom, light haloed the gloom. The steps ended. Darcy grabbed hold of the bottom rung, lowered herself down, and jumped to the ground.

The cylinder fed into an old watchtower. Moonlight scored the cobbled floor, its strong rays streaming in through a massive steel grate with iron slats welded at the seams. A red beam flashed across the bars. A laser detector.

At a safe distance, she stared out the grate into an excavated arroyo, the steep sides and basin encased in concrete. Judging from the terrain, the culvert had to be the same arroyo she and Ed had stumbled upon while fleeing from Cain. She remembered the torrent of water that had almost washed them away. Propelled by the thought, she leaped up, seized hold of the lower rung, and hoisted herself onto the ladder, anxious to escape the death trap.

At the top, she listened for voices but heard only silence. She pushed open the port and slithered out, happy to be back in the lab.

Isaac's boisterous laughter drifted through the room.

Darcy stole past the gurneys and hid behind a workbench. The men had been gone a long time. Probably drunk, she surmised, but they didn't act intoxicated.

Isaac crossed to the gurneys and bent over Sonny's body bag. A frown creased his brows. He straightened up. "The floor's sopping wet. Where'd all this water come from? A leak, maybe?"

Luke shrugged. "Beats me."

Darcy rocked forward on her heels, ready to run if Isaac investigated, but for some reason he dropped the matter and pushed both bodies to the conveyor belt.

An engine whined.

"Ready?"

"Almost there," Luke called back as he unlatched a series of extruded clips that ran along the base of the unit. After he freed the fasteners, he shouted, "Okay, go."

Isaac punched a button. Activated, the long metal body of the machine groaned as its shiny steel shrouds creaked upward to reveal five glass tanks. Luke sauntered toward the wall cap, forced it open, and gave a thumbs-up. Isaac hit a switch on the instrument panel. A segmented pipe inched from the machine, and metal clanged as the cylinder made contact with the chrome wall port.

Luke locked the tube in place. "Good to go."

Isaac unhooked a hose from the batch hanging on the wall and threaded a connector to a tank of compressed oxygen. He screwed the other end to a coupling on the machine, then repeated the procedure on a Dewar flask of liquid nitrogen. The sound of boiling water filled the room, and a white mist fogged the air.

"Rock and roll," said Isaac.

"Glad the stack's light." Luke grasped one end of Walt's body bag and Isaac the other, and together they flung the corpse onto the conveyor belt. As soon as Walt disappeared into the machine, on went Sonny. For Darcy, the ensuing minutes played out like a bad horror flick locked in slow motion.

The bag surfaced in the first chamber, and a high-pitched whine drowned out the hum of machinery. Disgusted, she watched a circular saw slice the corpse in half, then quarters, before a robotic arm fed the severed pieces into the second tank. There, the quarters floated in a bath of blue water ribboned with blood. A square plate descended to keep the body parts submerged in the liquid oxygen until a bell sounded.

After the buzzer died, the brittle remains traveled along the conveyor belt to a black funnel, where a loud grinding sound, like that of a supercharged garbage disposal, drowned out any other noise in the room. The rending finally ended, and a milky substance spewed into the fourth vat. Water showered from above, diluting the viscous material to a cloudy white. When the level rose to the halfway mark, Luke yelled, "Release valve."

The vat emptied. Liquid surged through the rigid hose coupled to the wall port. Now she made the connection between the cloudy water in the tank and the foamy deluge that had gushed from the culvert pipe and lapped at her boots. Pulverized tissue. Nausea washed over her.

"One down, one to go."

Luke's levity angered her.

"Remember the Maddox debacle?" said Luke. "Twenty-five in one night. What a mess."

Twenty-five people? The words blared in Darcy's brain. She recalled the thick mud she and Ed had trooped through to reach the concrete gulch. Could that have been the night they killed the twenty-five?

"I blame Enzo Duran, not Maddox, for the twenty-five," said Isaac.

Darcy sat forward. Maddox and Enzo Duran? Who wasn't involved?

"Fire's easier and cleaner," Luke said, "but the damn government screwed us by outlawing burning."

"Regardless, burning is a bad idea. Only raises suspicion, and we don't need the publicity."

The circular saw ripped through rubber, carving Sonny's body in half. Blood dripped from the serrated blade. Another cut came, and red spattered the glass. Darcy turned away. He's with Emma now. But the thought was no real consolation.

Keys jingled.

"Do you mind tearing down? The shift change is coming."

Isaac waved. "Go on. One final flush, and I'm done for the night."

In the distance, a door banged.

The water in the glass vat cleared. All signs of Sonny washed away.

A sharp clang snapped Darcy to attention.

Another clang as Isaac raised a second handle on the wing-shaped shrouds that rose above the machine and locked it in place. Done on one side, he came around to where she hid and shut down the section nearest her. Black scrub pants sailed by her. If he bent down, he'd be eyeball to eyeball with her. The muscles in her temples twitched.

Bang.

Isaac disconnected the stainless steel conduit from the wall port, and the pipe coiled back into the pulverizing machine. Next, he detached the hoses from the gas cylinders, as well as the unit, and stored them beside the sink. He wheeled the gurneys into a tiled room to hose them down.

Disinfectant wafted into the lab. Darcy pinched her nose to stifle a sneeze.

A telephone rang.

Isaac pivoted, the hose in his hand, and showered the lab. "Shit." He cranked off the nozzle spray and squinted at the monitor alongside the wall console. Words pulsed on the screen, too far off for Darcy to read. Isaac shook his head and let the phone ring. "Not in the mood, Gert."

The ringing stopped.

He toweled off the gurneys, washed his hands, and snatched up the wall receiver. "Is Steele in the building? Really, he's still here? Hmm, they're taking their time this go-around. Yeah, I know. The bitch called, and I ignored her. It's my turn to do rounds in hell. I could use some help. Say ten minutes or so? Yeah, meet me in cryo." He hung up and returned to the adjacent lab.

So she wasn't in hell yet, but she soon would be with Isaac as her ticket. Darcy crawled from under the workbench and snuck to the lab door. In the outer room, she moved stealthily to the glass wall and checked the hallway beyond, the passage as dead as a morgue. She slipped out of the lab, jogged to Isaac's vehicle, and squeezed between the open tailgate and the tarp. In the pitch-black, she listened to her heart throb until her mind took up a debate.

Twenty-five people murdered. A darn good reason to abandon her plan and get the heck out of Z-site. But how? She hadn't a clue how to find the nearest exit without Isaac or Sonny, and with him dead she had no option but to stick close to the enemy.

Sonny. Guilt pricked at her. She thought he'd lured her into a trap when, in truth, she'd probably led him to his death. No wonder he hadn't shown up in the elevator. Now, they were certainly on to her as well. The clock in her head stopped, the hands suspended in time.

A shout jump-started Darcy's heart. "Anything new in cryo?" She immediately recognized Perry's voice.

"Nothing you don't know about," said Isaac.

The cart ground into gear. Neither Perry nor Isaac said much on the miserable journey to hell. For her, the trip lasted an eternity. Her eyes watered and her nose burned from the new plastic. The temperature dipped. Her teeth chattered, and her body trembled, made worse by damp scrubs and the wet truck bed; the leftover condensation was from Walt's body bag.

The vehicle skidded to a stop.

Over the dull ring in her head, Perry said, "My turn."

A buzz sounded. Security, she presumed.

The cart moved forward, braked, and drove on, the change in the floor grade obvious. The vehicle bumped over a rise, veered sharply to one side, then the ride leveled out. Minutes later, the driver killed the engine, and the men climbed out. In seconds, their voices grew faint.

Afraid of losing them if she waited too long, Darcy wiggled out of the cargo compartment to find herself in a room about ten feet by ten feet. Opposite the parked cars were two doors, one marked MEN, the other WOMEN. Lockers most likely. She tiptoed into the men's room and crouched behind a partition.

Isaac and Perry sat on a steel bench with their backs to her. She glanced up. The orange and black biohazard symbol over the glass-enclosed chamber in front of the men confirmed her fears. This was a lot more than she had bargained for and damn dangerous.

Isaac kicked off his disposable foot coverings and looped his thumbs into the waistband of his scrubs, his movements fluid and confident in contrast to Perry's short, jerky motions. With his back to Isaac, Perry slipped off his scrub pants. He appeared ill at ease in his briefs and averted his gaze from Isaac, who stood motionless and completely naked as though making up his mind about his next move. She couldn't blame Perry for being self-conscious; God had cheated him and endowed Isaac in every imaginable way.

Impatient as to the holdup, Darcy transferred her weight to her other leg. A light near the glass-enclosed chamber turned green, and the mechanized door opened. The men filed in. The minute the computerized entrance closed, water cascaded from the ceiling. The spray changed from clear to a burnt orange before becoming clear again. When the shower stopped, the men moved into another chamber. The glass fogged. Once this lifted, the compartment was empty.

Darcy vacillated. Maybe she should stay put and wait for them to return, but what if they left by another exit? Or the automatic door sealed shut, cutting her off from following?

She stripped in a hurry, not keen on wandering around buck naked. She already felt vulnerable enough without her gun.

She hurried into the first chamber. Tepid water washed away the chill rooted in her bones. The bath grew warmer as the orange liquid spewed over her. The amber solution smelled like Betadine® laced with Lysol. The rinse spray cleared, and the water cooled.

Dry after a stint in an ultraviolet cell, she exited the compartment and found herself in a centralized locker room. So much for privacy. She rummaged through a unisex bin, found a workable size, and tore the seal on a plastic bag marked Sterile Wrapped. After several grueling minutes, she managed to tug on the skin-tight unitard and drag the hood over her head, no easy feat especially with damp hair. She stared into the full-length mirror. The outfit left nothing to the imagination, but anything beat stepping out in her birthday suit.

In the neighboring room, she paused to examine the gear hanging from the wall hooks. The hazard garments told her just how dangerous this investigation had become. Apprehension rippled down her spine, and her stomach knotted. Her gaze shifted from the equipment to the frosted entrance. She swallowed hard and inhaled deeply. Darcy never knew what horrors awaited her when she suited up for a hot zone.

32

Before she suited up, Darcy read the instructions posted on the wall. This was no time to be cocky; she knew from experience that mistakes in this business could be fatal, so she observed strict protocol. Over the spandex unitard, she yanked on an ultra-thin one-piece disposable scrub garment with full-cut legs. Sticky tabs closed the front opening, and strips of tape sealed the arm and pant cuffs. On her feet she wore thick cotton socks, the soles and ankles plastic coated. She wiggled her feet into white space booties, the soles rubberized. Next on the list, the spacesuit—in this case, white. And everything had to be sterile.

Darcy located the smallest size and inspected the suit, amazed by its lightweight design despite the impermeable lining, sewn-in insulated gloves, and attached hood. The white visor and helmet were shatter-proof plastic and the face shield bullet-proof Plexi, according to the labels. On the hood's exterior two dials protruded; controls of some kind, and inside a built-in audio set. Sewn across the breast pocket in bright yellow was "Prototype." This suit looked identical to the ones hanging in the locker, so she pulled it on, zipped and snapped the front placket, then scrutinized herself in the wall mirror to be sure she'd securely fastened all openings.

Ignoring the mandate to take her temperature, she brushed past the bins of sterile-wrapped thermometers to a metal box crammed with oxygen canisters. BACKUP SUPPLY, the sign read. Backup for what? Each tank had its own harness. She slipped her arms through the loops and hoisted the container into place, the compact canister remarkably light. She retrieved an extra to haul along. The instructions claimed each bottle lasted an hour, sufficient air for one person to make it from the lockers to the main lab. But where was the main lab, and what if the oxygen ran out first? With the helmet off, who knew what airborne contaminants floated through the atmosphere?

That thought dogged her as she approached the double doors, her anxiety heightened by the ominous black and orange biohazard symbol mounted over the entrance. A queasy feeling engulfed her. Anxiety? Fear? Like Dan once said, fear sharpened the senses, wired reflexes, and fueled brain cells—none of which meant a damn to her now.

Following instructions, she waited on the rubber mat that stretched across the double entrance. The floor lit up. Seconds later, the opaque panels opened. She braced herself, not sure what lay beyond, but all she heard was her pounding heart.

Flexible hoses automatically dropped from the ceiling. Their sudden appearance startled her. She snagged a line and with a quick twist attached the tube to her helmet. The narrow hose filled with oxygen, and her labored breathing eased to a rhythmic rise and fall as the suit billowed with cool air. If piped oxygen was available, then why carry tanks?

Darcy crossed the threshold into a room bathed in ultra-violet light. "Bug rays," Dan had called them. "They'll kill every damn virus known and unknown that hitches a ride." She proceeded through the amber rays to another set of double doors. A few feet from them, the panels parted, and a short hallway opened in front of her.

To her left a frosted glass wall obstructed her view. On her right, behind thick glass, colored lights blinked and yellow waves undulated from the darkness. Security command center or main computer room? No, wrong kind of equipment.

Since no one manned the post, Darcy moved in for a closer look. The bank of displays reminded her of an ICU monitoring station. Numbers flashed on every screen, one through one hundred, but she saw no names attached to the numeric list. From the monitor nearest her, a rainbow of wavelengths rippled through the displays, each color tied to a ledger at the base of the TV: red for respirator/ventilator, green for ECG/EKG, blue for a Swan-Ganz monitor, which measured blood pressure, blood gas concentrations, and so on. All common ICU devices, but only once had she ever seen a brainstem-evoked response instrument or an ICP to measure intracranial pressure—unless, of course, the patients were comatose.

Strong hands gripped her shoulders.

Darcy froze and stifled a cry. The gig was up. She turned, stunned to see Gale Clifford. The furrowed brows and blazing eyes conveyed vividly the director of hell's mood, but the words she mouthed were inaudible.

Red in the face, Clifford clapped both hands on Darcy's helmet, sending a hum through her brain. The woman fiddled with the dials over the earpieces, and an angry voice blasted Darcy, "Denahy, what in the hell are you doing here? You are Denahy, aren't you?"

While Darcy fumbled for an answer, Clifford flashed a

penlight beam across Darcy's chest. The light illuminated a name tag, invisible until now. The vibrant sapphire letters spelled out "Laura Denahy."

"You're Denahy, all right. Your shift started an hour ago, and I don't care who your uncle is, I won't tolerate tardiness, do you hear?"

Loud and clear. She mumbled a yes and followed Clifford as the woman marched at a fast clip down the hallway. She stopped outside an expanse of frosted glass, yanked the spare oxygen canister out of Darcy's arms, and ordered her to take a deep breath. Before she had a chance to inhale, Clifford disconnected the supply hose from her helmet. The flexible tube recoiled into the ceiling. Then Clifford pulled the tank off Darcy's back and deposited it in a plastic-coated bin, along with her own canister.

"One tank does the trick. Remember that. And they're only backups." Clifford caught a flexible chrome hose suspended from the ceiling and hooked it to her hood. She thrust a second line at Darcy. Connected to the main supply, Darcy sucked in and puffed out air, her lungs about to burst waiting for her next hit of oxygen.

A chime. "What's up?" Clifford spoke into a small box strapped to her shoulder. "Dammit, I told you . . ." She walked away and lowered her voice to almost a whisper.

Ignored, Darcy memorized her surroundings. She counted three levels; she and Clifford stood on the second, a catwalk above. She crossed to the white pipe railing to survey the floor below, a massive arena the size of a football field with seamless white terrazzo floors and walls that butted up against a glass-domed ceiling. At the far end stood a frosted glass-enclosed area. Ultraviolet light radiated from inside, the only warmth in this ethereal world of stark white. She raised her eyes to the ceiling, optimistic for a glimpse of sky, but a canopy of white glared back, its proximity oppressive. Had she finally arrived in hell?

A blinding light burst across the dome, then morphed to a gray haze. In one sector of the massive room, a red beam pulsed. Darcy glanced sideways at Clifford for a reaction and received one, but not the kind she expected.

"Not again," said the director, her sharp tone echoing through the audio system in Darcy's spacesuit. "Come on, Denahy."

Darcy caught up as Clifford bustled toward a staircase that led to the catwalk. At the top of the steps, someone waited. Everyone looked the same in these blasted spacesuits, which made Darcy feel safe but at times vulnerable. She sized up the person. Female, she deduced. As long as she didn't bump into Isaac or Perry. As she drew closer, the employee's features grew sharper, and the tense muscles in Darcy's neck eased, for she recognized the woman before Clifford introduced them.

"Laura Denahy, meet Dr. Janet Murasaki. Everyone reports to Muri, and she reports to me. She's the floor supervisor."

Another innocuous title.

Janet smiled. "Welcome aboard."

"Remember, Denahy, be on time in the future, and you'll work out fine." Clifford walked off.

Darcy half listened as Muri rattled on about protocol and job duties, her mind busy conjuring up a scheme to reach the lower floor so she could search for Johnny and Andrew. She passed a series of closed doors. The ones closest to Darcy read TISSUE LAB, CELL LAB, and BLOOD LAB, and all were marked with an order to keep the door shut.

Darcy tilted her head slightly, trying not to appear obvious. A surveillance camera occupied every corner of the room with one dead center in the ceiling; each probably programmed at different intervals. They'd be difficult to outsmart. She wondered why she hadn't noticed those earlier.

Something brushed her helmet.

Darcy turned.

Janet had popped the thumb lock on Darcy's air supply and given the hose a jerk. She watched the line disappear into the ceiling. "Sorry if I startled you, but I refuse to work on piped air. Too confining. Put this on. Another of your uncle's designs. He's constantly perfecting things. The new units are much better than those bulky backup models."

Darcy hid her anger with a false smile; she was mad at the bitch for not warning her to fill her lungs before she ripped away her life support. She hooked her arms into the netted harness. Nestled in the straps was a stainless steel cylinder no longer than a thermos—slim, ultra-light, and unobtrusive. "What's in the bottle?"

"Concentrated oxygen. The lifetime's six hours. Same as mine." Janet showed off her canister. "There are refilling stations throughout the lab, so don't panic if yours beeps. You still have twenty minutes to refuel. Plenty of time."

Darcy inhaled the cool breeze filtering through her hood. The buzz in her head subsided. A six-hour supply. She hoped her *real* lifetime lasted a whole lot longer.

"We'll start in Prep," said Muri as she headed down a hall with opaque glass on both sides. "Two cashed out. Two came in. Perfect opportunity for you to prep the new arrivals." She rounded a corner.

Darcy lagged behind, searching for a break in the frosted glass wall. She wanted a look inside, but the chance never came. The passage seemed to go on forever, with only muted light and blurred images shining through the translucent panels.

"In here." Janet punched a button with her elbow. The door to Prep swung in. "For a scrub nurse, this should be a cinch."

Scrub nurse? Darcy's heart shot into her throat. Janet held the door with her foot and motioned for Darcy to go first. The room resembled an OR. What in the hell had she gotten herself into? What if the patient relied on her expertise to save him?

Janet patted the membrane switches on a keypad located above the wrist of her glove. "You can remove yours as well and put on latex, but only in here. Before we leave, we'll both scrub again, and the space gloves go back on. Understood?"

"Yes, but aren't they sewn into the suit?"

"No, I'll show you." Janet held up her arm. "There's a tiny release button under the cuff. Hard to find and awkward to press if you're wearing these darn things. See it?"

Darcy struggled for a few seconds, her bulky gloves hampering her grip, but she finally managed to release Janet's pair. Curious, she inspected the array of buttons and dials on the keypads embedded in the back of Janet's gloves. The right-hand one had more bells and whistles than the left.

Janet cleared her throat. "I'll take those." She put her space gloves on a workbench by the sink and loosened Darcy's pair. "Step on the lever for me." She nodded toward a black bumper on the floor near the sink.

Darcy pumped the lever with her foot. Water spewed from the faucet.

"After you scrub"—Janet doused a brush in Betadine®— "double up." She gestured to a box of latex gloves.

Scrubbed and gloved, Darcy joined Janet, who was arranging instruments and other items on a tray attached to a cart. She lifted the lid on an autoclave, fished out scalpels, and fanned them out next to a sterile surgical pack.

A door squeaked open, which surprised Darcy.

"Hi, Janet." A man in a spacesuit entered. Behind him trailed another worker. Both pushed gurneys. On each lay a lifeless body shrouded in a white sheet.

"Hey, guys. Right on time. Meet Laura, Isaac's niece."

Darcy waved but avoided eye contact. The men didn't seem

to care. All business, they wheeled their charges to the center of the OR, locked the wheels, and departed.

Darcy sighed softly. Of course, cadavers. Janet was kidding about needing a scrub nurse.

"Grab one. I'll take the other." Janet gave one of the instrument carts a gentle push. It rolled across the room to Darcy. "Give me a few minutes, and we'll start."

Darcy parked her cart next to one of the gurneys and studied the cadaver, a Hispanic male in his early twenties; his head was covered, his ears exposed, and his dark leathery skin swabbed orange with antiseptic soap. Why bother with the Betadine® if he's dead? She lifted the sheet, puzzled to see wrist restraints. She looked at Janet, who was absorbed in measuring some concoction, then back to the man's hands. Someone had cleaned under his fingernails, but the stains from ground-in dirt had left an indelible black line. Thick calluses accentuated his palms, and the skin between his fingers was the texture of coarse sandpaper. A migrant worker? Sprawled on a table at LANL? One possibility swirled in her brain, one too gruesome to contemplate. A human guinea pig?

"Ready?" Janet's cheerful voice broke the silence. "Don't worry, Number Forty is sedated."

Number Forty? Sedated? Darcy dropped the sheet. Oh God. Calm down. Think. Remember those first aid classes. But why worry? Janet was an MD, which helped him but not Darcy, for Janet would soon discover she was no nurse.

Janet ripped open a long Tyvek pouch and pulled out foot after foot of coaxial tubing.

"Looks like serious stuff," said Darcy, trying to make light conversation.

"Not when you get the hang of it." And Janet had a handle on things, all right. She snatched the sheet off the man, bunched it into a ball, and stuffed it between his ankles. "Scalpel."

Darcy tore her gaze from the man's ankle restraints, whisked the instrument off the tray, and handed the knife to Janet, who carved a neat incision in the man's arm.

"Arterial line," said Janet, "but you know that. Catheter."

Darcy saw three on the tray. "Which one?"

"We'll need all three, but start with any of them—a Foley cath to drain the bladder, another to introduce fluids, and a third to feed him." Janet sliced into the man's pelvis.

Darcy clamped her lips together and averted her eyes. She skimmed the fine print on the sterile-wrapped packages, attempting to educate herself as much as possible in the seconds Janet took to insert the catheters.

"Now the NG tube." Janet fed one section of the nasogastric tube into the man's nose.

Darcy swallowed, but the urge to vomit persisted.

"Hold these." Janet thrust a tangle of surgical lines at her. "EKG, ECG, CVP, and ICP to monitor the pressure in the brain." Janet sorted through the snarl. "Think I got everything. Tell me if I missed one." She didn't wait for a reply. "We'll hook up the IVs next." She inserted a stopcock into the catheter bulging from the man's hand, connected two lines, then handed over a beaker of murky liquid. "Fill the plastic bag."

Darcy poured the concoction into the sterile pouch dangling from the IV pole.

Janet plugged the second tube into a bottle of saline laced with lidocaine and succinylcholine chloride. "A little something to inhibit the neurotransmitters."

No kidding. Quelicin. The neuromuscular block caused paralysis. The brain was alert, but the body dead. "What's in the milky mix?"

"Another of Isaac's inventions, a chemical/enzyme compound in a glucose base."

"What's it for?"

Anger flared in her eyes but quickly evaporated. "You ask a lot of questions for a newbie, Denahy."

Darcy covered the mistake. "Only trying to learn the ropes."

"You're right. Sorry. Your uncle's neurococktail fuels brain repair."

Repair from what? She didn't like the sound of that.

"Almost done. All these tubes are awkward but necessary until we reach the main floor. There we'll swap them out and hook him to the centralized dispenser/collection system once we're sure he's stable." Janet checked the time. "Good, right on schedule. We don't want him waking up before this next procedure. Unwrap the red package, and hand it over when I ask."

Darcy stripped off the wrapper, disgusted at the sight of the ugly titanium bolt. From the corner of her eye, she saw Janet lean across the OR table, pick up something, and spin back. She snapped to attention.

The drill in Janet's hand whined as she brandished the tool like a gun. She bored a neat hole in the man's head, demanded the subarachnoid bolt, and carefully screwed it into his skull. Horrified, Darcy didn't immediately respond to Janet's next command.

"I said," she repeated, "give the button on the wall a whack."

"Sorry." Darcy thumped the button with her elbow.

The same men who appeared earlier came through the door and wheeled the Hispanic man out of the room.

"He's off to ICU," said Janet, her tone jovial. "Push your tray my way, and we'll start on the next one."

Angry and confused, Darcy shoved the instrument cart toward Janet.

She caught it in mid-motion. "Ready?"

No, but she nodded.

On the gurney lay another Hispanic male in his early twenties, larger in build than his companion. He too had worked the fields. Troubled by Janet's callous attitude, Darcy had to force herself to prep the next patient. Patient indeed. More like a guinea pig.

"Confirm his numeric classification. My paperwork says ninety-nine."

A long silence.

"Denahy, I'm talking to you." Janet's sharp tone sliced through Darcy's dazed brain. "You'll find his number on the back of his hand."

The moment Darcy touched him, his palm warm in hers, empathy swelled her heart. Somehow, she had to free him. She gawked at the number tattooed into his flesh. Funny how history had a nasty way of repeating itself.

"Snap to it, Denahy. We're running behind schedule."

"Sorry. Ninety-nine."

"Thanks. That makes sense."

But none of this made sense to Darcy. Her brain in a fog, she went through the motions of helping Janet repeat the same procedure on Number Ninety-nine as she had on Forty.

"Okay. We're done here. Hit the button."

Darcy elbowed the wall knob. Again, the two men in white spacesuits came through the door and wheeled Ninety-nine from the OR.

"Let's scrub up and put our gloves back on. We're needed on the main floor."

Darcy washed her hands, apprehensive about what lay ahead.

Scrubbed and regloved, Janet backed out of the swinging door and crossed from Prep to Intensive Care. Behind the counter sat a woman in a white spacesuit. "Hey, hi Muri," she said as Janet approached the nurse's station.

"Hi. Are the neural cells on Ninety-nine and Forty firing?"

The woman gave Janet a thumbs-up. "Neurococktail levels are high, sedative low. They're ready for the glass house."

"Good. Have them brought out." Janet tilted a monitor toward her, keyed in her password, and scrolled through a list Darcy couldn't read from her angle.

The orderlies she saw in Prep approached the nurse's station. Each pushed a gurney.

"You take Forty," said Janet as she logged off. "I'll handle Ninety-nine. No help, I'm afraid. No one's allowed beyond here without Z-level clearance."

Darcy fell in step alongside Janet. The endless corridor crooked and curved. Beneath the thick gloves, her hands sweated. Janet stopped at a mirrored wall, and the reflective panels split.

"Watch your step. The floor slants downwards." Janet propelled the gurney over a slight rise and pushed it down the gradual slope.

Darcy paused. A soft rending sound broke the stillness.

"What's the holdup, Denahy?" Annoyance tinged Janet's voice. "You're blocking the laser."

"Sorry. Felt like the wheels had locked up." Darcy went forward.

They hadn't gone far when four employees in spacesuits walked up to Janet. She motioned with her hand, and without a word two of the four took over the gurneys. "Let's go. We've got a lot to do. Wonder what's keeping Bik? Oh, there he is."

A robot motored down the hall, its movements stiff and jerky. He wore a jumpsuit, similar to the unitard Darcy had on under her spacesuit, and boots. As he plodded his way up to her, she noticed his flesh-colored face lacked detail, the features crudely painted on. The machine slowed to a halt, his head forward and feet together like a good soldier.

"Bik's an old prototype—a Class 1. Around twenty work the main floor. All are programmed to carry out simple tasks. In this case, Bik's assignment is to watch you."

Darcy's defenses went up.

"New hires aren't allowed to wander the floor without constant supervision. Don't feel singled out. We all went through probation. Strictly a precautionary step."

"No spacesuit for our robot friend?"

"No, but we spray him down every morning and evening with disinfectant. He can't contaminate anyone or anything." Janet burst into a room marked HOLDING STATION.

Inside, the robot closest to the door snatched a clipboard off a workbench. Another machine lingered near Forty and Ninety-nine. Both Hispanic men stood erect, held upright by plastic rods attached to the floor and Lucite rings wrapped around their chests and waists.

"Vitals?" asked Janet.

The taller robot handed over his clipboard. "Ready for transport."

Janet scrawled something across the page, gave it back, and made for the door. "I've found the best tutorials are hands-on, so we'll skip the orientation and go straight to the main floor. Id said you're a natural. We'll see." Darcy detected sarcasm in Janet's tone. "I'll warn you—the first time down there is a bit disconcerting, but you'll get accustomed to it."

The warning made Darcy's imagination run wild. What would she find down there? She looked back. A few feet behind her puttered Bik.

A short jaunt from the holding station, Janet tapped the keypad on her glove, and a succession of automatic doors gave her access to an automated walkway. "The three chambers we just passed through . . . each wall is one-inch-thick bulletproof glass with gel pockets in between. They're great bullet stoppers. Early on, we had our problems with do-gooders. Not anymore."

Bullet stoppers? "By do-gooders, you mean saboteurs?"

"You catch on quickly. Isaac has his own way of dealing with traitors."

Darcy knew; she'd seen his handiwork.

"But security's much tighter these days," said Janet.

Really?

At a counter cluttered with terminals, Janet rotated a flat screen to face her and keyed in a password, short and easy to memorize.

"Are we on the main floor?"

"Not yet. Through there." Janet pointed to an expanse of frosted glass webbed in green. "Everything on the main floor is computerized, and all secondary support's cybernetic." A menu popped up on the screen. Janet scrolled through the list. "But we do have three nurses and three doctors, humans, on call for emergencies."

"What kind of emergencies?"

"Precautionary. Nothing notable." Janet clicked the mouse, and the display went black. "Slow shift. There's only one tonight. Normally, we have three or more, but only Number Eight is a viable extraction candidate."

The words made Darcy's skin crawl.

"Bik, the supplies."

"I remembered." The robot sounded defensive as he produced a covered tray.

"Hold on to it." Janet touched her glove. The green rays that crisscrossed the frosted wall vaporized, and the glass partition divided. A fine mist exploded from the interior, quenching the dry air of the outer room. On the humidity rode the smell of disinfectant overpowered by one of death.

A steady drone blended with the whine of equipment hard at work, interrupted only by the occasional beep from monitors toiling overtime or the low squeak Bik emitted when in motion. Darcy's heart thumped. At last, no more barriers remained between her and the truth.

"The minute you cross the threshold, your face shield will go photo blue. It's our UV protector."

Even though Janet had cautioned Darcy, the sudden change in color surprised her, but she welcomed the dark hue; the brilliant light in the lab harsh on the eyes. She blinked and squinted. Blurred forms grayed, then sharpened. She froze, shaken by the macabre scene that unfolded before her.

A quiver sizzled up her spine and exploded in fiery tentacles that splayed across the base of her skull. A tremor born of anger coursed through her. She fought for a plausible explanation to the ghastly scene, but none registered. In her helmet, a voice whirred on eardrums too numb to hear. Finally, the persistent garble of words penetrated her bewildered brain.

"Denahy, are you all right?"

Darcy seemed to float over the tiled floor as the world around her swirled in slow motion.

"Sit." Janet pushed her down. "Collect yourself. I'll be right back. Some natural."

Darcy heard the parting shot but wasn't the least bit ashamed of her reaction. She stared dumbfounded at the enormous blue-green prison with its aisle upon aisle of glass cells, the cages identical to the ones delivered to the loading docks at Z-site while she kept vigil in the freezing cold. The only difference was that these housed human beings. How mundane the boxes looked then, and how horrific now. Over the initial shock, she jumped up.

The crystalline walls snared her reflection, threw it onto those trapped in the transparent cells, then copied, magnified, and distorted everything it captured into infinity. She whipped her head from side to side but saw no way out. Everything around her was swallowed up in glass, the panes encased in green mesh, the lasers a death sentenced if compromised. Johnny. She had to find him. Free him.

Janet reappeared, a silver flask in her hand. "Feeling better?"

"Much," Darcy lied.

"There's a plastic circle below your chin. When I push a small lever on your helmet, it'll extend. I'm connecting this flask to the tube so you can drink water. Do you want some?"

Suspicious, Darcy nodded. The cold water tamed the bile trickling down her seared throat and quelled the fire blazing in her stomach. "Hot inside here."

"You're blood pressure's probably up. I'll fix that."

Cool air flooded Darcy's suit, the crisp draft refreshing.

"Your personal AC system," said Janet. "The button's on your helmet. Ready for the floor?"

No, but she muttered a yes.

"Follow me." Janet disconnected the silver flask from the tube on Darcy's helmet.

Intrigued yet repelled, Darcy stumbled through the glass maze, her eyes searching every blue-green cell for Johnny. Acidic smells floated through the ionic air, and the drone of monitoring equipment assaulted her ears, but the ugly visuals overwhelmed both senses.

"Z-site usually cares for two hundred cellmates," Janet said, breaking Darcy's concentration.

Cares for? A contradiction if she'd ever heard one.

"But at the moment, we only have a hundred."

The hundred Darcy had seen on the numeric ICU list.

"The cubes are four feet wide and seven feet tall," Janet continued. "We seldom acquire anyone taller."

Acquire or abduct?

"Number Eight's coming up."

How could Janet ramble on in such a lighthearted way about

something this grave? Maybe there was a simple explanation. Darcy stared down the aisle to the glass cell in front of her. Inside, a lifeless body hung from his acrylic braces, the same kind used on the Hispanic men in the holding station. No. Everything she saw added up to one thing: torture.

"Come on," Janet said.

"What's Number Eight's name?"

"We use numbers for our residents, not names."

Janet's firm tone didn't go unnoticed. Still, Darcy asked, "Why?"

"Shit. The server's down. This may take longer than I expected." Janet fiddled with the micro-computer on her glove and walked on.

Darcy lagged behind. Bik motioned for her to keep moving.

Number Eight, another young Hispanic man, wore white shorts, the material molded to his emaciated frame, and cotton foot coverings. Neck and waist haloes supported his body while wrist and ankle bands restrained him. A surgical tube hung off his sunken chest; another snaked into his jugular. Both lines fed into a centralized port on the exterior of his glass cell. But what disgusted Darcy the most was the bolt screwed into his shaved head. The man stirred, but his eyes remained closed. At the top of his cell, a thin circular metal plate gyrated at an arduously slow pace, the disk in tune with the steel rod jutting from the roof of his cage.

"What's"—Darcy swallowed and cleared her throat—"what's the plate for?"

"A brain wave stimulator. We think it stimulates cell growth, but our studies are inconclusive."

Darcy stomach churned with nausea. Acid burned her throat as it surged and trickled down. "And the line feeding into his jugular?"

"Isaac's invention. Remember the neurococktail drip? The

concoction promotes new brain cells. Never thought it possible, but brain cells do regenerate, and with Id's cocktail, at an amazing rate."

A low beep.

"About damn time. Server's up. We're online. Everything's controlled by these gadgets on my glove. When your probationary period's up, you'll have your own glove—similar, not a duplicate of mine. Okay, let's start the tutorial. Pay attention. I hate repeating myself."

"Mind if I jot some notes?" Darcy asked, forgetting she had nothing to write with or on.

"Sure. Bik, give Laura your Chipie."

The robot pulled a silver object from his breast pocket. Darcy reached for the thin, oval-shaped diskette, but Bik refused to relinquish the device. "No. Wait."

She yanked her hand away, eyes on the microprocessor cradled in Bik's palms.

"Body heat." His hands closed on the device. Red light seeped through his fingers. His eyes widened, and the corners creased with glee as a smile formed; obviously pleased with the results. "Chipie ready. Nanocomputer. Human chip inside," Bik said as he handed the device to Darcy.

A human chip inside? She stared in wonderment at the microprocessor. "I know how I can warm it, but how did you?"

Bik extended his hands. Phosphorescent circles burned bright red in both palms.

Janet cursed.

A clicking sound erupted from Bik.

Janet shook her head. "I wish Perry hadn't programmed that aggravating feature into your circuits." The robot repeated the sound. "Remind me to complain to Gert about the extraction server. Damn thing took ten minutes to wake up. Highly unacceptable."

"Nine minutes, two seconds," the robot said. "Damn Gert. Damn the server." Bik stomped his foot.

Janet snickered. "And damn Perry for creating a wiseass."

"Wiseass," he said, mimicking her.

"Okay, simmer down." Janet picked up the tray Bik had set on the Lucite stand near the cell. She peeled off the lid and removed a hypodermic filled with blue liquid. A sadistic smile curled her lips as she stabbed the needle into the catheter running along the exterior of Eight's cubicle. "Donation time. But first we have to flip him. The position makes cell extraction easier."

The glass cage rotated one-eighty, stopped, and locked automatically in the downward position with Eight's head parallel to the floor. His eyelids shot open, his irises frozen in fear. A rigid probe with yards of surgical tubing attached snaked from inside the glass cube and coiled toward the bolt fastened in the man's skull, like a serpent seeking its prey. Eight howled, a bloodcurdling cry that shattered the ever-present low drone of monitoring equipment in the cellblock.

White noise thundered in Darcy's ears. Dear God, were they doing this to Johnny as well? Nothing upset her more than powerlessness, but what could she do to help the men and still protect her cover? "Can't you give him something?"

"No way, Denahy. The whole point is to incite terror," Janet shouted over the man's agonizing wails. "We aren't sure why, but profound fear triggers a chemical explosion in the brain cells and makes them more productive in the lab."

Every gruesome moment left Darcy dreading the next act this cruel bitch would inflict on Number Eight. She had to do something. But what?

"Christ, I hate listening to this. Disgusting." Janet plucked a syringe from the tray and toyed with the sterile-wrapped needle, immune to the man's torment.

Appalled, Darcy watched blood and tissue flow from the man's head into a spherical sac halfway down the tubing line. When the capsule bulged, a plug sealed the pouch, and the bloody sample shot into a Plexiglas hose connected from the cubicle to the wire-grid ceiling. The screaming stopped the minute the probe retracted from Eight's skull.

Darcy tried to hide her discomfort, but it didn't matter; Janet seemed impervious to everything around her. How could she call herself a doctor?

"Denahy, pay attention. The central evacuation system extracts the sample and delivers it directly to the chip lab—contamination-free, never touched by human hands. This fancy garb"—she patted her chest with her glove—"isn't for our protection, but for theirs. We're worried about them contracting something from us. They're healthy specimens, and we plan to keep them that way. Isaac went through a lot of trouble to find . . ." Janet recovered from the blunder. "Notice we only house males? Men are much easier to care for than women."

Afraid she might vomit in her suit, Darcy suppressed the urge by continuously swallowing.

Janet tapped a button on her glove, and Eight returned to an upright position. His red, pleading eyes locked with Darcy's. "Help me," they beseeched her.

From the tray, Janet picked up a hypodermic filled with amber fluid and stabbed the needle into the catheter. In seconds Number Eight shut down, just as if she'd pulled the plug on a machine.

"Despite our efforts to protect them from disease, we've lost several to the constant emotional drain, but . . ." Janet shrugged. "Well, we have our sample, so we're off to the neural chip lab."

Reluctant to leave, Darcy lingered alongside Eight's cell, her mind working on a plan to free him and the others. Her thoughts became clearer as shock dissolved to anger.

"Hurry up, Denahy."

Bright light exploded across the glass ceiling and a shrill alarm sounded.

Janet shook her head. "Shit. Not another one for the cryo-torium. Bik, tell them to shut that damn buzzer off."

The robot shuffled to the nurse's station. Janet watched him go. Darcy snatched the last syringe off the tray on the pedestal and wedged it in her harness. The amber liquid might come in handy to shut someone down. The piercing blast died.

Janet sighed. "Guess at some point we're all expendable."

33

Think, McClain. She couldn't leave the main floor. Not now. This could be her only chance to save them. Flimsy excuses floated through her mind. Should she feign sickness? Stall by asking baseless questions? But nothing she conjured up resulted in a solid strategy. She had to do something—and fast. She wanted desperately to find Johnny, to free him and the others from these atrocities.

A crew in spacesuits paraded by. Janet nodded casually to her coworkers as they strolled past, her attention focused on the keypad on her glove. Darcy looked over her shoulder. The brigade in white lined up alongside one of the glass cells. The shortest among them wore a glove like Janet's. He placed his right hand over his left, and the front panel rose vertically.

"Dead as a doornail," a voice said. Liberated from his supports, the cellmate fell into the crew's arms. They dumped him on a gurney like garbage, threw a sheet over him, and wheeled the man away.

"Still can't believe the Brainwash team pulled this off," Janet said cheerfully as she walked down the hallway. "You know the odds were against us. In our case, conception began with chemicals by the ounce and brain cells by the pound. Such a humble beginning, yet we succeeded. We built the very first intelligent machine, one that reasons and experiences human brainwaves. Soon every computer will be a creative device equipped with a living brain chip instead of a hard drive. What we envisioned at Z-site was a robot farm where humanoids are bred for their intelligence. And we succeeded beyond our wildest dreams."

Yes, they had, but at what cost and at whose expense?

"Come on, Denahy. We've got work to do."

Reluctantly, Darcy followed Janet and Bik into the corridor outside the main floor. The doors to the lab closed, and green webbed the glass. Defeat dampened Darcy's spirits. She dragged herself up the stairs to the catwalk, several feet behind Janet. Bik brought up the rear.

If only she could find a phone. Maybe she could call out and warn someone. Or a computer. Maybe she could e-mail someone.

"The neural chip lab's up ahead. We'll enter an anteroom. From there we go into an airlock chamber where a disinfectant mist will kill anything we've hauled along. We take every precaution to protect the cell cultures. Remember that. You won't have to do anything inside the airlock hatch. Everything's preprogrammed. When the decontamination process is completed, the doors will open automatically. Enter the lab and wait. I'll catch up in a minute."

"Aren't you and Bik coming?"

"Only one person can be cleansed at a time."

Alone in the decontamination chamber, silence untangled

Darcy's jumbled thoughts. Her plan to overpower Janet gelled. She put her hand over the slight bulge in her chest harness, reassured by the package's presence.

A light mist fizzed from the side vents and covered her from head to toe. Seconds later, a warm current dried the droplets that spattered her face shield. The hatch opened, and she stepped into the chip lab. Impressive and expensively equipped, the room begged for a tour, but she'd lost all enthusiasm after her ordeal on the main floor.

She moved hastily around the area, searching for a suitable place to hide the package she'd stolen off the tray. Somewhere safe but accessible. She tucked it in a tissue box and was standing near the airlock hatch when Janet breezed in, a smile painted on her face. She headed straight for the only sink in the lab. "Same procedure as earlier. Off with the gloves, scrub, and on goes the latex, a double layer."

"Should I do yours first?" Darcy tried to hide the eagerness in her voice.

"One second. You can't remove them without a code."

Great, a code. So that's what Janet punched into the glove's keypad before she removed them in Prep. Good to know. Since Darcy had no idea how to pry the code out of Janet, she'd have to dream up another plan to get her hands on the gloves.

Scrubbed and regloved, she accompanied Janet as she strolled the lab making notations on a clipboard. She paused beside a table covered in jars. Glass shielded the cell cultures. A small sign read HUMAN BRAIN CELLS. Janet jotted a few lines on a pad, then moved on. "I want you to familiarize yourself with our central evacuation port."

Darcy scrutinized the four tubes dangling from the ceiling, each made of Plexiglas and approximately three inches in diameter.

"Number Eight's sample traveled from the main floor

directly to this lab, untouched by human hands." Janet spoke as though she'd said the same thing a million times. And she hated repeating herself? She leaned forward, raised the lid on a stainless steel box, and lifted out a glass vessel. "Take a look," she said, excitement in her voice as she held out the container.

Revolted, Darcy eyed the red and white clump swimming in a pool of clear fluid.

"The brain cells are suspended in a buffered solution to preserve and protect them until we're ready to build neural chips"—Janet looked at the wall clock—"which won't be for another hour or so. The lab has a different work schedule than the rest of Z-site. The techs should arrive in the next ten minutes. Then there's setup time involved."

Damn. Darcy hadn't planned on reinforcements. Thinking of reinforcements . . . "Where's Bik?"

"He'll be along shortly. I gave him permission to fix his annoying squeak. Worse than listening to a person shuffle their feet." Janet returned the vessel to its box, closed the lid, and roamed the lab. Darcy studied the woman. Robot—that's what Janet acted like. Dead inside. Could she be one of them?

Darcy noticed a box of syringes on a workbench. She picked one from the stack. The hypodermic resembled the probe used on Eight and appeared identical to the one she'd discovered in the arroyo on her property. At the time, she never imagined it was designed to inflict so much pain. "Janet, what's this? Some sort of syringe?"

"They're old extraction probes. Prototypes. We don't use them anymore."

Disgusted, Darcy dropped the hypodermic back into the box. Someone had used one on Johnny.

"Any other questions?" she said with a smile but no warmth.

"Yes, one. Why is everything white, including the spacesuits and undergarments?"

Janet laughed. "We call it an Altism—Gert's anal approach to security. She claims a monochromatic environment makes it easier for guards to spot an intruder on their surveillance cameras. You should've seen your uncle's reaction to the all-white policy. You know how he loves his black scrubs. Of course, when it came to the glass cells, Gert had no choice. The patients needed UV protection, and no one offered a blocker in white."

Darcy was glad she'd adhered to the innocuous point by dumping the blue scrubs.

"Enough mundane stuff. Come over here. This is where we build the chips. And over there, in the center of the room"—Janet pointed—"is a complete neural network: human brain cells growing on indium tin oxide."

Darcy gravitated to the center of the room, where a Corian® vat housed a trillion tiny wafers of ITO. On each miniscule disk wiggled fibers so fine, the naked eye could barely see them.

Janet handed Darcy a magnifying glass. "Notice the long, tentacle-like axons and dendrites? They connect to each other to form the brain's circuitry."

Despite her disdain for LANL's work, Darcy said, "Awesome."

"You'd better believe it. The human brain contains twelve billion nerve cells or neurons and can store and process more data than any computer out there."

"Hmm." Darcy stared through the glass top at the nano-chips, each no larger than a tiny eyelash. Hard to fathom that one of these microscopic chips housed the entire workings of a human brain.

A soft purr. The sound repeated.

"What's that noise?"

Janet smiled lovingly as she leaned over her brood of nano-brains. "They're hungry. Every three hours or so, we feed them."

Darcy cringed. "With what?"

"Your uncle's neurococktail. Remember? Watch."

Fascinated yet repelled, Darcy leaned in for a closer look. A haze clouded the glass. The vapor cleared.

The brain cells that languished on the conductive compound began to pulsate and squirm with life. They looked like a zillion miniature octopus legs waving in the air. "These feedings fire the cells' cooperative chemical network, inciting the growth of neurites."

"What happens if you don't feed them? Do they wither and die?"

A strange expression crossed Janet's face. "Deprived of food, they seek out humans, crawl up every orifice, and suck you dry. After all, that's what they're made of, human blood and tissue." She broke out laughing. "I'm kidding of course."

Bad joke, but Darcy forced a smile.

"Earlier, you asked what's in the cocktail. The mixture's sixty percent acetylcholine—"

"The most abundant neurotransmitter in the body. One crucial to learning," said Darcy.

"Right you are. Add a healthy dash of dopamine for executing smooth and controlled movements . . ."

"Too little causes Parkinson's disease."

"True. Throw in serotonin, add a hearty dose of epinephrine, and you have Isaac's neurococktail, more or less. Do you have any other questions?"

"Why do you use brain cells from only o negative patients?"

The question stopped Janet. She stared at Darcy for a few seconds, then asked, "Who told—"

"Isaac let it slip." The lie worked. Or had Darcy gotten past the point of caring? Besides, what difference did it make? She was privy to much more sensitive information than this.

"You and I haven't discussed the o negative factor yet, so I was surprised you knew. As for why o blood types, we aren't sure. We've tried others, especially o positive, but for some reason o negative has given us the best reproduction rate. We're studying the matter."

The airlock hatch whooshed open. One lab tech in a spacesuit tumbled out and waited by the door. Soon the hatch opened again and another entered. Janet didn't even acknowledge their presence until both said, "Hi, Muri."

"Perfect timing, Chuck, Zoe. While you set up, we'll swap canisters."

"You must be Laura. Welcome aboard," said Zoe on her way to the sink.

"Thanks," said Darcy, unhappy with the sudden arrivals but grateful when Janet steered her away from the lab techs.

"The fresh tanks are through here, in a small alcove diagonal to the lab."

But Darcy didn't move; her eyes were fixed on Zoe, who had the Kleenex box in her hand. Darcy sucked in air and exhaled slowly. "Janet, is your face shield spotted? Mine is. Let me grab some tissues."

"Bring the carton."

Darcy snatched the box from Zoe, smiled to cover her bad manners, then noticed Janet's gloves sitting nearby. She picked them up, along with her own.

"You can leave those," said Janet. "Put them over there."

Damn. Darcy placed the gloves on a workbench much closer to the exit than before and went through the adjoining door with Janet.

In a crammed alcove right outside the lab sat two crates: one stacked high with filled oxygen tanks and the other with spent CO_2 bottles. "What's in there?" Darcy motioned to the exit.

"An emergency exit that leads to the main floor and the level below. Why?"

"Just curious. Bad trait of mine." Darcy chuckled.

"Can also be a plus—in the right situation. Turn around."

True to form, Janet swapped out Darcy's tank first. "The last one had six hours, but these have ten. "I hate interruptions when I culture brain cells. Now mine." Janet leaned forward to make it easier to swap out tanks.

Darcy ripped tissues from the box until her fingers closed on the package. Her chance to overpower Janet had arrived. Her heart leaped, settled, and raced. Inside the latex gloves, her hands perspired.

Janet fidgeted. "Is everything okay?"

"The clasp's stuck. Move over a bit." Darcy replaced the empty canister with a fresh tank but didn't connect Janet's oxygen. "Dammit. Sorry. Put your hand on your shoulder."

"What for?"

"To ease the tension on the harness." Darcy pawed at the sterile wrap on the package, the cellophane difficult to open with only one hand.

"Weird. I've never had any trouble before."

"I'm new at this, remember?"

An exasperated sigh broke from Janet's helmet, but she complied. When her hand touched her shoulder, Darcy grabbed Janet's forearm and jammed the syringe into her bare wrist. Janet fought valiantly to free herself, arms and legs flailing and padded feet thrashing the tiled floor, but she proved no match for Darcy, a long-distance runner who pumped iron. Afraid the technicians might hear the ruckus, she dragged Janet away from the lab door, just as the sedative kicked in and the central air/vac system cycled on, drowning out subtle noises.

Darcy lowered Janet's limp body to the floor. The gory image of the snaking probe burned bright in her mind. How easy it would be to let this bitch suffocate in her spacesuit, but how inhumane. Her hand hovered over the dial to Janet's oxygen tank. The seconds ticked by. Finally, she switched the air on.

She paused to catch her breath and think through her next

move before she opened the lab door. Both techs had their backs to her, their shoulders forward and eyes cupped to microscopes. She tiptoed in, lifted Janet's gloves off the workbench, and retreated to the alcove.

After a quick tutorial of the controls, Darcy tapped "Alarm Deact" on Janet's glove and hoped the membrane switch would override the alarm system on the emergency door. Her heart pounded as she pushed against the horizontal exit bar; uncertain as to where to flee if the alarm sounded. The door opened to silence. Darcy blew air through her nostrils.

The gloves in one hand and an empty oxygen tank in the other, she wedged the cylinder in the open door, set the gloves on the floor in the hallway, and grabbed Janet by the ankles. Moving dead weight took energy and coordination, especially through a hydraulic access. All these automatic entrances and exits, and she had to pick a manual one.

Safe on the other side, Darcy lugged Janet across the landing and waited for the door to seal shut before she dumped her inert body in a dark corner of the passageway. Spurred by the clock in her brain, she scooped up Janet's gloves and jogged down the corridor, her footfalls muffled by the low and distant hum of the air/vac unit.

Ahead, the wall shimmered. Her pace slowed to a confident gait as she stuck close to the glass wall on her way to the main entrance. She glanced up. Good, no one on the catwalk. She crossed one glove over the other and tapped the laser control. The green beams disappeared. With a light pat on a membrane switch, the glass glided apart.

Darcy half walked, half ran to the nurse's station, keyed Janet's password into the same computer the doc had used earlier, and logged on. A file titled Cellmates appeared on the screen, the spreadsheet divided into three columns: Cell Number, Name, and Classification.

The first ten had the designation Und. A. after their names. Undocumented aliens? She opened the Details file. Of the one hundred listed, ninety-five men were blood type o negative. All ranged in age from nineteen to thirty, all in good health, and all active donors. The words sickened her.

She sensed eyes upon her and turned, but saw no one. The computer clock read 2:15 a.m. Darcy double-clicked the mouse. The next page materialized on the monitor. Glare from her face shield, or the screen, distorted the names. She shifted position. The name next to Number Twenty-two grabbed her attention: Johnny Duran.

Below him were Norman Carter and Andrew Silverbird. Her heart galloped. They're alive! She scrolled through the list, finding the rest of the names unfamiliar until the last entry: Enzo Duran. LANL listed him as recruiter with a classification of Am. C., the identical designation for Johnny, Andrew, Norm, and someone named Mando Olvera.

She checked the time; ten minutes had passed. The sedative Darcy had injected Janet with should last three, maybe four hours, but it wouldn't take the techs that long to investigate if she didn't return to the lab. And in the meantime, what if Bik showed? He'd sound the alert, then come gunning for Darcy. She closed the file and logged off.

Crouched below the counter, she studied the dials on Janet's glove, going over and over the sequence required to open the glass cells. A nagging concern resurfaced: even if she freed them all, how many had the strength to flee, never mind fight? Regardless, she had to try.

34

In her haste, Gert almost collided headlong with the sliding door that admitted her to Z-site's security command center. She threw up her hand to protect her face. "Shit." She smacked the tempered pane. "Bet the asshole is down here with Zeb." Sure, Isaac had nothing better to do than hang out in a dark control room talking shop with the nightshift guard, which was exactly where she found him, his feet propped on the narrow ledge that arced the bank of surveillance monitors, his silhouette lit by the score of computer screens. Next to him sprawled Zeb, a big man whose muscles tested the durability of his ill-fitting denim uniform. But his most imposing asset was the cannon strapped to his hip. The guard jumped up as Gert burst in. "Godammit, Denahy. You promised not to do this again."

Isaac, half-asleep in his chair, barely opened his eyes, which fueled her ire. "Huh?"

"Don't play games. I'm in no mood. You missed Steele's update."

In a calm voice, he said, "How'd things go?"

Zeb donned earphones and fiddled with the dials on his control board. It didn't matter if he heard. Actually, when Gert lambasted someone, she wanted everyone to know because it sent a clear message: "Don't cross me." Only one problem: the tirades had no effect on Isaac. You'd think she'd learn. Still, she said, "If you fail to show up for future meetings, I'm walking. I won't—"

"The only reason I tolerate these tirades is because we've been friends a long time and you're damn good at what you do. But don't push, Alton. Now how'd things go with Steele?"

Gert crammed her frame into a chair. "Steele's pissed. Said we've far exceeded budget—again. He hinted at reducing the grant to bring government spending more in line with our progress."

Isaac smiled. "So he feels Congress has sunk a ton into the program, but we haven't delivered what we promised by the deadlines. Good. His timing couldn't be better."

"I agree. He's making it awfully easy." Gert eyed Zeb. If the guard was eavesdropping, he gave no indication. Besides, Isaac had plans for the man; he'd never talk.

Zeb zeroed in on one of the terminals aimed at the main floor. Gert leaned over, curious to see what he'd focused on. The row of screens displayed various shots of the area, as well as individual views of the glass cells. She squinted at the monitor, angry at herself for forgetting her bifocals. She tapped a button on the console, and the lens scanned every cellmate housed in the basement. With a double rap, a close-up filled the screen, the picture almost as good as being there. Occasionally, as the remote video cameras panned their respective sectors, someone appeared in the picture, but most displayed motionless images. Not much activity this early in the morning.

"Given any thought to replacing Enzo Duran?" Gert stifled a yawn.

"I have a few prospects. I'll run them by you tomorrow. It's a shame he blew his cover."

"We aren't sure he did."

Isaac stretched. "Doesn't matter. His fate's been sealed. Too bad—Enzo brought in some good cellmates."

"You make it sound like a massive undertaking. I mean, how hard is it to drum up several hundred undocumented aliens, sort out the o negatives from the bunch, and send the rest to the cryotorium for disposal? Have you read the statistics lately?"

Isaac grunted. "Yes. Eleven million illegals in the US. So tell me why he had to go south to get his candidates?"

"You tell me. If he'd stayed in the US, he might still be alive. Face it, he got lazy."

"Still, Duran was a good recruiter."

She snorted. "Recruiter—great term for a hatchet man."

"How's my niece working out?"

Gert had been too busy doing Isaac's job to ask anyone. She fought the urge to tell him so. "I haven't had a chance to call Muri, but I'll check before I sign out." She stared bleary-eyed at the screen; Camera 5 pointed at the cellblock. Someone in a spacesuit drifted down the aisles of glass cubes. "Speaking of Laura, is that her?"

Isaac leaned sideways. "Can't tell. They all look the same in those white spacesuits. Couldn't be her, though. Bik's not around."

"You're right." Gert pressed a button. The remote camera zoomed in. The employee had her back to the lens and her arm extended as she examined the multiple dials and switches on her glove. "Must be Muri. It's her glove—Prototype 888. We only made four. We retired two, and the other belongs to Bo, but he's on vacation all week."

Isaac pushed himself away from the console and hooked his ankles on the armrest of a chair. "Wake me if I doze."

"Yeah, sure," said Gert, preoccupied with the figure roaming the lab. Something didn't fit. But what? She nudged Zeb.

"Whatcha need?" The guard yanked earphones from his ears.

"I want you to pan the main floor, independent of the remotes, and with a wider angle than both cameras give."

"Okay." He banged away on a keyboard built into the control panel. "There you are. Use the ball to sweep the lab, this button to zoom in, and the red one for focus. Holler if there's something I should check."

"It's probably nothing. Isaac claims I'm paranoid."

Denahy began to snore.

"Smarter to play it safe," said Zeb.

Like a hawk, Gert stalked the main floor, her keen eyes seeking anything that moved. But her own edict played against her; all this white made it difficult to discern small details. After several minutes, she blinked to moisten her dry corneas. Almost 3:00 a.m. She'd police the lab a while longer, see if Laura and Bik cruised by, rouse Isaac, and call it a day. She glared at him, asleep and content. She'd opposed hiring Laura but lost. Nepotism had no place in the workforce.

Movement on the screen drew Gert's attention. Muri hurried past one blue-green cell after another, walking fast. So unlike her. Slow and deliberate better described the supervisor. She bowed her head and placed her right gloved hand over the left.

Gert slapped a button on the console, magnifying the number on the glass cell: twenty-two. She rummaged in her scrub pocket for her Chipie and punched up the list for Z-site's cellmates. Johnny Duran? Why him?

Puzzled, she kept a wary eye on the computer screen, suspicious as the cell door to Twenty-three began to rise. She panned to the left, surprised to see Twenty-one's cube wide open and in lock mode. "This isn't routine."

"Ma'am?" Zeb said.

"Nothing." Gert zoomed out; all three cubicles were now in the frame. The body supports on Twenty-one broke loose. The man crumpled to the bottom of the cell and tumbled out. Muri ran to Twenty-three, arriving as the straps unlocked, and caught the man as he pitched sideways. With her hands under his arms, she pulled him from his supports and placed him on the floor.

"What in the hell is she doing, and where in the hell is Laura?"

A shrill chirp interrupted Gert. She jumped.

Zeb reached for the telephone next to his computer. "Security. One moment. For you." He handed the receiver to Isaac.

"Denahy. Where are you?" Isaac's feet hit the carpet.

Gert swung back to the terminals. Muri knelt on the floor, Twenty-one lying at her feet. She leaned over and slapped the man's face as if to wake him, but he couldn't be revived.

"Laura's stranded in White Rock. She slid off the road into a snowdrift."

At first, Isaac's statement had no effect on Gert; her concentration centered on Muri. But the minute she homed in on the face shield and struck the magnification button, she screeched like a wounded animal. "What in the hell?" She jumped up, dislodged her large frame from the chair, and lunged for Zeb's two-way receiver.

"What's wrong?" Isaac yelled.

"Con, Con. It's Gert," she screamed into the radio. "Release the 220s."

"Ma'am, are you sure?"

"Don't question me. Do it. Now."

Isaac wrenched the receiver from Gert. "Do you know what you're saying? What's going on?"

"Nothing I can't handle." She stormed from the control room.

35

Darcy pored over the dials and switches on Janet's space glove. Something was wrong. Why wouldn't Johnny's cube open? Frantic, she punched in the numbers again. Nothing happened. It made no sense. She'd followed the same sequence to free Norm, just as she'd freed Number Twenty-three not ten seconds ago. She tried again but failed. No way she could break tempered glass. Too noisy, and besides, with what? Remain calm and work through the problem. But the enormity of the situation overwhelmed her. She'd endured a lot to save Johnny. Now she couldn't even release him from his glass coffin. And if she freed him, what about the others? A hundred lives and only two syringes.

She'd hunted frantically for more, rifling every drawer in the nurse's station, desperate for needles and the blue liquid Janet had used to wake Number Eight, but she'd found only two syringes in a discarded surgical pack, along with an empty bottle of blue liquid. Thankfully, the needles were prefilled, and the code on the bottle matched the code on the needles, so she assumed they contained the same drug.

Come on, McClain, concentrate. Maybe Johnny's door was stuck. With that thought, she entered the access series for cell twenty-four, Andrew Silverbird. If his cube opened, then Johnny's must be jammed. The minute she completed the sequence, Andrew's cubicle door began to rise. Darcy seized hold of the side panels, leaped into the cell, and yanked him out. He looked pale and thin lying next to Norm. Now, she'd try Johnny again.

Hurry. No. Go slow. She keyed in the series, followed by the cell number, and rapped the ENTER key a bit too forcefully. A soft whine. Thank you, God. Darcy moved closer to the ascending panel, her eyes fixed on Johnny's face for any sign of life. His head bobbed, and his swollen lids fluttered open, the pink globes hideous as they rotated in a lazy circle. She wrapped her arms around his frail body and waited for the supports to open. He fell forward. She caught him and placed him on the floor beside Andrew.

Working quickly, Darcy tore the sterile wrap off one of the needles and stabbed Johnny in the crook of his arm. His body spasmed as the blue liquid drained from the barrel into his vein. Next, Andrew. With not a drop to spare for Norm, Darcy bent over the man and slapped his face, but he didn't stir. She might as well be whipping the dead. Damn, why couldn't she have found more than two?

The intravenous shots brought fast results. Andrew coughed and sat up. Johnny's head thrashed from side to side. Darcy knelt beside him and whispered, "Rio sent me to rescue you." His lids shot open. He made eye contact, sorrow evident in his tormented gaze. He tried to sit up but fell backward, his pupils dilated in horror.

Darcy saw the reflection in Johnny's eyes and pivoted, shocked to see Bik a few feet away.

The robot advanced. Darcy sprang off the floor and retreated, her eyes surveying the area for a weapon, but she saw nothing powerful enough to bring down a robot.

Bik barreled toward her, his arms raised above his head and hands clenched to form a fist. He swiped the air. She sidestepped him and leaped onto a Lucite stand in a futile attempt to fling herself on top of the glass cell nearest her. The plastic cracked under her weight and sent her toppling to the floor. Bik bore down on her.

Darcy shot off the terrazzo and hurled herself at another glass cube, her hands clawing the slick surface and grasping to reach the steel rod that protruded from the roof of the cage. She finally grabbed hold of the metal bar and held tight, even though the cumbersome spacesuit and the gyration of the rod threatened to throw her off balance. She swung one way and slid the other, her foot guards providing no traction on the polished glass. As she glided back and forth, Darcy slowed her pendulous swings by lunging at the mass of IV lines that choked the exterior of the cell. Steadied, and with both hands planted firmly on the steel rod, she heaved herself up and squatted on the roof of the cell.

Below, Bik stomped his foot and rammed a fist into a Lucite stand. Plastic shards bounced over the floor and pelted the neighboring cells. Andrew struggled to his feet. Bik's punch caught Andrew in the jaw. He landed on Johnny.

Darcy scoured the lab for an escape route. She considered vaulting from cube to cube, but doubted she could maintain traction on the slick surfaces. On the other hand, she stood a better chance up here than she did by letting Bik chase her on foot. Once she eliminated the robot, she'd return for Johnny and the others. In the meantime, she'd free the rest. They might all die, but at least they'd have a fighting chance.

She keyed in the release sequence. Freed, Enzo Duran rolled out of his cubicle and onto the floor. Next, cells ninety-nine and ninety-eight disgorged their captives. Some prisoners remained where they fell, but the alert banded together and attacked Bik. Chaos ensued.

Darcy's finger ached from repeatedly striking the membrane switches. At number forty, she noticed the Repeat button and leaned on it. The sequence automatically computed the start-up sequence. From there, she only had to enter the correct cube number. With this feature, the process went twice as fast, the digital signal flying from the glove to each cell. Twenty. Ten. Almost there. Four, three, two, one. In a trance, the more physically fit men staggered out of their glass cages and roamed the cellblock while the others remained passed out on the floor. The lab buzzed with incoherent voices and soft groans. Above the garbled words, one rang clear: "Help."

Darcy jerked in the direction of the plea. Affirming his strength, Bik had Andrew and Johnny by the wrists and was dragging them across the lab as if they were rag dolls. But the men failed to bog Bik down.

Darcy tore at the taped seams on her spacesuit. With her legs and arms freed at the ankles and the wrists, she ripped open the zippered front, shed the suit, and kicked it aside, along with the space booties and the layers of cotton foot covers. Barefooted, she had a firm grip on the glass top. She stuffed Janet's glove into her unitard and jumped to the adjacent cubicle, narrowly avoiding a nasty spill.

Bik shuffled around a corner and into another aisle, widening the gap between him and Darcy. She'd never catch him jumping from cell to cell; the strategy was too slow, but chasing after him on the ground was much too dangerous, so she crouched down then leaped upward. She hooked her hands on the wire-grid ceiling and moved rapidly from bar to bar, quickly making her way toward Bik.

When the robot stopped to watch her approach, Andrew seized his opportunity. He twisted out of Bik's grip. The diversion helped Darcy gain on the robot. Several cubicles beyond where Bik stood, she dropped to the floor and jogged across the lab to a crate filled with spent oxygen tanks. She snatched one from the pile and tossed it at Bik. She missed, but the second tank she leveled hit its mark. The wallop knocked him off balance. He pitched forward. Andrew fled, but Johnny froze.

"Run," Darcy screamed.

Johnny stumbled forward and fell. "I can't."

Andrew raced back, put his arm around Johnny, and carried him along.

Darcy followed, with Bik in close pursuit. "Head for the main exit."

Andrew picked up speed, and Johnny fought to keep pace.

The aisle ended, and the men rounded the corner, Darcy on their heels. She looked back. Bik had gained on her. She wrenched the glove from her unitard and leaned on a button. The main floor exit panels separated. "Go." She shoved Andrew through the opening. Johnny tripped but recovered. Andrew yanked his friend over the threshold.

"Darcy, look out," Andrew yelled as the doors closed, trapping them on one side of the glass and her on the other.

She whirled, prepared to defend herself against Bik, but the robot had disappeared. Her guard up, she motioned to Johnny and Andrew to keep going.

Movement in her peripheral vision.

Bik motored toward Darcy, Con by his side. They corralled her into a corner, blocking her only escape route. She expected them to charge and drive her back into the lab with the cellmates, but Con had other plans. He keyed in a code on his glove, the clicks loud in the dead silence.

Green beams shot from the surveillance cameras mounted near the ceiling and webbed the entire entrance to the lab. Now, she couldn't even backtrack to the cellblock. Darcy wiggled her hand into Janet's glove.

"Go ahead," said Con. "But any order you give, I'll override."

She cocked her head and listened.

He read her. "What you see is a laser gate. The wall prevents you from fleeing but doesn't stretch into the lab. The beams can't harm the cellmates." As he spoke Con shifted into position, stopping a few feet from Darcy. Bik lingered a short distance away.

"What happened to your modulated voice?" she asked, trying to buy time.

"Fake. Just like you . . . Darcy McClain."

If the comment was intended to throw her, it didn't. She lunged at Bik, her leg extended, and twirled. The kick struck the robot squarely in the chest. Pain stabbed Darcy in the foot and coursed up her calf into her thigh. She groaned. The impact had catapulted Bik sideways. The instant the robot made contact with the laser beams, they sliced him in thirds.

Con hurled his massive frame at her. She dropped into a prone position. From the humanoid's expression, the action surprised him. He sailed over her, slammed into the concrete floor, and slid toward the wall. He hit with a loud thump. Before he rebounded, she punched a button on Janet's glove and immediately another. The beams that netted the main exit vaporized.

In seconds, the automatic doors parted. Darcy didn't wait for the panels to complete their cycle. She squeezed through the tight opening and hit a switch on the glove, sealing the door shut.

On the other side of the transparent wall, Con sat up. He appeared stunned at her escape. She bolted down the deserted hallway, her feet barely contacting the terrazzo floor and her eyes searching for Johnny and Andrew. Given Johnny's condition, they couldn't have gone far.

Cocky damn humanoid. If Con had been smart, he'd have corralled her on the lab side of the laser gate and not the side closest to the exit. He would have stood a better chance of catching her with this strategy. He knew she had Janet's glove. Smart move tackling Bik, the weaker machine, first. If there'd been another Con, she might be dead now.

A wall panel cracked open, and Andrew leaned out. He waved excitedly. She dodged through to the other side.

"Saw you coming." He looked up.

Darcy stood in an endless corridor lit by low-voltage spotlights recessed in the glass floor. On one side of the passage stretched a moving sidewalk like those in an airport. Overhead hung TV monitors, the screens spaced every fifty yards or so along the length of the passage. The one above her pictured the cellblock. She saw no sign of Con or any worker, only the freed cellmates who wandered the area like zombies.

"Where are we, and where does this passage lead? Where's Johnny?"

Andrew took a deep breath. "One question at a time."

"Here," said Johnny from the shadows, his voice low. He sat on the floor, curled in a tight ball. He looked sickly, his bare feet a pale blue.

"You want to know where we are? Where this leads? I think this is a quick route for the guards," said Andrew.

"Circles Z-site," said Johnny. "Goes for miles. Never would've found it without Mando's map."

She had to listen carefully to hear him. "Mando Olvera?"

"Yes. Systems analyst . . . friend. You freed him after me. Mando shot me an e-mail with a classified address and password." The tempo of his voice picked up. "Mando said, 'On to something.' He wanted me to hack into Z-site's databases. Before I did...he disappeared. Next day, I did the hack and downloaded."

"The flash drive Andrew mailed me," said Darcy.

Johnny gave her a half nod. "Proof. I could've stopped there, gone to the feds, but what if the government ordered the experiments? Approved of them? I'd rather cross the Mob. Less dangerous. Downloaded the info, but couldn't believe what I read. So I did some detective work and came down here. Someone found out. Hunted me down." He slumped against the wall, his face drained of color and his body drained of life.

She touched his shoulder. Guilt ate at Darcy for the ninety-eight left behind. "Wish I could've saved them all."

"No, not my uncle," said Johnny, the burst of energy shocking. "Bastard. Isaac calls him the recruiter. His job? To supply the Brainwash program with . . ."

"I know." She patted his shoulder. "Come on. Let's put an end to this horror."

"You think so?"

"I know so." Her voice sounded more confident than she felt. "By the way, how'd you get down here to investigate without the proper clearance?"

"Special Eyedentacard. I stole it. It's hidden around here somewhere."

A muffled sound came from nearby.

Darcy held up her hand to silence him. The noise came from the other side of the wall. If Johnny had access to this route, so did Gert's henchmen. "This might be a quick way to travel, but I don't trust it. There's no place to hide. I feel like a rat trapped in a concrete maze."

"Been there." Johnny started walking. "Shortcut."

"Good," said Andrew. "The sooner we're out, the better." He patted Darcy's arm.

Several yards down the hall, Johnny paused to rest. "What'd you hear back there? Voices?"

The question made her think. And when she did, the hair on the back of her neck bristled, for she'd just recognized the sound: the same soft purrs she'd heard in the neural chip lab. "Yes, voices," she lied.

"Oh." Johnny shuffled forward, one foot in front of the other.

This didn't look good. He hardly had the strength to walk, never mind run. Andrew trooped alongside his friend, stronger yet uncertain in his footing. Anxious to move faster, Darcy set the example with a quick stride. Andrew and Johnny did their best to keep up, but they hadn't gone more than a hundred feet when Johnny stopped again. He gazed glassy-eyed up and down the hall.

Darcy tensed. "What's wrong?"

"Getting my bearings." He staggered. "Eyedentacard." He pointed to a slit in the wall joints.

Andrew tugged out the plastic card and handed the badge to Darcy. Not sure if her ID worked or not—not that it mattered at this stage—she inserted Johnny's card into a security slot not far from where Andrew had discovered the ID.

The door opened without a sound.

"I'll go first." She crossed into a lab drenched in yellow light. "Come on." She pulled them by the arms into the room.

Three robot heads like those from Perry's lab sat on a table. Andrew was immediately drawn to the human computers. Johnny held back, his eyes fixed on the Eyedentacard.

"Anything wrong?" asked Darcy.

"Here, you look. Carved numbers in plastic. Drugs. Pain"—he put his hands over his ears and shook his head—"All too much."

Darcy rubbed the ID between her fingers. The marred finish gave away the password's location. "The numbers are—"

"No, you memorize. My head hurts. Door." Johnny weaved an unsteady path to the back of the room. "Must outsmart guard. Go to the fire exit. The stairs lead up. Escape."

"Hey, this machine switched itself on," Andrew said.

Darcy ignored him. She inserted the stolen badge into the scanner, poised to enter the password, but spun back toward the room when a chair fell over.

"Darcy, something's happening," Andrew said with fear in his voice.

One of the computers had turned on. From the center of the screen burned a human face, the features bright red. "Intruders in lab," the head said in a baritone.

The other two chimed in. "Affirmative. Sense body heat. Three violators. Report security breach."

A pause.

"Command center warned," said all three.

"Time to go. Stick close." She entered the access code. As soon as she heard the familiar click, she pushed Andrew, then Johnny, into the adjoining area and waited until the door closed after her.

Shrouded in blackness, she groped her way through the dark hall, her hands swiping the sterile air to avoid colliding with something. "Andrew?"

"Here." Cold fingers grasped Darcy's arm. "Johnny's on your other side."

"Link arms," said Darcy. With Andrew on one side and Johnny on the other, she propelled them forward.

Ahead, light splashed across their path.

"Careful. Guard," Johnny said, leaning on Darcy.

"Stay with him. I'll check it out." She tiptoed to the security post. A uniformed guard sat behind a U-shaped desk. TV monitors surrounded him, but he had his eyes on a hardback, the pages propped open with a stapler and a Scotch tape dispenser so his hands were free to peel candy wrappers. Her mouth watered. She'd functioned too long without food, water, and sleep.

She scanned the section and saw two fire escapes, one within the guard's view and the other around the corner from his post. Above both doors red bars blazed. She hoped Johnny remembered which fire escape. She retraced her steps, pondering how to distract the watchman long enough for all three to scoot through the exit undetected. It didn't look promising unless he took a break.

She said softly upon approach, "Johnny, there are two doors. Which is the right one?"

"The one on our wall."

"You sure?"

"Positive."

Of course, the exit had to be the one within the guard's view. "Andrew, are you with us?"

"Locked onto Johnny."

The trek to the guard station gave her time to hatch a plan. A diversion. Worked once. Why not again? "Andrew. Stay alert. When I whistle, move."

"Will do."

Her bare feet skimmed the polished floor as she sprinted to the opposite wall and glided to a halt outside the wrong fire escape. She rammed both hands at the horizontal bar, the blow so hard that the door handle stuck into the drywall. A shrill alarm blasted the stillness and echoed through the hollow halls. She stole back into the darkness to watch.

The guard flew around the bend. He shouted orders into his radio and barged into the stairwell. The exit slammed shut. Darcy whistled softly. In seconds, Andrew broke from the shadows with Johnny. She launched her biometric pass into the key slot and pounded in her code, ready to insert Johnny's stolen card if hers didn't work, but the buzzer sounded on the first try. She wondered why Gert hadn't deactivated her clearance and why Johnny's card still worked if it was stolen. The door to the fire escape opened. She pushed the men through first, then stayed until the exit sealed shut.

A flight up she overtook them, their speed hampered by Johnny. Andrew must have read the urgency in her eyes. He wrapped his arm around his friend's waist and pulled him up the steps; the sound of Johnny's feet scraping the concrete echoed loudly in the confined space. Darcy let them pass, then followed, certain any attack would come from below.

The musty air triggered her allergies. She stifled a sneeze, then another. The dankness aroused bad memories, ugly scenes of the cryotorium. She dwelled on good thoughts—blue skies, sunshine—and prayed, for each flight of stairs brought the men closer to freedom. Only two. She could only save two. Her shoulders drooped. She'd seen so many horrors as an agent and a detective, but today she'd seen the darkest side of humanity.

Above her, the comforting thumps of Andrew's footsteps stopped. Alarmed, she ran to the upstairs landing. Johnny's frame blocked her path.

"He's badly winded." Andrew said, panting.

"Water," said Johnny.

"At the first fountain we find," she said. "What's on the other side of this door?"

"More hall," said Johnny. "Ends . . . at . . . cart station."

Thank God—the gates to Z-site. "I'm glad we're outbound."

"Amen," said Andrew.

Johnny wrapped his bony fingers around the metal railing and yanked himself to his feet. For half the trip, he stayed upright, but within eyeshot of the station he collapsed. His kneecaps cracked on the hard surface, and Darcy winced. She grabbed one arm and Andrew the other. Supported by them, Johnny alternated between walking and being dragged, the journey slow and cumbersome. She spotted the cart station, empty at this early hour, and her spirits soared.

"We're almost there. Keep going." But her encouragement failed. Johnny went limp, and the sudden weight toppled Andrew to the floor. Darcy stumbled forward. Her arms shot out to break her fall, her palms smarting as they smacked the terrazzo.

"Oh no!" said Andrew. "He passed out. Now what?"

"Don't move." Darcy jogged to the unmanned security kiosk near the cart station and circled the vehicles parked in neat rows behind the signature yellow line; most were key operated, but a handful were biometrically equipped. She placed her Eyedentacard on a square on one of the dashboards. Nothing happened. She tried another cart. The engine sputtered, then died. On a third try, her badge pulsed red. In seconds, the biometric strip read Deactivated.

"Shit." She tossed the ID aside and rummaged for Johnny's stolen badge. The minute she turned it over, she noticed Galvin Perry's name written across the biometric disk in miniscule print. Why hadn't he, Mr. Strict Protocol, reported the card missing? Skeptical, she slapped the Eyedentacard to the reader. The instant it made contact, the card shone blue.

The engine choked and threatened to die, then came to life. She flung herself behind the wheel, shifted into drive, and floored the pedal. Tires squealed on the polished surface. Glass clinked, and metal jangled.

Startled, Darcy glanced into the cargo compartment. The entire area was cluttered with cartons of steel flasks. She looked forward, saw the parked cart, and swerved. Her right tire clipped the vehicle's bumper, and she careened into the hallway. She steered to the right to avoid flipping and coasted down the passage, picking up speed as she neared Andrew. A few feet from him, she braked and vaulted out. With his help, Darcy lifted Johnny into the front seat and belted him in.

Andrew dove into the rear compartment. "We've got company," he said the second she took the wheel.

Robots poured from the stairwell door.

"Hang on." She gunned the engine, and the vehicle lurched into gear.

"Speed up," Andrew shouted.

She floored the accelerator. The cart skidded, but she kept it under control. If the vehicle drifted to the left, she steered to the right; the fight to keep the cart on track was a constant battle at this speed.

Metal clanged, the reverberation deafening as Andrew pitched flask after flask at the advancing robots, now visible in the side and rearview mirrors. In the distance, a gray cloud filled the cavernous passage.

"Oh God, no!" said Andrew.

The cry startled Darcy. Her foot slipped off the accelerator. The cart slowed, then sped up as she leaned on the accelerator pedal. "What?" she screamed, not daring to look back.

"The 220s."

The adrenaline charge pricked her senses. "Quick, the boxes. Rip out the insulation. Hand me a wad. Pack your ears and nose. And Johnny's."

Hunks of cellulose dropped into her lap. Using her fingernails, she forced the material deep into her ears and jammed it up her nose. She veered around a corner. Yards ahead, in the shadowy dark, someone had strung a tall black banner across the corridor. "Hold tight."

Darcy maintained speed as she hurled toward the barricade, bracing for a collision. As she drew closer, the blurred image sharpened. The sight stopped her cold. She braked, hardly believing her eyes. Ten humanoids obstructed her flight.

Over eight feet tall and built for battle, the machines wore black body armor, helmets, and combat boots. Cold, piercing yellow eyes glared from their face shields. Her heart hammered, and sweat dripped off her forehead. Some choice: blood-sucking gnats or bone-crushing humanoids.

Darcy made a U-turn and sped off in the opposition direction until she'd put a good twenty yards between her and the machines. Then she gripped the steering wheel tight, conducted another U-turn, and floored the accelerator, her sights set on dead center. As she headed for her target, the humanoids broke formation and lined up behind each other to form a spear, a manmade arrow pointed right at her. Their reaction threw her, but only for a minute. She closed in on them. Oh no, 890s. Telepathic robots like Con. The realization sent wild fear coursing through her. How could she win against them?

Clear your mind. Lock down your emotions.

As she barreled toward the humanoid barricade, Darcy concentrated on colliding headlong with this massive force of muscle. Mentally prepared for the impending crash, she dwelled on the gory details of her demise. If she survived, she still faced certain death at the hands of her formidable opponents. They'd probably tear her apart, limb by limb. A hideous way to die.

The closer she came, the more ominous they appeared, but instead of fearing them Darcy embraced death. A strange calm overtook her, broken by a fearful wailing—Andrew's cries to turn back. Ten feet, nine . . . she drowned out Andrew screams and drilled her gaze into the front robot. A cart length from the robotic chain, a loud report echoed through the passage.

"Gunfire," Andrew shouted.

A red beam skimmed the hood. A pop was followed by a prolonged hiss. The wheels spun. Darcy lost traction as the cart careened toward the robots. The bumper clipped the humanoid closest to her and sent him toppling sideways. He crashed into the machine nearest him. The collision created a domino effect as one by one the humanoids hit the floor. Jarred but unhurt,

Darcy jumped from behind the wheel and twirled around, searching frantically for an escape route. She'd just spotted the door when Andrew yelled, "Run," and scurried from the rear compartment.

A gray fog drifted toward them: 220s!

She tore her gaze from the gnatrobots to the humanoids. Remobilized, the ten advanced on them. She thrust Johnny's Eyedentacard at Andrew. "Go. 1080s." She read off the code.

Andrew fled. Darcy reached into the passenger's seat for Johnny. "Put your hands around my neck." His lids fluttered open and closed. She gathered him into her arms and ran for the exit. Pain, sudden and sharp, seared up her arm. Blood trickled through the black gash in her bodysuit. Johnny fell from her grasp. She hooked her hands under his arms and yanked him to his feet, but he went limp. Her right hand burned, and blood dotted the floor. Johnny fell away from her. She stared down at his broken, motionless frame; his eyes were shut. She checked for a pulse, his heartbeat so faint, she may have willed it.

A chirping drone filled the hall.

"Darcy, hurry!" Andrew said.

Mesmerized, she watched the gray cloud swirl toward her, moving faster than it had before. She broke into a run. On the threshold to the stairwell, she stopped for a last look.

"Close the door," Andrew said, his eyes wide with fear.

"Not yet."

The humanoids circled Johnny's body.

"Maybe they'll take him back to the lab. Care for him."

"Don't count on it," said Andrew.

One of the humanoids signaled to the gray cloud suspended near the ceiling. Slowly, the gnatrobots descended and swarmed Johnny's crumpled body, blanketing his thin frame in a sheet of gray. Then one by one they vanished.

A loud pop.

Johnny's head exploded. Brain tissue, blood, and skull fragments sprayed high into the air. On the red shower rode billions of gnats. Fear spurred Darcy into action. She slammed the door and threw the latch. Bile burned her throat.

A purring sound built on the other side. It grew to a loud, frenetic chirp, then died.

To think she'd helped program these microkillers. Darcy picked the felt from her ears and packed the keyhole with it. A black speck flitted out. The gnat alighted on her hand, this one much bigger than those that had pursued them. A scout. He flew off.

"Dar . . . cy. Help."

Andrew's pleading voice snapped her to attention. She turned. His eyes were riveted to the gnatrobot that inched up his arm, drawn to him by the scent of fear. He was sweating profusely, and the strong smell of body odor drew the pheromone-sensitive soldier like a magnet. She moved slowly toward the gnat, afraid of scaring him off. If he escaped, the gnat would return with a lethal army. Intoxicated by body odor, he made no attempt to flee as Darcy approached. She plucked him off Andrew, pinned him to the concrete steps, and drilled her fingernail into him. Andrew recoiled. He bounded up the flight of stairs to the landing and crammed Johnny's Eyedentacard into the door slot but fumbled the access code. The machine ejected the ID.

An angry buzz filled the air.

The wad of felt stuffed in the keyhole floated out and rose into the air, specked in black. The haze snaked its way up the stairs. She snatched the ID from Andrew, punched in the sequence, and flung open the door. "Head for the elevators."

Andrew fell across the threshold and ran. She locked the stairwell door and followed him. A soft, high-pitched whine, similar to an annoying mosquito, alerted her to the gnatrobot perched on her shoulder. Unlike his dust-sized friends, he too was larger in size. Another scout. She flicked off the piezoelectric hitchhiker. Tenaciously, he returned. Since it was dangerous to stop and immobilize him, she tweezed him in her fingers, put him between her incisors, and cut him in two—but not before his razor teeth bit a chunk from her lip. She spat both out.

"Darcy," Andrew shouted. His body was wedged in the elevators doors; he appeared oblivious to the metal panels that smacked him as they cycled and recycled. He backed up as she leaped aboard. "You've been shot," he said, his eyes on the red circle spreading across her shoulder.

"Laser burn. Superficial."

The ride up ended, and the doors opened.

Andrew dodged past her, but Darcy overtook him. "No. Stay behind me," she said. She slowed, and so did he. She stopped, and he hesitated. "Stay here."

His eyes widened. He looked about. "I . . . I can't."

She understood his fear. "Okay, but be quiet."

He nodded.

Darcy crept toward the lobby. She pictured the setup: glass entryway in front of her, elevators to her right, and across from them the guard post, occupied around the clock by four security officers. One covered the logbook, another circulated, and two commanded the block of computer terminals.

The closer she drew to the foyer, the more suspicious she became; the area was too quiet and too dark. Normally, overhead spotlights washed the corridor like a lighthouse beacon. She kept her guard up. They couldn't have quit this easily; too much was at stake. If only she'd had a gun. She flashed on another case where her 9 millimeter had proved useless against a laser-packing killer. Speed and agility—those traits had played in her favor.

Movement.

She froze. Andrew banged into her.

Something skipped across the murky lobby, too small for a person and too large for a gnatrobot. Besides, bots weren't smart enough to ride elevators? Or were they?

"Ready?" she whispered.

He clutched her hand, his touch weak and fingers cold.

Through the lobby glass, the cloud cover broke, and moonlight streamed across the floor. The subtle light illuminated the dark shadows but revealed no one hidden in their protective guise. Warm air flowed from the ceiling vents. The heat unleashed the faint odor of stale tobacco ingrained in aged paneling and old upholstery. The unit kicked off. The sharp scent of bleach wafted on the air. Robot? Sweat laced with perfume drifted across her senses. No, human.

A figure moved into her peripheral vision and advanced on her, but she couldn't make out who, because the room was too dark. Something swiped the air. Instinctively, she dropped to the floor to avoid the attack, rolled, and sprang to her feet. With her elbow, she struck her attacker between the shoulder blades, causing the person to fall forward. He landed hard at Darcy's feet at the same instant something clattered across the terrazzo. Moonlight shone on her attacker: Gert. Darcy knife-chopped her across the base of the skull and kicked aside the flashlight Gert had been carrying.

Whoosh. Something sliced the air. A second attacker stepped from the shadows. Darcy zeroed in on the baseball bat in his hand and ducked, but not fast enough. Pain radiated up her arm. Another whoosh, but this time he missed. Wood splintered as the bat crashed into the doorjamb. Darcy crouched down, drew her knees to her chest, and delivered a crushing blow to the attacker's lower back. He pitched sideways, banged into the wall, and lay prone on the terrazzo. She launched herself across the floor and collided feetfirst with the guard kiosk. The impact jarred her knees. She winced.

Darcy crawled to the far corner of the security post and hid under the counter, puzzled that no guards were on duty. Even stranger, her attackers didn't pursue her. She glanced about the command center. Every screen in the station televised the basement lab. Nothing had changed in the sublevel arena since she'd escaped. Freed cellmates lined the walls, their eyes vacuous and faces blanched, all in a catatonic state. Why hadn't someone arrived to lock them up?

The displays flickered and settled. Guards filed into the lab. Relieved, Darcy watched their numbers swell. No wonder no one was manning the security station upstairs; all of the guards were in the basement cellblock. But why?

Blinding white light burst from the terminals. Darcy covered her eyes with her hands.

A distant roar followed by a thunderous vibration rocked the building. Thrown backward, Darcy smacked her head against a shelf.

Another blast, this one more powerful than the last. She slithered to the back of the station, afraid the ceiling might collapse. Someone dove into the recess beside her—Andrew.

The computer screens faded to black, plunging the room into darkness.

Clifford's voice came over a speaker. "Evidence destroyed."

"They blew the basement," Andrew blurted.

Red laser beams shot overhead. A monitor exploded, and glass showered Darcy. Another blast.

"Go." She pushed Andrew. Petrified, he refused to move.

With a click, light flooded the room. Darcy squinted. Something hot grazed her neck. The smell of singed flesh and scorched hair fouled the air. She leaned out of the guard station, ready to run and seek cover somewhere safer.

Dozens of 890s poured into the hall. Above them a storm of gnatrobots swarmed, so numerous and close they colored the ceiling black. Isaac, dressed in riot gear and brandishing a laser gun, stepped from the cover of his army. He controlled his droids from a keypad on his death ray.

Darcy sized up the situation: not good. Nothing on or around her could serve as a weapon, so she judged the distance to the front doors. Not a chance.

Isaac took aim.

Andrew backed up.

"Get behind me." Darcy shielded him.

A shot rang out across from Isaac.

He bellowed in anger. Blood stained the front of his suit. Supporting his injured arm with his hand, he aimed his laser gun at a robot breaking formation and fired. The humanoid fired back, but too late. With an agonizing howl, the robot sank to the floor. Blood pooled from its fractured face shield.

Darcy rushed Isaac. She sprang into the air, drew her knees to her chest, and kicked out with all the force she owned. The blow, intended to strike Isaac in the lower back, struck too high, but still the tactic worked. Caught off guard by the sudden attack, he fell forward and landed hard.

Darcy stomped on his wrist to free the laser from his grasp, then dialed down the bursts to micro and zapped the switches on his glove. With the controls destroyed, he couldn't mobilize his 890s, but what about the 220s? Darcy spun. Evidently, Isaac controlled them as well, for they remained at bay, floating and purring at the ceiling like a pulsing black cloud.

Isaac tried to stand. She popped him in both kneecaps with a low blast from the ray gun. He grabbed his legs and bellowed in agony as he thrashed about on the floor.

"Andrew," she called out.

"By the front doors," he yelled back. "They're locked."

She sprinted across the lobby to the main entrance. Nothing she tried opened the automatic doors. "Probably deactivated by the shift guard." She inspected the latches. "Biolocked. Not sure this'll work. Stand back." She cranked up the energy on the laser, waited for the intensity to build, then pressed the Q-switch. A red beam shot from the gun and bored a neat hole around the latches. She knocked them out with the butt, and the doors opened. Andrew barged through the exit and disappeared into the night.

Headlights pierced the lobby. Not one vehicle but a steady flotilla wound a path up the hill.

"McClain." Maddox emerged from behind the immobilized humanoids. He had his arms at his side, his fingers curled around a .45. "You aren't going anywhere."

"Like hell I'm not."

Tires screeched behind them. Maddox holstered the Colt.

Charleton Cain hopped from a braking SUV. Tonight, he had traded green for blue. On his field jacket in bold yellow was "FBI."

36

FBI *Albuquerque Field Office*

Your typical government interrogation room—gray walls, drab green chairs, and weathered linoleum. A single light bulb hung from a tin shade. Every time the heater clicked on, the dull halo fanned the distressed tabletop and illuminated Darcy's iPad. Trapped here for the past two, now three, days, she felt like a prisoner and hungered for news from the outside world.

Two days ago, after a five-hour grilling (or as Cain called it, a "debrief") during which he never cracked a smile, Darcy had handed over Johnny's Zipgig. Cain's eyes lit up and he practically drooled. But all of them were stunned to learn the encrypted files had been corrupted and couldn't be deciphered despite the megaforce of G-cell.

Bored, Darcy scrolled through old messages while she waited for Cain to return from lunch. She'd refused his offer of pizza in favor of a coke.

The door opened, and in sauntered Ron Maddox, Special Agent in Charge of the Albuquerque Field Office. He brought along a G-man with a laptop. Behind him strutted Charleton Cain/Green/Mr. Dead. No one, it seemed, knew his real name.

The men nodded to Darcy, then took their seats. The minutes passed in silence. She was about to ask why the delay when a willowy brunette strolled into the room. Her sudden appearance commanded everyone's attention except for the G-man, who plugged away at his Mac. The woman introduced herself as Gina—no last name and the title of Director for Criminal Investigations. Darcy felt a twinge of jealousy as she wondered if she would have reached this level had she stayed at the bureau.

"As I mentioned yesterday," said Cain, "we invited you here, McClain—"

"No, you threatened me. Appear or lose my license, you said, which is the only reason I'm here."

Anger knitted Cain's brows. He snatched a sheet of paper off the table. "A government probe into the recent explosion at Los Alamos's S-site has been attributed to a gas leak in the boiler room. Once a plutonium storage facility, the building was shut down in 1950. Extensive testing revealed no traces of radioactive material, etc., etc. . . ."

"Oh, so it's S-site again. Sounds like a cover-up," said Darcy.

"No," Cain said, "just a matter we prefer to handle internally."

"Not much to investigate with the evidence destroyed. What about the key players? Someone will talk."

Cain paced. "Not likely. The think tank members are dead. Suicide pact."

"Guess no one told Clifford."

"She died with them," said Cain.

Darcy stifled a smirk. She didn't buy his remark.

"It's not our fault," said Cain, "that you failed to save Johnny Duran."

She grimaced. The truth still raw with emotion, and it would be worse when she had to give Rio the news.

Cain thrust a finger in her face. "But let me tell you, we paid a heavy price when Denahy killed Galvin Perry. Not only did Perry sacrifice eight years to Operation Brainmap, but he also gave his life to save yours."

The comment shocked her. "Perry was FBI?"

Gina tapped her nail on the table.

"Floor's yours, Gina." Cain appeared perturbed by the interruption.

"Ms. McClain, I'm Galvin's twin sister."

For the first time, Darcy noticed the woman's strong resemblance to Perry and groped for something sympathetic to say. "I—I'm sorry."

"Galvin knew the risks." She folded her hands. "My brother joined LANL's A-Life team as their top neuroscientist over eight years ago. All went well between Gert and my brother until the Brainwash project hit some glitches. Rather than give him the chance to work through the problems, she brought Isaac Denahy on board. The move was a terrible blow to my brother's ego and a permanent setback to his career at LANL."

Gina paused for a sip of water. "Bruised emotionally, he fought fiercely to regain his key position on the team, but it never happened. Four years later, Gert made a fatal mistake. Instead of meeting Brian Steele at their usual, undisclosed location, she invited him to LANL because she was too busy to leave the Hill. Steele bumped into my brother and commiserated with him on the failure of the team's fourth attempt to grow live brain cells on indium tin oxide. Galvin played along. In reality, the team had had phenomenal success, so Steele's remark threw Galvin. He did some digging, discovered Gert had been defrauding the government, told me, and I set up a sting: Operation Brainmap."

"So your brother was a whistleblower, not FBI. Damn. Galvin was trying to warn—not threaten—me."

Cain folded his hands, as though controlling himself from slapping Darcy. "And you came damn close to blowing our entire operation. He never should have given you that stupid note."

"Forget the note. He had even a better opportunity to level with me in the prototype lab. We could have worked together." Just what she needed—more guilt on top of the remorse she already harbored for Johnny's death and the ninety-eight who'd perished. No wonder Perry didn't report his stolen Eyedenta-card; it could've blown his cover. "Since you had the chance, on more than one occasion, why didn't you pull me out? Or why didn't Maddox warn me? He had plenty of opportunities."

Gina shot Cain a sidelong glance as if to say, "Don't answer," but the gesture went unheeded. "Why would we when you were doing such a fantastic job? Hell, better than us or our plants."

"So you used me?"

Gina stepped in. "Yes, and good for us, because Cain's team hadn't made much progress."

Cain glared at Gina.

With nothing to lose, Darcy asked, "Would you mind answering a few questions?"

Cain opened his mouth but quickly shut it. Gina nodded.

"Who killed Sonny?"

"Gert gave the order," said Gina. "Who carried it out, we don't know."

"Her motive?" Darcy had come to her own conclusion, but she wanted to hear what Gina had to say.

"Sonny remained an asset to the project until his daughter

Emma died. After her death his obsession with cloning wore on Gert. When the cloning process failed, Sonny became a liability."

Darcy let out a soft sigh. So Sonny hadn't been killed because of his association with her. "Why Walt and Norm?"

"Guilt by association. Johnny and Andrew worked for Walt, and Walt worked for Norm. If you eliminate the chain of evidence, you stop any possible leaks. Where Johnny failed, the other three may have succeeded."

Darcy weighed the rest of her questions, afraid Gina would tire of the counter-interrogation. "And Enzo Duran?"

She paused as if to contemplate the statement. "On one of his recruiting trips to Mexico, Enzo defied strict protocol, which was to hire only single men who were strangers to each other. He got sloppy, recruiting from only two villages rather than spreading the wealth. Of the thirty undocumented aliens, Gert learned twenty-five were related. One missing person from a village wouldn't be suspicious, but ten or more from the same village would be."

"The twenty-five she had killed," Darcy said more to herself than Gina, but the agent nodded.

"Enzo's house—"

"Razed," Gina said, "with Enzo's permission, in a way. After his recruiting debacle, Gert ordered him to tear down the house to remove any evidence of the aliens he housed there before moving them to LANL. Any other questions?"

"Why two different project names, Brainwash and Nanostart, when both had identical objectives?" Darcy had her own theory, but the pieces didn't fit, and she hoped Gina would explain.

"Before I answer . . . I loved my brother, but I don't condone his role in all of this. That said, Nanostart documented the truth, and Brainwash recorded lies. The only people privy to the truth were Gert, Isaac, and a select team at LANL, but later that changed when my brother started blackmailing Gert and Isaac. To keep him quiet, they agreed to bring him into the fold."

"How did this all start?"

"In a manner of speaking, Gert and Galvin had a brainchild but no money to fund their billion-dollar baby, so they pitched the premise to an investor—one with the deepest pockets in the world. They agreed to bankroll Brainwash because the project was in their best interest from a medical and military standpoint."

"The bank being the US government."

Gina nodded. "In the early stages, Gert and Galvin were astonished by their phenomenal success, which came thanks to my brother. Then, as I stated a minute ago, Brainwash hit a few snags. Impatient, Gert brought Isaac on board. That's when the project went from growing stem cells on indium tin oxide to using human brain cells to speed up their successes. 'Sacrifice a few for the good of all,' Isaac told Galvin."

"But your brother did nothing to stop them?"

"No, he didn't. I think creation had gone to his head and he cast aside humanity." She paused for another sip of water. "At some point, Gert decided not to hand over their revolutionary breakthrough to the US government. We speculate that she and Isaac planned to abandon the failing Brainwash project and regroup much later as Nanostart to complete their work."

"After," Cain said, "they embezzled millions from the taxpayers."

Gina continued. "They'd even identified some of the key scientists who would join Nanostart. If they didn't accept the offer, then they'd be killed."

"Maddox's role?" Darcy asked.

"Just doing his job," said Gina. "Shadowing my brother at my request. However, his contact with you wasn't authorized."

Cain pushed his chair away from the table. "Are we done?"

Darcy felt the same way. She'd been interrogated enough, but one piece of the puzzle still mystified her. "One last question."

Cain scowled at Darcy.

"Go ahead," said Gina.

"Johnny stole Perry's Eyedentacard."

Before Darcy could continue, Gina said, "And I promptly replaced it."

"What about the money hoarded from the Brainwash project? I assume all of the funds weren't spent."

"Deposited into a Swiss account. The money will be returned to the US government."

And squandered, but Darcy didn't voice her opinion. With the last of the puzzle solved, she stood.

Gina thanked Darcy, shook her hand, and opened the door.

Darcy hurried into the hall, eager to leave the bureau for the second and last time. How different her departure had been ten years ago. Then, she'd fought back the tears, the pain of resigning more than she could bear. Today, she practically ran for the exit.

Halfway down the corridor, Maddox shouted. "Hey, Darcy. Wait."

She stopped. "Don't tell me, you tried to warn me as well?"

"Hey, I wanted to do more, but I couldn't blow my cover. I had orders. You know the drill."

She held up her hands to silence him, more tired than angry. "Yeah, I know." She marched off.

Back at the rental house, she sat in her 4Runner and mulled over the best way to break the bad news about Johnny to Rio. Darcy hated emotional encounters, and this one ranked high on her unpleasant list. The only positive spin she could put on the tragic outcome was her promise to help Rio however possible, such as by hiring her as a full-time administrative assistant, an idea Darcy had kicked around for months, but she'd never had the time to interview anyone.

Rio stepped onto the front porch with Bullet beside her.

Darcy's pulse beat faster. Better tell her and get this ugly business over with.

Rio knocked on the driver's window. "Why are you sitting out here in the freezing cold? Hurry up. Let's go in." She shivered.

Darcy climbed out, petted Bullet on the head, then walked slowly up the path to the front door. The minute she entered the house, Rio said, "About Johnny . . . I've suspected the worst for a long time and have certainly done my share of grieving, but now I have to be strong for the baby and work out a plan to care for her."

Relieved beyond imagination at Rio's maturity, Darcy sank onto the couch and leaned back against the cushions, her dread fading, until Rio said, "Still, I must know . . . did he suffer a lot?"

After her parents' deaths, Darcy had taken Charlene to a counselor. "Lying won't help you deal with death," she'd told Darcy. "Grief is an intense and powerful emotion, and we all grieve in our own way. You can help Charlene get through the grieving process by being compassionate, understanding, and kind."

Darcy sighed softly. "I'm not sure what he went through before I found him, but during the short time we were together he appeared weak but not in pain. He had only one goal—to get back to you."

"Did he know about the baby?"

"No. We were so focused on escaping that I never had a chance to tell him. I'm sorry."

"If he'd known, he would've only worried more."

Good time to change the subject, McClain. "You said her? A girl?"

Rio's sad expression brightened. She smiled. "Yes. I had a sonogram yesterday. I'm going to name her Allison. Now I have to find a job because sooner or later you'll return to California and the money Randolph left me won't go far."

She'd forgotten about the ten-thousand-dollar inheritance, the sum puzzling and something she'd questioned at the reading of Randolph's will. Why such a paltry gift from a billionaire who'd pledged his love and support for his illegitimate daughter?

"Any idea when you're headed back?" Rio's question cut into Darcy's flashback.

"Mid-January, and you're coming with me."

"What?" Rio flounced onto the sofa beside Darcy. "Really? Been pretty stressed out wondering what I'll do."

"I never planned to leave you in Taos."

A sad expression crossed her face. "Unlike everyone else who's abandoned me—my real mother, my adopted parents, and through no fault of their own, Johnny and Randolph."

Rio had a point. Darcy hadn't thought about it that way. "Won't happen again."

Rio hugged Darcy. "Love you for doing this for me. Are you hungry? I can fix something."

"No, stay here and let's relax for a while. It's been a long two weeks."

"I'll say. Andrew called this morning. He found Ollie and has decided to adopt him."

The news warmed her heart. "Good, because Bullet doesn't like cats."

Bullet raised his head and looked at Darcy.

"He and Elena are engaged. June wedding."

"Wonderful," said Darcy, trying to be upbeat, but Charlene kept pervading her thoughts. As if on cue, her cell phone chimed. With mixed emotions, Darcy tapped the answer key.

"Hey, sis. As a compromise, since the snow is *so* much

better here, why don't you pack up and spend Christmas with me and Vicky?"

Driving or even flying to Canada held no appeal, not at the moment. "Depends. Where are you and Vicky?"

"Vail. We plan to ski through the holidays and drive down to Albuquerque after New Year's Day, and I'd fly home from there."

Too tired to argue and in no mood for more discord, Darcy decided to agree. "Hold a minute." She told Rio about the new plans for Christmas. "And you're welcome to come along."

"You'll only be gone a week, and I don't ski. I'd much rather stay here and dog-sit Bullet, if you don't mind."

"You sure?"

"Positive."

"Okay. It's a deal," Darcy told Charlene. Besides, the change in itinerary worked well for her. She'd keep the rental until mid-January, attend the new court date set for her easement hearing, then drive home with Bullet and Rio for company. The battle between her and Charlene had ended on a positive note, and the vacation hadn't been a total loss. She'd learned to be thankful for small blessings.

* * *

Meet The Carver—Albuquerque's most
brutal serial killer. Only one person
can end his carnage—Darcy McClain.
If The Carver doesn't kill her next.

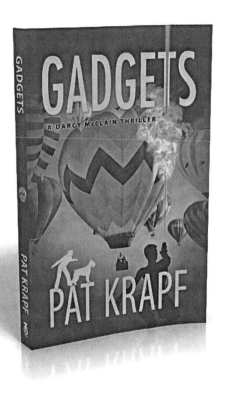

Winner of the Betty L. Henrichs Award for
Best Publishable Mystery Novel

AVAILABLE ON AMAZON OCTOBER 2014

Pat Krapf was born in New Jersey, but spent her formative years overseas and is still a globetrotter.

She worked in advertising and marketing for over thirteen years as a writer and product manager for the health care, aerospace, and architectural industries. She left the corporate world to write the Darcy McClain thriller series.

She lives in Texas with her husband and giant schnauzer.

CONNECT ONLINE
patkrapf.com

CPSIA information can be obtained at www.ICGtesting.com
Printed in the USA
LVOW08s2126150715

446359LV00001B/41/P